Novelists Against Social Change

Also by Kate Macdonald

JOHN BUCHAN: A Companion to the Mystery Fiction

REASSESSING JOHN BUCHAN: Beyond *The Thirty-Nine Steps* (*ed.*)

THE MASCULINE MIDDLEBROW, 1880–1950: What Mr Miniver Read (*ed.*)

JOHN BUCHAN AND THE IDEA OF MODERNITY (*ed. with Nathan Waddell*)

POLITICAL FUTURE FICTION: Speculative and Counter-Factual Politics in Edwardian Britain, 3 vols (*ed.*)

TRANSITIONS IN MIDDLEBROW WRITING, 1880–1930 (*ed. with Christoph Singer*)

Novelists Against Social Change

Conservative Popular Fiction, 1920–1960

Kate Macdonald
University of Ghent, Belgium

palgrave
macmillan

First published 2015 by
PALGRAVE MACMILLAN

Palgrave Macmillan in the UK is an imprint of Macmillan Publishers Limited, registered in England, company number 785998, of Houndmills, Basingstoke, Hampshire RG21 6XS.

Palgrave Macmillan in the US is a division of St Martin's Press LLC, 175 Fifth Avenue, New York, NY 10010.

Palgrave Macmillan is the global academic imprint of the above companies and has companies and representatives throughout the world.

Palgrave® and Macmillan® are registered trademarks in the United States, the United Kingdom, Europe and other countries.

ISBN 978–1–137–45771–4

This book is printed on paper suitable for recycling and made from fully managed and sustained forest sources. Logging, pulping and manufacturing processes are expected to conform to the environmental regulations of the country of origin.

A catalogue record for this book is available from the British Library.

A catalog record for this book is available from the Library of Congress.

Typeset by MPS Limited, Chennai, India.

Contents

List of Illustrations

Acknowledgements

I was able to visit archives and libraries while writing this book with the help of grants from the Fonds Wetenschappelijk Onderzoek, Belgium, and with visiting research fellowships at the Institute of English Studies, University of London (2010–12), and at the Bodleian Library, University of Oxford (2014–15). Earlier forms of some sections of this book were previously presented at conferences: *Historicising the Middlebrow* (Sheffield 2008), *Childhood in its Time* (Canterbury 2009), the Space Between (Portland 2010), Literary London (London 2010), and the Social History Seminar, Institute of Historical Studies (London 2010). Some material was previously published in my article 'Hunted men in John Buchan's London, 1890s to 1920s', *Literary London*, 7:1 (2009), and in the *Journal of the Alliance of Literary Societies* (2012).

The Estate of Angela Thirkell has generously given me permission to use the passages quoted from Mrs Thirkell's books, though this permission does not in any way reflect their endorsement or approval of my work. Permission was granted by A P Watt at United Agents on behalf of Camilla Kirkpatrick and Robin Humphreys to use the published works of Dornford Yates. I was unable to trace the copyright holders for the estate of A J Smithers, but would be happy to correct the acknowledgement made for the use of his unpublished letters and other writing in any future edition of this book.

My thanks to individuals must begin with the librarians: Eva Pszeniczko, Rik Vanmoerkerke and their colleagues of Ghent University Library; the British Library; the Bodleian Library, University of Oxford; Bristol University Library Special Collections; and Senate House Library, University of London, for their efficient help and unfailing professionalism in helping me see the books, articles and archives I needed. I want to thank in particular the Inter-Library Loan staff at Washington University Library, St Louis, for agreeing to send their second copy of Jill N Levin's MA thesis across the pond.

I would like to thank the members of the Angela Thirkell Society, and of the Angela Thirkell Society North American Branch online group, for their assistance, information and insights, especially Penny Aldred, Penelope Fritzer, Helen Hackney, Edith Jeude and Joanna Roberts. I am very grateful to the members of the Dornford Yates online group for their conversations and insights, and in particular to David Salter for his advice, introductions and conversation; to Richard S Greenhough for his indispensable bibliographical knowledge; and to Graham and Jennifer Harrison for their generous hospitality and access to archive materials.

Kenneth Hillier, Michael Redley and H E Taylor of the John Buchan Society, as always, gave me encouragement, advice and specialist knowledge when no-one else had a clue. George Simmers has been a valued source of ideas about popular fiction and facetiousness. Barry Rowe and Richard Adams made the cover I wanted possible. Ion Trewin gave me wise advice in the nick of time. Paula Kennedy and Peter Cary at Palgrave Macmillan have my gratitude for their good humour, equanimity and patience, over the years of our association on several projects. The anonymous reviewers of my earlier drafts gave me good advice, most of which I have used to my advantage. My beta readers Penny Aldred (Thirkell), Christine Berberich and Debra Rae Cohen (for critical rigour), Stephen Donovan (the ha'porth of tar), Sally Dugan and David Marsh (lay readers), and David Salter (Yates) read fast and wisely and showed me how and where to do things better. Responsibility for the remaining errors (hopefully few) is mine alone.

Finally, I want to thank David, Holly and Lucy for letting me just get on and write; and Lucy for the cooking.

While the 1920s Bugatti on the cover of this book is not a car that Buchan's characters ever mentioned, he would have undoubtedly admired its lines and horsepower as much as he did the Hispano-Suiza and its prey in *The Island of Sheep* (1936). It is faintly possible that a Bugatti might have appeared in Barsetshire, driven by David Leslie, and would most certainly have been watched with narrowed eyes by Jonah Mansel in Carinthia.

Kate Macdonald

1
Introduction: Politics and Pleasure in Language

> That the writer is interested in politics needs no saying. Every publisher's list, almost every book that is now issued, brings proof of the fact. [...] The poet introduces Communism or Fascism into his lyrics; the novelist turns from the private lives of his characters to their social surroundings and their political opinions.[1]

This quotation from Virginia Woolf's essay 'Why Art To-Day Follows Politics' (1936) was originally about novelists of the Left. It is equally applicable to the authors this book is about: John Buchan (1875–1940), Dornford Yates (1885–1960), and Angela Thirkell (1890–1961). They were politically and socially conservative but, as Woolf pointed out, it is how writers used their politics in their art that matters. She went on to say of the creative artist that 'society is not only his paymaster but his patron'.[2] I use her observations to shape my enquiry: what popular conservative and best-selling British fiction of the twentieth century said to its readers, and how we can understand the messages transmitted through this very popular fiction by Buchan, Yates and Thirkell.

They were extremely successful authors, in that their names alone became enough to advertise their new books. Their novels were about the conservative hero and heroine in a modernising world that was fast rejecting conservative ways of life and standards of behaviour. While it is impossible to know how enthusiastically their views were accepted by their readers, their continued high sales suggest tacit acceptance. Their prolific output was easily categorised into genres, which helped their sales. Their publishers, and the reviewers, referred to their new books by the authors' surnames, as brand names, and they attracted pastiches as appreciations.[3] Thirkell remarked of the title for her new wartime novel, 'it is really a label for another bottle from the same cellar';[4] the reviewer William Plomer remarked in 1933, 'this book must be taken as a Buchan'.[5] Hodder & Stoughton marketed Buchan and Yates in their trade paper *The Bookman* as competing brands, for instance filling the back cover of the June 1934 *Bookman* with a full-page advertisement for their new novels, headed by: "This month / *The Free Fishers* / John Buchan's New Novel / *Storm Music* / Dornford Yates' / New Romance'.[6]

These high-selling novels sold politicised rhetoric, but they are largely uncritiqued. Their conservative response to fears about social difference and social change is reflected in Raymond Williams's comment, on 'the well-known habit of using the past, the "good old days", as a stick to beat the present'.[7] British literary criticism about works published in this period generally focuses on writers and readers who are left-wing, minority, or otherwise struggling against social and political norms. These norms are usually understood to be being white, heterosexual, culturally Victorian, socially superior, authoritative (male), decorative (female), and economically affluent. Alison Light categorised this group as 'the worst excesses of a Tory politics [embracing] authoritarianism, dogmatic nationalisms, hard and fast prescriptions for sexual relations'.[8] By examining the novels by Buchan, Yates and Thirkell that display these characteristics, we can re-examine our assumptions about these readers, and re-examine how they felt about the norms of their world.

Bias and intentions

We are approaching the centenary of the beginning of the period that this book discusses, almost beyond living memory. As phenomena of a vanishing period and culture, these novels require more than ever to be understood: for literary reasons, responding to the prevailing critical tendency to overlook middlebrow literature, and to engage with the resurgence of conservative and ultra-conservative ideas in twenty-first century western culture. I will be connecting the style and idiom of these texts to their authors' politics later in this chapter. I want to establish here the importance of these novels, by virtue of their representational nature, as mirrors to the British social-political nexus of the twentieth century. By understanding their politicised rhetoric we can identify why these authors and their novels are important for integrating conservative politics into fiction, and why they appealed as middlebrow reading, enabling us to understand better how those who read it felt about changes in British society. The novels preserve the views, and fears, of the authors, like asparagus in aspic.

My approach to dealing with this material – over a hundred novels and short stories, and forty years of British social and political history – is to historicise its social and political attitudes, rather than the more familiar conservative tropes of imperialism and masculine adventure. I ask questions based on the half-hidden concerns of the authors in their fiction, and focus on the words and their implications that reveal emotional turbulence beneath the confident rhetoric. My approach is based on close reading – a technique developed and first theorised in the period under study – and uses cultural and social history to position the fiction in its original context. I have tried to be balanced in interpreting authors working in a social context long since gone, which we cannot fully appreciate now. By seeking to understand them and their context better through investigating their fiction, I have tried to maintain objectivity as well as a historical sense.

David Cannadine, the leading historian of the British upper classes, prefaced his revised edition of *The Decline and Fall of the British Aristocracy* (1996) with a short explanation of his own politics as context for why he is drawn to his subject. Following his example, it may be helpful for readers of this book to know that while I do not share the politics of my subjects, I like their fiction very much. While being Leftish-leaning all my adult life I have long enjoyed reading novels of the Right: a paradox that has been many times awkward to explain, and difficult to justify to those of stronger political shades than my own. Unlike the 'ravening hordes of left-wing critics, maddened sociologists, Marxist fanatics' and other 'enemies of contentment' so deplored by historians of right-wing popular fiction like Richard Usborne, William Vivian Butler and A J Smithers,[9] I have always enjoyed reading novels of entertainment that exude security, nostalgia, a fixed view of the world. These old-fashioned values attract me, but attraction is not enough to warrant spending so much of my professional life on their study. Authors long considered marginal in terms of their scholarly relevance have to have something additional to the inherent nature of their writing to make them worth talking about. The additional elements, for me, are the politics that influence such authors when they address historical change in their fiction, and the fact that they sold very well for decades. My socially predicated interpretation of how political conservatism relates to social conservatism in this fiction offers a template for reading politicised authors against the grain.

The authors

John Buchan (1875–1940) was a barrister, a civil servant, a publisher, a journalist, a historian, the Director of Information for the British government during the last years of the First World War, a Member of Parliament, deputy-director of Reuters, George V's Lord High Commissioner to the General Assembly of the Church of Scotland (1933–34) and, at the end of his life, Lord Tweedsmuir, Governor-General of Canada (1935–40). He published more than a hundred books, from 1895 to 1941. Whatever he was writing was undoubtedly coloured by his political engagement, and by his professional concerns.

He was the eldest son of a Presbyterian minister from lowland Scotland, and left Scotland for the first time to sit the Oxford entrance exam in 1894. Once he had begun his studies at Brasenose College in 1895, he never lived in Scotland again, becoming part of the Scottish diaspora, in Oxfordshire and London, and then Canada. His contacts with conservative circles while he was at Oxford led to his service in South Africa under Lord Milner in 1901–03. He was an assistant editor for the conservative weekly newspaper *The Spectator*, and joined the publishing firm of Thomas Nelson & Sons as their London-based literary advisor in 1906. He married Susan Grosvenor, a cousin of the Duke of Westminster, in 1907. During the First World War he became a war historian and war correspondent.[10] His authorship of Nelson's 24-volume *History of the War* (1915–19) led to his appointment in June 1916 as a press communiqué writer for General Haig, and he became the government's Director of Information from January 1917. He had become a best-selling novelist in 1915 with *The Thirty-Nine Steps*, although this was his twentieth book. In the 1920s and 1930s he produced many excellent thrillers, picaresque adventures, historical novels and short stories, as well as works of history and biography.[11] His plots look outward to national European and economic politics, using the personal vendetta to resolve these problems through private adventures in desperate situations.

Buchan's novels and his ability to write best-sellers, and keep producing them to the same irresistible high standards, made him continually visible to the man in the bookshop and the woman at the library. His family of a daughter and three sons grew up in an Oxfordshire home constantly visited by notables and interesting people from Buchan's many different professional interests: he was close friends with T E Lawrence, and Virginia Woolf was a friend of his wife Susan. When Buchan died unexpectedly in 1940, as Governor-General of Canada, the state funeral was for Lord Tweedsmuir, but Buchan was and is still remembered as the creator of Richard Hannay.

Dornford Yates, the pen-name of Cecil William Mercer (1885–1960), was born in Walmer, in Kent, the only child of a solicitor, and the cousin of 'Saki', the noted Edwardian satirist and short story writer. After Harrow and Oxford Yates trained as a barrister in London, but began writing fiction, and his first short story was published in 1910. After being invalided out from service during the First World War, he became a very popular contributor to *The Windsor Magazine*, and gave up the law to write full-time in 1920, shortly after his marriage to the actress Bettine Edwards: their son Richard was born in the same year. By the end of his life in 1960 Yates had created an oeuvre of 35 novels and collections of short stories. His sales kept up over time: even in 1948 novels published over twenty years earlier 'were still notching up nearly 3,000 copies each in the first six months'.[12] His readers followed him for his middlebrow fantasies of romance and his elaborate language. The defining characteristics of his fiction were social comedy and thrillers with mannered plots, using highly stylised language in three types of story.

The first was set in his 'Berry' world (1914–58). Berry (Major Bertram Pleydell JP) is the head of a family of five adult cousins living together, who engage in romantic and sentimental antics of pastoral comedy among the upper classes. These stories include a touch of the thriller to assert the masculinity of the male characters, but their principal characteristic is farce. The second type consists of intense and pared-down thrillers, where gentlemen with private incomes right private wrongs: a variant of the 'Gentleman Outlaw' genre.[13] These are largely narrated by Richard Chandos, but his leader and the chief vigilante, Jonathan Mansel, coexists in the Berry world. The characters of the remaining novels and short stories inhabit the same social world of the other two types, in tense and highly strung thrillers using dramatic set-piece social dramas to illustrate the dangers of failing to obey social rules. Yates's fiction had a powerful moral voice which did not acknowledge that he might have been wrong. His fiction represents attitudes that were shared by Thirkell.

Angela Thirkell (1890–1961) was the elder daughter of the scholar John William Mackail and his wife Margaret, and the grand-daughter of Pre-Raphaelite artist Sir Edward Burne-Jones. Her brother was the novelist Denis Mackail. She grew up in Kensington, west London, and in Sussex, and her memoir *Three Houses* (1931) gives vivid descriptions of a childhood spent among artists and writers, part of her reconstructed identity as the scion of an artistic and aristocratic family. She married the prominent singer James McInnes six weeks after their first meeting in 1911, when she was 21. In 1917 Thirkell divorced her husband, who was by then a physically abusive alcoholic and in debt. She married her second husband, George Thirkell, a captain in the Australian Imperial Forces, in 1918. After their move to Australia with her two sons, Graham and Colin McInnes,[14] her third son, Lancelot Thirkell, was born in 1921.

In Australia Thirkell began writing articles and journalism, but despite this mental stimulation she was homesick for British culture as well as her family. In 1929 she went back to Britain for a visit to recover her health, and realised that her marriage was failing. In less than a year she was back in Britain for good, leaving her husband and eldest son, by then an adult, in Australia. She began writing to earn a living, since her estranged husband and elderly parents could not support her, and she had her two younger sons to support. Her first novel, *Ankle Deep*, came out in 1933, followed eight months later by *High Rising*, the first of her Barsetshire novels, on which theme she would continue to elaborate for the rest of her life. She wrote 29 novels of rural life in her invented English county of Barsetshire, among other works (see Appendix). Jill N Levin notes that 'although her British sales probably never exceeded 60,000 per year [...] her American sales [...] were always substantial [...] well above what Q D Leavis called in *Fiction and the Reading Public* the category of middlebrow fiction "read as literature" (usual sales of 15,000 to 30,000)'.[15] By the mid-1940s two of her manuscripts had been requested by the British Museum and Yale University Library.[16]

After the war, Thirkell began to lose her sharp discernment. Her plots became stagnant and her characters lost the distinguishing features that made them intriguing. Thirkell was also suffering in her personal life, being lonely and increasingly waspish about declining social standards and political changes. She worried about not earning enough and felt driven by fiscal demands to publish a novel each year. Her relationship with her son Colin MacInnes, who had published his first novel in 1950, deteriorated due to his increasing drinking and resentment of her, and he was cut out of her will.

Thirkell's Barsetshire novels concern the lives and small doings of the inhabitants of an English cathedral county town and its neighbouring villages. She took many of the place-names and family names from Anthony Trollope's nineteenth-century Barsetshire novels, and updated them, reusing events and redesigning family alliances for comic and ironic effect. Her Barsetshire novels are effectively all one book, using overlapping characters and settings to continue the long story of how life was changing for the English middle and upper classes in the countryside. They are reassuring and retrogressive, extolling the comfort and desirability of Victorian ideals, pre-Second World War conditions and traditional English social structures untouched by the twentieth century.[17] In her wartime novels she documented and mediated these changes through satire that expressed compassion for the put-upon middle and upper country classes. As a pre-war pastoralist she had been soothing and very funny: as a furious wartime conservative she wrote vigorously against the changes to her preferred societal systems, for all classes.[18] Her novels look back to a better past, and fiercely resist attempts to force yet more change on society. Diana Trilling remarked of her in the 1940s, 'for all her gentle voice, she is one of the great haters on the contemporary fictional scene'.[19]

Over the forty years that this study covers, British society changed radically from the Victorian and Edwardian expectations that these three authors had grown up with. Throughout this period, society's understanding of sex roles, class categories and political affiliations was no longer based on a set of fixed norms, but on shifting and developing alternatives. International economic conditions changed British society's assumptions about earning and spending. The effects of war on the population altered permanently the social and economic relationships between its different groups. In the writing of Buchan, Yates and Thirkell we can see a rearguard action, a strong resistance to these social changes, because they hoped and believed that the changes they disliked, and often feared, could be reversed by a return to governments of the past and traditional social codes. They were hard-working outsiders who may have been goaded to extra efforts by the knowledge that they did not have a natural place in the upper strata of the society they were defending. Buchan was a self-made and aspirational Scot operating in the heart of Establishment England, Yates aspired to belong to more exclusive society than that of his middle-class origins, and Thirkell felt socially disadvantaged by her divorce and having to earn her own income.

What I find most interesting about these three writers is how they used their fiction to engage consistently, and, in the case of Thirkell and Yates, relentlessly, with the evocation of the old order against the onslaught of the new. Buchan did this for over twenty years, after the First World War, but his ascent into the British political class tempered the expression of his feelings in print. Yates and Thirkell fought their good fight in fiction for, respectively, fifty and thirty years. They defended their values and their standards against an increasing disregard for these in literature and the emerging popular media, as well as in political terms. They sought to influence their readers by writing with a conservative voice that lauded older values and the pre-war way of life. In this they were a striking contrast to the many British writers who used fiction to hasten social change, and consolidate the gains made by post-war reform to make even more radical change possible.

The power of popularity

The popular novels that these three writers produced are important cultural artefacts because they record the manners of their period. In this I follow Alison Light's observation that 'because novels not only speak from their cultural moment but take issue with it, imagining new versions of its problems, exposing, albeit by accident as well as by design, its confusions, conflicts and irrepressible desires, the study of fiction is an especially inviting and demanding way into the past'.[20] Fiction is a repository for the views of authors, their concerns, and most especially their fears. During accelerating social change and political polarisation in a turbulent world economy, we can observe how fiction collects and strengthens reactions to social change. The immersion of these novels in their own historical moment allows them to retain the record of dialogue about current events and, in the case of the conservative writer, about the far more preferable past.[21]

Using David Smith's methodology in his study of novels of the Left, since what is revealing for one political colour of fiction can work for all colours, we can view 'these books against the background of the political, and where necessary, the social conditions from which they sprang'.[22] By studying the fiction within its social and historical context, we can consider how its reception may enable a discussion of the socially and politically conservative novel as a complex social phenomenon that negotiates changing class rules and concepts of individual class and social mobility. The consumer of fiction is as important as its author, because the reader continues the process begun by the author, in agreeing or disagreeing with the points of view in the fiction for sale.[23]

This book is part of the new British middlebrow studies, in which scholars examine middlebrow authors and texts (fiction and non-fiction) for what they can tell us about the writing and publishing of the earlier half of the twentieth century and what these texts were telling their readers. I also align my work with the study of literary modernism, since these conservative popular novelists, while reacting to twentieth-century modernist culture, also show clear signs of adopting aesthetic and stylistic advances in literary techniques that modernism had produced. Yates's writing shows some evidence of this in his use of the carnivalesque in his comedies, and in his stylised descriptions that abandon narrative for impressionistic display. Thirkell's whole oeuvre is based on a conscious use of intertextuality, pastiche and parody, but she lauds the Victorians rather than dismisses them. She consciously embraced metafiction as her novels developed into a sequence, though her use of the narrative voice as a commentator on her own practice was not an obviously modernist act. Buchan's central trope of the thin line holding back the forces of anarchy from civilisation was an expression of conservative resistance to the modern, admitting and wrestling with the pessimism and world-weariness of the avant-garde. *The Spectator*'s poetry reviewer for many years, he explicitly attacked modernist poetry in *Huntingtower* (1922).

The cultural importance of these novels is that they were read by millions, and thus had immense influence, as well as representing the approval by millions of their views. They were not part of mass culture, which, typified by newspapers, was an agglomerate of the same thing said in the same way by many producers (though Thirkell's fiction did come to resemble this after the war).[24] Their writing displays aesthetic values, and was designed for culturally meaningful effect. Their work can be demarcated from that of their peers who also wrote thrillers, romances and social comedies. Their fiction is richly rewarding for the skilled intricacy of their plots as well as for how their stories were told. The sophistication of their techniques indicates that these writers deployed many influences from literary tradition, and should be read in parallel with the more widely discussed innovations by modernist authors of their period.

Reading these three authors with care, rather than belittlement or dismissal, can nuance our understanding of literary production in the interbellum, and during and after the Second World War, as it pertains to the encoding of social conservatism in fiction. There is a complex relationship between the views of the narrative voices, and the views embedded in everything the characters say and do, which will help us understand the fears and anxieties of the period.

The fears of the conservative novelist

The reactionary response of Buchan, Yates and Thirkell was based on nostalgia, undercut by fear. In *Politics and Literature* George Watson notes that 'the conservative mind feeds on nostalgia; its myth is always of a better time long past that can never be lived again. Any choice the conservative makes, for this reason, can only be in a mood of avoidance and out of fear of something worse. He thinks, speaks and votes against dangers, real and imagined'.[25] The idea of imagined dangers is particularly relevant for Yates. He resented all social change, except perhaps the increasing availability of cars. His income from authorship made him liable to pay more out in taxes than he thought was reasonable, but it also gave him the financial security to build his own home and live comfortably in the south of France. During the Second World War he and his wife fled to Portugal and then Rhodesia. When they returned briefly to their home in Les Eaux Bonnes after the war, they found a changed country, and disliked the new attitudes of their former servants and acquaintances towards expatriate Britons, especially those who had not experienced the Occupation. Thus, despite a morbid idolisation of England in his fiction, from 1921 Yates was only an occasional visitor to his home country.

Thirkell was less dependent on fantasy, and used her own experiences widely in her fiction, but she too had had an expatriate life. Although she had lived in Australia for the whole of the 1920s, her move back to Britain in the early 1930s was partly because the cultural and social climate in Australia was not enough to fulfil her creative and social aspirations. In the ten years of her absence her own culture and London society had changed. Her fiction thus can be read as a continuing critique of the changes in society that she resented, as part of a broader sense of entitlement.

Buchan used his novels to explore his concerns with international political instability, and with the integration of change within society. Compared to the writing of Yates and Thirkell, his fiction is less strident in his assessment of what was wrong with society, since he lived in Britain for almost all of his life until 1935. The changes that he incorporated in his fiction were handled more moderately, and with more understanding. His fiction was concerned with the national and Establishment response to political and cultural change that threatened economies and governments, rather than the fortunes of a family and a class.

Looking at the concerns of their peers, we can see how the writing establishment in interbellum Britain helped to shape the climate of conservative reaction that Buchan was already experiencing, and which Yates embraced with energy in his thrillers. When Thirkell began writing her response was mediated through social change, since it was this that struck her most powerfully on her return from ten years living outside Britain. Since 1919, the literary establishment in the mid-1930s had become politicised beyond all recognition.

Political writing

The critical landscape for twentieth-century British literature is uneven.[26]
There are very few studies of the commercially successful writers of the
Right, or indeed of any twentieth-century popular novelist who was
not of the Left. Most of the critical books I quote from were published
in the 1970s and 1980s, since almost nothing has been published since
on the interaction between twentieth-century politics and fiction. To
give a sense of how politics divided writers for this period, I will borrow
from George Watson's inspired analogy, in which he chooses a moment
from what Terry Rodgers calls 'the ideologically weighted and shifting
textual and cultural politics of the late thirties'[27] – the brief period when
Buchan, Yates and Thirkell were publishing simultaneously – to visualise the intellectuals of the Right and the Left in British literature 'as two
rival teams in an imaginary game, with the years 1936–7 as the point
of division'. In Watson's game of fantasy football, on the Right were W
B Yeats, Wyndham Lewis, T E Hulme, D H Lawrence, Ezra Pound, T S
Eliot, T E Lawrence, Roy Campbell and Evelyn Waugh. Playing for the
liberal Left were Team Bloomsbury, which included Maynard Keynes,
Virginia Woolf, Lytton Strachey, E M Forster, Bertrand Russell, Cecil
Day Lewis, Christopher Isherwood, William Empson, W H Auden,
Louis MacNeice and Stephen Spender.[28] This very subjective selection of
prominent outcrops in the intellectual and literary landscape of the day
contains no women writers apart from the inevitable Virginia Woolf,
and no writers of colour. It also ignores popular literature. Nonetheless,
it is a useful basis from which to work, as it shows us clearly the writers
who were, in the 1970s, thought worth discussing as politicised authors.

Buchan, Yates and Thirkell would not have been included for several
good reasons. By 1936 John Buchan was Lord Tweedsmuir, Governor-
General of Canada, and was out of the commercial fray as an author. He
was also not regarded as a politicised intellectual on the same terms as
the authors cited above, being more of a networker and political advisor
than a creator of original artistic statements and techniques. Despite his
many works of history and political biography, his authority as a historian has not lasted, and his reputation when Watson wrote his study
in the 1970s was 'only' that of a writer of excellent thrillers. Dornford
Yates could never be considered a literary intellectual: his black and
white views do not reveal intellectual curiosity, except that of a lawyer,
his former profession. Thirkell, too, was not remotely likely to have been
considered intellectual: she had received the education of a middle-class
Victorian girl, in which French was a more valuable accomplishment

than logic. Nonetheless, considering the likes of Pound, both Lawrences and Waugh as fellow travellers on the literary/political continuum with Buchan, Yates and Thirkell is helpful in positioning their fiction.

Other writers not included by Watson were the prominent right-wing interwar novelists who wrote for the mass market. 'Sapper', Sax Rohmer and Edgar Wallace wrote formulaic fiction of varying quality for a readership with particular requirements in their fiction (action, excitement, narrative tension, and forms of ritualised and abstract violence), and used their novels to reinforce stereotypes of alien fears present in the British interwar social landscape. Their scenes of violence could be crude and titillating, and were read explicitly for thrills.

Leslie Charteris, creator of 'The Saint', was less easily categorised. He opposed the Left-led National Strike by volunteering as a bus driver, though his conservative views were always moderate. The hyperbolic language in his novels from 1928 may have been an influence on Yates's experiments with style: gaudy, mock-formal, facetious. Charteris was too young to have fought in the First World War, and associated himself, through his hero Simon Templar, with anti-war sentiments from veterans who resented the war. His hero never plotted against Bolsheviks, and supported the Left in the Spanish Civil War. As a half-Chinese author, Charteris was also unlikely to have shared the explicit xenophobia of Yates and Thirkell.

The historical romances of the politically and socially conservative Georgette Heyer, published from the 1920s onward, did not comment on contemporary social ills, since they were set in an idealised past. Her plots were firmly conservative, in which older men married younger women by exerting a pleasingly physical dominance after demonstrating their intelligence and reliability, the feudal hierarchy was maintained without question, and inheritances were transferred between upper-class families by marriage. Her later detective novels of the 1940s and 1950s, sent the same messages by tackling progressive social evils, obliquely through characterisation, and overtly in dialogue.

Thirkell's work has nothing in common with the novels of 'Sapper', Rohmer and Wallace except their period, but she shares Heyer's superb mastery of comic writing within the romance. Buchan's novels rise above the mass-market novelists effortlessly by their literary quality and his scholarly background. Yates occasionally displays 'Sapper's intensity in his attitudes to foreigners and criminals, and in the sadistic detail of some of his scenes of violence and sexualised humiliation. However, his linguistic inventiveness and delight in wit and romance prevent him from descending too far down into the pit of right-wing formulaic crudities.

There was an increasing politicisation in reading during the 1930s, exemplified by the establishment of politicised Book Clubs. Terry Rodgers' research has shown that after the Left Book Club had been founded by Victor Gollancz in 1936, a Liberal Book Club was founded, run before 1939 'under the patronage of [journalist and novelist] A G Macdonell, who published work by Osbert Sitwell, Augustus John, J Maynard Keynes, Gilbert Murray, and A A Milne'.[29] The rather less well-known Right Book Club was founded as a direct response to the Left Book Club, by the leading bookseller Christina Foyle. 'From its launch in 1937, through the twilight years of the thirties and into the war years and beyond, the Right Book Club occupied a distinctive place in the publishing landscape as a locus of conservative values.'[30] Rodgers records that its existence, and indeed its success, 'reflected a widespread concern among Conservatives in the thirties to the effect that British culture, and particularly literature, was being assailed and subverted by Marxist propaganda masquerading as art'.[31] The target readership was 'the middlebrow and popular literary market', who would also have been readers of Buchan, Yates and Thirkell.[32] Foyle's motivation for establishing the Right Book Club was 'essentially socio-cultural and commercial in its trajectory' rather than political.[33] She went on a few months later to set up 'The Book Club', which effectively targeted the same membership as the Right Book Club, but could reach a wider social range, and in 1941 published Thirkell's novel *Cheerfulness Breaks In*.[34]

The references that these groups shared in their reading choices express cultural unities, and identify insiders and outsiders through language. To read Angela Thirkell can sometimes feel like training for a strenuous tournament of literary allusions from Victorian fiction, by which the winner demonstrates the right kind of moral and social values as well as formidably wide reading. Reading John Buchan can give the same impression, but competing in Biblical and classical allusions and the works of Sir Walter Scott. Dornford Yates's narratives are packed with very traditional echoes, described by his biographer as being located 'somewhere between the Pentateuch and the Bard'.[35] Reading fiction so saturated with these literary expectations introduces the reader to an encoded culture with specific expectations.

Following David Smith's approach to tracing socialism in literature, I would like to ask, in relation to the works of Yates, Buchan and Thirkell, 'to what extent is this book conveying its author's own conviction, and to what extent is it a satisfactory work of art?'[36] As Mary Grover notes in the context of studying authors whose work raises powerful emotions, 'our job as intellectual fissure-detectors is to map the contradictions and incoherence that underlie the illusion of a coherent worldview fraudu-lently constructed by the writer'.[37] Nothing may be taken at face value, even something as apparently simple as an opinion in the mouth of a fictional character.

Best-selling authors who were not obviously of the Left, or culturally privileged as followers of the modernists, have not been considered important or numerous enough to attract critical attention as a group. This has created a significant gap in the study of the popular literary culture of the twentieth century. Alison Light notes that even in the early 1990s the critique of conservatism in literary culture, as in every-day life, was well-nigh invisible. 'Anyone who wants to write about conservatism [...] must start from a kind of vacuum [...] conservatism, of the lower-case variety, has been even more unaccounted for; as one of the great unexamined assumptions of British cultural life its history is all but non-existent.'[38]

When we also consider political affiliation with class, the picture of the British interwar literary landscape becomes more complicated. George Watson notes that:

> The Left [of the interwar period] are more upper-class in origin than the Right. [They] might almost be said, in all essentials, to have led the same early life, and it was a life strikingly superior in its social advantages [...] there could be no clear and contrasting identikit portrait of the Right. It is not a set or a coterie between the wars, and it lacks a characteristic life-style based on a community of friendship or even acquaintance. [...] the Right may have existed powerfully in the literary world of the Thirties, but it did not exist as an entity.[39]

A similar lack of definition in what writers of the Right objected to may have weakened their justification for being taken seriously by more recent critics. Modern literary criticism has been interested in writing that focuses on political manifestations such as feminism, Marxism and its variations, and postcolonialism. It is predicated on writers of the Left as the norm, the model for literary activity, those who were deeply con-cerned with politics. Consequently those writers who were not solely political, and popular writers of the Right who focused most obviously on social rather than political disapproval, were not permitted the critical status that could have allowed them to function as counter-balancing voices. Janet Montefiore noted in 1996 that exclusion from the literary canon set by white male left-wing critics operated by back-ground, sex, age and education.[40] We should add politics to her list.

The major exception is Rudyard Kipling, who had been accepted into the critical canon by the 1970s. Evelyn Waugh and Anthony Powell have received scholarly attention more recently, but few others have been studied beyond the occasional scholarly article. Rosa Maria Bracco noted that in many of the novels published immediately after the First World War, assumptions about the rightness of the war and the just cause it represented were so accepted in national culture that they were rarely explicitly stated in that fiction.[41] The same may be seen of conservative popular culture in this period, especially when being assessed by scholars of the Left in literature. It was assumed that the right-wing, conservative, or non-socialist reader was the norm, without any critical value being placed on what these norms read or thought. We can find traces of conservative fiction on the edges of classifications drawn up by generations of liberal, socialist, left-wing and other politically advanced critics, in which the 'assumptions' of conservatism 'seem a strange and unfamiliar culture rather than the unexamined norm'.[42]

An additional reason for Yates, Thirkell and, until recently, Buchan being passed over by the academy is their status as writers of middle-brow fiction. Nicola Humble has noted that middlebrow writing 'straddles the divide between the trashy romance or thriller on the one hand, and the philosophically or formally challenging novel on the other: offering narrative excitement without guilt, and intellectual stimulation without undue effort'.[43] Much has been published since 2009 on middlebrow texts, authors, readers and theories, but middlebrow fiction that is angrily, dogmatically conservative, as it clearly is in Yates and Thirkell, has not received the critical attention its importance requires.[44]

It should not be assumed that a middlebrow reader only read middlebrow. A London newspaper of 1930 describes middlebrow as not representing 'the "middle-class" or even the middle-aged, but bridges all classes and ages and most activities', and that the middlebrow reader 'can be amused by, say, Aldous Huxley, without thinking him a particular tin god, or having any kind of illusions about the kind of people he celebrates: but so it can by Edgar Wallace and P G Wodehouse'.[45] More recently, I described middlebrow as a category of many dimensions along a continuum of relative positioning, because it had 'no single defining feature in terms of theme, subject, reader, form or message. Their markets were also disparate; middlebrow could be a mode of reading, a stratum of society, a class of book, or a state of mind'.[46]

There is a correlation here with what I said earlier about writers of the Right, based on a lack of central cohesion or unifying purpose. Both middlebrow and popular conservative fiction emerged not from an ideological movement or a single purpose, but as a market response that linked authors and readers very closely. If there is no obvious creative or commercial impetus external to the writer, then the writer's particular preferences will shape their writing: they will write themselves very deeply into their novels. This would explain the sustained political and social views throughout these writers' oeuvres, and their attraction to readers who desired consistency and reliability, fixed points of view in a shifting and changing world.

Readers who felt the need for this kind of reading need not have felt this all the time. It is perfectly possible that a reader could read 'up' or 'down' when reading Buchan or Thirkell. The fixed values in their writing (social and political) would attract aspirational and didactic readers, just as they would attract readers who wanted reassurance that others of their class felt as they did, and readers who wanted to relax rather than have their ideas challenged. While Buchan's histories and biographies, and his essays and serious journalism, might give him more gravitas as an author, most of his novels were exhilarating variations on the romp through the heather, invisibly supported with solid scholarship and literary skill. A Yates novel might be less easily acceptable as a reading choice for someone who normally delighted in Dorothy Richardson or Wyndham Lewis (I return to this point of reading range in Chapter 9), but for the reader who grew up devouring Yates's short stories and serialised novels in *The Windsor Magazine*, and who remembered his prose style with pleasure, a return to these early reading delights later in life could be a powerful temptation despite more recently acquired literary interests. As a novelist more commonly marketed to and read by women, Thirkell had an easier time achieving multi-level acceptance through her very high sales, not least to libraries. Requests to booksellers or librarians for her novels could have several categories of book in mind: delightful updatings of Anthony Trollope, wickedly satirical stories about the changing face of Britain, or comfortable romances at the end of which an engagement was guaranteed.

Buchan's unexpected death in 1940 meant that one of his best novels was also his last. His writing did not have time to deteriorate in quality, unlike with Thirkell and Yates, much of whose writing degenerated into circular memoirs at the end of their lives. The gradual decline in public interest in Yates and Thirkell during the 1950s was because the narrative voices of their novels did not change, whereas society did. In the 1950s, the messages that were popular in the 1930s were no longer comprehensible, and were not palatable to younger readers. I have already suggested that Yates and Thirkell probably drew upon their memories of a past Britain because they lived outside Britain for the whole of the 1920s, and in Yates's case, until his death in 1960. Their fossilisation of memory into fiction, and a gluelike adherence to their views of thirty years earlier, may be shared by other conservative novelists of this period. Buchan's writing may represent the more balanced views of the local inhabitant, set against the more strident and polarised opinions of the expatriates Yates and Thirkell. The popular critic Richard Usborne noted in 1953 that expatriates were 'often the most patriotic and xenophobic'.[47]

Yet fossilisation may also be regarded as preservation, even conservation. The resistance to change by the American writer H P Lovecraft, another author of profoundly conservative views, and also a genre writer, has been described as a positive trait: 'like many conservatives he turned to the continuity of tradition as a refuge against the forces of change'.[48] Yates and Thirkell were extremely strong on the continuity of tradition. In many ways this animated most of their novels, particularly their social comedies. Buchan too venerated tradition, and his narrative characters expostulated against change that ignored the traditions that he cared about. But expostulating, and sitting gloomily in silent worry, are as far as Buchan's characters go to express their objection to such changes. In his fiction, characters only express emotions when the most important traditions are violated. Emotions are vehement in Yates's novels, and in Thirkell to a lesser extent – although she was never as passionate in her fiction as he could be – but they are also continually present. By this continual suffering we learn that what matters to them is continually under threat.

Yates: Raised diction and diamanté vocabulary

By focusing on the emotional loading in Yates's vocabulary, I will show how decoding his use of language can let us read his politicised intentions, which will lead on to an examination of how Buchan and Thirkell also played with language with political intent. The 'hyperbolic floridity', to use the words of an anonymous early reader of the present book, of Yates's style may at first encounter be repellent, and also eye-catching. It is also one of his most characteristic traits. He may have been clinging to the vocabulary and syntax of his Edwardian education, but he decorates his sentences with complicated rhetorical tropes in a grandiose eighteenth-century style, and then rescues their teetering top-heaviness with an assured return to the metaphor first thought of. His style takes the reader away from the story for short games of word-play.

Yates's plots, particularly in his early 'Berry' short stories, have strong associations with 'the "filigree game" of faux shepherd and play-acting shepherdess' which Raymond Williams identifies as being key to the pastoral mode.[49] Pastoral plots remove characters from the real world to place them in a safe place to recover, to heal or to resolve their problems through play. They can also be allegorical. Using this intensely artificial setting, and language, Yates presented general truths in neo-pastoral settings that represented 'England'.[50]

Yates used the comic mode as one of his two default settings (the other was emotional tension). Berry Pleydell is Yates's best-known comic character. His normal stance towards his brother-in-law and cousin Boy Pleydell, Yates's lead narrator, is exasperation and joyful contempt, alternated during crises with brief moments of emotion expressed quietly when permitted by the stiff upper lip. Berry's playfully abusive tone and his fondness for loathsome physical descriptions are combined with irony to amuse the reader. His capacity for derision is also exercised in dialogue. Here, Berry returns from an inadvertent bicycle ride.

> He turned to Daphne. "Since I left you this morning, woman, I have walked with Death. Oh, more than once. Of course I've walked without him, too. Miles and miles." He groaned. "I never knew there was so much road."
>
> "Didn't you do any riding?" said Jonah. "I know they're called push-bikes, but that's misleading. Lots of people ride them. That's what the saddle's for."
>
> "Foul drain," said my brother-in-law, "your venomous bile pollutes the crystal flood of my narration. Did I ride? That was the undoing of the sage."[51]

As a barrister Yates clearly relished declamation. His deliberate, rolling phrases and exhilarating periods derive from exhibitionism at the Law Courts and are infectious, as is the humour derived from the sudden collapse from the haughty to the physical. Yates's biographer writes in the same style, and it is noticeable, after reading enough Yates, that ordinary correspondence takes on this Yatesian phrasing almost of its own volition, either in appreciative *hommage* or helpless imitation.

Yates admired Robert Louis Stevenson, Conan Doyle, W H Hudson and Anthony Hope, as stylists and storytellers. He also followed the writing styles of Thomas Hardy, Stanley Weyman and Maurice

Hewlett,[52] and the heavily stylised historical novels of Agnes and Egerton Castle. He was strongly in accord with the spirit of an age which used, as Paul Fussell has noted, a deliberately '"raised", essentially feudal language' for its war poetry. 'The tutors in this special diction had been the boys' books of George Alfred Henty; the male-romances of Rider Haggard; the poems of Robert Bridges; and especially the Arthurian poems of Tennyson and the pseudo-medieval romances of William Morris.'[53] Yates used 'assail' as a consciously archaic word for 'attack'. His 'gallant' meant 'earnestly brave'; 'staunch' was 'to be solidly brave'; 'deeds' were 'actions'; to 'swerve' was 'to show cowardice'; 'dishonour' was 'produced by cowardice'; 'naught' was 'nothing'; and 'save' simply meant 'except'. The overall tone produced by this elevated vocabulary suggested the polite values of a vanished society, and carried value judgements by its use. It is also what Ted Bogacz calls a 'further manifestation of English cultural resistance to the industrial age and most particularly to the traumatic new kind of warfare on the Western Front which was a long-range result of the Industrial Revolution'.[54] To use the words was to automatically be imbued with their qualities: a transference of sentiment to character.[55] Yates indulged this habit, too often and too freely for some tastes, in virtuoso displays of lexical excess.

The dedications to his books alone are an astonishing display of unselfconscious archness, showing archaic values on many levels. Yates's biographer wrote approvingly of a particularly theatrical dedication in Yates's first book, the short story collection *The Brother of Daphne* (1914), that it was 'merited, honest, and untainted by humbug'.[56] It reads:

> TO HER, who smiles for me, though I essay no jest, whose eyes are glad at my coming, though I bring her no gift, who suffers me readily, though I do her no honour. MY MOTHER.

One century later, we might admire the sentiment, but shift uneasily at Yates's expression. A selection of book dedications from the years that followed gives similar insights as to how he expressed strong feelings for the important things in his life.

> *And Five Were Foolish* (1924): 'To Bettine. They say that names are like chameleons, taking their colour from their bearers. And this I am ready to believe, for I never met one of my age that would say a good word for "Gregory" not [sic] one of your acquaintance that did not find yours, as I do, a sweet pretty name.'

As Other Men Are (1930): 'To Patricia, who married for love. This with my duty. Your husband will not object. Indeed, but for me, you would never have married the fool – a truth which has sometimes lain heavy upon my soul. But not for long: for so soon as I see you I know in my heart that if Time were put back and you were a maiden again I should do all I could to induce you to marry the fool.'

Adèle & Co (1931): 'To the Villa Maryland, Pau, which, with its English garden, made me a home worth having for seventeen years.'[57]

Safe Custody (1932): 'To the finest city in the world, incomparable London Town.'

She Painted Her Face (1937): 'To my beautiful dog, "The Knave", who, in his short life, gave me all that he had, and, by so doing, left behind him a bankrupt who can never be discharged.'

As well as giving snapshots of Yates's life, this sample of book dedications indicates Yates's preferred way of presenting himself to the world, and his concerns. An early dedication is long enough to bear close examination, from a 1930s edition of the story collection *Jonah & Co* (1922):

To Elm Tree Road.

My Lady,

It is hard, sitting here, to believe that, if I would call for a cab, I could be in St James's Street in less than ten minutes of time. Nevertheless, it is true. I have proved it so many times. Soon I shall prove it for the last time.

Better men than I will sit in this study and pace the lawn in the garden with the high walls. The lilies and laburnums and all the gay fellowship of flowers will find a new waterman. The thrushes and blackbirds and wood-pigeons will find a new victualler. The private forecourt, so richly hung with creeper, will give back my footfalls no more. Other eyes will dwell gratefully upon the sweet pretty house and look proudly out of its leaded window-panes.

The old order changeth, lady. And so I am going, before I am driven out.

Nine years ago there was a farm upon the opposite side of the road – a little old English farm. Going out of my door of a morning, I used to meet ducks and geese that were taking the air. And horses came home at even, and cows lowed. Now the farm is gone, and a garage has taken its room. And other changes have come, and others still are coming.

So, you see, my lady, it is high time I was gone.

This quiet study has seen the making of my books. This – the last it will see – I make bold to offer to you for many reasons, but mainly because, for one thing, this house belongs to you and, for another, no hostess was ever so charming to the stranger within her gates.

I have the honour to be

Your ladyship's humble servant,

Dornford Yates

Starting at the top, the dedication to the house where Yates had lived in London is a later addition: the book was originally dedicated to 'B.S.M.', his former wife Bettine Mercer, whom he divorced in 1933. He felt his divorce deeply enough to remove other book dedications to Bettine, and to exclude her completely from the rest of his life.[58]

By using 'if I would' for 'if I were to' Yates is establishing a consciously archaic tone, matched by 'ten minutes of time', 'waterman', 'victualler', 'the old order changeth', 'of a morning', and 'at even'. His fondness for the Elizabethan phrase 'sweet pretty' shows in its reuse in a 1924 dedication (see above), and its period is echoed by the Elizabethan 'leaded window-panes' that he is careful to mention.

Yates insists on being associated with a gentleman's natural habitus as well as his habitat. Elm Tree Road is in St John's Wood, an artists' suburb north-west of Regent's Park, London, and an area formerly notorious for the apartments of the mistresses of Victorian gentlemen. The street also lies parallel to Lord's cricket ground, home of the national game of English gentlemen. By indicating that he visits St James's Street so often, Yates is asserting his ease of movement between two social strata, and his acceptance in both. He also insists on privacy and control over his own domain: the garden's high walls are a source of pleasure, and his forecourt is private: an important distinction.

But there is also a sense of aggrieved beleaguerment. He says that he is leaving before he is driven out (but how could a speaker with such proud assurance be forced to do anything?). The farm is not only a symbol of all that is admirable about traditional, useful rural production, but it is also little (vulnerable), old (even more vulnerable), and English (it would hardly be anything else in London, but still: Yates is making a strong symbolic point). Turning to the interloper, Yates notes that the garage (symbolic of speeding, noisy, smelly modernity) has not only replaced the farm, but has 'taken its room': the phrasing is deliberately archaic, and 'taken' is an active, aggressive verb. Stepping back from the hyperbole, it is unclear why a garage across the road is enough to make Yates terminate the lease of a much-loved and convenient home. He was a passionate lover of fast cars, after all, and *Jonah & Co* is full of thrilling driving episodes. The changes that were still coming, the onset of the modern world that the garage represents, are driving Yates out, but he does not mention what they were. He sentimentalises about garden birds and flowers, and the 'quiet study [that] has seen the making of my books'. *Jonah & Co* was only Yates's fifth book, yet the phrase suggests a much longer publication list.

There is nothing wrong with such hyperbole: in Yates's hands it could produce spectacularly comic dialogue, as well as making adventure epic. It reads less admirably, and more egregiously, when he applies it to his own case in a bid for sympathy. After all, he is choosing to leave a way of life that seems perfectly pleasant, in search of an even more comfortable lifestyle. Most damning of all, the stories in *Jonah & Co*, first published in *The Windsor Magazine* throughout 1921 and into 1922, were all written in Pau, south-western France, in a rented villa. One reason for living in a warm climate was the chronic rheumatism Yates had developed during the war, another was a much lighter tax bill. As well as presenting a fantasised version of the past in this dedication, Yates was also offering a fantasy about his present, avoiding mention of his avoidance of tax by suggesting a highly emotive tale of persecution instead.

Turning again to his use of language to massage nostalgia into art, we can study a passage from his 1920 collection, *Berry & Co*.

Oxford has but two moods.

This day she was *allegro*. The Sunshine Holyday of Spring had won her from her other soberer state, and Mirth was in all her ways. Her busy streets were bright, her blistered walls glowed and gave back the warmth vouchsafed them; her spires and towers were glancing, vivid against the blue: the unexpected green, that sprawled ragged upon scaly parapets, thrust boldly out between the reverend mansions and smothered up the songs of architects, trembled to meet its patron: the blowing meadows beamed, gates lifted up their heads, retired quadrangles smiled in their sleep, the very streams were lazy, and gardens, walks, spaces and alleyed lanes were all betimes a-Maying.[59]

Once again Yates uses deliberately archaic words or phrasing. The initial capitals for words not normally so styled show Yates's interest in transferring status by association. Here he raises common nouns to a greater significance that draws on medievalised expression. He also enjoys the exuberance of the logical conclusion, expressed here in personification: spires glancing, grass trembling to meet its patron, beaming meadows, heads of gates, smiling quadrangles, and lazy streams.

Yates's hyperbole acts as a passport to his world. If you enjoy his descriptive style you will also enjoy similar excesses in his reactionary social politics or snobbery, his insistence on ossified male–female and inter-class power relations and his extraordinary retrogressive nursery society of forbidden consanguinity, without actually taking it seriously. George Simmers notes, rightly, that Yates's use of language can be linked to his political and social attitudes.

> Yates's readers are involved in a game. The language is hugely excessive, luxurious, unnecessary – so the reader is posed the question, how seriously do you take it? The reader is placed in the position of being able to wallow in the language, without taking it completely seriously – and this helps the reader enjoy the attitudes, too. They are so flamboyantly reactionary that the reader can pretend they are just a joke – while secretly sharing and enjoying them.[60]

The game can be played by readers of any political colour, but readers with less idealistic attachment to the Left will play it with most enthusiasm, without the knowing irony that other readers may feel necessary as an excuse. Yates made social and cultural nostalgia a political position that belongs most strongly to the Right.

With language as a vehicle, Yates employed his vocabulary to assert the values of the old, in defiance of the changing and the new. He processed messages through his word choices in quite remarkable ways. Symbols take flight to become outrageously extended metaphors in this passage set in the cramped and dirty attic room that Anthony the lovelorn ex-officer inhabits as a footman.

> It was more than a month now since he had seen the lady. At the moment he supposed gloomily that she had gone out of his life. Considering what his life was, it was just as well. (Melancholy smiled to herself, sighed sympathetically, and laid her head on Anthony's shoulder.) [...] There was a flap beneath the window [of his room] which, when raised, arrested the progress of such smuts as failed to clear it in their descent to the boards. (Melancholy smothered a

laugh and laid a wet cheek against her victim's.) [...] Scaramouche
Melancholy fairly squirmed with delight. Then she turned upon
Anthony eyes swimming with tenderness, put up consoling lips ...
The entrance of Polchinelle, however, cudgel and all, in the shape
of a little white dog, dragging a bough with him, spoiled her game.
Harlequin Sun, too, flashed out of hiding – before his cue, really, for
the shower was not spent. Scaramouche fled with a snarl.[61]

The reader can accept the metaphorisation of Anthony's melancholy
as a strangely two-faced fantasy woman. But when commedia dell'arte
arrives, the metaphor develops a completely new level of play-acting.
Ritualised relationships remind us of the need for balance in human
emotions. On one level this is a pleasantly whimsical word-game, but
on another Anthony is given a mythic, Everyman role as a gentleman
employed in unpleasant conditions a long way below his social station.
Yates's lexical exuberance raises the reader's imagination to sublime
heights to match his verbal invention, and forces the reader to affirm
his conservative view of post-war society, in which everything has
changed for the worse, as far as the gentleman is concerned.

Yates incorporated elaborate decoration and formal symmetry in
his sentences, to suggest a foundation of power. He summoned ideas
about class with highly specific words. The traditional vocabulary of
the mastery of horses, or dogs, was a particular favourite, especially
when applied to desirable women. 'The girl glanced up and down the
lane. Then she twitched her skirt to her knee. Under her right hock,
held in place by four straps, was a wallet.'[62] The unfamiliar juxtaposi-
tion of image and action can be unexpectedly erotic, as in *Blood Royal*
(1929) when Chandos is cleaning mud from the shoes of the Grand
Duchess Leonie. 'When I had cleaned them both, I knelt and shod
her.'[63] Shoeing the lady happens again in *Storm Music* (1934) and at
length in *Gale Warning* (1939).[64] Yates's language strove always to leap
backwards over the uncomfortable realities of the war, and even over
the nineteenth and eighteenth centuries, to recall to the reader's mind
through vocabulary a vaguely nostalgic period of history that was far
enough away to not be remembered accurately. His repeated verbal ref-
erencing of the past was also a rejection of a present that was becoming
increasingly inimical to him. Yates did not want to recall details, but
only glowing idealised images of traditional feudalism in perfect rural
surroundings.

Robert Scholes notes the potential in Yates's fiction for discerning his
readers' attitudes towards class and gender, and Yates's inclusion of tropes

that recall English cultural heritage. He is also alert to reading Yates's use of 'a distinctly modernist technique – the montage – in which images are blended or superimposed to produce a complex meaning that invites the interpretive activity of the reader'.[65] By linking this to Huyssens' phrase of 'suggestive intertextuality', Scholes argues that Yates's syntactical techniques fall within modernist criteria. Yates used intertextuality constantly (as indeed did Thirkell) by quoting from preferred texts from the past, as well as mimicking their style, vocabulary and register. The reason for this, Scholes argues, was to link past and present, 'insisting on continuity where many Modernists insisted on rupture, and he keeps his language within the reading range of the common reader'.[66] Arguing that Yates's style was essentially of a 'Modernism that dislikes modernity', Scholes's views are a strong encouragement to read Yates as a particular kind of modern writer for the interwar years: resisting change and upholding conservative values, but also using the language and techniques of writers and artists whose work he pilloried (see Chapter 8).

Buchan: Multiple dialects

When we consider how John Buchan used language, recall that his career had been long established when the period covered by this study begins. Predating the novels and stories discussed here are the first three Richard Hannay adventures (*The Thirty-Nine Steps*, 1915; *Greenmantle*, 1916; and *Mr Standfast*, 1919), his South African novel *Prester John* (1910), and many short stories and several excellent historical novels from the earlier part of his career which began in 1895. All these contributed to his later mastery of the chase, and the theatrical disguise. Buchan's earlier works show a strong use of Biblical language, heavily influenced by the rhythms of Presbyterian phraseology. His use of Scots was distinctive and also pervasive, moving from the characters' dialogue into the narrative voice as well.

In *Huntingtower* (1922) Buchan returned to using Scots for dialogue in a novel after a hiatus of over twenty years. There are two kinds: the first is where the English words are transformed into Scots by the syntax and the cadence, employed here by the lead protagonist Dickson McCunn, a 55-year-old retired Glasgow grocer, and his antagonist, Dobson, who tries to prevent him finding out too much about the apparently deserted house of Huntingtower.

"Well, I never!" said Dickson. "Is there any law in Scotland, think you, that forbids a man to stop a day or two with his auntie?"

"Ye'll stay?"

"Ay, I'll stay."

"By God, we'll see about that [...] Ye wee pot-bellied, pig-heided Glasgow grocer" (I paraphrase), "would *you* set up to defy me? I tell ye, I'll make ye rue the day ye were born." His parting remarks were a brilliant sketch of the maltreatment in store for the body of the defiant one.

"Impident dog," said Dickson without heat.[67] (emphasis in the original)

The cadence of these lines, reinforced at key moments by phonetic spelling, drives their delivery, and reinforces the characterisation. The narrative is given richness and flavour, and conveys deep pleasure in the rhythm. There is conservatism here too, in the sense that these lines could have been spoken by characters in fiction by Sir Walter Scott, or Robert Louis Stevenson. Buchan has kept his dialogue free from slang, and restricts the vocabulary to a core lexicon which remains undated, nearly one hundred years later. This choice was not unadventurousness, or a refusal to experiment, but a preference for language that endures.

The second form of Scots used by Buchan in *Huntingtower* is 'braid Scots', in which the phonetic spelling represents pronunciation (for example, 'Peer Pairson' for 'Peter Paterson'[68]) to evoke the rich and possibly impenetrable dialect of, in this case, south-west Scotland. Mrs Morran, an elderly countrywoman temporarily adopted by McCunn as his aunt, raises the alarm when he has been kidnapped.

Breathless, flushed, with her bonnet awry and her umbrella held like a scimitar, she seized on the boy.

"Awfu' doin's! They've grippit Maister McCunn up the Mains road just afore the second milestone and forenent the auld bucht. I fund his hat, and a bicycle's lyin' broken in the wud. Haste ye, man, and get the rest and awa' and seek him. It'll be the tinklers frae the Dean. I'd gang mysel', but my legs are ower auld. Oh, laddie, dinna stop to speir questions. They'll hae him murdered or awa' to sea. And mebbe the leddy was wi' him and they've got them baith. Wae's me! Wae's me!"[69]

There is assonance (speir, wi', sea, me) and consonance (grippit, fore-nent, bucht) in this brief example. The vowels in the stressed syllables chime with the repeated consonantal endings, stressed and unstressed, to make this 'barbaric keening' a choral lament. This changes Mrs Morran from being the provider of food and shelter into a Sybil or a Fury, urging on McCunn's enterprise to save the princess and rescue the jewels. Her very ordinariness, depicted with affectionate respect from what must have been a rich experience of old Scots ladies from Buchan's youth, make her a voice of the land, a voice of the people, a voice of Scotland even, repelling the invader, rejecting the unpleasant political changes in the world that had sent Bolsheviks to Scotland in disguise.

Buchan's descriptions of speed, of chases and episodes of great tension are his hallmark: no-one can match him for describing the cross-country flight of a desperate man. In *John Macnab* (1925), his epic narrative of poaching in the Highlands, Edward Leithen must not be caught trespassing, so when the ghillie Cameron nearly gets his hands on him, he hurtles downhill.

> Like a stag from covert Leithen leaped forth, upsetting Cameron with his sudden bound. He broke through the tangle of hazel and wild raspberries, and stayed not on the order of his going. His pace downhill had always been remarkable, and Cameron's was no match for it. Soon he had gained twenty yards, then fifty, but he had no more comfort in his speed, for somewhere ahead were more ghillies, and he was being forced straight on Haripol, which was thick with the enemy. [...] But the place grew more horrible as he continued. He was among rhododendrons now, and well-tended grass walks. Yes, there was a rustic arbour and what looked like a summer seat. The beastly place was a garden. In another minute he would be among flowerpots and vineries with twenty gardeners at his heels. But the river was below – he could hear its sound – so, like a stag hard pressed by hounds, he made for the running water. A long slither took him down a steep bank of what had once been foxgloves, and he found his feet on a path. And there, to his horror, were two women.[70]

Buchan's use of active verbs in the running commentary, and the slippage into and out of free indirect speech, gives immediacy and speed to the narrative, and demands the reader's attention for the details of the chase. Leithen escapes from the hill and ends up inside the estate from whose men he is escaping. The anxiety he feels is conveyed in his irritation at the obstacles in his way and the evidence of man's domination of the wilderness as he runs further into what we increasingly fear will be a trap. He is repeatedly compared to a stag: not just a deer, but a male of the species, and the most prized prey on the hills. Even the botanical details increase our awareness of Leithen's struggle to escape: we need not know for ourselves what wild raspberries look like, but because they are a 'tangle' that has to be broken through we can infer that they will be prickly and probably densely low-growing. To get through this formidable barrier at speed suggests strength and desperation aided by a downward impetus: every word helps us visualise his flight. The layers of detail in the impediments to Leithen's escape reinforce our awareness of his strength and the pace he can muster.

Thirkell: Language of literary persuasion

Thirkell, too, was a playful innovator with older forms of language, but her method was to use the conversational mode in the narrative voice as a didactic but disarming third-person omniscient narrator. Her 1948 novel *Love Among the Ruins* ends with the Barsetshire combined Conservative Rally and Pig Show.

> By this time the notabilities, including Mr Gresham the member for East Barsetshire, were on the platform, and Lord Pomfret who was chairman rose to introduce the speakers. At the same moment a car came along the back drive going towards the station. Lord Pomfret paused. What Mrs Tebben afterwards reverently described as a Something, made the audience turn their eyes towards the car in which unmistakeably was sitting ONE, recognisable even by the meanest reader of the daily press, foursquare as a White Porkminster, commanding as a Cropbacked Cruncher, but unlike these intelligent quadrupeds smoking a large cigar. A shout which reminded all the clergymen present of a Cup Final rent the summer air. The foursquare figure lifted its hat, waved its cigar in recognition towards its friends, and disappeared round the bend. [...] The meeting then behaved like any meeting where nearly all the hearers are of the same opinion.[71]

This rare sighting of a figure from history in Thirkell's fiction is of course Winston Churchill. He is a vision of reassurance and affirmation of Conservative values in the context of a great gathering of farmers, landlords, country folk and all good men and true. The tone is compellingly inclusive: it is simply not possible in Thirkell's Barsetshire to be an admirable character and not be a Conservative, and the reader is expected to share these views. Thirkell narrates conversationally here by implying familiarity with her invented pig breeds, and sharing the joke of associating football matches with clergymen. She interleaves jokes and rhetorical devices with impeccably correct grammar: a didactic technique which instructs not so much by example as by sheer force of personality.

Thirkell used immense amounts of literary quotation in her prose, often in her characters' dialogue, and adapted these fiendishly when a better point could be made by a witty parallel. She was a skilled parodist, an example of which is her sexually implicit Cavalier poetry by the lost Barsetshire poet Thomas Bohun.

"It is rather fascinating," said Oliver, "to think that by some trick of fortune this is the only copy known to be extant. [...] This poem, *To his Mistrefs, on feeing fundrie Worme-caftes*, has probably never been read until to-day." He held the open book so that she could see it. Miss Harvey, leaning towards him, looked at the yellowed page with its elegant italics and long esses and read,

> "'As *Wormes* their *Bodies'* earthen *Images*
> Vpon the *Grounde* (groundlings themfelves indeede)
> Do voide, themfelves a *Father*, yet a *fonne*:
> So I, my *Body's* race through thine b'ing runne,
> Do void (nor can avoid) th'immortal *Feed* – '"

"I mean Seed," said Miss Harvey correcting herself,

> "'Making (with thine) our true *Effigies*.'"

She stopped.[72]

Oliver and Miss Harvey are unable to discuss this poem about successful *coitus* in an objective fashion because, as Thirkell makes quite clear over our sniggers at the predicament of these unsympathetic characters, ladies and gentlemen do not discuss sex, certainly not if they are not married or even engaged. Unmarried agriculturally minded upper-class women may discuss animal husbandry, but not in the drawing-room. Thirkell goes on to reinforce this point through irony.

[Oliver] could think of dozens of young people, round about his sister Lucy's age of twenty-five or so, who would thrash out the whole question of worm casts with academic interest and no feeling of restraint. [...] As for Miss Harvey, she felt, not for the first time, how silly men were. Any child could think of the implications of the poem. She could think of dozens of intelligent women friends who would have analysed its biological and psychological significance. But men were so apt to be squeamish.[73]

The joke here is that Miss Harvey is pursuing Oliver in a very unmaid-enly, deliberate fashion, the behaviour of an ambitious woman who mixes gender roles to suit her own purposes. Thirkell heaped derision on women characters who did not follow her Victorian code of behaviour. In her Barsetshire canon, intellectual women are pilloried. Women authors are largely exempt (because to criticise them would be to criticise herself, since several were her alter egos), but there is no room in Barsetshire for a woman who does not make the domestic role her primary concern. In *Marling Hall*, above, Miss Harvey is a joke because she poses as an intel-lectual to lure Oliver in, but has not got the objectivity, or is too squeam-ish herself, to discuss a text without applying it personally.

By manipulating the reader's opinion of her characters with their care-fully chosen attitudes, Thirkell directs her readers' opinions: here, against 'intelligent women friends' and those who discuss such matters 'without restraint'. Only children would think, and speak, of the implications of such a poem. She was imposing Victorian manners and public conduct on a generation some forty years younger than she was by a rigid stand-ard of behaviour. The intellectual playfulness of her fragment of poetry, and her assumption that her readers would have the education to under-stand and appreciate its joke, and the good manners to understand about reticence in mixed company, adds another level of assumptions to her expected reader: they would be well-read, as well as conservative.

Thirkell only toyed with the seventeenth century: her preferred liter-ary playground was the culture of the expansive nineteenth-century novel. A reasonable knowledge of Anthony Trollope's Barsetshire novels (or a concordance) is essential to appreciate Thirkell fully, so this chal-lenge to the memory makes Thirkell intimidating, if one chooses to read her on her own terms. Thirkell's stylistic flights of exuberance were also a stern test, since her fiction employs literary quotation competitively as a metatextual technique. She expected her readers to already know, or at least recognise, her references. Her characters play at capping each other's remarks with quotations from Dickens, Victorian fairy tales or Henry Kingsley (brother of the more famous Charles, a particular favourite of Thirkell's, on whom she wrote a number of scholarly arti-cles). She was highly literate and exceedingly well-read, and demanded the same standards from her readers.

The critics

Before proceeding to the chronological analysis of their fiction, I want to indicate briefly the critical context that does exist for these three writers, to situate this book as part of a new wave of scholarship on twentieth-century British middlebrow authors and disregarded genres. Buchan has received the most critical attention.[74] Four biographies have been published, in 1949, 1965, 1990 and 1995, and the first book-length critical study of his work appeared in 1975.[75] The publication of extensive Buchan bibliographies indicates their importance for Buchan scholars in simply keeping track of what he published and where.[76] As well as an increasing number of articles in scholarly journals on Buchan's writing, as well as a long tradition of 'fan criticism',[77] several wider studies also have importance for an understanding of his work. However, this scholarly activity, much of it initiated after David Daniell's *The Interpreter's House* (1975), has been hitherto confined to the subgenre of 'Buchan studies'. Current mainstream literary criticism has only in the past few years begun to account Buchan an important figure in literary history, and his appearances in critical assessments are rare and short. The most influential popular work, in that it bracketed Buchan and Yates very firmly together in the minds of generations of readers, is Richard Usborne's nostalgic study *Clubland Heroes* (1953).

Clubland Heroes discusses Buchan and Yates as cultural phenomena, rather than for their literary achievement, because Usborne selected them for his pleasure in reading their works, and for their use of nostalgia.[78] By angling his discussion in this way, aspects of the fiction of Buchan and Yates that do not fall into the category of thrilling and energetic nostalgic adventure were neglected, and usually ignored.[79] Usborne consolidated the modern popular impression of Buchan as a thriller novelist and nothing else. It had already been warped by the dominance of *The Thirty-Nine Steps* (1915) in the Buchan canon, and the 1935 Hitchcock film *The 39 Steps*. Usborne recalled that during the Second World War while he was serving in the Special Operations Executive (SOE), 'practically every officer I met in that concern, at home or abroad, was, like me, imagining himself as Hannay'.[80] Thus we can see how plausible it might be that a generation who grew up reading Buchan in the 1920s was instrumental in maintaining Buchan's popularity into the 1940s and 1950s, after Buchan's own death. *Clubland Heroes* was republished in 1974, and again in 1983, indicating that the publishers expected three or more generations of readers to share Usborne's delight in Buchan's writing.

This cultural recasting of Buchan as the creator of Hannay alone, largely to the exclusion of his other novels, received additional impetus in the 1950s, when his original readers would have been reading Buchan to their children.[81] In 1953, the same year that *Clubland Heroes* was published, Penguin Books reissued the first of what would eventually be 11 Buchan novels as popular and cheap paperbacks.[82] The list was dominated by the five Hannay novels and the three McCunn novels, and thus produced the first major bias on the bookshelves for Buchan's novels. Usborne and Penguin together consolidated the post-war cultural meme that 'Buchan' equalled 'Hannay'.

Usborne's observations on Buchan and Yates are shrewd, but to appreciate fully what he says the reader needs to understand his and the authors' cultural backgrounds. His main focus is the importance of the socially demarcated concept of 'clubland', a word that has completely changed its meaning since the 1950s. For Usborne's generation and earlier this denotes the pre- and post-war male society that inhabited gentlemen's clubs in the St James's district of central London, adjacent to Mayfair. Living in or spending one's leisure time in clubland, the area bordered by Piccadilly, Green Park, the Mall and Regent Street, during the interwar period indicated that one had money, social and political access, and enjoyed class privileges. All these were central to the fiction of Buchan and Yates, and in the background for Thirkell's class assumptions. Using Buchan's shorthand term for men who shared common values, the 'totem', Usborne notes that 'the men of the totem joined the same sort of clubs, didn't quarrel with each other's politics (they sat loose to politics and party anyway), talked the same language, travelled adventurously when young, always kept fit and tried to make something of their lives'.[83] While discussing how easily the Buchan and Yates characters seemed to circumvent the rule of law in their adventures, he reminds us of the essential characteristic of a clubman or clubland hero: 'They had, they thought, as much right and indeed as much of a duty, to kill their crooks as they had had, as school prefects, to cane Jones minor for missing a catch in the house match'.[84] The important point for Usborne is that the readers of this fiction came from the same class and world that was evoked in the heroes' public school backgrounds, and readers contemporary to the novels' publication were expected to share this,[85] or at least understand the references. This is not the case today: by the 1980s so many of the references and attitudes in Buchan and Yates needed to be explained and sometimes excused, that almost all of their titles were allowed to go out of print. Buchan is out of copyright now, and thus many (though not all) of his novels are available again in several editions. However, a great deal in Buchan's fiction still needs to be interpreted for the modern reader, if not explained outright: the Oxford World's Classics editions have extensive endnotes.

There is a profound silence concerning Yates's existence in most surveys of twentieth-century popular fiction, or even in studies of the thriller. In Clive Bloom's very influential study of popular fiction and best-sellers (1996) he refers to Yates only once, as one of a group of writers (alongside 'Sapper', Buchan and Edgar Wallace) who had 'a fearsome and totally irrational hatred of all things foreign'.[86] No further discussion is offered. As discussed above, an unexpected chapter in Robert Scholes's *Paradoxy and Modernism* (2006) is perceptive on Yates's early experiments with metafictional narration, and is important as an exploration of resistance to the correction of literary taste, and the identification of pleasure, in concert with Usborne, as a crucial marker in the examination of Yates's fiction. Yates's biography by A J Smithers (1982) is the only source of biographical material on Yates, but it lacks critical distance, and is written in a style that is unnervingly close to the elaborate lexis and syntax that Yates employed. Such closeness in style does not give confidence that a subjective closeness in opinion will be avoided.

Both Yates and Thirkell were specialists in the light literature of dislike, and were self-appointed class guardians, repelling social encroachment vigorously. Thirkell shared many things with Buchan and Yates: personal politics, class consciousness, social milieu, readership and publication period: she was friends with Buchan's wife Susan. What Alison Light sees as Angela Thirkell's 'modernity, as in [her] reiteration of well-worked national and political themes'[87] also makes her ideal for analysis as a conservative author, since there are tensions to be explored between her tendency to rewrite Barsetshire with hindsight, and her faithful recording of rural British life through a conservative lens. Thirkell's attitude to writing as a commercial enterprise fits in well with the impetus for production exhibited by Buchan and Yates.

Thirkell's novels were initially only 'studied' in her reviews. In the 1950s reviewers became more critical of her writing, and produced some serious assessments that challenged her popular reception.[88] Subsequent critical work on Thirkell is sparse, and has tended to be either long but unsatisfactory, or perceptive but brief. Her biography by Margot Strickland was published in 1977, and remains the standard account of Thirkell's life and career. Jill N Levin's research is the most important scholarly work to date for its close focus on Thirkell as the main subject, and for her rigorous and scholarly approach. However, her publications are not widely available. Laura Roberts Collins wrote the first full-length description of Thirkell's fiction in 1994,[89] and Rachel Mather discusses Thirkell at length in her 1996 study of the twentieth-century comedy of manners, though she does not acknowledge the nineteenth-century

Trollopian model that Thirkell was following. She also appears to have an agenda of looking for feminism in Thirkell, which argues that she was expecting Thirkell to have written of the 1990s rather than the 1930s.[90] Penelope Fritzer has published two studies of Thirkell's novels, on ethnicity and gender, and on aesthetics and nostalgia, in 1999 and 2009 respectively, but these, like Collins, are descriptive rather than critically reflective.[91] The most recent study to have addressed Thirkell's writing in its historical context is by Jennifer Poulos Nesbitt in 2005, in which Thirkell's pre-war novels are integrated in her discussion of women writers of this period.[92]

Broadening the literary context, it might have been expected that Thirkell's major stylistic theme, of drawing from the Barsetshire novels of Anthony Trollope, would have been noticed by Trollopian scholarship. It seems, from a sample survey from one British university library's shelves, that this has not been the case, since it gleaned only three short paragraphs on Thirkell from 39 books on Trollope. As with Buchan, there is thriving 'fan criticism' on Thirkell's work, and many short articles on her fiction have been printed in the journals of the North American and British branches of the Angela Thirkell Society. These are particularly valuable for their crowdsourced detail. Considerable research has been done by the Society in identifying quotations and allusions in Thirkell's fiction, available online.

I have structured the book to follow the events of British political and economic history, with each chapter mapped onto significant political and social events. Thus, Chapter 2, 'From Communism to the Wall Street Crash: Buchan in the 1920s', and Chapter 3, 'Ex-Officers and Gentlemen: Yates in the 1920s', sets their fiction against this turbulence in British post-war politics. Chapter 4, 'Political Uncertainty: Buchan in the 1930s', begins with the collapse of the Labour government and ends with the outbreak of war against Germany. Chapter 5, 'Novels of Instruction: Thirkell in the 1930s', introduces Thirkell's arrival as a critic of 1930s manners. Chapter 6, 'Aggressive Reactions: Yates in the 1930s and 1940s', shows how Yates increasingly resorted to prescriptive writing in his thrillers and comedies, to demonstrate correct behaviour. Chapter 7, 'Thirkell in Wartime, 1940–45', discusses her six wartime novels that are a powerful record of her specifically conservative concerns on the home front. Chapter 8, 'Rewriting History: Yates and Thirkell, 1945–60', focuses on their attentiveness to the things that were worse after the war, rather than improved conditions, and how they attempted to rewrite the past to improve that as well. As a conclusion, or afterword, Chapter 9 departs from the analysis to consider how visualising and measuring the tolerances of a reader's taste can be combined with political ideologies. By using Franco Moretti's literary mapping technique, we can use our enhanced understanding of these authors in the context of British conservative popular fiction and popular taste to indicate how further research in more authors might extend the cultural field further to link politics more closely to the critical understanding of reading pleasure.

2
From Communism to the Wall Street Crash: Buchan in the 1920s

Turbulent politics

The end of the First World War left an uncomfortable Europe, adjusting to new conditions in most areas of life. Rapid changes in political leadership and social conditions indicate that traditional political models were struggling to adapt.[1] David Lloyd George, Stanley Baldwin, Andrew Bonar Law and Ramsay MacDonald dominated the political landscape in rotation, holding office once or more often as party leader, prime minister, or leader of a coalition or national government, in addition to various ministerial posts. The long-dominant Liberal Party effectively disappeared from the first rank as political players in this period, and British politics thenceforward became a battle between Labour and the Conservatives. Politics resembled quadrilles of politicians changing places.

Within the political parties, there was also change. David Cannadine records that 'between 1914 and 1939 there were 1,195 Conservative and Unionist MPs, of whom 17 per cent were related by blood or marriage to the peerage'.[2] This was a low average compared to the nineteenth century. Ennoblement was the traditional replenishing mechanism for the House of Lords, and, even before the First World War, more seats of power had been held by non-patricians, and by professional men, than by the grandees.

> Between 1886 and 1914, some two hundred people entered the ranks of the hereditary peerage for the first time. Of these, one quarter were the heads or scions of patrician families, the group that had previously provided the overwhelming majority of the new recruits. Fully one-third were professionals and state employees; lawyers who were increasingly important in politics, as well as the diplomats, soldiers,

and civil servants required to maintain the nation and the empire. And another third were the new, plutocratic rich, the men who had stormed the Commons and were now assailing the Lords.[3]

This trend continued after the war, and by 1929 Tory power was well on the way to no longer being represented by social rank, but by money.

The activities of the more radical political movements represented political impetus emerging from new constituencies. Membership of trades unions increased hugely. 'By the end of the war, one in three workers was unionised.'[4] The British Socialist Party (BSP) had been formed in 1911–12, and was the largest constituent part of the Communist Party of Great Britain (CPGB), which formed in August 1920.[5] The existence of other left-wing groups at this time, such as the Independent Labour Party, the Communist Unity Group of the Socialist Labour Party, and the trades unions, demonstrates that socialism was approaching maturity as a political force in British politics by the end of the war.[6] British Communist Party membership rose to just over 10,000 after the General Strike in 1926, but had fallen to 3,200 at the end of the 1920s.[7]

The British Fascists emerged as a political group in 1923, inspired by Mussolini, but remained a very small movement in Britain throughout the 1920s. The largely anti-Semitic Imperial Fascist League (IFL) was founded in 1928, but 'never had more than a hundred active members, and never fought parliamentary elections'.[8] The 1930s saw much more activity on this front.

Despite this situation of a socially and politically charged nation, with frequent changes in political leadership against a background of rising engagement with radical politics, riots and revolution did not happen. The British turned to political representation rather than direct action to make their views known. The electoral turnout during the elections of 1918 was 57 per cent, but in 1922, 1923, 1924 and 1929 (the year of the Depression), it was 73 per cent, 71 per cent, 77 per cent and 76 per cent respectively.[9] Political engagement over this period, in terms of active voting, rather than just agreeing with the rhetoric, was relatively high.[10] Adrian Gregory stresses that being on the winning side of the war had made a difference to the British political mindset.

The luxury of victory was such that it minimised the search for scapegoats and instead stressed universalism. The later 1920s saw a decline in sectarianism outside of Ireland, a more benevolent, albeit paternalistic, attitude to race within the Empire and perhaps a more conciliatory and in certain senses progressive outlook for gender relations. Class conflict climaxed in 1926 [...] the crisis passed peacefully by comparison with any other industrialised country.[11]

The social and political landscape of the 1920s

Statistical evidence suggests that, in many respects, daily life and the state of the nation during the 1920s and the 1930s was remarkably stable, with a few, important exceptions. The appalling losses of war and the 1919 influenza epidemic were restored by a large increase in the birth-rate (over 1.1 million babies born in 1921),[12] and inward migration. In 1921 there was a net gain of 70,000 immigrants and returning emigrants for the population, whereas in 1931 there was a net loss of 25,000 emigrants, which happened again in 1941.[13] Economic change had happened to these people, and they responded by urging political change to fulfil their new expectations.

Considering social change in Britain in the 1920s, to which the evolving political landscape was a background, conservative newspapers were receptive to the kind of tropes that Buchan and Yates wrote about. In 1924 a soap advertisement warned, with a strong visual image of xenophobia, that 'there is danger in every crowd', stressing the invisible but serious threat to readers, who needed to be vigilant to combat it.[14] If such advertisements are typical of the readers' preoccupations, they would have been very open to the messages in Buchan and Yates's fiction. The conservative *Daily Express* paid close attention to instability and violence abroad and the threat of it at home, and political change in all countries, but distracted its readers with celebrity and entertainment news as well. Its arresting photo-reportage would have reminded the British public of the enduring solidarity and strength within the British population, and showed them how Germany had become a defeated and desperate nation. Its pictorial summary of the interwar period, *These Tremendous Years* (1939), gives a contemporaneous insight into popular political and social concerns.

At the end of the war, the returning soldier, for whom the *Express* insisted 'it was our business to make Britain a land fit for heroes to live in', received attention.[15] Photographs of soldiers in wheelchairs and with prosthetic legs on London streets were set beside photos of men and women in military uniform relaxing together on Brighton beach. In 1920 the Unknown Warrior, later to be called the Unknown Soldier, was interred in Westminster Abbey. The inability of the returning soldier to find work was made more emotive with stories of undeserving 'officers' using snobbery to win public sympathy and donations: the *Express* told its readers that '1919 was the peak year for "ex-officers", not all genuine'.[16]

The *Express* reported news about women as minor social upsets. In 1919 Lady Astor was the first woman MP to take her seat in the House of Commons, and Suzanne Lenglen won Wimbledon in a knee-length dress without corsets (but still wearing stockings). In 1920 women were finally permitted to graduate from Oxford University with their degrees. Margaret Bondfield became the first woman to hold government office as the first Parliamentary Secretary to the Minister for Labour in 1924. In 1926 women's fashions displayed the shortest skirts ever known in public life, and in 1928 the Equal Franchise Act gave the vote to all women over 21. Women were seen as a problem, by the challenges they posed to traditionalists in their taking advantage of loosening social strictures, and of new opportunities in work, education and leisure.

The British class system was fraying at its boundaries. For the gentry and the landed classes, the war-changed economy was causing a slow loss of land and property, and with that their privileged social and economic status. There was a mood of idealising the nation in response to these changes, as an attempt to heal a national wound. Behind social changes, the increasing radicalisation of Britain's politics caused concern. In 1926 the General Strike, held to support the retention of national wages for miners after the mines went under new private ownership, ran from 4 to 12 May. The behaviour of the economy was also alarming: the crash of Farrow's Bank in 1920, and the 1929 revelations of the fraud perpetrated by Charles Hatry that led to the collapse of seven companies at a loss of £14,000,000, were symptomatic of financial scares.[17] In 1929 the 'Slump' began in America, later called the Great Depression.

Threats from abroad were reported faithfully, to a readership now painfully familiar with the effect of violence on civilian populations. In 1922 Mussolini, a former socialist, now a fascist leader, became Italy's prime minister, and in 1923 the French army occupied the German Ruhr in a dispute over coal. In 1924 the leak of the Zinoviev Letter, from a Russian commissar giving instructions to British Communists to prepare for revolution, lost hard-line socialism its popularity. In 1927 Britain broke off diplomatic relations with the Soviet Union. The message sent to conservative readers was clear: conditions abroad are worrying, and definitely un-English. This was the context in which Yates and Buchan were writing, and from which we find the political elements in Buchan's fiction of the period.

Reading politics in Buchan's fiction

Buchan had lived and breathed politics for most of his adult life. After Oxford, where he had been President of the Union, he became an insider in political and upper-class circles, as a civil servant in South Africa (1901–03), a staff writer on *The Spectator*, and through his contacts as a publisher, war historian and working for Lloyd George's wartime coalition government. Malcolm Baines notes that Buchan could as naturally have stood as a Liberal candidate, given his parents' backgrounds.[18] Buchan was adopted as a Conservative & Unionist candidate in 1911, but did not stand for election until 1927, his health and pressures of war service having been against him when opportunities arose earlier. In 1927 he was elected the Member of Parliament for the now abolished seat of the Scottish Universities with 87 per cent of the vote, and his maiden speech was reported in the *Express* as the best since 1906.[19] He was drawn to all-party working and served as an advisor to both Labour and Conservative prime ministers.

In his fiction his protagonists were largely also Conservatives, but Buchan was critical of extremist politics of any colour. As a progressive Unionist Buchan was probably regarded by die-hard Tories as practically a Liberal, and he was more inclined to centrist politics than the Right. From 1929 until he left for Canada in 1935, Buchan served on the management committee of the Bonar Law College of Citizenship, a training centre for Conservative Party workers.[20] This indicates his commitment to the long-term development of the party, as well as to maintaining its political ideals.

Buchan took great trouble in inventing alternative political scenarios for much of his contemporary fiction. His heroes were as often as not Members of Parliament, and all were Conservative sympathisers. Women's increasing participation in British politics, however, may as well have not existed for all the attention he paid to this. The two most important Buchan novels of the 1920s to reflect his politics were *Huntingtower* (1922), in which the villains are Bolsheviks, and *John Macnab* (1925), in which Buchan contrasts the attitudes to property of the international banker and the Cabinet minister who poach for fun, and the 'rotten sportsman' Lord Claybody, the war peer, who does not understand how to play that game.[21] *The Three Hostages* (1924) reflects different interests, also connected to Conservative ideology, in terms of the land, the national wound and the new enemy.

George Watson, one of the very few critics to examine politics represented in literature in this period, notes that the interwar years 'had left few writers [politically] unattached. Intellectuals tended to extremes; the mass parties were moderate, almost of necessity' (see Chapter 1).[22] Novelists could rely no longer on the Victorian and Edwardian political norm of Tories versus Liberals, interrupted by noises from upstart Labour on the sidelines. When rewriting the political and social landscape, novelists who felt strongly that there was a socialist menace to combat would make their more conservative views obvious in their writing. But this did not happen immediately: there was no mass literary uprising from the Tory shires against the forces of socialism when the British Communist Party was founded in 1920.

> In Britain at least, the polarisation of Left and Right was late, and belongs to the mid-Thirties. Documents earlier than that do not naturally see socialism and fascism as opposites. The clarity or crudity of Left and Right was to come later; and the myth of fascism as a conservative force, being fundamentally a Marxist myth, had to wait to be heard until Marxism itself was widely accepted.[23]

In the light of this, attempts to pigeonhole Buchan in the 1920s as a natural Tory opponent of the Left are forcing apart ways of thinking that, in some circumstances, lie closer together. His fiction reflects this.

For the remainder of this chapter, I want to consider in more detail how the fiction of Buchan responded to the changing social conditions, followed in Chapter 3 by an analysis of Yates's fiction of the 1920s. Bridget Fowler has suggested that popular fiction needed to 'restore belief in a justice which people suspected no longer existed'.[24] For novel-readers looking for 'justice' in the uncertain situation in Britain after the end of the First World War, realistic novels would not necessarily reassure those jarred by daily life. The experience of war had damaged a high number of people psychologically. Adrian Gregory points out that there were '4.5 million bereaved close relatives in Britain at the end of the war. This amounts, near enough, to 10% of the population'.[25] Romance, adventure, comedy and fiction evoking familiar pre-war settings and values would provide comfort.

There was no escaping the reality of returning soldiers, particularly those who had been wounded. Stories dealing with their situation, and forecasting how their changed lives would achieve purpose and fulfilment, were also a strong concern in popular fiction of this time. Returning soldiers and civilians alike experienced a new crisis in homelessness, exacerbated by the fluctuating economy, and changed social expectations. Uncertainty at home expressed itself in fiction as a search for the new enemy, who may or may not have been foreigners. Women attracted social suspicion, since they now had more economic and political power, and their opinions carried more weight. As well as a concern for the protection of society, and an intense urge to return society to pre-war conditions, popular novelists of this period were strongly aware of the importance of the land, as a synecdoche for the nation, and the idealisation of patriotism. This was closely connected with an insistence on reinforcing the boundaries of class and status.

Buchan's need for escape

In late 1919 Buchan and his wife bought a small country house in Elsfield, Oxfordshire, from which Buchan commuted to the Nelson's office in Paternoster Row in the City of London three or four days a week. In 1923 he became Deputy Chairman of Reuters, and in 1927 was finally elected to Parliament. In 1929 he left Nelson's, and became a full-time writer as well as what we would now call a consultant for many publishing and journalism interests.

With a base in the countryside again (his first since his boyhood holidays in the Scottish Borders) Buchan was able to enjoy country pursuits wholeheartedly. His characters became more obviously rooted in the country, and his political beliefs became less connected with the future of the nation as an economic or political entity, and more entwined with the land and its relationship with the landowners. His political engagement would become formalised by his seat in Parliament and greater access to the law-making process. Now that it was possible for Buchan to affect national policy, his fiction would show greater assurance about what the country and the British needed to improve their lives and consolidate the gains from the war. It would also draw closer to conservative ideology, and to a re-engagement with how conservatism itself might have to change to adapt to the changing world. At the end of the decade, his character Sandy Arbuthnot begins to show signs of extreme dissatisfaction with the British political process, and with Conservative party politics.

> "I can't begin to tell you how I loathe the little squirrel's cage of the careerists. All that solemn twaddle about trifles! [...] If I touched politics I'd join the Labour Party, not because I think them less futile than the others, but because as yet they haven't got such a larder of loaves and fishes."[26]

This is an explosive state of mind, because Sandy then goes off to start a revolution in South America. An essay Buchan wrote for *The Spectator* in the same year, 'Conservatism and progress', defined and defended conservatism as Buchan saw it at the end of decade.[27] How does Buchan's fiction reflect his awareness of post-war conditions in Britain, seen through the conservative lens?

Readers who turned to Buchan in the 1920s would read his novels for escapist reassurance. He wrote about the strength of the new barriers between civilisation and anarchy, since in his fiction the boundary was always held. When Buchan's characters discuss politics, or political aims, it can be hard to determine whether the views are Labour, Liberal or Conservative since he usually avoids giving characters' views party labels. But it is clear that Buchan's default political perspective is Conservative. Buchan's presentation of politics focused on individuals who could nurture as well as lead in times of crisis. This was a contrast to Yates, who reacted to threats by demonising those of whom he was afraid. For Buchan, crime was international, and generally had a politicised agenda, so although his villains usually had a powerful persona, their goals were political (usually international domination) rather than personal. There was a secretive, shadowy element in their organisation to attract the protagonist's animus, or a personal saving grace, thus offering a chance of salvation for the antagonist.

Huntingtower (1922) is Buchan's first truly post-war novel, in that the setting is a forward-looking vision of how post-war society may be repaired. After a prefatory wartime episode foretelling the collapse of the Russian Empire, the novel begins with a reiteration of idealised conservative middle-class values, with the early retirement of Dickson McCunn from his successful grocery business. McCunn goes on a walking tour to escape his former daily routine, with Izaak Walton to read for pleasure, but he is plunged into the very modern twentieth century. He encounters the lasting damage of war on people's lives, urban child poverty, the neglect of a house and estate after the death of the heir, a distressing absence of the respect he was used to receiving as a provisions magnate, and the bewildering nonsense of modernist poetry. His adventure acknowledges the emergence of Bolshevism from the First World War and offers a vision for the future, highly romantic but also attractively practical, of how the businessman's approach is the new model for conservative action.

Outside the detail of the plot, *Huntingtower* is a profoundly escapist reading experience, since it offers a modern fairy tale in the familiar holiday setting of Dumfries & Galloway. There are even a prince and a princess in disguise. The novel reinforces the patriotic British value of chivalry to the ladies, and encourages equally typical conservative emotions: fear and loathing of the foreigner, pity for and fear of the congenitally impaired, and pride in the war-wounded ex-soldier. The middle class still respects the upper classes ('Dickson like all his class had a profound regard for the country gentry').[28] One of the principal messages of the novel is that the strength of the British middle classes will be the country's future. But respect must be earned: the urchin Dougal has no respect for Sir Archie's rank or title, but he obeys the incognito Russian prince without a murmur since he is clearly the better soldier, even if this authority is still due, in the reader's subconscious, to rank.

The iconoclast on McCunn's journey is John Heritage, an unsettled modern character with a suggestively Everyman name. He has published his own, bad poetry, and worries McCunn by savagely criticising the poets of the past, invading McCunn's escapist idyll with scattergun modern opinions that startle and annoy McCunn the traditionalist from a hitherto very quiet existence. The novel enacts a tussle between the values of the past (presented here as the Scottish Victorian class hierarchy) and the infiltration of the modern, which means Bolshevism, international kidnapping and breaking Scots law. The conservative values of this novel are triumphant, because the modernist character is plunged into a world in which his opinions have no merit. Heritage performs an ideological *volte face* by burning his own poems while guarding a medieval tower from Bolshevik conspirators, and returns to a healthy love of Tennyson. Buchan's poetry metonym is revealing, because he had equivocal views about modernist poetry. In a 1922 poetry review he welcomed aspects of 'the modern' which was 'aggressively alive and snuffing the wind', in contrast to 'the conservative' which 'is, in a manner of speaking, dead'.[29] These lines suggest Buchan's openness towards elements of the avant-garde where it was active and alive. Heritage's discomfort with his ideas and aspirations reflects the confusion Buchan himself may have felt, and also his exasperation with the negativity he saw in literary modernism.

Other elements in the novel reinforce the idea of escaping into a conservative ideal. The troop of boy scout imitators, the Gorbals Die-Hards, follow the Scouts' values and practices without any resources of their own. They were 'a kind of unauthorized and unofficial Boy Scouts, who, without uniform or badge or any kind of paraphernalia, followed the banner of Sir Robert Baden-Powell and subjected themselves to a rude discipline. They were far too poor to join an orthodox troop, but they faithfully copied what they believed to be the practices of more fortunate boys'.[30]

Instead of continually combating the embodiment of conservative middle-class values, the slum children embrace those values through self-help and self-improvement. They aspire to a more prosperous way of life (they are effectively homeless), and follow the strongly conservative ideologies of the militarised Baden-Powell ideology.[31] They go further by actively rejecting Socialism, here the indoctrinational classes of the Independent Labour Party:

> To Dickson's surprise Dougal seemed to be in good spirits. He began to sing to a hymn tune a strange ditty.
>
>> "Class-conscious we are, and class-conscious wull be
>> Till our fit's on the neck o' the Boorjoyzee."
>
> "What on earth are you singing?" Dickson inquired.
>
> Dougal grinned. "Wee Jaikie went to a Socialist Sunday School last winter because he heard they were for fechting battles. Ay, an they telled him he was to jine a thing called an International, and Jaikie thought it was a fitba' club. But when he fund out there was no magic lantern or swaree at Christmas he gie'd it the chuck. They learned him a heap o' queer songs. That's one."
>
> "What does the last word mean?"
>
> "I don't ken. Jaikie thought it was some kind of a draigon."[32]

The only value the Socialists have for these immensely practical children is that their songs have good tunes and they make good battle anthems: Jaikie's declamation of 'Proley Tarians, arise!' [*sic*] is a stirring and ironic accompaniment to the final battle with the Bolsheviks.[33] They escape from their slum existence, through charitable donations, into the country to go camping. At the end of the novel they achieve the greatest escape of all: out of poverty into affluence, when the childless McCunn adopts them as his sons.

Within the novel there is also criticism of the government and rising inflation ("'It's awful the incompetence of our Government, and the rates and taxes that high!'").[34] This has a corollary in a fantastical escape from the rule of law. It is very common in Buchan's fiction – and in Yates's too, as we will see – for the conservative hero-adventurer to take the law into his own hands.

> "Do you realise that you're levying a private war and breaking every law of the land?"
>
> "Hoots!" said Dickson. "I don't care a docken about the law."[35]

The dramatic contrast of this passage is based on McCunn's earlier shrinking from trouble, an attitude now rejected by a forceful idiom in dialect. Of course, McCunn's escape from the restrictions of law does not contravene the law, since he is merely acting for the police who are otherwise slow to mobilise on a Sunday. But the true conservative, as Buchan sees it – loyal to the aristocracy, antagonistic to Bolsheviks, ready to risk personal safety for an honourable cause – will make a momentary escape from petty legal restrictions to do the decent thing.

Returning ex-soldiers and civilians

Fiction published during and immediately after the war frequently used a romanticised story of how a deserving ex-serviceman would struggle with a war impairment and be rewarded with a job, often with the prospect of marriage, after a trial of honesty, reliability or worth. War service and war wounds became the new trial of character. Bridget Fowler's question of whether 'justice', or a satisfactory peace for those who had fought for it, existed in the fiction of this decade, encourages us to consider how demobilised soldiers were depicted in peacetime fiction. The returning British soldiers who were not war-impaired expected to return to jobs, but might find that these no longer existed, or had been taken by women or younger, fitter men.

Buchan populated his 1920s post-war novels with gainfully employed ex-servicemen, but he did not often acknowledge the problem of unemployment. In *The Dancing Floor* (1927) more attention is paid to this aspect of the nation than in earlier post-war novels. Leithen acknowledges that he was lucky to be able to come back to his own profession. 'I had mighty little to complain of when you consider the number of good men who, far seedier than I, came back to struggle for their daily bread.'[36] Leithen also acknowledges the shaky economic state of the nation as a major factor in the immediate post-war mood. 'They were crazy days, when nobody was quite himself. Politicians talked and writers wrote clotted nonsense, statesmen chased their tails, the working man wanted to double his wages and halve his working hours at a time when the world was bankrupt.'[37]

In *Huntingtower*, Sir Archie's Galloway retreat is staffed by former soldiers.

Only cripples, I'm afraid. There's Sime, my butler. He was a Fusilier Jock and, as you saw, has lost an arm. Then McGuffog the keeper is a good man but he's still got a Turkish bullet in his thigh. The chauffeur, Carfrae, was in the Yeomanry, and lost half a foot."[38]

Such an arrangement is excellent for those who can afford to employ deserving causes, and accept the responsibilities of *noblesse oblige*. Buchan makes a point, in other novels, of his characters employing former staff who have returned in the war (keeping their jobs open for them), or creating jobs for those who have served under or with them in the war. This idealised policy is at once an example to those who might be in a similar position, and a reminder to all readers that former soldiers need employment. But while most of Buchan's solutions occur in a fantasy world where the conservative ideal is upheld by all, he does describe one former soldier who cannot find work. In *John Macnab* (1925), Lord Lamancha, engaged in poaching, is rightfully challenged by a labourer brought onto the hill to guard the deer. They wrestle, and the weaker man falls and breaks his leg.

> As [Lamancha] looked at the limp figure [...] he recognised something familiar. [...]
>
> "Stokes," he cried, "You're Stokes, aren't you?" He recalled now the man who had once been his orderly, and whom he had last known as a smart troop sergeant. [...]
>
> "What brought you to this?" Lamancha asked.
>
> "I've 'ad a lot of bad luck, sir. Nothing seemed to go right with me after the war. I found the missus 'ad don a bunk, and I 'ad the two kids on my 'ands, and there weren't no cushy jobs goin' for the likes of me. Gentlemen everywhere was puttin' down their 'osses, and I 'ad to take what I could get. So it came to the navvyin' with me, like lots of other chaps. The Gov'ment don't seem to care what 'appens to us poor Gawd-forgotten devils, sir."[39]

Setting aside the inevitable Buchan coincidence of Lamancha already knowing Stokes from his war service (which removes the need for a character reference) this episode reinforces Buchan's main point of *noblesse oblige*, that the upper classes take care of those who have a right to ask them for help. He sets up a textbook contrast between Lord Lamancha's impeccable behaviour and the ungentlemanly behaviour of the *nouveau riche* Johnson Claybody, Stokes' employer. Remarks are made in the narrative voice and in the dialogue to make it clear that Claybody deserves nobody's allegiance, since he expects to buy men's service, whereas true authority receives service by right in a feudal exchange of fealty.

This episode is only concerned with Lamancha's obligations as a *de facto* feudal lord to Stokes, and says nothing about the social or economic aspects of his predicament. Nothing more is said about Stokes in the story, but the reader is confident that Lamancha will continue to pay for his recovery, and will probably provide Stokes and his family with work on one of his estates. Stokes himself need do nothing more except work as his new master requires. The state needs do nothing to help this single parent get back on his feet and into work to support his family, because benign upper-class charity sees it as a responsibility of its class to step in and help the less fortunate. Buchan's conservatism is also conservative in its vision of the future, since it does not offer a new future within a putative Welfare State, but maintenance of the Victorian past.

Some of the difficulties faced by returning soldiers in rebuilding the better society emanated, Stephen M Cullen observes, from the civilian population that had not served.

> Disenchantment in ex-combatant writing is [...] with the England that they felt had emerged during and after the war. Ex-combatant writers identified wartime civilian attitudes and failings as the source of the failure of England to renew itself in the post-war period [...] it is, broadly speaking, a right-wing [critique] – attacking profiteers, trades unionism, materialism, modernity and mass society [in the form of] abandoned ex-servicemen, greedy businessmen, politicians, newspaper barons, profiteers, striking or wage-hungry war workers and complacent civilians.[40]

In Buchan's fiction it was not possible for a man of the right age and condition to have been a civilian during the war, and remain morally sound. When he wanted to shame the attitudes of those who had harsh things to say about 'malingerers', and who failed to understand mental and emotional trauma, he gave them no right to criticise if they had not served themselves.

> Mr Claybody announced that he was sick of hearing the war blamed for the average man's deficiencies. "Every waster," he said, "makes an excuse of being shell-shocked. I'm very clear that the war twisted nothing in a man that wasn't twisted before." [...]
>
> Something in his tone annoyed Janet. "You saw a lot of service, didn't you?" she asked meekly.

"No – worse luck! They made me stick at home and slave fourteen hours a day controlling cotton. It would have been a holiday for me to get into the trenches."[41]

In Buchan's conservative world, the decent civilian man would be aware that not having served in the war was an intolerable handicap, preventing him from being accepted as an equal by Buchan's ex-soldier characters, and their women.

The new enemy

Civilian anger at the state of the nation flared in the first months of peace, and thereafter was subsumed into a permanent grumbling state. Adrian Gregory notes that 'all of the poisonous ingredients of extreme right-wing politics existed in Britain – particularly southern England – by the end of 1918: middle-class grievance and resentment of both big capital and big labour, xenophobia including anti-Semitism, disillusionment with parliamentary government, conspiracy theories and even perhaps a tendency to reluctantly condone violence'.[42]

Anyone who did not look British was a potential target, especially in the immediate post-war years. There were serious outbreaks of racist attacks, against 'Arab seamen' and others, during 1919.[43] Michael Diamond identifies several important categories of the 'Other' who were vilified in fiction, before and after the war: the 'Yellow Peril', and Arabs from north Africa and Egypt, and 'Levantines' (a euphemism for 'Greeks, Syrians, Maltese and Jews'),[44] were the subject of complicated imperial and Christian attitudes towards foreigners in general. Anti-Semitism was endemic in British popular culture, as were casual racist attitudes towards all non-whites, 'Levantines' included. Susan Kingsley Kent observes that 'aliens and alien ways were expelled from the newly complete story of the nation, by identifying them linguistically, visiting violence upon them (in fiction) providing relief from intolerable trauma [including] Irish Catholics, Jews, Bolsheviks, Indians, West Indians, Africans, women'.[45]

Leaving aside for the moment the question of how women may have been vilified as alien in the 1920s, we can see that in Buchan's fiction anything foreign is immediately suspect, until it is revealed as the right kind of foreign. Yet there are also 'good' foreigners: the Russian prince and princess of *Huntingtower*, because they are of the aristocracy, serve the White Russian cause. It would be an interesting exercise to rewrite *Huntingtower* from the Socialist perspective, since its polarities are so clearly defined. Buchan could not sympathise with Bolshevism as depicted by these extravagantly villainous characters, because it, and they, signified anarchy, destruction, and the loss of an older and a better form of society.

Two years later in *The Three Hostages* Buchan is specific about the new enemies of civilisation, whose intentions he predicts using the example of post-war Germany, where 'power lay with the bloated industrials, who were piling up fortunes abroad while they were wrecking their country at home. The only opposition, he said, came from the communists, who were half-witted, and the monarchists, who wanted the impossible'.[46] Once Hannay has infiltrated the enemy organisation, he encounters another type inimical to his notion of civilisation: 'It was the thin, high-boned, high-bred face of the hillman; not the Mongolian type, but that other which is like an Arab, the kind of thing you can see in Pathan troops'.[47] Careful readers of Buchan would recognise this look from his 1916 novel *Greenmantle*, in which a Turkish gypsy chief was transformed into a high-ranking Islamic leader. There is also admiration and respect in this description: it is a divided gaze. Buchan was inviting the readers to join Hannay in fearing and loathing the mysterious Eastern enemy, and then puncturing their expectations. He was perhaps pointing out that appearances are deceptive, or that if we look for devils we will find them in ourselves.

The problem of women

After demobilisation, women workers were resented by the general public, and by ex-soldiers for retaining 'their' jobs. This was a response to the increasing public role that women had played in the war, and (nervously) as a response to women's partial enfranchisement in 1918. Kent connects women's newly public visibility with fears about the dangers of women's sexuality, of men's vulnerability to disease spread by prostitutes, and attacks on women that mirrored the pre-war attacks on politicised women during the suffrage campaign.[48]

Women's advances in society were not noted with enthusiasm by Buchan. In *The Three Hostages* and in *The Dancing Floor*, Buchan, through his highly critical male narrators, is stern about cosmetics: 'her face was loaded with paint'.[49] His narrator Leithen objects to how women use their new social freedoms. 'One could forgive a good deal of shrillness and bad form in such a case. My one regret was that they made such guys of themselves. Well-born young women seemed to have taken for their models the cretinous little oddities of the film world.'[50] Even modern hairstyles are objectionable. Koré Arabin's bobbed hair not only 'desecrates the gifts of the Almighty', it cannot properly support her riding hat.[51]

I have written at length elsewhere on how Buchan used women characters in his fiction.[52] His fictional women were largely powerless and normally subordinate, and exist because of their relationships with more active male characters. But in the 1920s, more women characters appeared in Buchan's fiction. They were also more interesting, and less conventionally handled, although they were still restricted to a very narrow upper-class stratum. Apart from an experiment in his 1900 novel *The Half-Hearted*, Janet Raden in *John Macnab* (1925) is Buchan's first focalised female character, in that we see the action through her eyes, and understand her perspective on the action.

Buchan was rarely openly critical of women in his fiction, but his most severe strictures, relatively speaking, appear in the 1930s, in *The Gap in the Curtain* (1932) and *A Prince of the Captivity* (1933), discussed in Chapter 4. In the 1920s in *John Macnab* he pokes fun at Lady Claybody, part of the composite parvenu that the three Claybodys represent. In general, Buchan's preferred female character is one who 'does not challenge, she does not oppose, and she nurtures'.[53] In the 1920s, there are no female characters in Buchan who challenge or oppose. He reserved his ire for girls who failed to dress correctly (he praised the girls who looked well soaked through on a moor, *because* they were correctly dressed), or who behaved in too independent a manner. Koré Arabin of *The Dancing Floor* is the most rebellious woman that Buchan managed to write, and even she is tamed, first by attempted human sacrifice, and then by marriage to the inhumanly perfect and god-like Vernon Milburne, which may amount to the same thing.

Buchan only wrote women who were part of, or in a feudal relationship with, the upper classes. This naturally narrowed the opportunities or probability of such women being a threat in the fiction, or a destabilising influence on society. Conservative women simply did not do that, even if many of them had by now received the vote. Janet Raden of *John Macnab* is an unswerving and deep-thinking Conservative, but there is no suggestion that she, the 'best brain of the family', might stand for election herself, in place of the nervous and scatty Archie.[54] This brings us back to the nurturing and supportive role: by standing for election Archie will regain confidence and the psychological manhood he lost through his wartime and sporting injuries. Marriage to Janet will make a man of him, as we will see in *The Courts of the Morning* (1929), when he is a fully mature heroic protagonist at last, rescuing his wife. Buchan's response to aggressive female encroachment on 1920s society was to show them an idealised route to supportive, nurturing womanhood.

Saving the land

The readers to whom Yates and Buchan were speaking in the 1920s were under pressure. The landowners were losing their land: David Cannadine notes that 'in the years immediately before and after the First World War, some six to eight million acres, one-quarter of the land of England, was sold by gentry and grandees. In Wales and Scotland the figure was nearer one-third, and in Ireland it was even higher'.[55] The upper and middle classes were suffering change. C F G Masterman asked in 1922:

> if [...] the land is passing, to whom, one may ask, is it going? In the main to one of three classes. There is, first, the War Profiteer, climbing upwards towards gentility, a title, and a seat in the House of Lords. There is, second, the tenant-farmer, buying up the house in which his ancestors had lived and the land which they had farmed for genera-tions. And there is, third, the County Councils, Rural District Councils and other public bodies, who are purchasing land for various purposes, mainly, in specially favourable districts, for a closer settlement of smaller farmers upon the soil.[56]

Buchan's fiction rarely considers councils. Since Hannay could buy himself an estate after the war, he may have been a war profiteer of the right kind, since he profited by his war experience to install himself firmly among the landowning classes. But Hannay, as a representative of Buchan's self-made Tories, is rich because of his fortune-hunting, prospecting days in Rhodesia.[57] Most ex-soldiers did not have that financial cushion.

Stephen M Cullen has noted that in the fiction published immedi-ately after the war by ex-combatants 'it was upon images of England that their conceptualisation of patriotism chiefly centred. These images were traditional ones, drawing upon myths of England as an essentially rural country with an ancient heritage'.[58] The rural landscape was the focus, rather than the urban or industrial. Raymond Williams points out that 'seeing land as an index of revenue and position' is problematic. 'Its visible order and control are a valued product while the process of working it is hardly seen at all.'[59] It is certainly true that in Buchan, workers are very rarely seen working the land, although the gamekeeper and ghillie, as stewards of the landowner's living property, are common secondary characters.

The Three Hostages (1924) is the sequel to *Mr Standfast*, set after the First World War. Its first two paragraphs are a rich source of state-ments by Buchan about ownership, nationality and stability. *The Three*

Hostages itself is important for being the novel in which Hannay finds his place as an English landowner, the embodiment of the imperial adventurer made good, the pride of the British secret service, and a general and a knight to boot. The one area of life in which Hannay does not shine is politics: he does not have subtlety, finesse or intellectual nimbleness. This can be seen in his behaviour in the Prologue to *The Courts of the Morning* (1929) in which he throws his weight about uselessly in diplomatic circles like a bull on the rampage. For the average reader, a man of action and a man who loved the land was perhaps a more engaging hero than an aloof Foreign Office spy. It was clearly important to Buchan to connect his hero with the common experiences of England.

That evening, I remember, as I came up through the Mill Meadow, I was feeling peculiarly happy and contented. It was still mid-March, one of those spring days when noon is like May, and only the cold pearly haze at sunset warns a man that he is not done with winter. The season was absurdly early, for the blackthorn was in flower and the hedge roots were full of primroses. The partridges were paired, the rooks were well on with their nests, and the meadows were full of shimmering grey flocks of fieldfares on their way north. I put up half a dozen snipe on the boggy edge of the stream, and in the bracken in Sturn Wood I thought I saw a woodcock, and hoped that the birds might nest with us this year, as they used to do long ago. It was jolly to see the world coming to life again, and to remember that this patch of England was my own, and all these wild things, so to speak, members of my little household.

As I say, I was in a very contented mood, for I had found something I had longed for all my days. I had bought Fosse Manor just after the War as a wedding present for Mary, and for two and a half years we had been settled there. My son, Peter John, was rising fifteen months, a thoughtful infant, as healthy as a young colt and as comic as a terrier puppy. Even Mary's anxious eye could scarcely detect in him any symptoms of decline. But the place wanted a lot of looking to, for it had run wild during the War, and the woods had to be thinned, gates and fences repaired, new drains laid, a ram put in to supplement the wells, a heap of thatching to be done, and the garden borders to be brought back to cultivation. I had got through the worst of it, and as I came out of the Home Wood on to the lower lawns and saw the old stone gables that the monks had built, I felt that I was anchored at last in the pleasantest kind of harbour.[60]

The novel opens with Hannay describing how he does the rounds of his country estate in Oxfordshire. On a certain evening in March he is 'coming up' the meadow, by which name we infer that the 'Mill Meadow' is an old field with a name referring to a pre-industrial site, suggesting a long-settled part of England. The house has gables built by monks, but the name of the manor is more ancient, since 'Fosse' refers to the Fosse Way, the Roman road that runs from the south-west of England to the north-east, connecting Hannay's land to its oldest historical inhabitants.

Hannay describes the precise kind of light that appears at sunset in March, suggesting that he is familiar with life in the outdoors, and that he can observe differences across seasons and time. This familiarity with the natural world is apparent in the virtuoso passage of nature description that follows, which pays close attention to the behaviour of birds, to the flowering of plants and the timing of nest-building. In southern England, March is the end of the winter, and the beginning of spring; it is a transitional month in which the world is indeed 'coming to life'. Blackthorn normally flowers in mid-April, so its flowering in March is indeed absurdly early. These are also rather early primroses, but not impossibly so. The stream has boggy edges, indicating that this is low ground, and that the water table is still high; the winter rainwater has not yet begun to be drained by new plant growth. The fieldfares are indeed early, but not implausibly so. Woodcock forage for worms on agricultural land, but might nest in woodland, as is suggested here. An ornithologist's opinion on this passage is that Buchan was describing here the habits of birds in his native Scotland, which are later than the birds of Oxfordshire, where he had lived for only a year or so.[61]

Such close attention to nature, and such a close alignment with the author and his character, suggests that watching for signs is important for Buchan's estimation of the right kind of country landowner. He can read a landscape and read the natural world, so he will be able to decode the mystery that the novel unfolds. Such reading also suggests ownership, and a mediating role. Buchan and Hannay interpret the ways of nature to the reader: they will also interpret politics, social behaviour, and class expectations. We are to be guided by them because their expertise and knowledge are greater than ours. Buchan placed great importance on taking the advice of an expert, which was done by all his heroes *in extremis*, and before a great adventure. The reader is here also advised to take the author's advice, and to abide by it.

Hannay is also master of this domain, the land of Fosse Manor is his to look after. 'This patch of England was my own', and he looks after the '*wild things*' as part of his responsibilities. But he has more than responsibilities; he claims a kind of ownership over wild creatures as well: they are 'members' of his 'household'. Such a strong emphasis on his personal responsibility suggests a metaphor connected with Hannay's recent adventures saving the Allied cause, and civilisation, from the Kaiser's armies. In his previous adventures he protected Britain, and in his most recent adventure, *Mr Standfast* (1919), Hannay formally self-identified as an Englishman (he was originally written as South African or Rhodesian). Now he has 'something I had longed for all my days'. He has bought the manor, and is 'anchored' in a 'harbour', a place of safety. So we read several strong statements that this novel concerns ownership, security, responsibility and England as a landscape as well as a people. But a harbour can be left, it is a temporary shelter: we can sense that Hannay may be about to go adventuring again.

Paragraph two describes the people in Hannay's landscape. At the end of *Mr Standfast*, the earlier novel, Hannay and a Foreign Office secret agent called Mary Lamington, were engaged to be married. Two and a half years later, in this novel, they have a son, named after two of the other male protagonists in that novel, Peter Pienaar and John S Blenkiron, a South African and an American, respectively. This choice of names for the new life that Hannay, the new-made Englishman, will nurture, is a nice metaphor for the 'British world' of Anglophone colonial and ex-colonial interests. The infant Peter John does not decline; rather, his existence becomes a powerful trigger for Hannay's decision to take on the task of recovering the kidnapped children in this novel. Peter John's existence also gives Mary, his mother, the ideal cover story for her last and greatest undercover work. The notice taken of Peter John's health prepares us for the task ahead. The estate, not the child, is the patient that needs care and recuperation, and is described in this paragraph in very clear terms. These also describe the then state of Britain and the Empire, which have 'run wild during the War'. Things need to be 'thinned', 'repaired', drained and thatched before the land can be prosperous and healthy again. Metaphorically, there is much work to be done on the land, and in British society too. This becomes the theme of the novel, since it is concerned with the moral breakdown of society, and the regular maintenance needed to prevent long-term damage.

Buchan's anxieties were primarily concerned with the breaking down of barriers. He externalised this in his famous trope of the thinness of the barrier between civilisation and anarchy, first articulated in his fiction in 1901 in 'Fountainblue'. As Buchan developed his role as a cultural authority, this barrier became his most frequently used metaphor. In the first two paragraphs of this novel, Buchan shows us the barriers that need to be repaired, to make Britain fully safe after the depredations of the war. The tone throughout is assured, the voice of ownership, and responsibility. The reader is invited to share the sentiments expressed, of pride in the land and the importance of being vigilant, and aware of the gaps in the hedge through which marauders might creep.

In *John Macnab* Buchan challenges the complacent view of conservative politics that demands the retention of the status quo by virtue of birth, advocating an active conservatism, in which landowners must defend their right to own the land. Terry Gifford notes that the novel 'challenges the concept of ownership of wild Scottish landscape'.[62] If a parvenu fights harder to defend what he owns, he has more right to it than a landed family who 'settled down and went to sleep and became rentiers [...] Their only claim was the right of property, which is no right at all [...] Nobody in the world today has a right to anything which he can't justify'.[63] Janet Raden's political pep talk realises for Archie his political vision, because she makes him see the difference between party politics – 'scraping into Parliament' – and 'real politics – putting the broken pieces together [...] Papa and the rest of our class want to treat politics like another kind of property in which they have a vested interest. But it won't do – not in the world we live in today'.[64]

This is a radical view, and is mistaken several times in the novel for Bolshevism, since on the surface it seems to be no more than a rejection of the rights of property. But Janet's point, which Archie very quickly adopts, is that to own land, or any other property, you must justify your ownership, or give it up. This competitive attitude, in Buchan's view, is part of the post-war world, and explains why the old landed gentry are dying away and the complacent aristocrats are shrivelling. *John Macnab* is a stirring celebration of conservative values that are linked to ancestral land ownership, because it shows what owning the land means for a community, for the successful preservation of nature, and for the amenity it gives to those who live there. From a present-day perspective there is no particular reason why these should not be socialist or even nationalist views, but in Buchan's day Conservative views with such an active stance came the closest to offering a way of allowing the landowners' way of life to survive. The invention of John Macnab, a character who cocks a snoot at the rights of property and challenges the owner to defend what he holds, is a deliberate incentive for stronger 'Toryism – the courage to give the lie to impudent rogues'.[65]

Defending the right of John Macnab to exist and carry out his goading task is also a delightfully paradoxical position. 'Here was a laird, a Tory, and a strict preserver of game working himself into a passion over the moral rights of the poacher.'[66] Of the three landowners under challenge by Macnab, the parvenu peer, and his businesslike son who has no understanding of fair play, are at a loss first to understand the game, and, when all is revealed, to comprehend why these three eminent public men have masqueraded as rogues and poachers in search of a little sport. The Claybody family (and their name is apt) simply cannot understand this need. Lord Claybody's plaintive enquiry, '"Why – why this, this incivility?"',[67] makes it painfully clear to the reader that if he cannot understand an upper-class sporting endeavour, he had better learn, or give up apeing the aristocracy.

The Claybodys respond by assuring the influential conservative public figures that they have never stood in the least danger of exposure since the three target landowners would never have let down one of their own class. It's a depressing and anticlimactic conclusion at the end of this wonderful poaching novel, that there is no freedom even to be disgraced if you are embedded in the national web of class, political and landowning obligations. Of course, the Claybodys are afraid of copycat Macnabs invading the countryside, who will not have the class allegiances of the original threesome, and will steal, damage and destroy as well as poach: 'There may be a large crop of Macnabs springing up, and you'll be responsible. It's a dangerous thing to weaken the sanctities of property'.[68] In the end, the exploits of John Macnab have been conducted in a closed system, in which there was no risk and no chance of anyone outside the landed or conservative classes being allowed to play. The lower-class characters are not involved in the competitive poaching, since they have no stake in the game, unless acting under their employers' direct orders, as does Benjie. Buchan gives the end of the novel a cynical twist on conservative values for land ownership, despite his robust and radical proposition for preventing loss of the land itself. The last we hear of John Macnab is that one of his real names – the Earl of Lamancha – is proudly displayed on a stag's head in Lady Claybody's hall. His name is as much a trophy for the new conservative landowners as the animal.

Class and status

Reinforcing ideas about class was a significant factor in these novels. John Atkins offers a useful definition of class as:

> an aggregate of persons, within a society, possessing approximately the same status [...] a man is judged in accordance with the judging person's perception of his income and wealth, his occupation, his level of achievement within his occupation, his standard of living (including the location of his residence), his ethnic characteristics, his kinship connections, his educational level, his relationship to the main centres of the exercise of power, and his associates.[69]

All these are invoked by the three authors under study, in different works. In addition, George Watson suggests that 'we might choose to talk of rank rather than of class, for instance, since rank is a descriptively subtler tool for depicting social differences'.[70] A point made by David Cannadine offers ways to distinguish further between the upper and other classes. 'Whereas small landowner, middling proprietor, and territorial magnate are class designations, signifying particular gradations of wealth, landed gentleman, baronet and peer are status designations, signifying precise degrees of rank.'[71] Rank also suggests an earned (or inherited) status, a position that has been awarded through merit as well as birth, whereas a change in one's class is somehow arrived at through changes in one's understanding of oneself and one's relationship to others. In the fiction we are dealing with here, class matters more than rank, since the novels are all about characters' perceptions of each other.

Nicola Humble notes that 'an intense interest in class' in middlebrow fiction 'spoke to [the] increasing middle-class fascination with status'.[72] Sentimentalising the fall of the landed, by casting out the privileged from their ancestral rights and territories, was a simple way to construct attractive characters who would appeal to those who felt cast out themselves: I discuss Yates's use of this trope in Chapter 3. Generating sympathy for the socially and economically beleaguered upper classes generated sentiment. Everyone loves a lord, and a lord in hard times, enduring them nobly and with patient endurance, especially if he is an ex-officer, just as if he were nobody in particular, was a calculated appeal to conservative instincts in all classes of reader.

These categories are subject to the threat of belittlement: class, and status, were contestable; rank could be lost or gained. What makes

Buchan and Yates interesting within the wider literary landscape of politicised popular novelists is their introduction of the modernist intellectual to the battlefield. Anna Vaninskaya has pointed out that 'Chesterton and Orwell [on opposite sides, politically] were fighting a culture war on behalf of the so-called democracy against a self-appointed highbrow elite'.[73] Buchan and Yates were fighting a class-based rearguard action against an elite of the intellect. The sense of the victimhood of the social elite is a recurrent idea with other conservative writers. Mary Grover notes that for novelist Warwick Deeping, 'the idea of victimhood at the hands of those in superior positions within the cultural hierarchy is integral to the power of Deeping's fantasies: the notion of an oppressive force, hierarchical or not, is essential to their construction'. For Yates, and Buchan to a lesser extent, the threat would come from lower-class attack or domination. Grover's identification of 'fear of belittlement' is also valid for them: who does the belittling makes the difference.[74]

Huntingtower has much to show us about class. There are subtle variations present throughout the novel, because it is a story of conservative values resisting onslaughts by a new order that nobody yet wants. Dickson McCunn's firmly middle-class identity is praised several times in the narrative, for longevity and for embodying its attributes. He refuses to aspire to a higher class, and his wife is laughed at gently for her enjoyment of her class rituals and leisure choices. But he is also valued for his economic stability, which the emerging post-aristocratic societies need to acquire before they can build a nation again. The exiled Russian prince acknowledges McCunn's stability as a function of his class.

> "He is what they call the middle-class, which we who were foolish used to laugh at. But he is the stuff which above all others makes a great people. He will endure when aristocracies crack and proletarians crumble. In our own land we have never known him, but till we create him our land will not be a nation."[75]

John Heritage, on the other hand, is of a higher class than McCunn, since he is a gentleman and an ex-officer. Rank comes into play within the upper classes. By falling in love with Princess Saskia, Heritage, who is lower in rank than Sir Archie and Quentin Kennedy, who are in turn lower in rank than the princess, has fallen in love out of his rank. There is a barrier between McCunn, Mrs Morran and Dobson, and Heritage, Sir Archie and the Russian nobles, just as there is one between the middle- and the working-class characters, and the upper classes. The Gorbals Die-Hards (the very poorest) have more class access to the respectable middle-class McCunn, than they would have with the Englishmen and the Russians, since in Scotland the class system is considerably more fluid than for the English.

The potential for conflict between the different class groups is exacerbated by their military capability, the new mark of a hero after the war. Dougal the street urchin is a born military strategist. McCunn the retired grocer is a cunning undercover agent but not a military type. As ex-officers Heritage and Archie Roylance have recent military experience, but they were volunteers, and have no sense of the long game that the professionals – Dougal and the Russian prince whom (we assume) has survived the Revolution and the war by his natural military acumen – understand instinctively. Conservative expectations of leadership by the gentlemen of the army are also neatly undercut by the immensely practical expertise of the lower ranks, who, as we have seen since Kipling first began to publish, know a great deal more about warfare than the officers from being perpetually in the thick of it.

In *The Three Hostages* Buchan wrote about class in brief remarks, designed to develop characters as well as urge on the action. These have a didactic effect, functioning as hints to the ignorant as to how a gentleman should, and should not, behave. Hannay hopes that Julius Victor, the richest man in the world, will not offer him money to find his kidnapped daughter, because that 'would have spoiled the good notion I had of him'.[76] By this we are reminded that gentlemen do not work for money, and nor do they offer money to their equals. When Lord Mercot recovers from the hypnosis that had kept him a docile kidnap victim, he 'had begun to see [his kidnapper] no longer as a terror but as an offence – an underbred young bounder whom he detested'.[77] With the return of health comes the return of class-based courage. Hannay draws on this when he asks Mercot to return to captivity. '"If you think it out you'll see it's the only way. We must do nothing to spoil the chances of the other two [kidnap victims]. You're a gentleman and are bound to play the game."'[78] When Sir Archie is threatened in a seedy nightclub, he pulls rank to gain an advantage. '"I tried to solemnize 'em by sayin' who I was, and [the Marquis de la Tour du Pin] was there, so I dragged his name in. Dashed caddish thing to do, but I thought a marquis would put the wind up that crowd."'[79] Archie is a little clumsy in his methods, but his status is secure, as is his understanding that pulling rank usually has a positive effect. But the reader learns that having to mention one's rank in public is the action of a cad, antithetical to that of a gentleman.

Buchan gives an interesting class lesson in the Claybody family, who represent the new transitional people moving between classes in post-war society. Lord Claybody is mentioned at the end of *The Three Hostages* in fairly disparaging terms: 'a certain middle-aged Midland manufacturer [...] who had won an easy fortune and an easier peerage during the war'.[80] Archie too is jovially critical.

> "Rather a good old fellow in his way, and uncommon freehanded. Rum old bird, too! He once introduced his son to me as 'the Honourable Johnson Claybody'. Fairly wallows in his peerage. You know he wanted to take the title of Lord Oxford because he had a boy goin' up to Magdalen; but even the Herald's College jibbed at that."[81]

Archie's voice is of a titled man so secure in his rank that he scarcely thinks of it, but is critical of a new peer's ignorance of the extraordinarily complex social codes that accompany the new title but which are expected to be already known. Lord Claybody commits solecisms by using his son's title when introducing him to others; and he attempts to claim the city of Oxford as his baronial title on no grounds of ownership or family residence (the usual means), but simply because his son will attend university there (as do thousands of others). In *John Macnab* (1925), two years later, Lord Claybody has become an almost sympathetic character, because his insensitive son and his pretentious wife are much worse, in social terms. '"He's rather a good old bird himself. Don't care so much for his family."'[82]

Buchan also plays with the expectations of other classes in *John Macnab*. Leithen, intent on surveying the river from which he has to poach, first disguises himself as a lower middle-class tourist. The key class signifiers are the pocket camera, inappropriate footwear, the butler's watch chain and tartan bow-tie, and 'a vulgar green Homburg hat of Archie's'.[83] No-one recognises him, especially when he drops his aitches by code-switching. When he is taken unawares and captured by the enemy, as well as forgetting to mask his upper-class accent, he forgets that his own watch-chain has been dislodged, and that his miniature Eton shield is now in full view. Agatha Raden, his captor, assumes that he is a gentleman down on his luck, to which Leithen suggests that drink has been his downfall. She lets him go, and because 'she could not give away one of her own class', she does not discuss him when she rejoins the house party.[84]

'Playing the game' in *John Macnab* is a crucial indicator of class. The game is set up by the upper classes, a sporting proposal against heavy odds, to perform an illegal act for the fun of risking public notoriety. They understand the concept perfectly, since playing and games are activities common to their culture for showing membership of a class, and of their background. But other classes in the novel fail to understand the rules. Benjie, on returning secretly to base against orders with the stolen stag, is sent right back into the enemy's camp to return the corpse, which had been fairly won by the enemy. He doesn't understand at all. 'Something in Palliser-Yeates' eyes cut short his triumph. '"Benjie, you little fool, right about turn at once. I'm much obliged to you, but it can't be done. It isn't the game, you know. I chucked up the sponge when Miss Raden challenged me, and I can't go back on that."'[85]

Buchan's own political involvement would naturally draw him to populate his fiction with protagonists who are active in the Conservative Party. *John Macnab* is particularly rich in this, starting with Lord Claybody, now a Conservative peer, who is involved with 'A Grand Conservative Rally', at which Archie and Lord Lamancha (one of the Macnab syndicate), the Foreign Secretary, are to make speeches. Archie is the prospective Conservative candidate in a constituency of 'the most obstinate reactionaries on the face of the globe, but they've been voting Liberal ever since the days of John Knox'.[86] Class is also important for this political allegiance. '"In this country, once you start in on politics you're fixed in a class and members of a hierarchy, and you've got to go on, however unfitted you may be for the job, because it's a sort of high treason to weaken."'[87] Buchan's fictional worlds are Toryised, to the extent that no other politics seem possible for his protagonists. Variation, and transference between ideologies, only becomes possible for Buchan's fiction in the 1930s with *A Prince of the Captivity*.

Looking forward to the 1930s

At the end of the 1920s, Sandy is off to South America to foment a revolution on behalf of the indigenous aristocracy and free the people from criminal capitalism. This is a desperate fling by a lonely Earl to find a purpose in life. He finds his purpose by getting married, because by this he will propagate his line, and perpetuate the conservative hierarchy of class. Hannay seems to have sunk himself in home farm agriculture and does not appear again outside his gates except for urgent national reasons. Leithen has had an emotional time in *The Dancing Floor*, and is also feeling his age: he will from now on play a passive role in fiction until Buchan's last novel, *Sick Heart River* (1941). The setting of *The Runagates Club* (1928), the private dining club first seen in *The Three*

Hostages, is an old boy's club for pre-retirement adventurers. All their stories in this volume are of the past, past exploits, pre-war adventures, things done by younger men some time ago. Buchan speaks to his readers implicitly with a plea for their continued appreciation of the values and strengths of the past by showing his heroes as such strong proponents of these. The defence of the old is more apparent in Buchan than resistance to the new but, as we have seen, Buchan does resist some altered social conditions. His rhetoric carried authority, and was overwhelmingly persuasive through his trademark plots – fast-paced adventures in the outdoors among decent people and written with the confidence of traditional linguistic patterns. These gave Buchan's fiction timeless appeal, and a highly effective impact on his readers.

The McCunn boys are not interested in being grandees, or asking for their help. Jaikie is an undergraduate (students had never appeared in Buchan's fiction before), who cannot be cowed by social bullying, and Dougal works for a newspaper magnate and is as Red as they come. McCunn himself has timid landed pretensions, with his own little estate, but on strictly middle-class terms of comfort. Archie has grown up, because Janet has got him onto the political treadmill, and he speaks in the House of Commons on agriculture and the air. New one-off characters appear, in single stories or novels, whom Buchan invents to work out his views on increasingly alarming European politics, and the polarised and competitive state of politics at home. *The Gap in the Curtain* (1932) is a key novel for the latter, while *Castle Gay* (1930) and *The House of the Four Winds* (1935) cover the former. There is also a new Buchan protagonist, the important but one-off character Adam Melfort of *A Prince of the Captivity* (1933), who is Buchan's major contribution in addressing European politics of the 1930s. *The Island of Sheep* (1936) is less overtly political, but returns us to Buchan's pre-war world where a national political arena can be used to sort out a private matter between gentlemen. There is a pattern to Buchan's overriding concern with conservative values in his fiction of the 1920s, of a repeated return to the norm, rebuttals of the new, and a reiteration of the familiar and safe.

3
Ex-Officers and Gentlemen: Yates in the 1920s

Dornford Yates came to prominence as a writer in the 1920s. He had gained an enthusiastic readership through short stories and serialised novels in *The Windsor Magazine* since 1911, and his books were published by Ward, Lock & Co. His 1920s fiction expressed profound agitation, responding to the new disruptions in society that Adrian Gregory describes as 'some anti-Semitism and colour prejudice, anti-Irish sentiment, elements of gender backlash and class conflict, all of which were strong for a year or two after the war'.[1] Laura Beers and Geraint Thomas observe that 'the decline of the landed classes' and the 'redefinition of gender relations' were key indicators of social change after the war.[2] These were at the foreground of Yates's stories.

Yates presented figures of authority struggling to maintain social as well as physical or political authority. William Vivian Butler describes the reader's situation: 'four years of slaughter, plus the spectacle of the Bolshevik bloodbath and mass unrest at home, meant that thriller readers now wanted, above everything, a "sound-chap" hero – if possible one reminiscent of the safe, glorious, golden Old England they thought they used to know'.[3] Yates's authority figures are upper middle-class gentlemen, who had usually held officer rank during the First World War. They are identifiably conservative, though Yates paid no attention to party politics as such in his fiction. For him, the good were conservatives, and the bad were everyone else, but even the bad were rarely characterised in political terms. His more thuggish protagonists might have subscribed to the early fascist organisations, had it been acceptable for gentlemen so to do. For Yates, socialism was an aspect of villainy, rather than the other way round. In his short story collections *The Courts of Idleness* (1920), *Berry & Co* (1920), *Jonah & Co* (1922), *And Five Were Foolish* (1924), *As Other Men Are* (1925) and *Maiden Stakes*

(1928) Yates works in miniature, exploring a single characteristic of an individual as a foil for the genial idiocies of the Pleydell family or their wider social circle. In these stories, there is little room to give villains and antagonists a fully realised description, so their essential wrongness is signalled by the cut of their waistcoat, or manners towards women, or servants. Departing from the gentleman's codes condemns a man in Yates's fiction. The use of comedy and indulgent romantic playfulness – the dominant tones in Yates's early short fiction – likewise signal the ease and generous spirit of the gentleman and his ladies. Comedy's function of social restoration reiterates the unquestioning conservative values of Yates's protagonists. Some of his 1920s short stories express violent feelings based on socially conservative fears. 'Ann' (1924, originally entitled 'Mésalliance') of *And Five Were Foolish* is a savage response to social miscegenation. His uncollected 'Valérie' of 1919 is an alarming statement of the ownership rights of the husband, and the punishment of the erring wife. These moments that indicate an urge to control social rebellion were characteristic of his fiction as a whole.

The Yates novels of the 1920s use the themes of the control of women and the defence of conservative social values on a much bigger canvas. In *Anthony Lyveden* (1921) Yates makes his definitive statement about the plight of the unemployed gentleman ex-officer, tortured by inarticulacy amid modern Gothic horrors. Its sequel, *Valerie French* (1923), was based on a painful insistence on retrogressive relationship criteria that forbade men and women from transgressing some very fixed codes. *The Stolen March* (1926) is an anomalous dark satire on relationships between the sexes and classes which repays close study for its conservative responses. His first thrillers – *Blind Corner* (1927) and *Perishable Goods* (1928) – are powerful explorations of how might will ignore the law, and restore a proper sense of conservative social views to society.

Throughout the 1920s, in parallel with his developing range of tones, his writing increasingly expressed resistance to post-war social, political and economic change. To deal with this adequately, Yates developed how he wrote, demonstrating a talent for perfectly mannered styles, literary pastiche, lexical exuberance, and sophisticated plotting. This technical creativity transformed the formulaic foundations of his fiction to such an extent that it is wrong to place his novels in the marketing categories also occupied by, for example, Edgar Wallace, a stupendously prolific novelist who delivered distinctively undistinctive formula fiction. *Anthony Lyveden* showed what Yates was capable of by being simultaneously a modern allegory, a Gothic drama, a legal thriller, and a romantic love story. *Perishable Goods* (1928) is at once a love story, a thriller, a novel of escapology, an episode in an ongoing family saga, and an incitement to vigilantism. Yet these shared the same message. Yates's fiction offered his readers complex social criticisms of a world gone, or going, to the dogs, in adventures that showed how the good men and true could resist this change.

In terms of how Yates's fiction related to the universal social problem of unemployment, *Anthony Lyveden*, with *Valerie French*, is also a paean to the idealised jobless ex-officer, an attack on the social injustice that forces gentlemen to take employment beneath their station in life, and the value of army training that makes such appalling injustice endurable. This was not uncommon: an important best-seller of the early 1920s, Warwick Deeping's *Sorrell and Son* (1925), uses the same tropes. Many of Yates's 1920s short stories begin with the story of what happened to the hero after the war, and how finding a job was difficult, or impossible without sliding down the class scale.

The good man in Yates's world was rarely anyone who did not have lineage and a family home built by ancestors. The rise of the new, plutocratic rich was causing, in Yates's view, the decay of the gentleman's world. The war had made 'good' society more accessible. The 'right kind' of people were altering: class was becoming so much harder to determine. Jill Greenfield writes: 'the entry of new groups to the middle classes and the downgrading of others – the "new rich" and "new poor" – exacerbated status anxieties'.[4] We can see that this mattered to Yates because he began to specialise in stories about class indicators that could not be mistaken: breeding, manners, and authority. Novels of the 1920s by Evelyn Waugh, Ronald Firbank, Michael Arlen and Aldous Huxley (joined by Nancy Mitford in the 1930s) used derision in their ambivalent criticism of the generational values that had been so severely challenged by the war.[5] Yates did precisely the opposite, valorising where they criticised, and writing in an elegiac mode while they employed satire.

His social concern stopped at the personal, and hardly extended into the community. There is no interest in Yates's fiction in rebuilding ravaged post-war communities or regenerating the economy, because he did not depict interwar England as having suffered (though he did write retrofitted fiction in the 1950s to show how the upper classes suffered political oppression from the Left in the 1920s: see Chapter 8). Upper-class individuals suffered by losing their estates or their income to taxes, but no other losses are mentioned, and no other classes. Instead, Yates's characters are only interested in re*gaining* their status, homes, land, or privileges. The strongest examples of this need for restitution are his idealised deserving ex-officers.

Many of Yates's short stories from this period are about the loss and retrieval of the right kind of home for the right kind of people, where 'home' means a landed estate that gave privacy from the world as well as servants. Increasing emancipation for women in society and in employment impelled Yates to praise those aspects of his heroines that he could control: their hair, clothes, manners, and destiny on the arm of the right man. Interestingly, he maintained his preferred standards out of Britain. Almost all the episodes in Yates's escapist adventures happened abroad, where the natives were friendly, policemen could be bribed and enemies buried without fuss. Yates's gentlemen vigilantes and picaresque travellers made lordly progresses through France, Austria (especially Carinthia), Germany, and the invented state of Etchechuria. These travels were sometimes pastoral escapes from trying times at home, or simply from the miserliness of the pound. Sometimes they were urgent missions to find hidden treasure, rescue ladies, or exact revenge, with fast cars and back-up support from silent automaton servants. They all had in common a positive resolution or restitution that gave the reader pleasure. Aspiring novelist Winifred Holtby knew the importance of the post-war happy ending in 1922: 'every one says that a book with a sad ending has no chance of a sale these post-war days. People are too much concerned with living down their own tragedies to take much interest in other people's'.[6]

The world gone mad

Yates used the supernatural to describe the upside-down condition of society. *The Stolen March* of 1926 is in the different category of portal fantasy, and *Wife Apparent* (1956) is discussed in Chapter 8. The Gothic and the supernatural are so important for the plots of *Anthony Lyveden* and its sequel *Valerie French*, and drive so many of the characters' actions, that they must be considered as an example of how Yates was exploring a new world of unnatural strangeness in his fiction. He uses Gothic drama to crank up the tension for his hero, to heighten the reader's fears and multiply the agonies the reader will undergo as Anthony and Valerie continually fail to be reunited and understand each other. To maintain this tension, Yates used the artificial stimulants of a malignant ghost and a dark enchanted forest: both were expertly depicted, and make these two novels the most emotionally exhausting of his works, torturing the reader with the undeserved travails of a gentleman. The elaborate plot alone is an indication of how strongly Yates was writing at this time. It was the moment that his career changed up a gear, when he began to explore his skills and concerns by extending himself in terms of length, stylistically, and thematically.

Anthony is destitute because his uncle left him his fortune only on condition that Anthony achieves a knighthood. Naturally no gentleman will angle for such an honour to gain money, so this leaves Anthony penniless after demobilisation. He endures class-based humiliation steadily while he is earning his living as a footman, but he cannot endure the strain of falling in love with a rich girl who wants him to marry her, who then thinks (wrongly) that he is trifling with her. Anthony thus disappears, driven out of heaven by mutual inarticulacy. In the next paragraph, Yates tells an apparently unrelated ghost story, which is a four-page hair-raiser, leading to the discovery under the floor-boards of a letter that recalls to the finder's mind a secret that will restore Anthony's fortune to him. But now Anthony is in a new job, and no-one knows where he is. He is working as second-in-command to Colonel Winchester on the great work of restoring the forest of Gramarye, somewhere in the Cotswolds, with a team of war-impaired soldiers, and just enough money for tools and food. The work is physical and demanding, and would be perfect, if it were not for the unnerving obsession of the Colonel for the work, which Anthony is beginning to share, and the interruptions of André, the girl who has been engaged to the Colonel for far too long.

She is a casualty of the wood, which rejects women, and demands the ritual sacrifices of male votaries. The wood sends Winchester mad in a remarkable scene of warped dimensionality out of Edgar Allan Poe and Lovecraft where only the road saves Anthony by not letting the crazed Winchester pass. Other portents become apparent when André is there to show Anthony how affected he has been by the enchantment. He hasn't laughed since he began work, because he and the other men are serving as priests, not workmen. He can't eat, he can only drink; he is a fasting acolyte. When a stranger infiltrates the forest, he breaks a leg, is never found, and dies there. When one of the men goes mad, digging graves for the corpses only he can see, this is a clear suggestion of breakdown from war trauma, and an indication of continued, unrelieved suffering.

The scenes in Gramarye are written in a very high allegorical style, as if Edmund Spenser had been rewritten by Dr Johnson. Such a mixture of haughtiness and invention would raise even the most trivial of subjects by such exuberant literary decoration. Yates insures against an imbalance of mode and subject by ramping up the tension with abbreviated sentences, outbreaks of italics, single word utterances. He pays as much attention to the rules of fantasy structures and myth as he does to the pacing of André's overwrought dialogue and Anthony's interior digressions on Fate and Romance.

But why do all this? What was Yates's purpose in these novels? His playfulness with myth and the Gothic would have been a strategy for maintaining reader interest in the story while it was being serialised in *The Windsor*. After some very high-tension flirting and romantic misunderstandings in the first four chapters, the fifth chapter focuses on physical and psychic torments, rather than wallow again in the emotions. The remainder of the novel buffets Anthony between female emotional demands (two women and one forest), while inadvertently eluding the men of the law who have a future to offer him. These may be metaphors for the confused state of a nation not at rights with itself, where men and women are not in their right places. The restoration of the forest boundaries as a project is another metaphor, for the restoration of the nation, of which only ex-officers are capable (and has resonances with the opening of Buchan's *The Three Hostages*, as discussed in Chapter 2). *Anthony Lyveden* and *Valerie French* demonstrate the torments and passions that ensue when one man's world has been turned upside down.

The world turned upside down

Yates's didactic fiction reiterated the maintenance of social standards by judging those who did not understand their importance. He focused his instructions on correct modern manners, and the treatment of inferiors, of women and of one's betters. By always writing from a poetic and romantic point of view, Yates made the instruction very attractive. The stories are reassuring to the man who doesn't quite know how to behave like a gentleman. They show a cautious woman how to respond like a lady when placed in situations of social difficulty, as well as of high melodrama. Negotiating modern social norms, for all classes, required instruction, because in the 1920s many people were finding themselves in unfamiliar social territory. There is little joy in these fictions of an upside-down world, and no celebration of the carnivalesque, because the world should not be upside down: the results are inimical to the conservative perspective.

Ross McKibbin describes the type of fiction that Yates wrote as 'the literature of conflict'. It 'was anchored firmly in the early 1920s and the angst with which much of the middle class experienced those years. Class conflict was, directly or indirectly, central to this genre. Such conflict is usually seen by the reader through the eyes of an ex-officer and it is often around his status in post-war Britain that the plot flows'.[7] Yates appealed for readers' sympathy through a technique called sentimental or romantic disproportion, 'the use of incongruity to introduce the emotion of the wonderful or the pathetic'.[8] P N Furbank coined this term when discussing the writing of Dickens and Warwick Deeping, both of whom shared Yates's tendencies towards emotional melodrama. Such characters undergo a journey between exaggerated extremes, from poverty to riches, from loneliness to family warmth. Yates also used what Furbank calls a 'congratulation system' in his plots, in which a character's sufferings are itemised as evidence of their inherent worth; and had a dependence on nostalgia, in which 'past things are moving and significant simply because they are past [...] to create pathos'.[9] Yates used these three techniques intensively. In writing his stories of characters cast down by Fate, sentimental disproportion was a key generator of his readers' empathy.

Come down in the world

The most common social evil that Yates addressed was the plight of the unfortunate gentlemen and women who had come down in the world through no fault of their own. Yates used recognisable difficulties caused by the unstable post-war economy and the effect of death duties on large estates to destabilise his heroes. In his story 'Spring' (1923) in *And Five Were Foolish*:

> When he had come back from the War, things were in evil case. A cold rain of demands beat upon his diminished income; the stream of outgoings were like to burst its banks; over all, the cloud of a heavy mortgage, once no bigger than a man's hand, was blotting out the heaven.[10]

Here Yates is invoking the landowning classes, who were struggling financially throughout the interwar period, no longer with a reserve to draw on. 'By the inter-war years, many landed estates had ceased to be economically viable. [...] The combination of reduced incomes, increased exactions, and eroded confidence, meant that most patricians were obliged to economise and to retrench, compared with the earlier and more prosperous period when, in retrospect, money had always seemed to be easily available.'[11] Many of Yates's characters are placed in this position, in fiction that produced personalised tragedies out of familiar social and economic conditions.

For those gentlemen who did not have ancestral homes to lose, simply having to earn a living was a bad enough step down the social scale. Yates invented fantasies to show how gentlemen and ladies could endure it. In *Anthony Lyveden*, after two very unpleasant jobs with vilely low employers, Anthony lands on his feet with the very humble Bumbles. They have become rich during the war, and now employ Major Lyveden, and Captain, Mrs and Miss Alison to be their footman, chauffeur and housemaids, because these gentlefolk are simply the best applicants for the jobs. To show the essentially perfect qualities of the gentry classes Yates makes the point that true gentlewomen will know exactly how a room ought to be cleaned and how to look after a house that deserves it. Ex-officers will obey orders from an inferior employer as they would from a superior officer, no matter how incompetent or foolish. But thankfully the Bumbles are not foolish, and are gratefully inferior to their perfect servants. Lyveden and the Alisons retain some class privileges, by paying one of the kitchen maids a shilling a week for her to lay their table and serve their meals, which they eat in a private dining-room, reintroducing Victorian servant hierarchies of privilege.

While insecure employment and approaching destitution are classic indicators of sentimental disproportion in fiction, these conditions can also be bracing for characters who are behaving badly and need chastisement. Yates enjoyed constructing elaborate legal problems by which he could drag his suffering gentlefolk through tortuous social indignities until, at last, the lawyers do their work and the fortune is retrieved. In 'Oliver' in *As Other Men Are* (1925) the Pauncefotes lose their money just as their marriage is crumbling. This crisis does not permit them to forget their *noblesse oblige*. They pay their bills immediately by selling what they own, but Oliver is not able to find work. 'A soldier's not much good outside his own job [...] Three ghastly months had gone by and Captain and Mrs Pauncefote were down to seven pounds.'[12] Jean learns to shop for food in market stalls, they abandon their brittle, fashionable manners, and are finally given a perfect post as caretakers for a country home. Poverty chastises them, real work (very suitable work for gentlefolk) retrains them for their station in life, and allows them to admit their love for each other. Only then are they given their reward, money out of the blue, only presented when Captain Pauncefote remembers to pay the last of his debts. It's a blatant prescription as to how gentlemen and ladies should behave.

Young penniless gentlewomen acting as paid companions were used by Yates for retellings of *Cinderella*. The eponymous heroine of 'Susan' (1924) in *And Five Were Foolish* is placed in a difficult situation in a lavish house party populated by monsters. She is rescued by the quiet and diffident Duke of Culloden in incognito, who has very little money, but an estate and a name. Susan has nothing but her good name, and lost her home in Maine due to her father not making a will. Yates piles social indignities upon the tragedy of her past (her evil cousins even took her home-made curtains) and her increasingly desperate present-day situation. He then allows the Duke to rescue her with a terrific set-piece of social revenge and class approval that cuts down Susan's foreign predator and the false Duke with one masterly plot twist, and enables Susan to have accepted a proposal of marriage from a duke without knowing who he really was, thus absolving her of being merely an American gold-digger.

Once again, those who are cast down the social scale are rescued because they demonstrate nobility of character. This very simple equation of being deserving equalling financial and social salvation was undoubtedly emotionally reassuring to Yates's readers, but it has deeper resonances with the times in which he was writing. As well as the people who found themselves struggling in the post-war years, there were also those who were unexpectedly on top. Yates's fiction showed people how to behave whether they were on top or pushed under, and projected a very simplistic reflection of society that reinforced beliefs about fate and fortune's wheel. They also stressed the importance of good behaviour and hard work. Yates offered moral guidance in these fictions of reassurance, but refused to question the conditions that had brought about the changes that he so disliked. Instead, he looked for easy victims by accusing those who had climbed up on top of all the social crimes he could find.

Climbing up in the world

Going back to *Anthony Lyveden*, which is the *ne plus ultra* of Yates's loathing of post-war social change, we are very early on presented with the spectacle of Mrs Slumper, Lyveden's first employer whom Yates sets up to deserve no mercy. No detail is spared us. She has rented a house in whose kitchen she would not normally have been fit to work, from a titled lady whom she does not know; she is a bully to her well-meaning, though equally low, husband, who is a City swindler; she attends society weddings uninvited; she has no positive traits, existing only as a caricature symbol of the destruction of all upper-class (meaning civilised) values and standards. Yates cleverly mediates her vileness in letters written by Anthony to a friend, so that we can assume that if even this mild-mannered and perfect gentleman criticises his employer in a private letter, she must be appalling. It's interesting that Yates's bile is reserved for the woman of this unpleasant couple, perhaps to indicate that she insults the hallowed status she seeks to take.

Yates expects the reader to agree that social divisions are necessary, and must be maintained. Sometimes this is simple snobbery, as in *The Courts of Idleness* (1920), in which a character observes that Biarritz is 'gradually filling up with the sort of people one leaves England to avoid'.[13] Properly separated class divisions have to be maintained without patronage. There should be no snobbery based on assumed superiority. In *Anthony Lyveden*, the humble but proud Mr Bumble lends his car to Lady Touchstone after her car has broken down, but refuses to accompany her.

"I shouldden dream o' takin' advantage of an acciden', me lady."

Regretting very much that she had never noticed the ex-grocer before, Lady Touchstone sought desperately to pull the position round. [...] The quiet determination of his tone was unmistakeable. The little man was clearly stoutly resolved not to improve an acquaintance which his wife did not share. Wealth had not clouded his memory nor corrupted his simple heart. Lady Touchstone hauled down her flag.[14]

This novel uses its narrative space to investigate many kinds of patronage, and incorrect behaviour to and from the lower orders. The overwhelming message is that those who have so risen have a responsibility to rise also to their new position, and change themselves to suit society's expectations.

Reinforcing class indicators

A novelist contemporary to Yates but with diametrically opposite politics was Ellen Wilkinson MP, a former member of the Communist Party and a Labour Party member from 1924 until her death in 1947. Her 'semi-autobiographical' novel *Clash* (1929),[15] set during the General Strike, features her alter ego, Joan, who has 'no doubts at all about the selfish inadequacy of the middle and upper classes. "They wanted inequality. They could not conceive of a society without someone to bow before and others to cringe to them"'.[16] This could also be said quite accurately of most of Yates's characters. For Yates the nation was represented by the experience of the upper middle classes, the gentry and the aristocracy. The rest of the population existed to serve. The indicators of who served, and who was born to receive service, were therefore very important. Yates's view was that there was a distressing amount of slippage across this boundary. We can now turn to what the boundary markers were, and how they could be upheld.

Valerie French begins with a destitute man in rags realising that he has no memory, and that he is being followed by a small dog. They carry on their journey together, and we see that this is a good man: he goes back to collect the dog when it collapses, even though he is in the same state of starvation. Some hours later, Anthony Lyveden (for it is he) comes across a lorry at the side of the road, and asks for help. The driver knows that he is a gentleman, or a 'toff', as Yates will have it, because of how Lyveden speaks. The driver responds to him as an 'other rank' to an officer, and feeds and clothes him freely. He and his colleague take Lyveden to a pub to rest, and the landlord gives him unlimited credit. On their departure, the lorry drivers give Lyveden two ten shilling notes, claiming they'd been found in the ragged old clothes Lyveden had been wearing. This fantasy episode – as far from probability as the enchanted forest – performs the function of reminding readers of whom this character is, and the proper relationships he should have with the world around him. He is utterly trustworthy, he will pay his bills as soon as he's found his feet again, and he should be helped as a matter of cross-class loyalty as well as humanitarianism. This is acceptable, though far-fetched. Lyveden next gets conned into helping a thief into stealing a car's spare wheel (at this period these were kept on the outside of the chassis), but, because of his accent, is instantly believed by Sir Andrew Plague, the car's owner, to be innocent. In a later episode, Sir Andrew notices that Lyveden is being tried at the magistrates' court, and steamrollers the magistrates into dropping the case, regardless of the accusation, because of his assumption that Lyveden is a gentleman. Yates's fantasy here is that gentlemen never appear in the dock, that all men should help each other, and that suspicion and distrust will not occur in a proper social arrangement where everyone knows their class.

The spectacular transgression of class barriers and allegiances in 'Ann' (1924), in *And Five Were Foolish*, is one of Yates's most tortured stories, in class terms. Lady Ann has married her father's groom, because she is in love with him, and with the romantic dream of love in a cottage, isolated from the world. Bob Minter is a good man, but he has dreadful relations, and we know from the opening page of the story that this will not end well. Ann's aunt is 'on her knees with tears running down her face'; they marry in a registrar's office where the registrar has a 'face like a mask', and Ann hears 'the cameras click as she and Bob passed out, felt the insolent stares of the waiter who brought them lunch'.[17] These are clear signals of class indicators breached: the sister of an earl or duke does not kneel to her niece; the daughter of an earl or duke does not marry in a registrar's office; ladies are not photographed in public, nor do they put themselves in a position where they can be stared at by an insolent waiter. Yates builds up the torment slowly, as Ann and Bob travel by third-class train to the seaside resort of Suet, to meet his family. She has to go through with this because she is married and he is her husband. She must obey, she must esteem, but after only eight hours she can no longer love him. She cannot bear his aspirations for her, or his innocent and loving stratagems that cut across all the training of her class. 'Nothing, it seemed, was to be spared her – nothing.'[18] Yates spends a lot of time making sure we see her agonies, and understand why she is suffering so much. In this way, he shows us how class indicators work, why they matter to his view of the world, and how crass it is that anyone should think they should be ignored. The final tragedy of the story is that Ann is released from her torment by her husband's defence of her against a socialist bully, and his conviction that the upper classes have the inborn right to have authority over the lower classes. Yates's reasoning is questionable, since a man who acceded so strongly to the view that each class should keep its place would never have married so far 'above' himself. S P B Mais, a noted critic of the period, gave 'Ann' particular attention.

> There is real unexpected power in 'Ann', the story of the girl who married her father's groom. As a warning to any foolish young thing about to marry out of her caste, this grim tale could scarcely be bettered. Mr Yates has an astonishing flair for creating a crude atmosphere, all the more horrible in so far as he keeps his descriptions always on the light note.[19]

The 'light note' is questionable, when the readers' emotions are so determinedly harnessed to Ann's situation and sufferings. It is a story written from a patriarchal perspective, and its emotional impact is the victory of class-based propaganda over common sense.

In *The Stolen March* (1926), Yates deals with a class etiquette problem when mules become talking animals (this novel is set in a Mittel-Europa Wonderland). What social class are mules? In 1911 Yates's cousin 'Saki' had tackled this problem calmly, presenting Tobermory the unexpectedly talking cat as the same class as his victims in the drawing-room.[20] Yates follows his example and does the same with the mules, giving them the same gentry vocabulary as his protagonists. They also provide humour and counsel, helping Yates's suggestion that the English travellers would treat them as rather good-class local guides, with whom they might socialise had they met them at home.

In *Blind Corner* (1927), servants are used to show how rigid are the class boundaries in Yates's worlds. When the heroes plan their mission, Mansel sends Bell, his recommended candidate as a servant, to Chandos for inspection, as if Bell were a dog. Only Yates's senior servants had surnames, and were automatons, especially those on active service with Mansel and Chandos.

> He seemed to notice nothing, yet was exceptionally observant, and he always wore the same agreeable, but sometimes resigned expression, as though his face were a mask. I never knew him volunteer a statement unless he thought it might be of service: he never once complained: he was most faithful, and I think he thought Mansel was a god. In this tenet he was not peculiar. Rowley and Carson, Mansel's servant, held the same view.[21]

This is not a man but a collection of requirements and services, lacking personality or any vestige of character. His function and purpose is to serve, and to act as faithfully as a soldier in peacetime. Even when, at the end of this adventure, he has been rewarded with one-ninth of the vast treasure (the upper-class participants get two-ninths each) and has enough to live on easily for the rest of his life, Bell asks to stay in Chandos's service. Here we can see that, for Yates, service as a vocation was a strong indicator of the lower classes' proper function. Two books later, Bell is still the obedient automaton. In *Blood Royal* (1929) Chandos leaves Bell with Rowley to sit in a wood overnight with no food, water or shelter, at a moment's notice, and no complaint is made.[22] Later (no sleep, little rest), trouble looms, and Chandos issues his orders, in the third person, to his automatons. '"One," I said, "will stay at the foot of this track, and the other will go to where he can see the abbey at the end of the road. The first sign of movement, please."'[23]

I want to discuss the first paragraphs from *Blind Corner* in close detail, to show how Yates worked his views about class, politics and gentility together to produce a narrative drive that exuded unanswerable authority. Yates wrote this thriller for Hodder & Stoughton after several volumes of frivolous short stories and the romantic thrillers of *Anthony Lyveden* and *Valerie French* where the psychology of class was a motivating factor. In *Blind Corner* he was refining a consciously masculine style that was profoundly reactionary. There is an interesting political dimension to this novel that is rarely seen so openly in Yates's fiction.

> When the first of these things happened, that is to say upon the twentieth day of April, 192-, I was twenty-two years old, a little stronger than most men of my age, and very ready for anything that bade fair to prove more exciting than entering the office of my uncle, who was a merchant of consequence in the City of London.
>
> I had lately been sent down from Oxford for using some avowed communists as many thought they deserved, and, though George Hanbury – for he had been with me in the affair – and I received much sympathy and more complimentary letters from complete strangers than we could conveniently answer, I think we were both more distressed than we would have cared to admit to take our leave of Christchurch [*sic*] before our time. For my part, I had been glad to get out of England and to put the matter as far away from my mind as ever I knew.
>
> I had, then, spent five weeks at Biarritz, the guest of some people called Pomeroy, with whom, such was their benevolence, I believe I might have stayed indefinitely; but a letter from Hanbury, with whom I was to share a flat, threatening to forego the agreement if I did not return to Town, at length precipitated my departure.
>
> I returned as I had come, alone in my car, making for Dieppe and spending the first night at Angouleme and the second at Tours.
>
> From Tours to Dieppe is a comfortable day's run, and I rose that April morning, intending to pass my third night on the packet which should take me to England.[24]

The first thing we notice in the opening paragraph is the fact that if the date and the means of transport are left out, this could be the opening of a novel set in the 1750s. It shares the syntax and tone of Agnes and Egerton Castle and Baroness Orczy, champions of the pre-Regency historical romance; and also of their imitator Georgette Heyer whose first novel was published in 1921. It does not, however, have the true ring of the eighteenth century, since it uses the first-person narrative voice outside the epistolary tradition. The narrative voice does not profess piety as part of the character's discourse, and there is a focus on bodily strength, rather than, for example, sentiment, or rationality, and a professed refusal to take up offered patronage. Yates uses a faux-historical syntax to offer an impression of manners and attitudes from a time long past, yet set in the reader's present day. He does this to reinforce the fantasy setting, but also to woo the reader, to produce a satisfying aural effect.

We are not told the name of the protagonist, only that he is 'stronger than most men my age, and very ready for anything', except a free job working in an office when he had no other prospects. This bodes well for an action-packed thriller with a hero who has a certain unconcern for how he will earn his living. For a novel written in the Depression, this carries class messages: no matter how desperate, a gentleman prefers not to soil his hands with trade.

The second paragraph tells us that Chandos has been thrown out of university for 'using some avowed communists as they deserved', and that he was apparently up at Christ Church (spelt wrongly in the original), an Oxford college considered to be the most aristocratic in the university. Yates would have known this: he himself went to University College, and his biographer notes that 'none of his better class of character admits to having been at University College. All are either Christ Church, New College or Magdalen men'.[25] Notice that Yates does not commit Chandos to actual violence, only to 'using'. This suggests physical violence, but the caution of the lawyer, and the old-school reticence of the gentleman hero, occlude the facts. The reader is thus invited to demonstrate his understanding of such language, and political stance, and not find it necessary to be told exactly what 'using' means in the context of communists.

I find it interesting that Yates would make this point so early in the novel, that his hero and his friend were violently anti-communist, and thus right-wing, and that so many 'people' applauded and supported their actions, even if the university did not. It is clearly an important part of Chandos and Hanbury's characterisation. Chandos (his name is not revealed until the second chapter) did not leave Oxford but waited for the university's decision, suggesting that he felt that his actions were reasonable. Yates's description of how 'complete strangers' and the 'people called Pomeroy' shower Chandos and Hanbury with praise and hospitality has a strong whiff of self-justification and wish-fulfilment about it. Given the decrease in their popularity at this time, was beating up communists a risky business in 1927? Whatever the facts, in Yates's fantasy world political nuance was not important. One beat up communists, ergo one was a good fellow, deserving of praise, and the university that sent you down was an ass. It's also interesting that the communists were 'avowed', as if people only suspected of being communists would have been a safe target. For a lawyer like Yates, details like this would matter.

Chandos then spends five weeks staying at Biarritz with 'some people called Pomeroy'. This apparently off-hand reference for generous hosts is also class-nuanced understatement: one does not gush about generosity, or bandy their names about in public. Biarritz was a desirable resort, but one with a curious reputation. It was extremely chic, but also a little déclassé, with a growing British expatriate community in the vicinity. By 1927 Yates had lived in the area around Pau and Biarritz for some time, and was eventually to build his own home there. He would have regarded it as the ideal location for a gentleman, because he was one. Yates lays down the standards for the behaviour of a gentleman just a little too vehemently for one who on his own estimation ought to have accepted them as the norm. His messages to those who need reassurance are not only that these were the models to follow, but that he was the authority to obey. Through Chandos he is sending messages about how a young man of spirit (and conservative values) should behave. Chandos is a gentleman in behaviour, expectations and resources. He is also an adventurer, and plans to share rooms in London, a classic jumping-off point for adventure.

Homes

When Yates's characters were not struggling to maintain their class status, they were busy looking for and rescuing their homes. An important post-war expectancy was the right to a home, much encouraged by the politicians. The number of new homes built in Britain increased dramatically from 25,000 in 1920 to a peak of over 350,000 at the beginning of the Second World War: around half of these were semi-detached houses.[26] The market also changed considerably in terms of ownership, and renting. 'Of over 4 million houses' built in the interwar period, '2½ million [were] for private sale, and the rest for rent by local authorities'.[27] Private ownership meant increased security, and a change in social expectations of where and how one lived.[28] There was consequently an expectation that a house, or at least a flat, of one's own, was the right of every tax-payer, and certainly the right of a returning soldier. Even though Yates did not live in Britain for much of the 1920s, he would have been aware from the newspapers that housing was a social concern. His own home was very important to him. We have seen in Chapter 1 how he eulogised his last British home in the dedication to *Jonah & Co*, and he made house-hunting a frequent issue in his short stories. Though some of his characters were idealised with large incomes or family mansions, many were so cast down the housing or employment ladder that they lived in lodgings, and had to clean their own shoes.

The home as a metaphor for England

The regenerative action of buying land in danger was often used by Yates, and his fiction tends to describe the transfer of such land from the point of view of the owners who might or might not lose it. Naturally, he allowed miracles to happen to prevent such sales; incoming heiresses and wealthy ex-soldiers were allowed to marry into struggling estates, rather than take the estates away from the rightful family owners.

In two early Yates stories from 1920, he makes a straightforward case for how England can be saved through the metaphors of the sale of land and recovery of stolen property. The Pleydell family manage to prevent the sale of Merry Down, an idyllic estate neighbouring their own, by effectively kidnapping the loathsome (German and Jewish) would-be buyer Mr Dunkelsbaum until the auction is over. Instead, Merry Down goes to the right kind of 'purchaser, who had paid a good price, was of English blood, and had known Derry Bagot at Eton, and soldiered with him [...] The place had passed into good clean hands and was to be cared for'.[29]

In 'Spring' (1923), Willoughby's ancestral home is bought by a pork baron, which is a very clear statement that the heritage of England is being sold to the wrong sort of people who have not even the decency to become rich in a gentlemanly way. The pork baron and his wife are delighted with their new toy, and exhibit it to anyone they can get in the doors. But they are not true owners: they sell the house and estate rapidly for ten times what they paid.

> "Wot else could I do? You can't turn away money like that. You 'aven't the right. I tell you straight, I'm dotty about this place, but 'Business First' 's my motter, an' – an' it's pretty nigh arf a million," he concluded absently.[30]

Willoughby had originally sold the house to them because he has had no choice. He ensured that he was kept on as a servant, incognito, to make sure his home was looked after properly. As a final message of how such salvation may come about, Yates invokes the recent but now traditional trope of the American heiress. This story is typical, presenting a metaphor for the proper conduct of English gentlemen towards their homes, and towards the nation, to counter the rising population of businessmen only concerned with money.

He attacked threats to the physical integrity of the home in 'Titus' (1925), in which Blanche and Titus Cheviot have to earn their own living, and turn to interior decoration. They are completely untrained, and force abominations on a market only too happy to pay inflated prices in return for their aristocratic name and artificially inflated seal of approval. Their design solutions for modern living are a vandal's dream for the period manors and Georgian mansions that Yates hands over to their care. In this grimly satisfying satire he is criticising modern decorating fads, and also the ignorant snobbery that compels owners to hand over their homes to such treatment.

Homes, we must realise, are to be treated properly (as must England), and if you do not have the good taste to understand how this must be done, then you do not deserve to own such national treasures. Naturally, these idealisations of the English country home would have come from Yates's expatriate reading (of *Country Life*, perhaps?) and nostalgia. In the 1930s he would move the Pleydells permanently to join him in the south of France, but throughout the 1920s they and his other characters spend increasing amounts of leisure time touring France, and Spain. White Ladies, Bell Hammer, and the other gracious, desirable houses in his fiction, assume the lineaments of a dream, and drift out of reality.

Women

As I noted in Chapter 2, women's advances in society were not noted with enthusiasm by Buchan or Yates in the 1920s. Yates went further than Buchan, by punishing women's behaviour when they broke his own particular gender rules. In his 1920s fiction, the most repellent example is the short story 'Ann' (1923), already discussed above. Yates applied rigid rules for the behaviour of his women characters (according to his biographer, he also did this to his first wife[31]), and was repeatedly insistent about their sexual purity, rather than, say, kindness to animals, or willingness to have children. But he also enjoyed writing occasional episodes of sexual voyeurism, titillation and cohabitation in his fiction, for example in the short story 'Derry', in which two married couples exchange partners until fear of their photographs appearing in print brings them back to correct behaviour.

It isn't clear why Yates was so vehement about sexual purity for his characters. Most other writers producing fiction for his markets did not share his intensity of focus, or his limited set of fears about what would happen if a woman smiled at or went for a drive with an unapproved man. Yates's view was predicated on an assumption that social reputation was all-important (more important even than divorceable acts), and that a woman found guilty would be condemned, for all time, by everyone. It is a polarising and unforgiving world-view, as well as an unrealistic one. It is also relentlessly class-ridden. By his aperçu, 'spotted silk is so much worse than stained sackcloth',[32] women with the class, or character, of sackcloth are not expected to be stainless, while it is a tragedy when a lady behaves so carelessly as to spot her silk. In 'Susan', discussed above, Susan is expected to socialise with unfit company, either on a yacht or in the house party. We're not told why the yacht's guest-list is unfit, but, given the tone of this story, we could assume that it is sexually promiscuous. She is assaulted by the wolfish attentions of fellow guests, until Culloden steps in to rescue her. Yates dwells on the riotous goings-on that occur when the host and hostess have lost control of their own guests, making it an inevitable consequence that young women will have their reputations compromised unless older and sounder men take charge. Yates's inventiveness with innuendo and flirtatious dialogue makes this story about the discernment of good and bad taste titillating as well as instructive. He may have been assuming that exclusive society behaviour as reported in tales from the Lido, the Riviera, the London nightclub scene, and so on, were becoming the new norm, and did not like the way women were behaving. He also may have noticed, uneasily, how the revealing fashions and public display of the woman's body that had been admired so by his fellow officers in the pin-up spreads in, for example, *Nash's and Pall Mall Magazine* during the war years, were not now restricted to print media, nor were they confined to the stage.

The war had also given other opportunities to women that may have repelled Yates. Buchan's most well-known woman character, the secret service agent Mary Lamington, was hymned in 1919 because 'she can't scare and she can't soil'.[33] It is usually forgotten that Mary was also a VAD (an unpaid nurse in the Voluntary Aid Detachment corps), as were thousands of middle-class British women, anxious to serve in hospital during the war. In *Mr Standfast* (1919) she is a tea-tray carrier in a convalescent hospital for shell-shocked officers, a very easy line of service, with nothing shocking described. Historically, VADs were usually given the messy and tedious cleaning work of the hospital, and were rarely allowed near the soldiers. Trained nurses did the real nursing, and women trained as nurses during the war precisely to serve this need. Consequently, during the war, women of all classes and ranks had cleaned, dressed and held the hands, and other body parts, of all classes and ranks of men. The graphic experiences recorded in women's memoirs and fiction of the war, by Irene Rathbone and Helen Zenna Smith among many others, have been discussed in this context by Jane Marcus.[34] David Cannadine observes that 'at home and overseas, titled nurses abased themselves to perform menial tasks for their social inferiors which they would never have dreamed of doing for themselves in ordinary life [...] after such sudden and unprecedented social mixing, the distancing aura that was such an essential aspect of aristocratic hegemony would never be inviolate again'.[35] In this context, Yates's strong interest in policing women's behaviour in his fiction, and restricting the men with whom they might associate, can be linked to his equally strong interest in how they might be soiled, and why. There are no nurses in Yates's fiction, and very few scenes of wounded men, since these are post-war stories. But I think it is possible to detect a gendered squeamishness in how Yates wrote about women 'soiling' themselves by the wrong kind of contact with the wrong kind of man.

Bad behaviour

Women often risk disgracing themselves in Yates's 1920s fiction. There is a feverishness about the stories in *And Five Were Foolish* (1924), *As Other Men Are* (1925) and *Maiden Stakes* (1928) that typify the Roaring Twenties, and the firm line of conservative behaviour must be indicated. In *Anthony Lyveden* Yates sets up a magnificent scene of Anthony sacrificing everything he had just struggled to earn for himself (a house, and worthwhile work he loves) to save the good name of André, whom he had met only that day. Colonel Winchester, her fiancé and Anthony's employer, walks in on them in the dark outside just as she has thrown herself at Anthony and kissed him. Anthony's reaction is to take the blame for her shocking behaviour. His nobility only heightens her intolerable actions, and emphasises by how a gentleman behaves, how a lady ought not to.

Women smoking in public (no longer a taboo in 1920s society) is criticised in some of these stories in certain circumstances, but it is not a major crime. In 'Childish Things' (1925), and in 'Vanity of Vanities' (1928), both published in *Maiden Stakes*, women smoking cigarettes is a signifier of class, good taste, even of a modern youthfulness, and, if done privately, can also be approved of by the men. But alcohol is a different matter. In 'Jeremy' (1924), Eve behaves very badly to her husband because she has the money and refuses to obey him as she should. She also drinks more cocktails than he thinks a lady should, and when he remonstrates they have a two-page argument that shows how strongly Yates felt about this issue: he even made sure that her retort, 'I suppose you realise that this is 1924' was updated in successive editions to 1930,[36] to pointedly blame modern society for Eve's unfortunate adherence to fashion.

A more serious case, of a wife bullying her husband, appears in 'Peregrine', in the same volume of stories. Mrs Carey Below is a monstrous creation, a mouthpiece for vindictive social bullying that uses expectations of class and gentlemanly behaviour as her weapons. Her husband Peregrine Carey Below won't stand up to her, being too gentlemanly to use her own weapons against her, and by now, too browbeaten to do so. 'The man was in thrall to a personality – a vigorous magnetism, which sucked the marrow from his bones, and, waxing fat on it, grew more exacting and savage every day.'[37] This wife is a succubus, an affliction which is inhuman in its indifference to mercy, or its devouring of Peregrine, and shows clearly what Yates thinks of wives who bully their husbands. There is nothing demonic about her actions, just simple human nature, unforgettably associated with a woman behaving not just badly, but cruelly. Yates developed this portrait with a full-length version, in *This Publican* (1938; see Chapter 6).

Selling themselves

Being a lawyer by training, Yates was fond of using his legal knowledge in plots that turned on wills, property and agreements to marry. In 'Sarah' (1922), later published in *And Five Were Foolish*, Sarah and Virgil have to marry each other if they are to also inherit James Tantamount's fortune and houses. They agree to do this, after petulant bantering, because they both secretly do rather want to marry each other, but are too proud to admit it. Naturally, Sarah is accused of mercenary motives. '"I don't mind admitting", said Margaret Shorthorn, "that I could have done with Virgil. They talk about Sarah's selling herself. Well, what if she is? We're all trying to do it. The only difference is that in Sarah's case the conditions of sale have been announced in the Press."'[38] This brutally straight condemnation (and assertion that this is how society works) is caused by the announcement of their engagement, which appeared four days after the announcement of the will.

In the same collection, Lady Elizabeth Crecy of 'Elizabeth' (1923) is about to marry a self-important parvenu for money, but flings his jewels and her drink in his face when she finds out that he has been slandering her closest friend (whom she goes on to marry). In 'Simon' (1924) in *As Other Men Are*, Patricia thinks that she has to marry for money, but thankfully marries Simon for love instead. None of these romances leave their principals penniless, since Yates implies that there will always be a spare ten thousand or so between them and want. These are retellings of *Cinderella*, a tale of entitled virtue rewarded that Yates used habitually since it expressed a familiar truth even while he ensured that it enforced the social codes he admired. Ultimately, no woman should sell herself, even though her function as a commodity was the foundation for the safe transfer of land, wealth and property, and the class system that Yates's fiction venerated. This paradox expresses the triumph of the romantic in Yates's writing, over his more political and social concerns.

Laws for women's conduct

When Yates describes women's behaviour in his fiction he is concerned with the rules they must follow, and with celebrating a particular kind of feminine grace and beauty. In 'Force Majeure' (1928) in *Maiden Stakes*, runaway heiress Elaine is hidden by Ammiral in his tent. 'His guest was, of course, as safe in his keeping as if she had lain in a hospice governed by nuns [...] Her present position was unheard of, had only to be coldly focused to be found big with confusion – a very Caliban of abashment, to haunt her days.'[39] The reference to pregnancy is deliberate: her sexual reputation is at stake.

For a traditionalist like Yates, the true sources for women's correct behaviour were stories of courtly love and chivalric romance. In *Perishable Goods* (1928), his second Chandos thriller, Adèle is kidnapped and Jonah Mansel leads her rescue.

> Adèle was his cousin's wife, at once his *liege lady* and his familiar friend [...] Throughout our *venture* Mansel *bore* himself with such exalted *gallantry* that I have often thought since that, though he could not have known of the speech I had had with Adèle, yet he knew in his heart that she would know why she had been taken and that he was *carrying her colours* for the first and last time.[40] (emphasis added)

The formality of Chandos's narrative tone in this novel is intensified by the overtly archaic vocabulary used here, making the point that Mansel's behaviour is truly *sans reproche*. This reflects a Guinevere-like lustre on Adèle, the married lady of this love triangle in which her husband is Yates's authorial alter ego. The now familiar technique of disproportion has an additional effect here of increasing the largely absent

Adèle's purity and bravery as her body is symbolically offered to Mansel by her captors. First her hair is sent: an obvious symbol of despoliation and sexual availability, and of her (temporary) ownership by another man. Soon afterwards her blouse is sent in an envelope. Not even in a box: this indignity is an even more explicit signal of her vulnerability, and the risk to her body and honour. The final threat was to tattoo her back with Mansel's name, an astonishingly vivid branding exercise that says as much about Yates's lurid imagination as the characters he invented who enacted these thoughts.

In *Blood Royal* (1929) Yates is equally attentive to the social codes that women must follow, but these are also a measure of class, and rank. The Grand Duchess Leonie reminds her fiancé, Prince Paul, that he cannot eat alone with her late in the evening (the only way she can prevent him entering her house).[41] Chandos, the narrator, explains her code. 'As her affianced husband, the man had a right to demand that, when they met or parted, the Grand Duchess should give him her lips.' This is not an astonishing attitude, but the haughty and aggressive way it is expressed – he may *demand* – negates completely the excessive concern elsewhere in the narrative for the Grand Duchess's comfort, safety or wishes. The rights of the husband, or near husband, are clearly of great importance in this narrator's world-view, to rather alarming lengths. 'Had he asked, and she objected, vile as he was, he could not, I think, have been blamed for insisting on his right.' [42] Chandos's own conduct as a married man, to another woman, in the sequel, *Fire Below* (1930), reveals an interesting double standard that Yates seems to have missed or ignored (see Chapter 6).

The desirable child

Buchan and Yates shared a tendency to describe women characters at their most desirable as beautiful children. Buchan used the trope of the girl-as-boy, and the girlish hero, as a way of celebrating androgyny and the non-existence of sex.[43] For Yates, the innocence of a child was his heroines' most idealised feature. In 'St Jeames' (1927), later published in *Maiden Stakes*, the heroine is described as having the 'unconscious glory of a beautiful child'.[44] Women at their most desirable were not women, but neuter, children, innocent and unsexed and inexperienced and needing protection. Big eyes are an indication of this. In 'Force Majeure', the driver of the car climbing the steep and dangerous pass is 'a girl – a child' with 'big grey eyes', and she is resolute and fearless and alone.[45] All these suggest that she will soon need protection because she doesn't have it at present: the pregnancy reference I noted above from a page or two further on doubles the effect of the vulnerability suggested here.

Yates's heroes and heroines can be children together. In *Perishable Goods* they are caught by the enemy 'with the effortless ease of a nurse outwitting a child', and Adèle is 'like some old picture of a beautiful boy'.[46] It is interesting that, in this novel, as soon as Adèle is physically present, the imagery of juvenilia is employed, invoking her infantilisation (in contrast to her sexual vulnerability noted above), thus removing all blame from the emotional tangles that will lead to her implied adultery with Mansel. Chandos himself reverts to being a worshipping boy with Adèle rather than the physical man of action he is under Mansel's influence. Adèle and Chandos sit 'down on the floor, like two children', and she tells him secrets as if he were her brother.[47] Given that the reason Adèle has been kidnapped is her status as Mansel's secret love, and as the wife of another man – both are sexualised roles – it seems evasive, to say the least, to depict her as an androgynous child in speech and character. Yates seems to be trying to avoid any 'stain' on her character in a situation that he has set up to allow the reader to enjoy the emotional titillation of Adèle joyfully being stained. The answer is, of course, that Yates was beginning to experiment with metatextuality within the Berry world. *Perishable Goods* creates an Arcadia for Jonah and Adèle so that the reader can enjoy their dalliance knowing it doesn't affect her marriage, and they return to their real world unchanged. Boy's marriage with Adèle is unbetrayed by her liaison with Jonah, because the action and characters are set apart from the orbit of Berry & Co, the central, bonded group, and the novel is not (crucially) narrated by Boy.

I think there is more to be found in the idea of childish retrogression for women and men in Yates's fiction, which may also connect to the idea of escaping the world. His romantic characters rarely move beyond the honeymoon stage. In *The Courts of Idleness* (stories dating from 1914 and published in book form in 1920), a married couple called Fairie share a house with their cousins, Robin and Fay Broke, and there are no children. They winter in Madeira, and meet a further single man and woman, producing the inevitable betrothals. In the Berry stories (*The Brother of Daphne* was published in 1914, and the stories in the next volume, *Berry & Co*, first appeared in 1920) the characters inhabit an eternal children's paradise, with no interruption or interloper tolerated. There is a perpetual infantilism of the characters, with their servants as nannies or footmen to feed the hungry children on the lawn or in the drawing-room after they have played. This was not a novel trait: Kenneth Grahame's *The Wind in the Willows* (1908) is also a retrogressive world (some 'Saki' stories inhabit this territory too), without children, because the characters *are* the children.

Is it possible that for Yates's comedy characters the nursery is the only safe place, where one need never grow up? Cousins marry, couple after couple marry, but no children appear to be born. The only exceptions are Jill's twins (only one childbirth needed), but so strong is Yates's need to avoid children, that they are killed in a plane crash, with their father, which ensures that Jill will breed no more, and that she will be safe to marry her cousin Boy (much later), and maintain the inviolate unity and strength of the Pleydell family.

Nobody leaves the nursery. Life in the Berry world revolves around meals, outings, games, clever tricks, the acquisition of new paintings for the walls, playing with dogs, and losing and finding their toys and special jewels. Their personal relationships are stylised, perfect as foils to the verbal fireworks and entertainment of the plots. It is noticeable that with these much-loved characters who are maintained as part of a saga of short story events, there is no development, and no change in what they do or who they are. That is not their purpose. Stories with one-off characters engage more explicitly with the real world.

Escape

Throughout the 1920s, Yates's characters were escaping. The theme is dominant in one of the two collections of short stories he published in 1920, *The Courts of Idleness*. The bright young characters escape to Madeira (in the stories, Rih) to avoid the British winter weather. While this would have appealed to readers of the 1920s longing for an escape from memories of war as well as from the climate, over half of these stories had been written before the war, and were published in *The Windsor Magazine* by the end of 1915. Yates collected them into a book along with five 'Berry' stories originally published in 1919, and transformed them from light-hearted social comedies of the rich and underemployed into an elegy for the men who died in the war. He framed the pre-war stories of leisurely frolics with accounts of the male characters' heroic and tragic wartime deaths.[48] The book's purpose in offering an escape from war, and unsatisfactory everyday life, is strong. By presenting these stories as a bitter-sweet reminder of the way of life and the ease of mind that had existed before the war, Yates is invoking powerful nostalgia in his readers. This was not so much for a lost way of life for a particular class, but for a lifestyle that had not known the horrors to come. It was also Yates's own lost idyll: he was mourning the passing of a view on life that he had enjoyed in his twenties, even if he had not had the income or the leisure to frivol as his characters did. Perhaps the key to the success of the Yates short story milieu and style was that in these stories he rewrote his salad days.

The escapes by Yates's characters out of England to a more unrestricted arena began again with *The Stolen March* in 1926, several years after he had made his own escape to live permanently at Pau. In *The Stolen March* (the title was a pun on lost borderlands) romance and comedy were combined jarringly with nightmarish danger in the invented country of Etchechuria, but this was a Wonderland of coded puzzles rather than a functional kingdom modelled on Ruritania and the well-established genre of the cardboard kingdom.[49] Yates started to develop his own Ruritania in *Blind Corner* in 1927 and in *Perishable Goods* in 1928, where Jonah Mansel leads his team to Carinthia, a real-life region in Austria, now just north of the Slovenian (then Yugoslavian) and Italian borders, but in the 1920s conveniently little-known to British tourists. Yates uses place-names convincingly to wash his compelling plots with verisimilitude, though unfamiliar but real names like Villach and St Martin might just as well be invented. This for Yates's readers was the point: the settings of his thrillers were all about crucial details of topography, not about sight-seeing. In his short stories and Berry novels he played around with toponymy most satisfyingly, hurtling through the well-known and familiar Rouen, Chartres, Tours and Dieppe. These were still pleasantly, Frenchly exotic, but real. Back in English settings Yates invented outrageously romantic English place-names that carry a suggestion of authenticity because they are so improbable. To take one collection as an example, *As Other Men Are* of 1924, we have Castle Breathless and Peering Gap (in 'Simon'); Garter Spinney, Stomacher Place and Sweeting Valley (in 'Oliver'); and Mow Corner, the village of Sundial, Pullaway Brow, The Doublet (an inn), Minever Park, Domesday Hall and Witchery Drive (in 'Christopher'). Serious stories in this volume don't fool around with names (as in the story of Peregrine's torture at the hands of his wife), but in the comedies, the reader was invited to escape to stories so wittily romantic that even the names of its setting were part of the delight, as well as an invitation to escape to an Arcadia.

As well as demonstrating a certain resistance through didacticism to hideous social changes in his 1920s writing, Yates offered alluring escapist fantasies as an alternative. The tension, eloquence and descriptive decoration of his style would have encouraged his readers to ignore reality, rather than rise up and challenge it. He prescribed in detail how to behave, as if changes in manners would roll back time, and persuade the economy or political trends to falter. His strength was in describing perfect aspirational manners and ideals, and his readers devoured them avidly.

4
Political Uncertainty: Buchan in the 1930s

The 1930s saw seven changes of British government or prime minister, and ended with the outbreak of war against Germany. The second Labour government, formed by Ramsay MacDonald in 1929, was made up of (for the first time) non-public-school men and one woman. Parliament was also populated by a large number of Conservative MPs who were ex-soldiers. Richard Carr notes that 'despite recording 260 seats to Labour's 287, Baldwin could call upon the support of over four times as many ex-servicemen as MacDonald'.[1]

MacDonald's government collapsed in August 1931, and was replaced by an interim National Government for a few months, still led by Ramsay MacDonald. The Labour Party expelled MacDonald and all other Labour members associated with the National Government from the party, producing the odd result that, after October 1931, MacDonald, now a 'National Labourite', won elections for the new National Government as a member of no recognised political party. He resigned as prime minister in June 1935, due to ill-health, and was succeeded by the Conservative leader Stanley Baldwin (Angela Thirkell's second cousin). He resigned from politics in May 1937, on the suitable occasion of the coronation of George VI, and was succeeded by the professional administrator and Conservative politician Neville Chamberlain. Chamberlain brought Britain into the Second World War with what A J Taylor calls a 'government of national pretence',[2] but was forced out by Labour in May 1940, who brought in his deputy in the government, the Conservative Winston Churchill, as prime minister.[3]

John Buchan resigned his seat in Parliament in 1935 on becoming Lord Tweedsmuir, as Governor-General of Canada. His political involvement after 1935 was understandably bipartisan and discreet: this has been studied in depth by J William Galbraith, and also by Buchan's biographers, Andrew Lownie and Janet Adam Smith.[4] Galbraith observes that when Canadian prime minister Mackenzie King welcomed Buchan to Canada as Lord Tweedsmuir, he noted in his diary: 'It has been a real shock to me to lose the John Buchan I had known, and discover a Tory [with] a sort of royalty complex'.[5] This says as much about public expectations of Buchan the novelist from a plebeian background as about King's fears from Tweedsmuir the potentially threatening political force, yet King was perfectly aware of the governor-general's restricted role. This chapter will consider how Buchan incorporated his Tory politics and his veneration of the ruling classes into more generalised concerns over social change, and national and European politics, in his fiction and journalism.

His novels in the last decade of his life personalised political anxiety, particularly *A Prince of the Captivity* (1933), which is about one man's mission to steer the dangerously drifting course of British and European politics. *Castle Gay* (1930) and *The House of the Four Winds* (1935) are the sequel and conclusion to *Huntingtower* (1922), and take his working-class Scottish heroes into the Establishment. *The Gap in the Curtain* (1932) is a series of linked short stories using politics as a backdrop, intriguing for their detailed use of an alternative British political establishment, developed further in *A Prince of the Captivity*. As with Chapter 2, I do not examine Buchan's historical fiction in this study. Although Buchan could use historical fiction to make a case for a modern concern, for example seventeenth-century non-conformism and twentieth-century religious doubt,[6] in general his historical novels did not address present-day concerns. I also do not discuss here the final Hannay novel, *The Island of Sheep* (1936), or *Sick Heart River*, published posthumously in 1941. Both are final adventures for ageing men, and address interior anxieties and personal concerns, but do not engage with the wider world to the extent that his other 1930s novels did.

The turnouts for the two general elections of the 1930s were similar to those of the 1920s: over 70 per cent but under 80 per cent.[7] These numbers indicate a broad sense of public concern with the direction in which the country's government was taking the economy, and how it was providing jobs and homes. We can see this concern in *A Prince of the Captivity*, with the interweaving of Labour politics with the mission to produce political stability, but Buchan adds his own twist to the outcome by depicting the shift in the politics of the Labour character from being a staunch union man to becoming a creature of the Conservatives. The economic and social conditions that drove the National Government's attempts to maintain a grip on the economy were a contributory factor to changes in British right-wing and left-wing politics in this decade. The attempt of the Communist Party of Great Britain (CPGB) to form a 'popular front' and unite all opponents of fascism and the National Government in 1935–36 was not a success, though CPGB membership increased during this period. But there was not a full flowering of social-ism in 1930s Britain. Andrew Thorpe considers that the influence of the Labour Party 'was generally greater the less it stressed its Communism'.[8] Politics of the centre-Right would dominate the decade in Britain.

By May 1930 Sir Oswald Mosley, a Member of Parliament since 1918, had changed political party several times. He was first elected as a Conservative (natural for his class), but 'crossed the floor' of the House to become an Independent in 1922. He joined the Independent Labour Party in 1924, but did not win a new seat in Parliament under their aegis until 1926. He resigned from the Labour government in 1931, and formed the New Party, which was proto-fascist and failed to gain any seats in Parliament. In October 1932 he led the new British Union of Fascists (BUF) in a takeover of the New Party, absorbing the British Fascists (see Chapter 2) as well. Under Mosley the BUF attracted 20,000 members in two years,[9] but after the BUF's involvement in the Battle of Cable Street had revealed the danger of uniformed and politicised thugs on the streets, the Public Order Act of 1936 banned the wearing of politi-cal uniforms. British Union of Fascists candidates were roundly defeated in by-elections after the outbreak of the Second World War. In May 1940 Mosley, his wife and over seven hundred British fascists were imprisoned for the duration of the war. The BUF was suspended in July 1940.[10]

Buchan himself had commented in a *Daily Mirror* article of 1928 that although there were doubts about fascism continuing to be successful in Italy, its efficiency and the power of its leader (a 'great man') were to be noted, whereas Bolshevism was a 'poison'.[11] This is the only instance known of Buchan commenting in the public press on fascism, and he did not address British fascism in his fiction. It may be that he felt that doing this would encourage its supporters by taking them seriously. The left-wing novelist Winifred Holtby felt this way, noting in a let-ter on 17 November 1925: 'Our merry Fascists are showing us the way to revolution. Let us hope we can learn to laugh at them. There is no other way'.[12] Literary history shows that belittling comedy was used as a warning instead, by other writers, for example in Nancy Mitford's novel *Wigs on the Green* (1935), in which she mocked her brother-in-law, Mosley, and by P G Wodehouse in *The Code of the Woosters* (1938).

Buchan addressed European fascism in two novels. In *A Prince of the Captivity* (written between February 1931 and April 1932)[13] the fascist characters are vague, and are overshadowed by Buchan's more energetic depiction of anarchists and communists. In *The House of the Four Winds* he deals in more detail with fascism in Eastern Europe, within the confines of the Ruritanian setting of Evallonia, which gave him a fictional political arena with which to experiment. Buchan's invented Evallonian proto-fascist movement was led by a woman (unlike real-life fascist parties, despite prominent support of fascism by women), and is so closely associated with monarchism that the Evallonian fascists give up their militarised aims to support the new young king without any apparent ideological struggle. This solution suggests that fascist authoritarianism is merely monarchism under another name, but it would be echoed in a real-life iteration after the Spanish Civil War. Buchan was applying wishful thinking to his romantic plot in an effort to obviate, in part, a looming European political nightmare.

Domestically, law and order was an increasing concern throughout the 1930s: the crime rates doubled between 1920 and 1940. The number of murders, on the other hand, decreased, and the prison population remained stable at around 10,000 for England and Wales over the interwar period.[14] Police numbers increased slowly.[15] From 1932 there were annual outbreaks of violent protest against different grievances, for example against the means test in 1932 (a socially loathed enquiry which determined whether the unemployed were eligible for state support), the campaign against agricultural tithes which the BUF attempted to dominate in an attempt to win support from the farmers (1933–34),[16] unemployment assistance (1935), anti-Semitic campaigning by proto-fascist groups (1936), and the start of the IRA bombing campaign on mainland Britain (1939).[17] It is strange, given the great popularity of the crime novel and the detective novel in this period, which told stories of the restoration of civil order for the reassurance of the middlebrow reader, that Buchan did not use his fiction to address civil unrest and social dissatisfaction, until *A Prince of the Captivity*. But Buchan was not a detective novelist, and the focus of his thrillers was the continuing maintenance of civilisation, rather than of the welfare of individuals: the political rather than the personal.

An immediate concern for individuals would have been their earnings, and their value. Economic historians John Stevenson and Chris Cook note that there 'was a quite perceptible improvement in the standard of comfort witnessed by many people, especially the middle classes' for this period.[18] Retail prices in general were highest in 1920, but thereafter fell and remained largely stable until 1940.[19] In contrast, the cost of a pint of beer almost doubled over the period.[20] Unemployment was a more serious concern, since to be unemployed took away all the benefits of increased earnings and values, and depressed the markets in badly affected areas. It fluctuated strongly. 'By July 1930 there were over 2 million people out of work'; 22 per cent of the population were unemployed in 1932, almost three million people.[21] After 1932, the unemployment level did not go below 10 per cent of the population: a considerable and alarming increase not seen before in the twentieth century.[22] There was a split in the experience of living through the interwar years, for the population as individuals and as a group. The rich stayed rich, and the middle classes, upper and lower, stayed comfortable, though they were being made nervous by increasing fiscal responsibilities if they owned land. Those with little income or spending power, especially the 10 per cent of the population who were unemployed, suffered more as the decade wore on. This sense of stability for those who had money, voices and influence, was inaccurate in terms of the population as a whole, but it is important to explain the apparent lack of concern for the living conditions of the poor and disadvantaged in the popular reading of the day. The poor and disadvantaged did not buy many books, and were not a target readership, and were not a direct concern of those who were comfortable. John Atkins considers that 'those who controlled society appeared to find the situation bearable'.[23] The unemployed and their families were surviving, rather than living, often in terrible hardship, but Stevenson and Cook show that 'living standards, and the quality of life, actually improved for the majority of the population [...] faced with the worst depression in British history, the electorate voted massively for Conservative-dominated governments'.[24] Widespread generalised content would have contrasted with the struggles of the immediate post-war years. Stevenson and Cook note that 'there were never less than three-quarters of the population in work during the 1930s and for most of the period considerably more. Alongside the pictures of the dole queues and hunger marches must also be placed those of another Britain, of new industries, prosperous suburbs and a rising standard of living'.[25] Their view reinforces 'the paradox which lay at the heart of Britain in the thirties, where new levels of prosperity contrasted with the intractable problems of mass unemployment and the depressed areas'.[26]

In his essay 'Inside the Whale' (1940) George Orwell rejects the accepted understanding of how writers responded to the 1930s by framing his peroration with a review of Henry Miller's novel *Tropic of Cancer*, discussing the difficulty in writing resistance to mass emotion and mass persuasion. He makes a casual mention of 'a huge tribe of Barries and

Deepings and Dells who simply don't notice what is happening',[27] a
dismissive recognition of the writers who did not pay proper attention
to political and social change. Orwell unwittingly describes Dougal
Crombie of *Castle Gay*, the now adult Die-Hard from *Huntingtower*,
when he observes that the new kind of literary man is 'an eager-minded
schoolboy with a leaning towards Communism'.[28] No such creature
would exist in Yates's 1930s fiction, and would only appear in Thirkell
to be ridiculed. Their writing in the 1930s was part of what Andy Croft,
a commentator of the Left, has described as 'the one moment when the
ruling class was intellectually isolated, backward-looking and exposed
as the friends of tyranny'.[29] The reading environment of Yates and
Thirkell can be seen in how Croft talks about 1930s literature.

> The novel was the most popular literary form among readers of all
> ages and classes; enjoying sales and circulation far in excess of any
> one of the poets who have dominated literary history. The realist
> conventions of novel writing and novel reading allowed little room
> for the sort of generalised political hectoring characteristic of much
> contemporary poetry. And many socialist novelists took to popular
> generic forms in order to popularise their hopes and fears.[30]

We could replace 'socialist' in that quotation with 'conservative' to
show that political colouring may not have been as important in the
kind of writing and what it dealt with, as the 'generic forms' that produced high sales. If authors wanted to express their hopes and fears,
and those of their readers, they had to write novels at the level that lots
of readers would buy. Consequently some fears and anxieties would
be given simultaneous popularised treatments by opposing political
stances, but possibly not for the same readers.

Croft is also alert to the changes that took place in the 1930s in
popular reading. Drawing on left-wing commentary in the late 1930s
he suggests that the established norms of 'chauvinism, snobbery and
anti-semitism' were those in which

> villains [were] dangerous Bolsheviks, cunning Orientals or rough
> dagoes, always planning to do bad against the good Englishman and
> whites: a roll-call, in fact, of flatly caricatured threats to the social
> order [...] So long as the fears of the British ruling class were kept at
> bay by the combined intelligence and courage of Sexton Blake, Lord
> Peter Wimsey, Bulldog Drummond, 'Blackshirt', Allan Quatermain,
> Sir Henry Curtis, Richard Hannay, Sandy Arbuthnot, Sir Edward

Leithen and Archie Roylance, the scales were 'loaded against the criminal' in popular fiction, 'as befits a society grown timidly fearful of impending doom'. The hero fought against fantasies.[31]

Croft cites four of Buchan's protagonists in that list of the defenders of the ruling classes, but he does not include Yates (Thirkell does not write in this genre), and seems also to have conflated three sub-genres in that list, pitting the sophisticated writing of Dorothy L Sayers and Buchan against the entirely different Victorian romance quests of H Rider Haggard (Quatermain, Curtis) and the formulaic fiction of 'Sapper' and Bruce Graeme (who created the Raffles-esque gentleman thief 'Blackshirt' in the 1920s). Other anti-communist and pro-fascist novelists of the period whom Croft mentions in this context were Mrs Wilfred Ward and her 1927 society novel *The Shadow of Mussolini*, and J J J's novel *The Blueshirts*.[32] Along with Dennis Wheatley, Croft has grouped Buchan, and Sayers, for that matter, with interwar anti-communist, right-wing popular authors whom he suggests were also pro-fascist. It is an awkward selection, since the only thing these writers have in common is that they all approved of a ruling class, and that their novels sold very well. The differences in their approaches to presenting solutions to socialist threats are thus ignored, when they ought not to be. 'Sapper', for instance, was criticised in 1939 by a contemporary commentator, along with Sax Rohmer and Fu Manchu, for valorising 'the cult of brutality, the complete inversion of values, the exaltation of cunning before all other intellectual qualities'.[33] Buchan's resolute opposition to right-wing thuggery and the forces of fascism and his support of free democratic debate, as we shall see, are the antithesis to the 'Sapper' approach.

Castle Gay

Buchan's first novel of the decade, *Castle Gay* (1930), is a commentary on social change and politics, in its plot and characterisation. At the heart of the novel is a fascinating portrait of an approaching election in Calloway, in south-west Scotland, featuring public meetings and speeches by rival candidates for the seat and visiting speakers. This atmosphere of vigorous debate and keen local interest in politics provides entertainment and intellectual exercise for the voters, which Buchan expected his readers to share as an interactive experience for all classes.

While Communist voters among the quarrymen outside the town (working-class and transient) are considered to be normal, Buchan's narrative stance is quietly Conservative. 'After dinner [Jaikie] put in an hour at a Unionist meeting, which was poorly attended, but which convinced him that that candidate of that party would win, since – so he argued – the non-political voters who did not go to meetings and made up the bulk of the electorate were probably on his side.'[34] Craw, the nervous and intellectually flabby newspaper magnate in hiding, makes a success of his emergency speech in favour of Labour, in an episode that Buchan reprises from Hannay's (Liberal) turn on the hustings in *The Thirty-Nine Steps* (1915), and from Archie's terrified début as a Tory candidate in *John Macnab* (1925). Craw's impersonation of a 'red-hot' Socialist is clearly opposite to his natural views, though we should be wary of assuming that Craw the important media figure is naturally Conservative: this episode criticises his caution.[35] There is a slight suggestion of bias from Buchan, in terms of a Conservative resistance to women in the public sphere, in the only portrait of a political failure in the novel: 'a woman, who had a real gift of scolding rhetoric [...] She was vigorous and abusive, and had a voice like a saw, and five minutes of her were a torment to the ear'.[36] Any political acumen she may have had is unremarked: the exterior qualities of her voice, antithetical to the universal dictum that it should be 'soft. Gentle and low / An excellent thing in woman',[37] are more important here. In contrast to this candidate's attempt at a public role, the novel's two leading female characters, Mrs Brisbane-Brown and her niece Alison, only function in the drawing-room, and in gardens, up trees or on the hills. They are wise voices, and have influence on the male actors in the plot, but they are excluded from the public sphere. The difference between these two sets of portrayals may also be due to class. The woman candidate speaks of 'huz puir folk', and she comes from a 'Glesca stair-heid'.[38]

The women in *Castle Gay* reflect two of its themes: how Buchan depicted political engagement, and how class had become more nuanced. They cause reactions in the protagonists, Dougal Crombie, an opinionated and loyal newspaperman, and Jaikie Galt, undergraduate, rugger Blue and endearing romantic. Both former street children from the Gorbals have grown up, eight years after *Huntingtower*. Jaikie is politically neutral, but Dougal is a rampant ideologue for the Left. He is apparently standing for Parliament without expecting to get in, this time. This is important for his characterisation, since he is one of the new class of professional politicians, and a new character type for Buchan. He seems representative of the new age, when youth and skill have a chance of succeeding without money and position. But, as we will see, like Utlaw in *A Prince of the Captivity* his rise to power over time will dilute his ideology to a bland conservatism.

Dougal works for the Craw Press, a vast newspaper conglomerate built up by Mr Craw through a clever understanding of the market, and a natural skill in providing readers with easily digestible opinions and reassurance that mean little and have a soporific effect. The Craw papers are conservative, that is, smug, secure and safe. Craw is his own chief political editor, and refuses to admit Communism into European politics. He thinks that Fascism might work, calling it 'that bold experiment', but he has no interest at all in actual political endorsement, because, as readers can see, actually giving an opinion might involve him with politics in the real world, rather than the safety of armchair theorising.[39] Although Dougal has sharper political acumen, he lumps together all foreign political groupings: 'When a foreigner gets a notion into his head he's apt to turn into a demented crusader. They're all the same – Socialists, Communists, Fascists, Republicans, Monarchists – I dare say Monarchists are the worst, for they've less inside their heads to begin with'.[40] These confidently xenophobic remarks are too sweeping for the reader to take seriously, and indicate that Dougal the junior reporter has an arrogant non-understanding of foreign politics. Thus he and Craw have a lot to learn from their encounters with the Evallonians.

Two rival political groups from Evallonia – Buchan's Ruritanian country located somewhere near the eastern borders of Hungary and Austria – come to Craw in the expectation that his fame and the widespread distribution of his newspapers means that he also has immense political power. Setting aside the irony aimed at famous British newspaper editors like Robertson Nicoll, Beaverbrook and Northcliffe, Buchan intends us to understand that this of course could not be the case, and that while lesser, foreign countries might allow their press to wield political power, or might muzzle it completely, this cannot happen in Britain. The Evallonian Monarchists have come to ask Craw to arrange for Britain to act as a kind of League of Nations referee and keep the Evallonian struggle clear of outsiders, since they fear external (Soviet?) support for their bitter rivals, the Evallonian Republicans. This unrealistic request is presented in a gently comic mode, patronising the Monarchists for such silly, foreign misunderstandings about British press powers. It also reflects how Buchan would like his readers to think of Britain's international reputation. The Republicans are not given the same benign treatment, since they are all depicted as gangsters and fanatics (aided, tellingly, by a double-crossing Craw employee who is not quite a gentleman).[41] The dramatic ending of Craw's interview with the Republicans, at the end of the novel, produces violence, the only political dialogue offered by such criminals and anarchists. At this moment Jaikie, the calm, sane, onlooker, realises that the boundary between anarchy and civilisation, Buchan's long-standing principal metaphor for the danger that perpetually threatens British, and western civilisation, is here in the library. But the melodramatic moment is disrupted by the arrival of British common sense, in the form of retired grocer Dickson McCunn and a policeman. Revolvers are placed in a waste-paper basket, ending the episode with the reassurance of bathos.[42]

Turning to class in *Castle Gay*, we see how Buchan describes the difficulties of the out-of-work ex-officer in a rather different manner than Yates had employed in the 1920s. Craw's secretary, Frederick Barbon, is a rather ineffectual character who has had a trying time since 1918 in finding and keeping a job. His problem is not fecklessness, but incapacity. He simply doesn't have the character or the staying power to hold a job in a tough market, or the luck (which is important) to find a job with an employer who will not disappear.

> He knew only too well what it was to be a poor gentleman tossed from dilemma to dilemma by the unsympathetic horns of destiny. Since the war – when he had held a commission in the Foot Guards – he had been successively, but not successfully, a land-agent (the property was soon sold), a dealer in motor-cars (the business went speedily bankrupt), a stockbroker on half commission, the manager of a tourist agency, an advertisement tout, and a highly incompetent society journalist [...] The dread that haunted his dreams was of being hurled once more into the cold world of economic strife.[43]

This is a more nuanced story than Yates was telling about ex-officers in the 1920s. It depicts the insecurity of temporary employment, and the fear that dogs the confidence of a man who has been unemployed before and may be again. This sense of economic dependency and the group investment in the success of the Craw empire is important for the plot, for the reader must feel that all Craw's employees have a stake in the continued maintenance of its newspapers, for their monthly salaries. Sigismund Allins, too, is a gentleman struggling to stay afloat in a world where class no longer gives automatic privileges. Allins is Craw's fixer and contact with the world, but his approach is to bribe journalists with drink, socialise with undergraduates so that he can sell them racing tips, and accept employment from his master's enemies. He exudes a déclassé aura of untrustworthiness that ten years later would be associated with the spiv. Barbon is a nervous and rather useless gentleman; Allins sacrifices his class markers for easy money. Neither are admirable role models, though the reader is asked to be sympathetic to Barbon's uselessness in a tough world.

Jaikie is introduced as 'a scholar and a gentleman', a Cambridge undergraduate playing rugby for Scotland, who wins the game with a body swerve perfected in his extreme youth in the slums.[44] Thus indicators from an underprivileged childhood and present-day class security are combined in a character whose modesty and unassuming doggedness make him a new kind of hero for the Buchan canon. It seems extraordinary now that a character most often described as 'slight' could have the stamina to survive an international rugby match as a winger, but Buchan's intention in putting this character in that situation is to make him the moral heart of the novel. Simon Glassock notes that 'civilised behaviour is defined by moral and *physical courage*, honesty, a sense of fair play and a commitment to putting the needs of society before those of the individual [... This] demonstrates to Buchan's readers that the values his heroes endorse are not only central to a well-ordered society but also universal in their application' (emphasis added).[45] Jaikie's affiliation with the University of Cambridge places him securely as a gentleman, and is quietly reinforced by his clothes (old flannels, instead of Dougal's unwieldy tweeds), and his accent, now changed to 'pure English' with a slight but attractive lilt.[46]

Buchan fills in the background to Jaikie's term-time activities with an interesting episode that might be a pointed antithesis to the Chandos episode at the opening of Yates's *Blind Corner* a year earlier in 1929, discussed in Chapter 3. Jaikie has just met the Socialist speaker and militant pacifist David Antrobus, whom he had previously encountered at Cambridge. 'Mr Antrobus had been invited to lecture to a group of young iconoclasts, and Jaikie, in company with certain Rugby notables, had attended. There had been a considerable row, and Jaikie, misliking the manner of Mr Antrobus's opponents, had, along with his friends, entered joyfully into the strife, and had helped to conduct the speaker safely to his hotel and next morning to the station.'[47] While Yates's Chandos was probably also a 'Rugby notable', it is significant that while Chandos had been violent, Jaikie protects the right to free speech.

He is contrasted with Dougal, formerly his Die-Hards commander and his best friend. Cambridge has habituated Jaikie to socialising with the upper classes, but Dougal has not had the same training. When they are invited to lunch at the house of the aristocratic Mrs Brisbane-Brown by her very attractive niece, the Honourable Alison Westwater, daughter of Lord Rhynns, Dougal

> was acutely aware of being in an unfamiliar environment, to which he should have been hostile, but which as a matter of fact he enjoyed with trepidation. Unlike Jaikie he bristled with class-consciousness. Mrs Brisbane-Brown's kindly arrogance, the long-descended air of her possessions, the atmosphere of privilege so secure that it need not conceal itself – he was aware of it with a half-guilty joy.[48]

Dougal's encounter with the upper classes is his grooming for Establishment respectability, but it sits awkwardly, and very honestly, with his avowed radicalism. Just as Craw has to face the real-life examples of the theory he has spouted in his papers, Dougal has to face the class enemy he has hitherto resented. Dougal's experiences indicate how complex this process is, of adjusting to what is normal, what is acceptable, or what is inimical, in terms of accent, social assumptions, even the simple fact of how to behave to a butler. Throughout this novel Dougal is only comfortable when he is in command, returning to his teenage role of military strategist. This allows him to adjust to the alien comforts of castle living, and the easy assumption of social authority that the others have and he does not. Perhaps this is the crux of Dougal's dilemma, which Jaikie has somehow bypassed by entering the class stream via Cambridge. Dougal's natural entry point into the class struggle is as a member of the working class, albeit with advantages accrued by his adoption into Dickson McCunn's middle class. He does not see how he can rise in his profession without abandoning his natural class position. Buchan shows us that for Craw and Dougal, theory has to give way to accepting the standards of other people, probably not of the same class or ideology, to achieve professional success. As Dougal's life experiences are expanded, he will become less fiery, and more attuned to the classes who hold power, especially – as we will see in *The House of the Four Winds* – when he ascends that ladder of power as a professional journalist and editor. Professional achievement trumps class loyalty, and is the *raison d'être* for Buchan's working-class characters of the 1930s.

The Gap in the Curtain

There are no working-class characters in *The Gap in the Curtain* (1932). The novel consists of five excellent short stories, each about one individual, linked by a framing narrative verging on the supernatural that allows the characters to be shown a single fact from their personal or professional future as a headline in *The Times* of a year hence, and follows their stories in how they use that knowledge. It is set in Buchan's invented alternative political context in London of the early 1930s. Politics is the principal occupation of the older men in the novel, and it forms the subject of most of their conversations. By this mechanism, Buchan can describe subtle variants in the upper-class view of how politics should work, and the differences between Conservative, Labour and Liberal points of view. For most modern readers, these differences will be meaningless, and so the political colourings serve as character delineation rather than as indications of their motivation. But political uncertainty is important as a driver in two of the novel's episodes, represented by the social changes associated with it. Buchan's preoccupations in this novel are the new professionalisation of occupations that used to be vocations, and the public role of women.

Professionalism in politics was a new career in the late 1920s and early 1930s. Buchan's disapproval of 'trimming', the practice of changing sides for personal gain, is the impetus for the plot of 'The Honourable David Mayot'. In his story, Mayot sees the name of the prime minister in a year's time, and jettisons all his political alliances and loyalties to become the confidant and close associate of that man, hoping for his own advancement. He is a professional politician,[49] and is consistently criticised by the narrative voice and other characters through the novel. His personality is also dubious, being the unsatisfactory result of being both professional and a politician, rather than a loyal colleague. His abilities are 'doubtful';[50] during the First World War 'he had opportunely remembered that his family had been Quakers, and he had something to do, from well back in base, with a Quaker ambulance' (Buchan did not object to pacifism that was sincere).[51] Mayot's plans are brought down, quite suitably, by the demands of national concerns: the public's response to increasing unemployment figures, which had 'obliterated party lines'.[52]

Professionalism in politics is not, however, condemned in this novel. Commitment and loyalty are more important, in taking a public role, or in resigning it, whereas strong politician characters can be described approvingly for their professionalism. The protagonist of the story 'Sir Robert Goodeve' does neither, because he saw his obituary headline in the future, and so his story is a very personal problem. He allows his personal concerns to sap his courage and commitment, and destroys a potentially magnificent and valuable political career. David Cannadine describes 1930s politics as 'a new world with a new ethos: of full-time work, of probity, loyalty, self-effacement, and secrecy, of detachment from high politics and high society, of rational promotion, and of rewards and honours. This new civil service was self-consciously a middle-class profession: the old aristocratic amateurs had gone for good'.[53] The Goodeves in Buchan's fiction – 'aristocratic amateurs' – simply cannot function with the new way of running the country.

Another instance of Buchan's distaste for the new professionalism is at the centre of 'Mr Reginald Daker'. Reggie is the gentle dilettante who decides to turn his hobby of antiquarian bibliophily into a small business, and then finds it taken over and horribly commercialised by the smiling face of professional capitalism. Buchan exacerbates Reggie's horror of professionalism by making the Cortals, his new colleagues, 'the type which in my irreverent youth we called the "blood stockbroker" – the people who wanted to be gentlefolk first and city men afterwards, but were determined to be a complete success in both roles'.[54] The Cortal brothers have chosen a good time to capitalise on the lifestyle and history of the upper classes by selling it to eager new money. '"A new millionaire in the States, as soon as he has made his pile, starts to found a library, though he may be scarcely literate. He knows what is certain to appreciate."'[55]

This profit-focused approach is contrasted strongly with Reggie's beliefs. His love of traditional occupations and the seasonal round of English society drives his love of books, and has given him natural good taste and acumen for finding treasures for sale in the houses of his extensive acquaintance, with whom he hunts and has probably known all his life. He has no qualms about selling these items of portable English heritage – 'he took to frequenting sales, cultivated dealers and collectors, enlarged his American acquaintance'[56] – so making money from his gentlemanly status is not at issue. The differences between Reggie's aspirations and those of his new Cortal partners appear in the tone of the narrative voice, which emphasises their interest in professional management in terms that suggest the military and the soulless.

"You must get a staff together, and lay down your lines carefully, for what you want is an intelligence department and a scientifically-arranged clearing-house. You have to organize the buying side, and know just where to lay your hands on what you want. And you have to organize your customers [...] Your watchword must be organization [...] rationalization" [...] He was excited, too. He saw himself becoming a figure, a power, a man of wealth, all that he had ruled out as beyond his compass – and this without sacrifice of the things he loved.[57]

The last words are, of course, the key: Reggie is faced with the old-fashioned temptation of money. The Cortals represent modern business management, with which there is nothing inherently wrong. Leithen, Buchan's narrative voice in this novel, has no problem with mixing business, class standards and aesthetic values. What he objects to is the exploitation of Englishness, of the attempt to sell the intangible to eager buyers who want to own English heritage without contributing to it or nurturing it. This one-sided bargain is represented by the catalogue for Reggie's business, now called by the Cortals 'The Interpreter's House':

> which was to be circulated to a carefully selected list in England and America. [...] It was a kind of [Army & Navy] Stores List of the varieties of English charm and the easiest way to get hold of them. [...] Relentlessly it set down in black and white all the delicate half-formed sentiments we cherish in our innermost hearts and dare not talk about. It was so cursedly explicit that it brushed the bloom off whatever it touched. [...] I could see the shoddy culture of two continents seizing upon it joyously.[58]

Reggie's story personifies narrative resentment of a 'shoddy culture' grabbing greedily at the remnants of a more fastidious one, which has been forced into this position by brutal economic forces. The class-consciousness resisting this distasteful alliance is made clear. 'I'm going to be a sort of Cook's guide to culture.'[59] The problem with the Cortals is not so much their smiling appropriation of a coveted social position, but that they do not understand it, nor are they of it. 'Their efficiency was a little too naked; they were too manifestly well-equipped, too elaborately men of the world.'[60] Buchan's invention of the Cortals shows that he regards being a gentleman as not a job but a state of mind. It can be acquired, and it can be developed, but it requires sensitivity, and an awareness of intangible values, and is ultimately a state of being, not simply performative. A modern-day analogy might be that the Cortals, and the social characteristics that they represent, are like a stately mansion, a showplace for how the stately used to live, rather than a home. The kitchens and the gardens are never left untidy when they are on show to the public, and neither are the Cortals; '"everything tidied up and put to its best use"'.[61]

The most chilling of the Cortals is the sister, Verona (a name undoubtedly chosen for its closeness to the popular sleeping pill and sedative Veronal). She meets Reggie while hunting at the house of a country friend, and becomes his confidante. He tells her how he would like to develop his modest dream of selling the books he loves to make a living by conveying the essential charm of English life and history, and she brings in her brothers to help him develop this dream, as we have seen. In applying herself to business, rather than, say, the traditional domestic occupations of ladies, Verona enters the public sphere, begins to manage Reggie, and soon brings other women into the business. 'She had got him a secretary, a girl who had been at college with her, and she had started a system of card-indexes, on which she dwelt lovingly. [...] There would have to be a good deal of work at the Museum, and for this she could enrol several young women who had been with her at Oxford.'[62] Once he has been devoured by the Cortals' vision of his business, Reggie is expected to propose to Verona, but this is the last straw. A man should do his own proposing, not be expected to do so as if it were a business partnership, and he also ought to love the lady, not fear her. Buchan's brief depiction of this masterful young woman is arresting, because of the power of capitalist domination that she represents.

In more traditional areas of life described in *The Gap in the Curtain* Buchan's attitude to women is the same as in *Castle Gay*. A concerned society mother is annoyed with her daughter for suddenly refusing to take an interest in the very suitable marriage towards which she had been heading dutifully. '"She says that he's too good for her; and that his perfections choke her – doesn't want to play second fiddle to an Admirable Crichton – wants to shape her own life – all the rubbish that young people talk nowadays."'[63] The exasperation that the mother feels on seeing her previously well-behaved child turn sulky is not a new complaint in the Buchan milieu: Pamela Brune's moment of rebellion owes a lot to Koré Arabin's shockingly independent behaviour in *The Dancing Floor* in 1927. These young women may have echoed the experience of Buchan's eldest child Alice. She was 19 in 1927, and still unmarried and without occupation at 24 when *The Gap in the Curtain* was published in 1932. She too had been rebellious, disguising her copy of James Joyce's *Ulysses* with a dust-jacket from *The Pilgrim's Progress*, and 'enduring a London season or two as a deb [before she] became a student at RADA'.[64] Like Koré, Pamela Brune redeems her bad behaviour by turning into a heroine, when she discovers her true calling and saves Charles Ottery's life by giving him something to live for. This is not much for a modern young woman to aspire to, since it is a sentimental role and a vague idealisation of married love. Verona Cortal, on the other hand, is entrepreneurial, a networker, and a fine, though rather insensitive, manager of people and systems. Her problem as a model for Conservative womanhood is that, although she is undoubtedly willing to marry and settle into running Reggie's home for him, she is unlikely to stop running his business for him as well.

A Prince of the Captivity

In the year after *The Gap in the Curtain* came out, Buchan published *A Prince of the Captivity* (1933), which also deals with contemporary society, modern mores, and the nature of commitment. Yet it lacks the light-hearted elements that characterise several of the *Gap* stories, and is rather too much a mature work of serious political consideration. Buchan combines different genres in an attempt to make a thriller out of economic and political theory: the adventure quest in which one man battles impossible odds on his own, the condition of England novel, and the political *bildungsroman*. The action covers twenty years, from the hero's trial for fraud some years before the First World War, to his dramatic and sacrificial ending in central Europe while combating the forces of anarchy, communism and fascism simultaneously. Adam Melfort is on a self-sacrificing mission to save civilisation, and this service takes the form of secret-service work in occupied Belgium in the First World War, the rescue of an American millionaire stranded in the Arctic, and then a ten-year search to find leaders to save Britain from an inevitable economic crash. The leaders are not necessarily Conservative: Buchan spends a lot of time in this novel exploring why and how Labour leadership must work for the people. He does not rewrite the history of the 1920s, but revisits it, explaining through the stories of different characters how Britain had got itself into the mess it did, and how it still needs saviours in the then present day of the early 1930s.

His villains are the forces of apathy, cynicism and selfishness, symbolised by Warren Creevey, a fashionable economist (apparently based on Maynard Keynes),[65] and Mrs Pomfrey, a society leader of the self-absorbed who corrupts by pandering to the ego. '"She is making a sentimentalist out of an idealist. And the next step, you know, is a cynic."'[66] Their methods are to take the energy out of their most promising opponents by persuading them that their efforts are worthless. The 'half-baked' whom they attract are aligned with those who follow fads in literature as well as theology or politics: another instance of Buchan's uneasiness at the pessimism of the avant-garde. In brief, the novel describes how leaders who abandon their posts are not the right men for the job, and is a study of those who abandon the country. By succumbing to apathy, Britain runs the terrible risk of being unfit to withstand the forces of evil and anarchy gathering on the other side of the Channel, against which there will soon be an inescapable battle. The novel's tone is not overtly apocalyptic, but when the social history and the politics are isolated from the fiction, it seems clear that *A Prince of the Captivity* is a novel of dire warnings for the mid-1930s.

Organisation is once again Buchan's concern. Falconet, the energetic American whom Adam saved in the Arctic, is out to find leaders to fix the post-war crisis in America, while Adam is detailed to do the same for Europe. Falconet's methods are based on method rather than instinct, and use committees and underground enquiry. Adam is a lone inves-tigator, penetrating the darkest places, listening to his friends in high places, and nurturing the men (it is always men) whom he thinks will have the stuff in them to save Britain. Falconet is promiscuous in his search: "'I want to spot the men who might be leaders – in business, politics, I don't care what – for its leaders we're sick for the lack of'".[67] He is also attracted to quick fixes and easy answers. "'Do you mean Warren Creevey?" [...] "I never met a fellow with such a lightning brain. *He* understands organisation, if you like. If you throw out a notion he has a scheme ready before you have finished your sentence."'[68] This glibness is a warning sign, as is Creevey's association with the 'get-rich-quick mania' of the 1920s that Buchan uses as his motif of all that is rotten in British society. "'What's the sense of wanting to acquire if you haven't the sense to know how to do it. [...] Everybody wants to take short cuts [...] nobody is trying to understand the rules.'"[69]

From the landowners' perspective, the political activity of Kenneth Armine, Adam's first candidate for leadership, reflects how the patrician classes were responding to social change by using the arena of local politics.[70] He becomes Mayor of Birkpool (for which read Liverpool or Manchester) as a way to influence local people with whom he might no longer have a feudal relationship, but whom he instinctively feels he can lead by virtue of his class and family history. He is an enlightened landlord, but is defeated by his tenants' desire for greater autonomy. This wastes their slender resources and renders the landlords unable to help with their capital when the inevitable economic slump reduces the value of the tenants' investment.[71] Armine tries to take the established political system head-on, turning himself into what his wife calls a 'mixture of High Tory and rampant Bolshie'.[72] As an indication of the frustration felt by the landed classes at the mess society has got itself into, and their inability to do anything practical to fix it, he is an ideal-istic and affectionate portrait of a man doing his best to turn back the clock to a patriarchal system and simple leadership. But Armine gives up, because he cannot defeat socialism's insistence that the rights of the workers must take precedence over economic facts.

When Joe Utlaw, the second of Adam's protégés, does (momentarily) defeat his socialist opponents, he defies the union he works for, breaks the strike and submits his men to lower wages, to ensure their continued employment rather than the meagre rewards of idealism that are limited strike pay and then no job at all. With Utlaw's story Buchan was depicting the complexities of 1920s labour politics, and economic policy as a very uncertain science. Typically, he personalises the conflict in the novel, showing how Utlaw's rise in politics will give him personal advantages but leave his colleagues behind in the Depression with only their ideals. Idealism is pitted against pragmatism, but it is not clear on which side Buchan's narrative voice stands, since Adam's potential leaders all fail the test of their times. Utlaw abandons the workers and becomes a Tory, and Lord Armine abandons the workers and retires to the country to breed horses.

In Frank Alban, the third candidate, Buchan is critical of spiritual laxity, and short cuts to mental and emotional comfort: '"the gentry who minister to minds diseased. The mystics who lift you to a higher plane. The psychotherapists who dig out horrors from your past. The Christian Scientists with large soft hands and a good bedside manner"'.[73] Frank the slum preacher and minister of religion was a beacon of hope for working people because he worked for them, suffered with them, and supported them when they were in hard times. He is seduced away from the drudgery and impossible work in the working-class parishes, to become a society preacher to the rich who seek uplift, rather than bread. Buchan presents his failure to serve his people faithfully as a betrayal of Christ, because '"Christ was a red-hot Socialist"'.[74]

Class and character are evoked in telling details of characterisation. When Adam meets Utlaw, the man whom he will spend years nurturing as the next great political leader of his generation, Utlaw is fishing (a classic sign of a good man in Buchan), wearing an old trench coat and trench boots, indicating war service, reinforced by a slight limp: service and a war wound are automatic guarantees of good character in Buchan's canon.[75] Utlaw is a trade union district organiser in the steel industry, and has a history of effective and well-received negotiation between men and their masters.[76] He is engaged to be married to Florence Covert, a welfare worker in the factories. She is of good birth, denoted at first by her appearance, which is shabby and poorly styled (this is noted because Buchan's women have a duty to present well), and later by her genes. 'The moulding of her face was fine, and the deep eyes under the curiously arched eyebrows made her nearly beautiful. [...] She was untidy, but she suggested haste rather than slovenliness.'[77] She shines against Utlaw: 'his smartness only accentuated his class. He was a child of the people, and the girl, for all her dowdiness, was not'.[78]

The new Mrs Utlaw has definite ideas about not accepting patronage, but her rise in class status as Utlaw rises in political importance also increases her acceptance of the world's expectations. She dresses better, she does accept social patronage, and she is clever enough not to patronise in her turn. She is not free from snobbery. 'She would have Utlaw stick to his class, but she was determined that he should be high in his class's hierarchy.'[79] She admires another politician, Sir Derrick Trant, ostensibly for his professional approval of her husband, but 'Adam remembered also that Sir Derrick Trant belonged to a family that had fought at Crécy'.[80] Ultimately she becomes a political wife and a lady who lunches, talking politics at second-hand. She becomes a looker-on, no longer working as an activist in her own right.

It is significant that Buchan ignored the possibility of Florence taking to politics herself. After the 1931 general election there had been 33 women MPs, 14 of them in the Conservative Party.[81] Florence is an active, shrewd and courageous person, her husband's spokesperson, but her destiny in the plot is only to support Utlaw, to comment on his successes and failures, and embody the more socially risible aspects of his translation from Labour man of the people to the pet of the Conservative masters. She is a lightning-rod for the opprobrium that Utlaw's evolving political position will attract, since, as we have seen, Buchan is severe about those who abandon their principles for their own advancement. Interestingly, once Utlaw has abandoned his post, he is not seen again in the novel, and is only spoken of. His breaking of the strike is explained in patriarchal terms, for the workers' own good. His translation to the Tory benches is Florence's social triumph, and she disparages those whom he used to represent in particularly power-based terms: '"You see, he is working with white men now"'.[82] She is an apologist for his abilities in terms that say as much about her own perspective of their former colleagues as where she wants her husband to be – '"One oughtn't to use a razor to peel potatoes"'.[83] She values his career rise for what opportunities it will bring him, not for what he will be able to do for other people. She shows us all we need to know about the corruption that power brings.

In the story of Utlaw and Armine, there is a strong sense of the Establishment taking the best of the working-class out of their natural environment, giving them all the chances and resources they need, but inevitably putting them to work for the good of the ruling classes in the name of the country. There is no sense in this novel that a man of the people can stay loyal to his class and constituents and have power to do them good: Buchan does not depict Labour as a party that will ever succeed. Utlaw ignores the warnings because he has been engrossed in Creevey's arguments, and, a few pages later, he is out of a job. '"He'll have to get his friend Creevey to find him something else."'[84] And so he does: Utlaw is whisked out of the world of union negotiation and worker representation, and is sucked into full-time patronage. '"Mr Creevey has found him a post in Addison's – he is to look after the labour side of the business, and he is on the board of the new evening paper. He ought to be quite well off soon. A seat in the House? Yes, of course we want him there as soon as possible."'[85] 'We' are the malign powers of Creevey and Mrs Pomfrey, who are speaking for their own little interest group that seems now to be tightly aligned with the Conservative Party, and the Establishment, hierarchical politics that run the country.

One of the voices of power, Jacqueline Armine, Lady Warmestre, is in the novel to comment on class encroachments, a process she views with amusement rather than outrage since she is secure in her own position. Jacqueline makes pointed remarks about incomers to her own class whom she entertains at Armine Court when her husband is the Mayor: '"war knights, you know – and the Clutterbucks, who have just bought the Ribstones' place and are setting up as gentry"'.[86] But her role in the novel is also to observe and praise Utlaw. She admires his ability to transcend class. '"Do you know, Adam, that's an extraordinary fellow? He can lay himself alongside any type of man or woman and get on with them."'[87] The walk-on character Lord Lamancha doesn't bother with ceremony or titles when talking to Utlaw, whereas he uses elaborate and formal manners for the Clutterbucks and their ilk. This is explained also by Utlaw's background as a soldier, and an officer risen from the ranks. For Buchan, war service is the male finishing school to render most men equal. He seems to value a limited egalitarianism in the society he presents in this novel, as long as certain values are respected. A man with the abilities of an officer can leave the class he was born into, but by moving into a role traditionally owned by the upper classes, he must also accept that social hierarchy, and the system that puts titled families and their political masters above the rest, with more pay and advantages.

There are hints in the novel about 1930s threats from abroad: 'He spoke of evil elements, the financiers who flourished in any *débacle*, the hordes of the restless and disinherited, the poison of Communism filtering through from Russia'.[88] In the last section, Adam has encounters with anarchic agitators and fascist politics, which seem much more dangerous and powerful out of Britain. The norm for the 1930s thriller combating right-wing forces was to pitch the battles on mainland Europe, and Buchan does this with the sequel to *Castle Gay*, in 1935.

The House of the Four Winds

In *The House of the Four Winds* (1935) Buchan focuses very obviously on the conflict between the politics of the old and the young. The novel is the continuation of Jaikie's role as Buchan's new Hannay, as he encounters Ruritanian politics in Eastern Europe. The Evallonian Monarchists of *Castle Gay* are struggling to secure power in this small but volatile country, but their methods and ideology are flawed. The 'gentle fanaticism' of the Monarchists[89] seeks to overthrow the 'effete' Republican government founded by 'rootless Communists'.[90] This familiar post-war dyad has been disrupted by a third political force, a youth party called Juventus, drawing on on the Hitler Youth for its insistence on militarism, nature worship, and strict discipline and loyalty, but does not share its eugenicist or anti-Semitic ideas.[91] Rather, Juventus is a forceful voice of hope and fresh energy, though its militarism is depicted as a little ridiculous, through British eyes. Jaikie the former boy scout is associated with Juventus throughout the novel, as he ends up wearing its uniform (temporarily), and acts as its agent and strategist for much of the novel. Juventus's authoritarian intervention is presented as a rejuvenating force. '"Youth is the force in the world of today, for it isn't tired, and it can hope."'[92] Yet at the beginning of the novel one of Juventus's opponents speaks darkly of how dangerous 'youth' can be, especially when it is 'disappointed, aggrieved youth, which has never known the discipline of war. Imaginative and incalculable youth, which clamours for the moon and may not be content until it has damaged most of the street lamps'.[93] The novel ends with a triumphant 'revolution of youth which is also a restoration'.[94]

If this novel is read for its politics, rather than as the sequel to *Castle Gay* or *Huntingtower*, its structure is based on a political equation, padded out most entertainingly with Buchan's set-piece adventures. Buchan uses this novel to explore how a political intervention can solve political impasses; in this case, youth intervening when the older generations are stuck. He invents Juventus as 'not only a trained and disciplined force, the youth of a nation in arms for defence and, it might be, offence; it was also an organisation for national planning and economic advancement'.[95] Buchan spends some time explaining the economic reasons for Juventus's emergence, and the existence of an academic pro-letariat who give the uprising a philosophical basis, and jargon.[96] This sounds like a political party with a military core, the National Socialist Party of Germany being the obvious parallel, though the novel's central struggle of monarchists versus republicans anticipates the Spanish Civil War (1936–39). Its backers, and leaders, appear to be wealthy aristocrats who can exploit Evallonia's oil fields. Juventus is more like an occupy-ing army emerging from the population, 'the resurgence of the spirit of the Evallonian nation'.[97] Buchan also emphasised the theatricality of European fascist events to reassure readers that this kind of thing would never take hold in Britain. This is echoed by the feminist playwright Cicely Hamilton on observing fascist marches in Britain: 'our British brand of Fascism has always seemed to me to be an imitative body – its theatrical manners and gestures of homage, which may be right enough in the country of its origin, are not the natural expression of an English faith and enthusiasm'.[98]

In contrast, the British protagonists of this novel intervene, in an auto-matic assumption of habitual colonial rights, to solve a sticky political problem caused by the arrival of Juventus. The function of the British protagonists is to persuade or cajole native Evallonian political oppo-nents to set aside their regrettable tendencies to melodramatic excess (here Buchan's sympathies are opposed to the real-life fascist dramatics of mid-1930s Germany and Italy), to work together for the greater good of the country, and to avoid bloodshed. The British adventurers per-form people management on a national scale, out of the limelight, to enable 'a nice law-abiding revolution' to take place.[99] The involvement of Dickson McCunn as an ardent Royalist is not so much for his insis-tence on helping Prince John to a kingdom, but because his common sense, and business experience, rather than ideals, enable him to find a solution to the impasse based on cunning. His actions are sanctioned by the class values of Sir Archibald Roylance, a Member of Parliament and delegate to the League of Nations (the active roles of MPs may have been intended to prove that they could do more than speak on their benches), and by the media, Dougal Crombie of the Craw Press. Their adventures are gaily high-spirited, and alarmingly casual, stepping into political conflicts as if they were enjoyable social contretemps.

In a Dornford Yates novel of the 1930s, for instance *Fire Below*, these actions would be expected, for Chandos and Hanbury are gentleman adventurers. Yates usually offers a strong chivalric justification for his heroes' inadvertent but unavoidable interference in foreign politics, just as there had been in the original Ruritanian escapade by Anthony Hope, *The Prisoner of Zenda* (1894). But Buchan, unable to write romantic love convincingly, cannot offer the passionate affair that ought to be the impetus for the story, a conflagration between the Countess Araminta of Juventus and Prince John, perhaps, whom she puts on the throne in this novel. Instead, he makes the political implications of the restoration of a monarchy the focus of attention, and has trouble with the subsequent questions that would arise if a British MP, recently attending sessions at the League of Nations in Geneva, disguised the Monarchist pretender to the throne as his chauffeur, and risked being killed in a shoot-out in a Republican dungeon. Ruritanian politics should not be exposed to rational examination, nor presented as an amusing *opera bouffe*, as Buchan has done here. Buchan uses Evallonia as a cardboard arena for a political experiment, but in choosing the Ruritanian mode, rather than the more robust military thriller, as he did with *The Courts of the Morning* (1929), the mood is wrong, and the weaknesses in the hypothesis cause the experiment to produce only weak results.

The messages in these Buchan novels are complex, and almost too insistent in their political application for their original readers to read them as escapist pleasure. Taken together, these four novels comprise the modern politics canon in Buchan's oeuvre, which, as can be seen in the Appendix, was large. They show how concerned Buchan was with national and European unrest and political instability. He took the ruling perspective, narrating automatically as one of the ruling classes (which he certainly was not by birth). Individual stories of suffering and experience were illustrations, rather than the subjects of his stories, and his leaders are remote from the people they purportedly represent. It is clear that Buchan was responding to national unemployment levels and economic hardship for some, but, as I noted at the beginning of the chapter, there was a split in the economic experience of this decade, and Buchan was never on the poorer side. His 1930s novels lack felt experience (except in the episodes of outdoor endurance), and give extrapolations from figures on paper rather than from the experience of being out of a job, or being unable to pay the rent. Wrapping his political lectures in superb storytelling did not wholly work. *A Prince of the Captivity* and *The Gap in the Curtain* are the least popular of his contemporary novels, and are regarded as curiosities by those looking for more Hannay. The politics, and the strictures about professionalisation, muffle the romance that the Buchan reader would normally expect.

5
Novels of Instruction: Thirkell in the 1930s

In the first scholarly study of Angela Thirkell, Jill N Levin observes that Thirkell created 'an irreplaceable record of the imaginations and yearnings of the classes which interested her – the gentry and the professional upper middle class'.[1] David Pryce-Jones notes that Thirkell 'responded immediately in her novels to shifts in the system, so that unreflectingly she wrote a fictionalised journalism',[2] which agrees with what Thirkell had said of her novelist alter ego Mrs Morland: '"She has the makings of an excellent reporter in her if only she could keep to the point"'.[3] Thirkell's occasionally riotous comic satire presented contemporary anxieties about class and failing traditions by employing 'nostalgic melancholy and satirical malice'.[4] Even though she could be stridently conservative, her critiques of social change sometimes insert unexpectedly progressive notes into how she depicts contemporary lives. Alison Light notes that studying Thirkell, among other conservative novelists, would show that 'their interest would none the less lie as much in their modernity as in their reiteration of well-worked national and political themes'.[5] Thirkell's relentlessly unsentimental view of the housewife's daily round contradicted the imagery of advertisements, for example, and made female-centred commentary possible within a conservative framework.[6]

Yet, the romantic marriage plot lies at the heart of all Thirkell's novels. In this she was bucking the trend for what Nicola Beauman and Nicola Humble identify as the feminine middlebrow novel, the genre in which Thirkell's work would normally be considered, where 'marriage is seen as the antithesis rather than the apotheosis of romantic love, and the domestic sphere as a cage rather than a haven'.[7] Thirkell's novels are notoriously marriage-minded, and the multiple betrothals at the end of her novels have a socio-political purpose. Jill N Levin explains Thirkell's insistence that the upper classes needed constant replenishment with either money or fresh energetic bloodlines: 'since their survival is problematic, Thirkell's stories strive constantly to inject the blood, brains and breeding of people like herself into Barsetshire'.[8] Thirkell's own status as a writer led to her populating Barsetshire with a statistically improbable number of authors of her own class, as well as architects, barristers and civil servants. Their marriages provide stability and healthy growth for the upper middle classes and the gentry, since nearly all produce children. Domesticity is described at a distance, since all her characters have servants, and the nearest thing to a domestic crisis occurs when the servants are not working properly.

Her focus on the upper and lower strata of the class system – the middle and upper classes, which included the nobility, and 'a corps of feudally devoted domestics' – meant, as Levin says, that 'the lower middle class, the teachers, managers, petty civil servants, and clerks' were either ignored, or, especially during the war when their existence could not be ignored any longer, ridiculed.[9] Her novels are set in the home, and revolve around social gatherings and meals at home, or in other people's homes. Q D Leavis's attacks in the 1930s and 1940s on upper-class women novelists, in the intimidatingly highbrow journal *Scrutiny*, as Janet Montefiore observes, had 'contributed to a generally dismissive consensus that bourgeois women's contribution to writing in this period could be considered negligible',[10] and that their age and education excluded them from serious scholarly analysis if they were not born between 1900 and 1914. Thirkell was born in 1890, grew up in Kensington and was educated privately. The 'dismissive consensus' that ignored the views of women like her was as elitist as they were supposed to be.

As noted above, Thirkell was interested in the reportage of daily doings – Hermione Lee notes that Thirkell's 'pleasure is in the ordinary, the everyday, and the recurrent'.[11] Her novels were a literary commentary on the bewildering changes of her times, in which balance was always desirable. Diana Trilling notes that the 'amiable inanity' of her characters disguises 'but never hides Mrs Thirkell's opinions and prejudices. It is a disarming device for persuading us that a powerful class of grown men and women – England's upper middle class, gentry and minor aristocracy – are lovable children'.[12]

The function of these novels as conduct literature is also important, since Thirkell was a didactic author, considering her readers to be as much in need of instruction as her characters, who learn social nuances as life lessons. The manners and social usage of all aspects of English middle- and upper-class life are set out throughout her oeuvre, with examples of how not to behave used as a source of comedy and gentle derision. Nicola Humble notes that through conduct instruction, the readers are given 'access to the jealously-guarded rituals and values that mark the borders of upper-middle-class identity, allowing them to "pass" if they read correctly and apply the results of their reading' to their own lives.[13] The repetition in Thirkell's instruction served to fix social usage by rote.

Readers would recognise correct behaviour in those characters who performed it without comment from the narrative voice. In the writing of middle-class femininity between the wars, women writers codified a particular language of reticence.[14] The unspoken in the woman's middlebrow novel was a challenge to the right kind of reader, who would pick up the cues as an assurance of correct, and desirable, behaviour.[15] Thirkell's characters hardly ever intruded on each others' feelings, making reserve a barrier to the baring of emotions, not a ladylike screen. Thirkell's domestic settings are private, always excepting the presence of servants, invisible until they interrupt. When characters go out it is usually only to the house of a neighbour or friend. Like Mrs Miniver, Thirkell's conservative woman was an ideal maintainer of the home and domestic routine, conserving and maintaining what was already there.[16]

Many things were ignored. Jill N Levin notes that 'in Barsetshire no character suffered poverty for long or felt real pain; paid work was unimportant but usually pleasant; and only the old had to die'.[17] Sexual attraction and desire in Thirkell's fiction are severely played down in the novels, and her characters could display a disconcerting innocence in using or even hearing sexualised vocabulary.[18] Divorce only appears in Thirkell's first novel in 1933 (in a sophisticated London setting), and even there it feels rather too risqué and bitter for the tonal qualities of her writing. Divorce became much more freely available in 1937, yet Thirkell barely mentions it thereafter. In contrast to the characters of her contemporary Nancy Mitford, Thirkell's Barsetshire gentry have no liking for modern art, music or literature, and seem to be intellectually void, concerned only with maintaining a Victorian way of life that already seems out of date in the 1930s. Mitford's novels show the aristocracy acting as cultural trustees,[19] because she had the confidence of her very secure aristocratic background, whereas Thirkell, without titled descent herself, relied very heavily on the grandness of her friends, and on her relationships with famous people, for her cultural validation. Her middle son Colin MacInnes wrote after her death: '"a curious aspect of her portrait of the English gentry was that she was never of them, and didn't really know them"'.[20]

Background

In 1929, the shock – both exhilarating and terrifying – of being back in her own country, in which she had to make her own living, gave Thirkell the impetus to write her first published book. This was her memoir *Three Houses* (1931) in which she describes living in Fulham and West Kensington in London, and Rottingdean, in Sussex, where she was the much-loved eldest grandchild of Sir Edward Burne-Jones, playing with her best friend Josephine Kipling and listening to cousin Ruddy reading the *Just-So Stories* aloud for the first time. Bearing in mind that Thirkell was at this time in her life re-establishing her identity, *Three Houses* is an excellent insight into how she wanted to remember her early life and family connections, and how she presented herself *vis-à-vis* her celebrated relations. Written from a child's perspective in an adult's voice, the memoir is about clothes, food, furnishings she loved or was scared of, the games she and her younger brother and sister played, and the explorations, treats and events of their young lives. It is a perfect evocation of the end of the nineteenth century in surroundings where the Pre-Raphaelites and other artistic luminaries were ordinary friends of the family: the Holman Hunts, Tadema, the De Morgans, Morris, and Mrs Patrick Campbell who lived across the square.

Three Houses also makes us aware of Thirkell's uncompromising critical tendency. She regards the furniture designed by her grandfather as being among the most uncomfortable known to man. She is scathing about changes in London architecture, about buildings that have sprung up to replace the sites she had known. 'Mean houses and ugly pretentious flats' and 'the hideous tide of commerce' exist because 'the great aim of democracy is to make everything as uncomfortable as possible for the greatest number'.[21]

Three Houses was a critical success, which must have encouraged Thirkell to complete the two novels she had brought with her from Australia in manuscript.[22] Thirkell says many times, as Mrs Morland, that she only wrote novels for a living, that she depended on them for her income and to support her sons' education. This was clearly true, but there are other factors to be considered. She had written a lot in Australia, but nothing came of it because she could not write about Australia with love or passion. There was nothing there that she wanted to defend, for instance as a bastion of culture or civilisation, because she felt alienated socially and culturally. Thirkell needed her own culture to stimulate her unexpressed creativity which would be most eloquent when critiquing social change.

Her first novel was *Ankle Deep*, apparently in draft in 1929 and accepted in 1932 by James Hamilton, proprietor of the new publishing house Hamish Hamilton Ltd. He would publish Thirkell's fiction for the rest of her life. Elizabeth Bowen considers that *Ankle Deep* (1933) 'could not have been written by a young woman'[23] (Thirkell was 43 when it was published). Her biographer Margot Strickland was convinced that Thirkell had had a romantic episode in 1929 that fuelled Aurea's dizzy and irresolute passion in the novel.[24] It is an over-long dissection of social dilemmas amongst the dining-out classes, and reads too often as a floundering sequence of social engagements without purpose or direction. Yet images and tones rise from the depths to give the story a strong sense of felt experience, and the narrative voice has an exasperated patience with the characters' painful progression through their romance. Without knowing it, Thirkell was experimenting here with types who would develop in the next few years into two of her most successful characters: the opinionated schoolgirl as guardian of conservative values, and the older married woman addicted to acting a part for her own aesthetic enjoyment. *Ankle Deep* is dominated by its women characters and social expectations of the parts they have to play. This would become Thirkell's enduring concern as she grappled with social and, later, political changes, in her fiction.

Ankle Deep was followed by *High Rising* (1933), a novel about writers and publishing, narrated by Thirkell's alter ego Mrs Morland the detective novelist. This was followed by *Wild Strawberries* (1934), set in the country estate of Rushwater, home of the maddening and interfering grandmother, Lady Emily Leslie, who presides over a permanently summered existence with family and friends coming and going. Thirkell's targets in this novel were effete youths working for the BBC, educated women, pompous gardening bores, the French, and young men who don't take their flirtations seriously enough. She next published *The Demon in the House* (1934), four novellas focusing on the High Rising world and the aggravating Tony Morland, which may have been written for the *Just William* market. The different childhoods of her own sons were her inspirations for the character of Tony Morland, fully anglicised and promoted to the upper middle classes and prep school society. Reflecting adult society through the persona of an articulate child, Thirkell reinforces social codes by showing how even the anarchic child protests against their relaxation.

Her fourth novel, *Trooper to the Southern Cross*, a non-Barsetshire satire based on her emigration to Australia with her sons and second husband in a sabotaged German troopship, was published in 1934 by Faber &

Faber under the pseudonym of Leslie Parker. Otherwise critical, Colin MacInnes thought this much the best of all her works. In the summer of 1934 James Campbell McInnes, Thirkell's former husband whom she had divorced in 1917 amid unpleasant publicity for his cruelty and adultery,[25] visited London, where he offered to meet Thirkell, but she refused. Her fifth novel, *O, These Men, These Men!* (1935), was completed some months later, and there are powerful connections with this, and the memories of her first marriage that Campbell McInnes's unexpected contact may have aroused.[26] Given that *High Rising* and indeed *Wild Strawberries* show a considerable amount of literary skill, *O, These Men, These Men!* is unaccountably clumsy: Thirkell herself described it as 'crashingly bad'.[27] It seems to be three separate stories combined into one plot: a conventional romantic novelette set among the middle classes; an ur-Barsetshire novel containing embryo characters and themes; and a potentially very interesting novel about a woman recovering after a divorce, and the tension between her well-meaning relations' views on how she should carry on with her life, and her own anger. The novel is unique among Thirkell's works in seeming to suggest that a happy ending could be achieved without the heroine getting married again, but in the last pages the predicted dénouement arrives, with an undercurrent of resentment at what women suffer when they leave their husbands.

After this book, Thirkell continued to explore other routes into print, by writing more children's stories, *The Grateful Sparrow and Other Tales* (1935), and a historical biography of Regency courtesan Harriette Wilson, *The Fortunes of Harriette* (1936). She enjoyed trying new subjects and exploring new stories, and took to research very easily.[28] With the publication of *August Folly* (1936) Thirkell finally enters her kingdom of Barsetshire with brio and panache, though, as Margot Strickland points out, Barsetshire – the characters and settings of High Rising and Rushwater – isn't actually mentioned in this novel, in which are introduced many future Barsetshire characters.[29] The satire in *August Folly* is about family relationships, with a new and welcome strain of comedy sending up academic scholarship, the glamour of Oxford and painful incommunicativeness between parents and children.

Thirkell made one more writing experiment away from contemporary social comedy into historical fiction. *Coronation Summer* (1937), which is about the coronation of Queen Victoria, incorporates a great deal of historical research to structure its plot, but this was her last attempt to see if she could shine in other forms than the domestic comedy. Six months later *Summer Half* (1937) was published, and *The*

Times and *Punch* gave her high praise: 'Mrs Thirkell at her liveliest and best, laughing gently at her people'; 'one of the great humorous writers of our time'.[30] From this point Thirkell settled into a hugely popular and lucrative writing pattern. By reinscribing, in its true sense, a Victorian landscape with its values and standards upheld by modern characters, Thirkell indicated, in novel after novel, the standards that she expected her readers to approve of, learn from and also uphold. In *Pomfret Towers* (1938) and *The Brandons* (1939) modern pretensions in writing and art, and the breaching of good manners, are her targets, and her last pre-war novel, *Before Lunch* (1939), has a theme of unsatisfactory marriage.

By considering Thirkell's 1930s novels as a corpus it will be seen that there are some recurring themes of great importance. Her close attention to moments of domestic pleasure gives conduct instruction. She responds to alarming 1930s politics with derision, leaving her reader only the Conservatives to choose from if they wish to have her good opinion. Where people live, their houses and the relationship of those buildings and their owners to county history and current society, are recurring ideas throughout her novels. Class and snobbery are engaged with persistently by the narrative voice and through her characters. Money is positioned against class, again reflecting real-life concerns. Her own enjoyment of intertextuality is echoed in the novels by Barsetshire's large population of professional writers, to whom she gives a lot to say about the modern profession of writing. Less socially universal concerns include the university woman, and the wrong university college, but also the ubiquity of cinema in modern life. The final theme is Thirkell's unusual resistance to the cult of the child, and her use of the child in socially critical ways. These themes are relevant to her output in the 1930s, but, as we will see, altered as she began writing in wartime. Her post-war fiction also had new concerns and fears. This progression in themes demonstrates the innate flexibility of her writing, which was more ready to address modern living than Yates and Buchan, perhaps because of her use of the domestic setting, and certainly because she was interested in social change as experienced by those living it, rather than those standing aloof from it.

Domestic instruction through pleasure

Thirkell excelled in lyrical writing about instantly recognisable domestic pleasure, which in itself was instruction. This example is from *The Brandons* (1939), on Delia's preparations for the arrival of Miss Miller, the worn-out companion of a just deceased tyrant mistress, who is coming to recuperate.

> By this time Delia's blood was up. She stripped the garden of practically every white flower she could find and arranged them all in the Green Room, choosing several rather valuable white Chinese vases that were kept in a cabinet and never used. By the time she had decorated the dressing table, the writing table and the mantelpiece, and massed white phlox in the fender, the room with its pale green curtains and chintzes and its pale green walls, was like a dwelling under a glassy, cool, translucent wave, and Delia was filled with admiration for her own work.[31]

The reader is reassured by the beauty of the description, and the commonplace objects and actions that achieve the soothing effect. Physical comfort and pleasing surroundings are evoked by the names of the pieces of furniture, and by the space suggested in a 'Green Room' (not just the spare bedroom) that can hold them all. The passage emanates refreshment after toil, and comfort after poverty. It enhances the reader's opinion of Delia, a rather galumphing and obsessive schoolgirl, unnervingly eager to assist with First Aid. That she can arrange a room so imaginatively and simply speaks of an innate sensitivity and love of beauty, and we read this as a promise of approaching maturity. If the immature Delia can display such tact, which reflects well on her occasionally dotty mother, we can think the worse of the graceless Mrs Grant, Lady Norton and Aunt Augusta, who pass through this novel as examples of how women should not behave, and how ladies of social standing do not demonstrate a proper sensitivity to others.

There is also a strong emphasis on gracious living. The Brandon garden must be vast to produce so many flowers of one colour; the valuable vases kept in a cabinet speak for themselves; the size of the room is not so vast, but the impression given in the description is similar to the instruction in the women's magazines of the period, for instance *Homes and Gardens* or *Ideal Home*, 'suggesting expensive settings for gracious upper-class married' women and their families. Historian Ruth Adam describes Delia's class expectations: 'if you did not find the whole absorbing world of shopping, cooking, knitting and bringing up children sufficient to occupy your time and talents, it could only be because there was something the matter with you'.[32] Similar moments describing the pleasures of a domestic interior or the comfort of a room occur in all Thirkell's novels, and are not all confined to the graciously appointed country house.

Political loyalties

Thirkell's characters were defined by their social lives, rather than their political affiliations, and her pre-Second World War characters were vaguely pro-Conservative, and thus against Labour, rather than actively Tory. Her fiction did not become truly politicised until the outbreak of the Second World War. She mistrusted any imperative for change because, as Alison Light notes, 'socialists and radicals are those who "interfere" or tamper with people and their lives'.[33] But Thirkell was willing to notice the Liberals, formerly a dominant force in British politics, when she could make a class-based joke (see Chapter 8).[34]

She noted current politics through people's behaviour. Socialism first appeared as an adolescent aberration displayed by Martin Leslie in *Wild Strawberries*. In *Pomfret Towers* 'communist' is used as a synonym for skimping, short-measure, and functionally useless.[35] In *Before Lunch*, Lady Bond's character is established with politically sweeping generalisation. '"But not that young couple over at Beliers," she said. "They are Communists and the woman wears shorts and the young man has a beard."'[36] In *Summer Half* (1937) Philip Winter the Communist Classics master at Southbridge School learns to be less boring, and properly Conservative, over the course of this very funny novel. He takes any remark about socialism personally, whether about typical Communist literature,[37] or when the boys place Hacker's chameleon on his desk dressed in a red paper frill.[38] His plans for visiting Russia are foolish,[39] and his rage at rather vaguely expressed local conditions of poverty are demolished by county girls Lydia and Kate Keith, who explain the local housing and employment problems to him. They are the local Conservatives who understand and deal with local problems when they arise, upholding a feudal system that they, and Thirkell, see no reason for changing.[40] Further evidence of what Thirkell presents as typical of Conservative thinking is the political spectrum in the school, which offers 'middle' as an equally strong possibility to the left or right,[41] but 'middle' in this context means Conservative, and 'right' merely means peculiar foreign fascism.

In *O, These Men, These Men!* (1935), Thirkell creates a running joke between two immature middle-class brothers sneering about each other's extreme political affiliation, one Communist, the other a Fascist. 'Wilfred was anxious to be confirmed in his feeling that Soviet Russia was on the whole Antichrist and an underbred Mongol one at that, while George counted on Hugh to support him in his view of Hitler as a second Attila and Russia as a rather better version of the Millennium.'[42]

Notice the use of 'underbred': these barely adolescent boys are political enthusiasts using a very middle-class filter. They also have no commitment. 'George gave up a very dull evening party at which he had hoped to meet a Communist, and Wilfred ran a pencil through an entry in his diary which read, "West Kensington Blackshirt Rally, 7.45?"'[43] Thirkell caricatures these boys and their beliefs as no more than fads of the day. '"Wilfred is an English Fascist, but he can't be bothered to go to the blackshirt meetings much, because they are apt to happen on nights when he has a theatre or dance."'[44] Thirkell also diminishes the fascists by adding a frivolous aesthetic observation. Caroline admires the black shirt of the Blackshirts because it looks so becoming on the good-looking young men, but '"I don't think the low, rather deformed looking spotty sort look so well in it"'.[45]

In *Wild Strawberries* (1934) David and Martin walk through a crowd of hikers who have just got out from the London train. 'A few gave the Fascist salute',[46] which is their ironic comment on the masterful, aristocratic demeanour of Thirkell's heroes, but also a record of how the 1930s passion for nature, rambling and cycling was associated with adherents of extremist politics. In *The Brandons*, counterpointing a muddled conversation about Phalangists, Communists, and the Spanish Civil War, Mussolini is admired by foolish Mrs Grant.[47] Thirkell wrote in 1939 to Jamie Hamilton that 'what depresses me about *The Brandons* is that so many people think Mrs Grant "the funnier character" – while she is really a little bit cheap as humour'. [48] Thirkell does not grant socialism or fascism the status of a serious threat that many thought they were. Political feeling, for Thirkell, was reflected through other aspects of the way one lived.

Where people live

"Can what they call civilization be right, if people mayn't die in the room where they were born?"[49]

This outburst from Mrs Wilcox in Forster's *Howards End* (1910), to the younger and uncomprehending Margaret Schlegel, epitomises the Victorian perspective that Yates and Thirkell regarded as natural, and desirable. One should live in the house one's family had always owned, and to be driven from it was to live a rootless life. Both were very concerned in their fiction about where their characters lived, and the ownership of the land. The country house with its own grounds and servants was the ideal. The gracious townhouse was also acceptable, as long as invitations to stay in the country with friends were plentiful and frequent. For both writers the countryside was the ideal place to live, and they reinforced their fiction as pastoral romances, or comedies, with characters who belonged in the countryside that they owned. The cultural critic Raymond Williams observed that the eighteenth-century mode of pastoral also indicated an interest in developing 'a new kind of society: that of a developing agrarian capitalism'.[50] In the twentieth century, the neo-pastoral concerned itself with the country house and its estate, and reacted against modernisation in a 'militant resident Toryism'.[51]

As well as politics, Englishness is strongly evoked in the country settings of these novels. Alex Potts has noted that 'dwelling on the beauties of the English countryside is usually associated with social and political conservatism – a garden of England refuge from the tensions and ugliness of modern urban society. Here, among familiar lanes, meadows, hedgerows, copses, brooks and ponds, the embattled and weary upper-middle-class consciousness can briefly find peace and comfort'.[52] Thirkell followed the 1930s fashion for affirming in fiction what Englishness could or should look like, and created a new home in each novel. With the inconvenient and incompetent features of the Tebbens' house and the easy cool luxury of the Deans' home in *August Folly*, the expansive country home of Rushwater and the hideous pile of Pomfret Towers, she was establishing what Pierre Nora calls *lieux de mémoire*, places of memory and identity that reassure and confirm.[53] But unlike Yates, Thirkell was not sentimental, and relied on humour as much as she did a rose-tinted recollection of the past to affirm a sense of continuity in her fictional settings and places.

Some of Thirkell's businessmen buy country estates for their families to play with, in *August Folly* (1936) and *Before Lunch* (1939). They are contrasted with those longer-established families who dwell comfortably in landed estates inherited by primogeniture. Thirkell's characters own land and receive rents from it, take their responsibilities to their tenants seriously, and do their duties as landlords. John S Su notes that 'literary texts' had a 'tendency to downplay nostalgia', but Thirkell, and Yates, made nostalgia the primary emotional trigger in their novels.[54] By using nostalgia, their fiction presented a vision of the glory of British living, and of a decline already in progress. 'Only in the midst of decline can the purportedly true ideals of Britain be recognized', Su notes.[55] Barsetshire houses, in their decline and in their glory, can be read as a metaphor of both the society they adorn, and the families who live in them.

Thirkell resists the tendency that Su identifies in literary fiction of this period of undermining the idea of the estate as a 'symbol of nation'.[56] Throughout all her fiction she writes elegies for times past, not for 'Britain'.

Her recurring complaint is that things, not the country, are now not as they were. In *Wild Strawberries* (1934), the toadying serial houseguest Mr Holt laments the loss of his accustomed round of Edwardian house parties. 'These glories had diminished. The War broke up the happy life of county England. Many of the houses where he used to visit were shut or sold. Old friends and patrons were dead, dividends had fallen, game no longer reached him.'[57] Yet, despite this grumble, Barsetshire estates still prosper, because the old homes are rejuvenated by a younger, energetic generation who have a proper appreciation of times past.

Thirkell acknowledges one solution to the upkeep of impossibly expensive homes that is rarely found in contemporary fiction. David is showing Mary around the ruins of Rushmere Abbey, on his father's land.

> "We used to go in and out as we liked, but now it is a National Trust or something and costs sixpence." [...] "Afternoon, Sutton. We haven't any money. Can we come in?" Sutton touched his cap and let them in.[58]

Thirkell combines the *noblesse oblige* assumption that they too should pay their entrance fee with David's easy arrogance in assuming that, as a son of the estate, he can still come and go as he pleases. In *Before Lunch* Lord Pomfret buys the disputed strip of land called Pooker's Piece and gives it to the National Trust in memory of his wife.[59] Land should not be sold to developers, or to people like the Liberal MP and Lloyd George knight Sir Ogilvy Hibberd, whose suspect politics make his intentions suspect as well.

Continuity is also maintained by simply refusing to let go, or to let progress occur. In *Pomfret Towers* (1938) Thirkell creates Nutfield, a town that will never change.

> Most of the land around is owned by families who have remained rich enough not to be obliged to sell their estates, so the speculative builder has been kept at bay, and the town is very little larger than it was in the eighteenth century [...] The town itself is on the estate of the seventh Earl of Pomfret, who refuses to allow chain stores or cinemas, and exercises a personal and terrifying supervision over the exterior of shops and garages.[60]

Nutfield's liege lord, the crusty but endearing Earl of Pomfret, is an all-powerful safeguarder of traditional systems for living, and keeping newcomers, and modernity, and convenience for the less well paid, out.

Class

When, in *Pomfret Towers*, Sally Wicklow the agent's sister married Mr
Foster the heir to the Pomfret earldom, this caused much annoyance to
the pushing Mrs Rivers, who had rather wanted her daughter Phoebe
to be the next countess. Both young women were similarly well-born,
yet both had close relatives who earned their own living: Roddy in the
Pomfret estate office, and Mrs Rivers by her own pen (she is a vicious
satire on Thirkell's contemporary, the novelist Ann Bridge). But neither
are 'noble', in that neither have titles, and neither, for that matter, does
plain Gillie Foster who, in *Cheerfulness Breaks In* (1940), will become
the eighth Earl of Pomfret. In *Before Lunch*, the not particularly well-off
Denis Stonor is instantly registered by the reader as from the same class
as The Honourable C W Bond, son of Lord and Lady Bond, because they
went to the same prep school.[61] The signifiers of the British class system
are difficult to understand when the nomenclature of the upper classes
is actively obstructive in linking families and class strata. Thirkell was an
expert on the subject, and used her fiction to explain and instruct, and
to actively engage with the changes that were happening to the class
system in the 1930s and after, which Nicola Humble notes 'were a time
of heightened class tensions and of [an intense] class-consciousness'.[62]
Mrs Rivers's campaign of doing down Sally Wicklow as not being
suitable to marry the next earl reflects this anxiety, since it had been
perfectly possible in fiction for over a century for a nobody to marry
an earl. Sally was also not a nobody, but a thorough county woman,
more knowledgeable than anyone else about how the estate should
be run. Mrs Rivers's anxiety assures the reader of her foolishness, and
her snobbery.

Thirkell was also acting as a social historian with an approach that
appealed to readers (everyone loves a lord) rather than academics. Social
historians, especially those who focus on gender and culture, find class
a useful research lens, but, as Alan Kidd and David Nicholls say, it is
'rarely the predominant analytical tool reached for by the historian'.[63]
A way of thinking about how Thirkell uses class as a didactic tool is
offered by Len Platt, who notes that in the early twentieth century
'aristocratic status, actually declining in the real world of landed society, becomes the central absence of prestigious literary culture, a vanishing orientation point around which modernity is constructed and
judged'.[64] The depictions of the aristocracy in Thirkell's fiction, and also
of the gentry classes and the upper middle classes, legitimise the class
system by positioning the aristocratic good, unselfish and deserving

against the feckless lower classes. This is aligned to the novels' world-view that aspects of modernity (lower class) are most often bad, and the preservation of the past and old traditions (upper class) is almost always good. Platt shows that when opposing cultures take sides and intensify their opposition, literature also has to take sides, with the result that social and cultural conservation emerges as a social good.[65] There is also the question of what the upper classes had to offer. Humble notes: 'as the influence and standard of living of the upper-middle-class declined, they defended their class values with ever more intensity, and with even sparser cultural capital'.[66] If the upper classes sensed that they had less to offer a society increasingly independent of aristocratic leadership and patronage, conserving the past for the good of the nation was an obvious demonstration of the legitimacy of those classes since they had the specialist knowledge to defend and conserve their own culture.

Thirkell crushes the wrong kind of politics solely on class grounds, not because fascism is inherently offensive.

"It was a man selling little books. One of those blackshirt fellows, you know, like Puss in Boots in a polo jersey. I don't know why, but it was awfully funny." [...] "I'll tell you another funny thing about those blackshirts," said Lydia, "No-one ever knows who they are, or where they go. I mean, have you ever seen one, except standing on the pavement in waders, looking a bit seedy. You meet quite a lot of Communists and things in people's houses [...] But you never go to tea with someone and find them sitting there in their boots."[67]

Thirkell's upper-class disdain for fascist supporters is belied by the real-life upper-class enthusiasm for Sir Oswald Mosley and his beliefs. In the world of writers and intellectuals, it was the other way around. As noted in Chapter 1, successful writers of the Left tended to come from the upper classes and the public school system, whereas those of the Right were more likely not to have had those social advantages. Thirkell expresses the intellectual tendency, which would have challenged some of her readers' views.

Thirkell's attitude to the working classes was feudal. The tenants and peasants on the estates of her gentry and aristocracy were perfect because they were faithful, and they liked their conditions of squalor or amusing cottages. For Thirkell, domestic service to the gentry and working on the land were the only possible functions for the working classes. Even the servants can be class snobs. The butler Simnel in *Summer Half* is easily crushed by Colin's effortless ownership of the things that Simnel cravenly worships.[68] In *The Brandons*, Miss Miller is able to encounter Mrs Brandon's domineering head servant Nurse with perfect class positioning.

> "How do you do, Nurse," said Miss Morris, coming forward and giving her hand with what Nurse considered exactly the right nuance of deference as from an unplaced companion to a pillar of the house, equality as from employee to employee, and proper condescension as from a clergyman's daughter to a children's nurse, which won her complete approval.[69]

In *Before Lunch*, Mrs Pucken, the former kitchenmaid in Staple Park, 'knew her place to quite an alarming extent. It still pained her to think that her husband was still one of the lower class'.[70] Her assurance in her own position is supported by her complete confidence when she meets Lord Pomfret, with whom she is on comfortable but respectful terms. He rises to greet her and makes his way across a crowded room to ask after her family.[71] Such is the very attractive vision of class relations inside Thirkell's Barsetshire which has as yet suffered no failure in its country sufficiency. All this would change with the Second World War.

Money

Money and the need of it is a much more definite concern in Thirkell's fiction than in Buchan or Yates, possibly because her settings were grounded in reality rather than fantasy adventures. She borrowed Trollope's interest in the power of money on home and happiness, but with caveats. No-one is really hard-up in her pre-war novels, but there are significant differences that can rankle, or merely cause exasperation. In *Wild Strawberries* Mary is anxious to retain David Leslie's attention.

> "Never been to the Riviera?" said David, looking at her with interest.
>
> "No, nor the Lido, nor Algiers, nor winter sports."
>
> "Good Lord, we must go there some time. I know heaps of people who are always making up parties and going," he added vaguely. [...]
>
> She realised that to him an existence which did not imply at least a couple of thousand pounds a year of one's own was fantastic.[72]

David's attitude is similar to that of Dornford Yates's 1920s characters, who have financial independence as a birthright. Circumstances may take that money away, but they began with it, and so it helps to establish their class status.

The Tebbens in *August Folly* have barely enough money to maintain one home, and Richard's unpleasantness to his parents is partly due to his ignorance of how much income one needs to live comfortably like the Deans. Mrs Tebben's managing and scrimping ways are mocked in the narrative, but they represent reality for many people. Managing and scrimping ensures that the family can have even modest comforts. The impoverished Daphne Stonor, the professional secretary for hire in *Before Lunch*, is cheerfully straightforward and firm when negotiating her fees, as she has to be when working for a people who assume that everyone has a private income.[73] In Thirkell's 1930s fiction everyone has enough to live on comfortably, and those who do not are excluded: money gives class status. But during the war, and certainly when rationing begins, the spending power of the Barsetshire characters will fluctuate, and perfectly nice people whom one invites to dinner will have very little money to manage on at all.

Intertextuality

It is impossible when reading Thirkell to miss her passion for integrating literary allusion, pastiche and direct quotation into her novels. The Thirkell indexer Hazel Bell has noted 'the sheer mass of references to writers and artists, quotations from the works of literature. Thirkell's prose is dense with quotation; I know of no author who quotes more'.[74] Dickens (mostly *David Copperfield*), Shakespeare and the Bible are her most frequently used sources, followed by Trollope, Browning and Kipling. She uses quotation, adaptation and allusion to supplement the characterisation, to enhance the register, or drop it wildly into bathos for comic effect. Her characters' literary awareness can give them an extra dimension of literary *nous* that can alter as they reappear in later novels. Some of the time the quotations are there to enhance the language of the scene, for its own pleasure. Rachel Mather notes that 'if Thirkell is a snob she is a snob about language. In the comedy of manners language and speech patterns reveal social class and degree of education and culture'.[75]

Thirkell developed a running joke of parodying well-known genre conventions. In *High Rising* she drops heavily weighted hints to suggest that the story is a detective thriller (as is suitable for a novel about a detective novelist).[76] In *August Folly* she uses Mr Tebben's role as a Norse and Anglo-Saxon scholar as an opportunity for an appositely gloomy parody of *The*

Battle of Maldon.[77] In *Summer Half* she pastiches *Young Woodley* (1925), in which a young schoolmaster falls in love with the headmaster's wife. This is followed by an episode borrowing from 'Sapper's very low-brow *Bulldog Drummond*,[78] which contrasts well with her magnificent Miltonic simile in *Before Lunch*, in which two milk-white bulls representing rival young women fight it out over the unconscious heads of their admirers.[79] That episode is one of several in this bittersweet novel in which characters long for forbidden cultural delights which do not fit their public position. Mr Middleton secretly reads a thriller called *All Blood Calling* in his study, and Lord Bond is childishly excited to be given an illicit private evening of Gilbert & Sullivan. Mr Middleton himself speaks in epic periods which have an air of parodying one of the more pompous broadcasters, but his flights of puffed-up self-aggrandisement fall flat since no-one pays him any attention. By such literary devices Thirkell encouraged her readers to laugh at highbrow cultural snobbery by employing the modernist technique of intertextuality. This is slightly different from the stream of allusions noted above, since the tone of the narrative is different. Characters who know their Dickens are admirable; whereas characters with pretensions to artistic or personal authority are laughed at with the revelation of their passion for mass-market pleasures and middlebrow music.

The professional writer

Very few of Barsetshire's many authors are allowed to be proud of their literary status without justifying their success by their sales. They avoid what Cyril Connolly would later deplore as the 'enemies of promise' – domesticity and the time-consuming details of daily living – being the bar to literary achievement, as it is quite clear that almost every author in Barsetshire (and there is at least one in every novel) has the help of servants and often a spouse with money of their own. William Deecke has shown how Thirkell parodies the detective genre, with Mrs Morland and (after the war) Isabel Dale aka Lisa Bedale, later the Countess of Silverbridge.[80] Mrs Tebben is a serious writer of works on economics, an unexpectedly heavyweight intellectual whose acknowledged scholarship is undercut by her domestic fussiness and tunnel-visioned managing ways. She is modest about her writing, and effaces herself and it to the drawing-room, whereas her husband has a study to himself. The reader is expected to approve of this, and also of the modest attitude of the successful historical novelist Mrs Barton in *Pomfret Towers*, although there is implicit criticism of her for neglecting her lonely husband for her writing.

A woman writer who is not modest, diffident and unpretentious is not behaving correctly, as epitomised by Mrs Rivers, the aggressive modern author who doesn't keep her writing in its proper place. From internal evidence we can see that Mrs Rivers is a parody of the novelist Ann Bridge.[81] Bridge's pre-war plots were usually about a perfect but misunderstood older woman of artistic genius having a chaste affair with an adoring younger man in exhaustively described exotic surroundings, narrated with stifling self-importance. This model is ruthlessly parodied by Thirkell seven times in *Pomfret Towers*,[82] in which novel Mrs Rivers first appears, and again in *Before Lunch* where she brings together an older woman and a younger man in an almost tragic mutual renunciation against a backdrop of farce.[83]

Mrs Dean and Mrs Brandon are also the victims of tiresome crushes from young men, in whom they have no interest, in several novels until the mid-1950s. Mary Grover notes that

> it is through the figure of Mrs Brandon, the apparently indolent mistress of a large family house that Thirkell most subtly negotiates her middlebrow cultural status [...] Mrs Brandon's authority is closely linked to her power to assert control over what is read to her by a sequence of infatuated, aspiring male authors, who need her approval far more than she needs theirs.[84]

Mrs Brandon wields power over these men by acting as the audience whom they must please, but her attention is an impassable test, since she has no concentration or interest in their work. Avoiding the temptation to read aloud one's work to others is thus another instruction from Thirkell to authors, because to be boring is a social crime.

In contrast, discussing your work with publishers is one of the most satisfying activities an author can have, because they will be reassuring and practical, and guide you best towards the joyful certainty of selling your book. Thirkell was very strong on the practical aspects of being an author, and invented publishers for her authors with thinly veiled identities. Laura Morland publishes exclusively with Adrian Coates, from *High Rising* onwards. The Oxbridge Press (*Three Houses* was published by Oxford University Press) is the place to publish your scholarly work or school textbook,[85] but for the popular market the gentlemanly Johns and Fairfield are the men to see. Johns and Fairfield have a lucrative but often strained relationship with Mrs Rivers, and decide to take on Lord Pomfret's riotously indiscreet and successful memoirs, fending off aggressive poaching attempts by the lower-class Bungay & Bungay (who may be a disguised Hodder & Stoughton).[86]

By normalising authorship and publishing in her novels – each one has at least one aspiring or successful author – Thirkell was reflecting the democratisation of writing in Britain that Christopher Hilliard discusses as a strong aspect of social change in 1930s Britain. Thirkell's position is that the proper purpose of authorship was to please and also absorb the public's reading attention, reinforcing Hilliard's argument that 'the majority of the population read not for self-cultivation but for "escapism"'. In the 1930s 'there was an implicit but clear cultural conservatism in advising aspirants to write to entertain others rather than, say, "to express an ideal which burnt to be expressed"'.[87] Since the most satirised authors in Barsetshire do only write to express an ideal, and snoot at the idea of merely supplying entertainment, we can see that Thirkell's vision of authorship is unexpectedly in the service of readers, rather than of the author's Art. This is an interesting departure from her usual stance of resisting all change, because this is most truly her subject. She understood exactly what writers did and how, whereas, in her other concerns of country life, Thirkell was an onlooker and a passionate advocate, but not part of that life. Her personal engagement made her support a democratic cause that she would not entertain in other areas of life.

The university woman

By rejecting accusations of seriousness in her writing, Mrs Morland, and Thirkell herself, betrays her staunch anti-intellectualism. There are few professional intellectuals in Barsetshire before the war, except the subject specialists like the Tebbens, and the Classics masters of *Summer Half*. They are associated with education, and with university teaching, and are thus traditional models of the intellectual, unlike a more modern version who could be a classless, even foreign, autodidact. She admired those who went to university (which in her eyes only meant Oxford or Cambridge) and created a running joke throughout her novels about the rivalry between Paul's (a reuse of Henry Kingsley's Oxford college of St Paul's from his novel *Ravenshoe*, on whom Thirkell was an authority)[88] and Anthony Trollope's college of St Lazarus (also Oxford, from *Barchester Towers*). Thirkell pilloried Lazarus's reputation with sloppy scholarship and eccentric tendencies, although (and also because) the shy chameleon-keeping and Classics genius Hacker is to go there at the end of *Summer Half*.

Like Buchan, Thirkell expressed annoyance and distaste for the university woman and the independence, even the feminism, that she represented. In *Wild Strawberries* (1934) the 'university woman' Joan Stevenson is asked to lunch by David Leslie and insists on paying for her share (a breach of manners). David thus enjoys taking her to the most expensive restaurants he knows until she admits that she cannot afford to eat at his level of income.[89] When David invites both Joan and Mary to lunch, Mary resents Joan for attracting David's interest, and also for her background. 'University women were always hard – unsympathetic and conceited as well.'[90] Miss Stevenson is affectedly intellectual, and also pointedly professional, another aspect of education for women that Thirkell was often ready to criticise.

Mrs Tebben, in *August Folly* (1936), is in Thirkellian terms an admirable product of the universities, since she has used her intellect to continue to write important work, while maintaining her duties as a housewife and mother. Her modesty about her intellectual work, and her focus on her domestic role, are approved of in the story. But, as she is an incompetent housewife, a desperate nagging mother and a catastrophically bad cook, we cannot escape the conclusion that she is doggedly working hard and badly at the job she is least suited to do. If Mrs Tebben settled down to write full-time, thus doing her 'real' job, in the terms that Dorothy L Sayers debates in her feminist university novel *Gaudy Night* (1935), would the Tebben family be any better off? It is unlikely, since authorship of economics works is not an obviously lucrative profession. Mrs Tebben would be an excellent don, since she need never go near a kitchen, her scholarship would adorn any college, and she is an unexpectedly good substitute moral tutor for the tiresome Betty Dean. This adolescent bore is insistent about 'going up', i.e. going to university, and is given much to think about when Mrs Tebben punctures her hero-worship of a very unsuitable role model. Mrs Tebben is far more than just a comic character, but as a representative of the university woman, she is an unusual anomaly in Barsetshire, which Thirkell reserves for domestic women and matriarchs.

From the later 1930s Thirkell's tone changes about the university woman. She creates the monstrously gracious Miss Pettinger, headmistress of Barchester High School for Girls, in *Summer Half* (1937), who will become one of her most delightfully awful characters. Her first appearance is officious. 'Miss Pettinger then broke in upon a quiet talk that Everard was having with Mr Birkett about the Lower Fourth, and drew them both into the conversation with the easy tact of a university woman.'[91] We see much more of Miss Pettinger and her graceful antithesis Miss Sparling, in *The Headmistress*, in 1944, but for now it is enough to notice that Thirkell had found social comedy that would support her anti-intellectual bent by combining a critique of modern women's education with bad manners of the modern age.

Cinema

> The inter-war period was one in which the English began to see images of themselves and their cultural behaviour – gestures, bodily movements and facial expressions – 'at the pictures' and in magazine photography as never before.[92]

Alison Light reminds us that the cinema would reinforce differences and similarities between social groups. Buchan completely ignores the ubiquity of the cinema in modern life, but it was relished by Thirkell. The difference between their approaches was that Buchan's characters were out to save civilisation from the forces of anarchy, in which the amusements of daily life were not relevant, whereas Thirkell wrote about everyday life for county people by which means anarchy, in the form of social change, was resisted. Buchan had himself helped to create the fantasy world of romance for cinema consumption. His 1910 novel *Prester John* was apparently filmed in 1920, *Huntingtower* (1922) in 1927, and *The Thirty-Nine Steps*, famously, in 1935, and later in 1959 and 1978.[93] Films like these were seen from the shilling seats in Thirkell's novels, an easy alternative to reading books, by the younger and less scholastic characters who would seek to impress each other with their cinema-minded references. In *O, These Men, These Men!* George and Wilfred show signs of moving their devotion from Communism and Fascism to the cinema by adopting the vocabulary of the cinema detective.[94] Their easy assimilation of the moving image was one of the speedy aspects of modern life that the older, more conservative generations found less easy to emulate. The adults in that novel do actually go to the cinema, in a rare contemporary description of what it was like to sit in a cinema theatre in a group, to watch the film and be emotionally affected by the music.[95] Adolescent Thirkell characters who ought to know better speak airily of 'going on the films' as if this were a viable career option – Stella Gibbons's *Cold Comfort Farm* (1932) satirises this as well – which shows how Thirkell regarded such a choice.

The lure by which young Barsetshire is attracted to the cinema is Glamora Tudor, a film star in which to sublimate their hopes and dreams for decades. She first appears in 1939, 'the one that they called in Hollywood "The Woman Who Cannot Love"', playing Princess Alix in *Moonlight Passion*.[96] In *Before Lunch* Miss Tudor can be seen in *The*

Flames of Desire, 'when she told wicked Lord Mauleverer that it was really the Duke that she loved'.[97] Both these descriptions come from the free indirect speech of servants, a superior parlour maid and a scatty temporary kitchenmaid, showing that Thirkell sees cinema inhabiting the mass-market entertainment niche occupied only ten years earlier by the romantic novelette she parodies in *O, These Men, These Men!* While the more knowledgeable Hilary Grant notices that some films were made outside Hollywood, Thirkell reserves her affectionate scorn, as if for a vulgar but endearingly cheerful new neighbour, for the Hollywood film worshipped by those who know no better (see Chapter 8).

Controlling the child

> Laura had once offered to edit a book called *Why I Hate My Children*, but though Adrian Coates had offered every encouragement, and every mother of her acquaintance had offered to contribute, it had never taken shape.[98]

Most of the social changes Thirkell addressed in her novels were old traditions under attack by the forces of modernity, and she fought these using nostalgia as a weapon. Yet there was one significant area in which, as a woman writer, and as a mother, Thirkell did not conform to social expectations. She had the audacity to write about children unsentimentally, because she had brought up three sons and knew the worst. 'When, for about a quarter of a century you have been fighting strong young creatures with a natural bias towards dirt, untidiness and carelessness, quite unmoved by noise, looking upon loud, meaningless quarrels and abuse as the essence of polite conversation, oblivious of all convenience and comfort but their own, your resistance weakens.'[99]

Her depiction of public schoolboys and the infants of the nannied classes was an expression of her need to control and contain elements inimical to her ideal society. In *High Rising* (1933) boys, in the mass, and as individuals, are the light relief in this novel: categories of how Thirkell used them could include 'boys' enjoyment of chaos', 'tiresome-ness of', 'wickedness of', 'the mother's experience of', and the 'obtuse-ness of'. Tony Morland's exploits and his mother's struggles can be seen as a cruelly unequal battle between the forces of chaos and those of civilisation.

The most sustained relationship Mrs Morland has with her son is while she is trying to contain his excesses. This simple formula, repeated in all successful schoolchild stories of the period, opposes the parents, who represent controlling society, to the anarchic child. This pattern is also seen in the oppositions of fairy tales, romance and quest literature. The reader is invited to participate vicariously, and the entertainment derives from how the resulting chaos is handled. Thirkell's particular cleverness with this trope was to range Tony as the force of chaos <u>within</u> adult society, and to disrupt it from the inside, thus presenting questions and challenges to societal codes, and to affirm those codes that Thirkell particularly wanted to be maintained. Tony is a locus for parental ambivalence. 'He suffered from what his mother called a determination of words to the mouth, and nothing except sleep appeared to check his flow of valueless conversation.'[100] But in sleep Tony is enchanting, immobile and contained, and thus a perfect child.

In *Wild Strawberries* the characters include Agnes Graham's three children, looked after by two nannies, and her mother, Lady Emily, who is indulging in an affectionately described chaos of class-based privileged behaviour that will, after the war, become dementia. Lady Emily is beginning to play the child herself, and requires her own 'nanny', Miss Merriman, who is one of the strongest characters of control and command that Thirkell was to create. Agnes's idiocy over her children is ridiculed (she is one of those Thirkell mothers whom Nicola Humble has described as 'benignly eccentric'[101]), but she is also a perceptive daughter, assuming the matriarchal role without fuss or resentment as her own mother loses control. The Graham children are barely present as personalities in the plot, since they are bodies to be fed, cleaned and taken for walks, and sometimes removed from the pond.

The disruptiveness of Lady Emily becomes an important and continuing trope until her death after the war. She is continually described as 'enchanting' and a 'spirit of love', but she is also a domineering, possessive, controlling and erratic presence, aggravating and maddening the reader who does not enjoy eccentricity as a character asset. Her entourage is equivalent to the nursery staff of an infant at the same social level. Lady Emily's increasing obliviousness to the wishes of others is a strong example of the infantilisation of adults that Thirkell used to make the importance of controlling childish behaviour a metaphor for the maintenance of societal codes.

Tony Morland reappears in *Summer Half,* in which he attends a private school where boys of age 11 and upwards are educated and boarded.

"One of the strongest primal impulses known to humanity is to get away from, or get rid of, its offspring. Every new child is a shattering blow to its parents' privacy and independence. They will pay pretty well anything to get rid of their children for long periods in every year. The older the child, the more parents will pay."[102]

Their teachers are unsentimental, much like a good nanny, and so the private boarding school is shown as the ideal environment for the eccentricities of the child approaching adolescence. By separating the children from the adults, rational adult life was able to carry on, while the potential disruption and chaos of the child, or the infantilised adult, was, temporarily, contained. Containment is the most satisfactory solution Thirkell can see for the problem of uncontrollable society.

In *The Brandons*, Thirkell returned to the idea of infantilising adults by the simple idea of retaining the under-occupied Nurse in a family where the children have long since become adult, but who still live at home. The inherent humour in the tyranny of family servants who cannot be withstood comes from how Mrs Brandon allows her staff to fuss over her like a child, because she revels, without shame, in comfort, and because by allowing them to nanny her, they gain professional and emotional satisfaction. A class dimension to a social duty of care is introduced with the Thatcher family from Grumper's End. The ignorant Mrs Thatcher has an indeterminate number of children rolling around in squalor in her filthy kitchen and yard, and her elder daughters have their own 'children of shame', who roll around similarly with their young uncles and aunts. The future wife of the vicar treats them all as a competent nanny would treat the neglected children in a gentry household, showing that she is the ideal occupant of the rectory by her management skills.

The more resources available to the family, the more controlled the child. The sign of a poor family, or an ill-managed one, is where the child or children is not controlled (as with Richard Tebben's shocking manners), or even clean, as with the Thatchers. Thirkell consistently attributes bad behaviour in adolescents or young adulthood to the uncontrolled or uncontrolling behaviour of their parents. A correct bringing-up is crucial for the maintenance of this society, even into old age, as we see with Lady Emily. Thirkell only permits parents to break these rules, by taking over the care of the children on the nanny's day off, as a treat for a very motherly mother.

While Thirkell's approach in her pre-war fiction was quite different to that of Buchan, and, seen in the next chapter, of Yates, her concerns were the same. Her concentration on the upper classes and their marriages expresses the importance of stability and healthy growth for this social stratum. Her attention paid to the home, and the families in it, demonstrates that social critique was possible, and devastatingly effective, because of its limited settings. Her use of upper-class characters delivered coded messages about how one expressed emotion, shock, disagreement, or unhappiness, with appropriately modulated reticence. Her novels were conduct manuals in all but name, instructive for all classes and guides for the unconfident. At a sociological level, her depictions of the upper and gentry classes legitimise these classes for the good they do and the traditions they represent. But she was not wholly in accordance with the expectations one might have for a woman of her class and rigid attitudes. Her use of child control as a metaphor for social maintenance could be merely authoritarian, but was in actuality an expression of solidarity and sympathy for struggling parents. She was also a passionate advocate of the right to be an author, an uncommon encouragement in a ferociously crowded market by a very competitive practitioner.

6
Aggressive Reactions:
Yates in the 1930s and 1940s

The 1930s brought about a crisis in Yates's personal life. His biography gives an account of the difficulties in the Mercer marriage, and the conditions under which Yates and his wife lived in Pau, and divorced in 1933.[1] After interviewing Bettine Mercer in 1976 Tom Sharpe published a long article in the *Sunday Times* discussing Yates and the divorce. This includes further information on Yates's life and character, including the long letter from Yates to his wife that told her why he was about to divorce her. Some of those who had known the Mercers personally disputed Sharpe's interpretation of events and motives in Yates's life, but the article re-established Yates's reputation posthumously for those who otherwise had never heard of him. The divorce was undoubtedly traumatic for both parties, and devastating for their son, Richard, aged 13 at the time. Yates forbade Bettine from seeing her son again, or risk losing the maintenance he offered to pay her.[2] In 1934 Yates dedicated *Storm Music*, his first book to be published after the divorce, to Richard, but Richard, whom his mother described as having a 'sensitive nature', seems to have suffered from his father's behaviour. Bettine feared Yates's behaviour to their son: 'crushing him and driving him and shutting him up if he says anything he does not want to hear'.[3] As an adult Richard Mercer lived as a recluse in Denmark, and was cut out of his father's will.[4] Yates remarried in 1934.

These sad facts inform our reading of Yates's novels from the mid-1930s. He systematically deleted Bettine from the dedications of six of his books as they were reprinted (see Chapter 1).[5] In 1936 Yates published a new set of Berry stories, *And Berry Came Too*. He tells his readers that these were set shortly after *Berry & Co*, that is, in the very early 1920s. In these linked stories Boy is not married, and Adèle no longer exists (even though she had been a leading character in many novels and stories up to *Adèle & Co* in 1931). Instead, Boy flirts easily through these stories with an English girl (Bettine, and Adèle, were American) called Perdita, the 'lost one'. These stories are Yates's Canute-like attempt to rewrite his lost youth or even his lost marriage, with a different woman, his strong feelings clearly apparent in the mood and tone. In another story, 'Missing, Believed Killed' (1941), he reused some of the facts of his own life in a murder mystery in which a famous thriller novelist is found guilty of having buried the body of his wife, with whom he claimed he had never got on, in the garage inspection pit underneath his treasured Rolls Royce. Yates too liked a Rolls, and the novelist in the story was also obsessive about order in the home, one of Yates's own traits. The story is clearly about admissions of guilt, trial by adverse newspaper publicity and rewriting the past to make a new story. Yates's personal attention to the process of serving divorce papers on his wife is reused in *Lower Than Vermin*, over 15 years later.[6]

He was highly successful in the 1930s – the 1943 reprint of *Jonah & Co* (1922) gives these print runs: 'Reprinted 10,000 August 1930 / Reprinted 10,000 February 1933 / Reprinted 8,000 December 1935 / Reprinted 8,000 March 1939'. These are high sales for a book of stories over ten years old. The most evident themes that we can see Yates returning to in the 1930s and the 1940s are what he wanted his readers to feel about punishment and justice, class and service, and about how women should be controlled. He published ten novels (if the linked short stories of *And Berry Came Too* are counted as a novel) between 1930 and 1945. Apart from *Period Stuff*, which is a miscellany of previously published short stories, and the bucolic comedy and high farce of *And Berry Came Too*, Yates's novels of the 1930s and early 1940s are all thrillers, which William Vivian Butler describes as a classical 1930s genre, especially in fiction magazines.

> In the thirties [...] thanks to the circulating-library bookshelves [...] and thanks, also, to a smallish but fantastically prolific group of writers [...] public interest in thriller heroes was at its peak.[7]

Yates was, of course, one of the writers who supplied this market, and he published at least five of these novels as serials in magazines. Thrillers were now Yates's oeuvre, a long way in tone from his glory days of poodle-faking in his post-First World War short stories. He was also a market leader. After seeing Yates do very well with eight thrillers with Hodder & Stoughton, Ward, Lock & Co welcomed Yates back in 1936 with *And Berry Came Too*, and were rewarded thereafter with the rest of Yates's output.

The language of names

His thrillers are all Ruritanian in setting, and – excepting *Adèle and Co* – are narrated by grim-voiced, serious young strongmen who fall shatteringly in love with the woman in peril. The settings are his invented principality of Riechtenburg, or the neighbouring and real-life countries of Austria and Carinthia. Yates enjoyed exaggerating the formality of Austrian manners in his fiction, extending social usage to almost any aspect of his story that he wanted, to reinforce the Ruritanian archaism of the settings. These stories derive from the *fin-de-siècle* Victorian male quest romance model, which invokes chivalry as well as adventure, and a Victorian veneration for royal houses. This model was not necessarily stuffy, since the original Ruritanian novel, *The Prisoner of Zenda*, had humour and pace, and lightness in its villain and hero alike, but Yates's narrative personality is a leaden weight. Richard Usborne admits that 'there is a pomp and pedantry about Chandos's style that perhaps suits the solemn, humourless man [Chandos] who is supposed to be writing them'.[8] The vocabulary is so stately, and lifeless, that it disappears into its own syntax, leaving only faint traces of its original resonance. This linguistic taxidermy makes the sentiments in the story feel old-fashioned, but contrasts unexpectedly and effectively with the fast pace. 'Yates is writing a fast-moving action story but his language forces you to take it steadily and to consider and savour what he is saying.'[9]

The dialogue of the Riechtenburgian and Carinthian peasantry – ostensibly translated from German into the narrator's English – has a heavy poetry of its own that Yates achieved by using an Elizabethan prose style by way of Maurice Hewlett. One of his Austrian peasant characters says: '"and there," said he, "you will find me if ever you stand in need, for from now I am at your service by day as by night"'.[10] Such archaisms in syntax reinforce the Arcadian setting that is a fantasy existence not in the real world. On occasion Yates would deliberately ignore modern usage when he preferred an older, now extinct meaning of a word, and the effect can be unfortunately risible: 'enlarge' for 'release', and 'uncover' for 'to take his hat off'. His obliviousness to such comic juxtapositions – very odd for a writer so finely aware of the possibilities for humour in language – gives an unfortunate sense of self-importance, and pomposity.

As in the 1920s, Yates's 1930s place-names provide an antique resonance from the antiquity of the words that he uses for villages, fields and castles. In *Storm Music*: Plumage, Lass, Annabel, Witchcraft, Sabbot, Starlight. In *And Berry Came Too*: Broomstick, Hammercloth, Shepherd's

Pipe, Brooch, Cockcrow, Thistledown, Ribbon, Bloodstock, Coven, Quality, Warfare, Relish. In *She Painted Her Face*: Brief, Tracery, Gabble, Raven, Usage, Palfrey. These names are clearly private jokes made by Yates for the pleasure of language used audaciously and strikingly. Few are plausible as place-names for English or Austrian locations. We are mildly unsettled by the exotic effect of foreignness, and the sense that these stories are set in a strange culture, where normal rules may not apply. Yates's attraction to the fantasy mode that created *The Stolen March* in 1926 had not been quelled.

Europeanness as a literary and cultural presence, as well as a political context, is relevant here, as Yates's Europe was a playground, an Arcadia for escape and adventure. Europe was only a setting for his fiction, not a culture: the French, Austrians, Carinthians and Riechtenburgians that his characters encounter are barely foreign at all, since they all conform to British norms of behaviour, and obey the English heroes unquestioningly. On occasion it can be hard to remember that Yates's thriller heroes are human: they are machines of muscle with prehistoric ideas about justice and revenge that would make them hard to integrate socially in the modern world. Of course, that was the point. Yates was not writing a modern world, he was writing gloriously tailored fantasies that invited his readers to share his social views, and enjoy the breathtaking skill of his plotting. Realism was not expected.

Read against the characters in novels published by his contemporaries, for instance Nancy Mitford, Evelyn Waugh, Rosamond Lehmann or Leslie Charteris, Yates's protagonists are old-fashioned. Even in 'Period Stuff', a short story set in the Second World War and first published in 1943, cocktails are drunk as if they are a new invention, and the young male and female protagonists call each other formally by their surnames until they are on the point of admitting their love for each other. Taking this social step towards requesting and admitting intimacy is gruelling, for such is the rigour of their manners. '"You'll never know what that cost me – to use your name." "I did it somehow," said Thane, "but I nearly died."'[11] Yates's point with this formality is to insist that even when the world and its standards are collapsing, the right kind of people will maintain the right standards of behaviour. He says in a Preface to this collection that these stories belong to 'an era which has come to an end' and that he 'shall always remember the era in question with affection'.[12] It is not only the upper classes who hold to these standards in Yates's fictions; the servants, too, are decorously perfect in Edwardian manners, and '"all they're afraid of is change"'.[13] This attitude colours all of Yates's fiction.

Blood relations

There are strong bonds of homosocial loyalty and admiration between men in the thrillers, plainly and devotedly expressed. The cousins Jonah Mansel and Berry and Boy Pleydell are unquestioning loyal comrades for over thirty years. Yates uses the model of Jonah the older man with the brains and his younger acolytes Chandos and Hanbury as the brawn in *Blind Corner* and *Perishable Goods*. In *Safe Custody* and *Storm Music* he developed the model with blood relationships: John Ferrers and his older cousin Hubert Constable, and John Spencer and his cousin Geoffrey Bohun. Women are won as marriage partners in these stories where male cousins are the protagonists, and their honour and reputations are extremely important for plot purposes, often exaggeratedly so. I am not suggesting that there is a secret homosexual subtext in Yates's fiction, but these men's open devotion to each other is most often between blood relations.

This blood relationship between protagonists can be read as a metaphor for trustworthiness and comradeship. Given the medieval character of the traps and architectural puzzles by which these cousins are often tested, their cousinship is also a tribal or clannish bond that will be stronger than any others. This is reflected in the villains' associations that are constructed by hate and vengeance in contrast to unquestioned family loyalty. Family loyalties become more pronounced when the group is besieged by aggressive invading forces. Buchan's heroes were all of the same 'totem', a loose band of friends and acquaintances who formed different partnerships across novels to suit the circumstances and skills needed. Yates directs his resources more tightly inwards, withdrawing his heroes to castles and isolated forest and mountain landscapes where they, like Buchan's protagonists, resist the forces of anarchy and maintain the values of civilisation in a focused battle between symbolic individuals. Even the Pleydells follow this pattern: by withdrawing to isolated family homes they consolidate resources and forces, and resist threats. The Berry stories of the 1930s show how victimised they are: as representatives of their class, for their money, for their mode of speaking and behaving, and in law. The stories are about their overcoming of adversity, and so the reader is induced to feel sympathy, through Furbank's idea of sentimental disproportion (see Chapter 3). Sympathy normally goes to an underdog, but here the reader gives it willingly to a group of highly privileged people with all possible resources.

In the Berry books, Berry is married to his cousin Daphne, and they and Boy, Daphne's younger brother, are cousins to Jonah and Jill Mansel.[14]

These tightly bonded cousins also don't have children, and are living in a consciously infantilised world (see Chapter 3). This would explain the atmosphere of perpetual holiday and playtime with friends, and the irrelevance of most adult responsibilities that the Berry stories invoke.

In *Adèle & Co* Jill is the mother of pre-school twins, but barely seems to consider them as her responsibility, behaving towards them as if they are toys or pets. The children are lovingly referred to by the narrator as the Fauns: toy baby animals for the family's amusement. When the Pleydells rent a house in northern France to carry out their private investigation of the jewel theft, Daphne is the one to think about bringing Jill's children over from Rome, not Jill herself.

> "I'll tell you what," said my sister. "Why don't you wire for the Fauns? This place would be perfect for them and they can go on to [the Pleydells' Hampshire home] as soon as the painters are out." [...]
>
> "Shall I?" said Jill. "I'd love to. Nanny's splendid at trains and we could meet them in Paris and bring them down."[15]

Jill's apparent disconnection with her own children is striking. Daphne is also the one to take them back to Hampshire, while Jill stays in France watching the progress of the investigation. The other Pleydells play occasionally with the children, but Jill is affectionately uninterested. Her absent-minded asking of permission above can be explained by Daphne's role as group hostess, and as Jill's mother figure, but it also suggests that Yates did not know how to write relationships with children except as adorable temporary toys. In *She Fell Among Thieves* the children are wired for to come to France to entertain Jill and Jenny, but that is their only other appearance. It is a mystery why Yates gave Jill children at all. They are reported in *The House that Berry Built* (1945) as having been killed in a plane crash with their father, thus releasing Jill to marry her cousin Boy, which results in two married couples in this extraordinarily tight-knit group of five first cousins.[16]

To live with one's devoted cousins is to always have playmates, supporters and protectors, and to have a multiplicity of resources on call in moments of emergency. Adopting futuristic imagery, is it too much to consider the Pleydell and Mansel characters as a collective mind, or characters who share a common personality since their function is to be a unit? Their only moments of internal dissent are when they are roused by Berry's clowning; otherwise they think, speak and act with a single purpose ('she spoke for us all'[17]), and appear to be socially self-sufficient, though always glad to welcome visitors into their circle. The family group at home represents an Eden peopled by individual aspects of the perfect male and female. Their homes in the different novels, in England and in France, are an extension of the group's integrity (an Englishman's home is his castle). When violence is done to the group, and possessions (usually jewels) are taken, they are recovered in a group effort. Leaving this magical, protected space is risky, and undesirable. They do not allow others to threaten the home's integrity (or its views, or the quality of its neighbours). Such defensive mechanisms to protect a locus of identity that is a metaphor for England, or Britain, make sense when the protectors of the home are one family, one identity.

Consanguinity can be a threat to Yates's women. Most Yates thriller heroines are threatened by their close relations who want their title, family inheritance or property. The Grand Duchess Leonie of Riechtenburg is battling her cousin Paul in *Blood Royal* and in *Fire Below*; Countess Olivia Haydn of *Safe Custody* and Countess Helena Yorick of *Storm Music* are pitted against their male cousins; Jenny of *She Fell Among Thieves* is threatened by her own mother; Lady Elizabeth Virgil of *She Painted Her Face* is fighting her uncle and cousin. The aristocratic elements are a natural consequence of the Ruritanian plot, which, as Raymond P Wallace has noted, requires a 'wicked uncle' adversary,[18] but also owe something to the useful familial context in which conflicts over inheritance and family secrets must arise. Even the Pleydells have this problem: they have yet more cousins to whom they do not speak, due to a disagreement over ownership of the family home and heirloom portraits. The Pleydells recover the hidden family silver by outwitting their cousins through farce, instead of the muscle and drama of the thrillers, a neat doubling by Yates of his thriller plot.[19] The insistence in the novels of self-sufficient characters in a secure and uninterrupted arena (the police are rarely involved) speaks to Yates's very conservative desire for the gentleman's right to pursue his own business privately, without state interference or the eyes of the world upon him. Keeping things in the family is as much a requirement of his characters as the right to mete out justice without officious intervention by the law. In such equivocal circumstances, perhaps it is better that one's confederates are also one's blood relations.

This Publican: social terrorism

Before I discuss Yates's use of punishment and justice in his thrillers, I want to spend some time on what I consider to be his most remarkable novel, *This Publican* (1938). Yates is writing here in his most deliberately strident terms about the evil that some women do, expressed at length and in excruciating detail, always through the vulnerabilities of social usage, Yates's particular bête noire. The title comes from the Bible, in Luke 18.10–11: 'I thank thee that I am not, as other men, extortioners, unjust, adulterers, or even as this publican'. A modern translation of the Authorised Version gives 'tax-gatherer' for 'publican', so the social sense is clear: someone who takes money, by the law, but possibly also without heed for human decency. It is a novel of social violence about a worldly woman victimising her gentleman husband. It clearly channels Yates's anger, possibly at the wrongs he felt he had been done by his former wife, but more probably the wrongs he could see now, in the 1930s, made possible by laxity in morals, and slackness in class respect. The novel points out with vicious clarity the vulnerabilities in the social codes that Yates imagined were still the norm in British society: his vision of the ideal world was always Victorian-Edwardian. By pointing out vulnerabilities Yates was warning of the strangers at the gate (in very class-conscious terms), but also the terrible damage that the infiltrator within could do to a complacent society. Buchan had been warning about the thin line between civilisation and anarchy since 1900, and European fascism since 1933 in *A Prince of the Captivity* and *The House of the Four Winds*, but he was looking outward. Thirkell's novels from this period – *Summer Half* and *Pomfret Towers* – are also concerned with the maintenance of class boundaries, but she and Yates shared a socially based concern for the integrity of conservative Britain, while other commentators were looking anxiously at Germany.

This Publican was also eagerly received as a woman's novel. Yates arranged its serialisation in the British monthly magazine *Woman's Journal*, under the rather more comprehensible title of 'She Knew Not Mercy', from November 1937 to March 1938.[20] There is also a personal interpretation. Yates wrote *This Publican* about a hapless man evilly deceived by a ruthless gold-digger, whose life is made happy again by the love of a good woman. He had already written a powerful indictment of a bullying wife, the repulsive Mrs Carey Below of 'Peregrine' (1924), published in *As Other Men Are*: *This Publican* is an extended version of the same plot.

The illegitimate teenage actress Elsie Baumer has murdered an innocent girl and stolen her name. As Rowena Howard she marries David Bohun, scion of an ancient house. He is too gentle and too gentlemanly to stand up to his wife's greater mastery of how to manipulate society against him, for her own gain. The peculiarity of this novel is in how vicious it is, since Yates tests his readers' emotions by extreme events in the plot that break social codes for maximum effect. Rowena's main target is the public manners of gentlemen. As she violates social codes again and again Yates establishes the rules on what one should and should not do in good society, thus enforcing a didactic message on the readers of the novel through the shock effect of its plot. Thirkell did the same, but her aim was comedy through shame, rather than public mortification.

Yates uses metaphor and allusion to express the inexpressible, and uses inferences to produce high drama. Rowena sacks two servants who have worked for David's family all their lives, and lies to them that this was his decision. She replaces them with a Eurasian couple, and so the housemaid leaves as well (since no decent Yates servant will work with non-whites). Rowena does not wait for the servants to leave the room before telling David his offences of the day. She speaks perfect French, but it is the French of the gutter and the bar, not that of a gentlewoman, and because David speaks French poorly (a very British trait), he cannot tell the difference. When David meets Helen, Rowena changes her plan from simply bullying her husband, which is not getting her anywhere, to manoeuvring David and Helen into an affair from which Rowena can demand a very public divorce, thus ruining them both socially, and gaining her all David's money.

Elsie/Rowena represents not a type, but an incoming wave of have-nots and gold-diggers who can no longer be restrained by the old social codes. Another character typifies Rowena's circle: 'the future Countess of Churt would be able to boast that she had been the daughter of a usurer, the wife of a book-maker and the mistress of the leader of a band'.[21] This off-stage character is presented as a stern warning to society, typical of the social infiltrators who Yates feared were preying on good society and rotting it from the inside. The climactic set-piece of social terrorism occurs when Rowena arrives at David's club, sobbing for all to see, and falls on her knees to beg him not to leave her for Helen.[22] Naturally he has to resign from the club, since he has been publicly shamed in multiple ways, and Helen's name has been publicly traduced: all Rowena's objectives have been achieved. But the real power of this scene comes not so much from David's humiliation and impotent rage at his entrapment, but at Rowena's calculated attack where a gentleman would feel most secure, in the sanctuary of the gentleman's club. David now has no home left to him, since Rowena has appropriated everything.

It should be remembered that Yates was depicting a society he did not inhabit himself. He barely socialised in Pau, where he lived, and certainly did not know contemporary London society except, possibly, through cinema, newspapers and magazines, very much like his readers. His fixed views produced a fossilised image of how society had been, and what it was becoming, and this was presented as a lesson for readers to absorb. Upholding the correct social codes was only part of the message. Another lesson learned from the ghastly example of the destruction of David Bohun is that society must be on its guard, that the gentlemanly and middle classes must beware of infiltrators into their class territory because they will not recognise them. No-one defends David in the club scene because no-one present expects or even suspects such an attack in such a way. They behave in predictable ways, which Rowena had used to her own spectacular advantage.

The most interesting aspect of *This Publican* is that Rowena is not punished for her crimes. For a novelist so concerned with the restoration of order in all his other fiction, it is uncharacteristic that he allowed Rowena to continue her career into blackmail and other unknown horrors. It is telling that, having borrowed a text from the Bible to reinforce the moral force of his novel in the title, Yates did not use the remainder of the verse. The Pharisee gives thanks for not being as vile as the sinful publican, and also points out to God how well-behaved he has been. Yet the publican

> beat upon his breast, saying "God have mercy on me, sinner that I am". It was this man, I tell you, and not the other, who went home acquitted of his sins. For everyone who exalts himself shall be humbled; and whoever humbles himself shall be exalted.[23]

In the novel Rowena is free to continue sinning, while David and Helen become humble in their happy life together.

Rowena functions as a dreadful warning to society, and is only unmasked because she is found to have a Jewish and foreign lover, and her original name suggests that she too is Jewish. These details are unnecessary to the plot, and are characteristic of Yates's demonisation techniques, which reflect the prevalent anti-Semitism of the period. Anti-Semitism was endemic as a background feature of casual speech in fiction by most authors of the period, some using it more deliberately than others. Buchan has become a by-word for anti-Semitism on misunderstood evidence, which I have written about elsewhere,[24] and there are unreflective scatterings of it in Thirkell's fiction and in her private letters (and see also Chapter 7). It is occasional but not common in Yates's fiction, and most often occurs in the Berry world. Berry, and Boy as narrator, are unwarrantedly unpleasant to named or unnamed Jewish characters because they are invaders, either of terri-tory (see the monstrous German-Jewish Mr Dunkelsbaum of *Berry & Co*), or of cultural property. In *And Berry Came Too* (1936), Yates mixes implied homosexuality with anti-Semitism in the briefly encountered characters of Mr Stench the kingpin antiques dealer and his 'willowy, pale-faced' underling, and makes anti-Semitic jibes about bidders in an auction house.[25] But Mr Stench is acknowledged to be an expert in his subject, and is deferred to by Berry, who follows the dealer's judgement on a piece of furniture, the highest accolade a tradesman could be given by Yates. It doesn't remove the stain, to use a Yatesian term, of the anti-Semitism, but it is an unexpected nuance in the depiction of the character which is worth noting in this period, and in Yates's defence. In Yates's wartime collection *Period Stuff*, anti-Semitism is, if anything, more apparent, which says much about the relaxing of any restraints he may have put on his views about Jews hitherto, and an extraordinary insensitivity to the fact that Jews were suffering so much in the war. By using anti-Semitism as a new slur on Rowena, Yates was simply using the worst insult he could find for that character, within the rules of his own understanding of what should be punished, and how.

Punishment and justice

Yates's attitude to punishment and justice has much to do with his for-mer profession as a barrister. As a best-selling author, he had to provide the reader with entertainment as well as cunningly planned justice. William Vivian Butler notes that 'almost any reader can revel in a crime, so long as it is made clear that it is someone's else's punishment'.[26] But the punishment must still abide by certain codes, and the codes of a gentleman and British fair play were more important in a foreign land than law. In *Fire Below*, Chandos understands how his gentlemanly codes will disadvantage him when he goes to untie Greig, a villain who is out to kill him. 'I must free the man, of course. That went without saying. And when the man was free, I must give him some law. If he did not run, I must stand back the width of the road...'. But this gentle-manly planning will not work, for a lady's future is at stake. Greig must die so that his unwilling wife Marya can be free. 'It seemed that I must play the butcher.'[27] Even though the servant Rowley is willing to kill Greig for him,[28] Chandos the gentleman must take the responsibility and set the lady free with his own hands.

This assumption of the extra-judicial right of a gentleman to sentence and execute has been seen before, in *Perishable Goods*, when Jonah, Bell and Rowley quietly murdered a minor villain for the crime of handling Adèle's blouse. The locations are very similar: in the backwoods of Austria any man can be an executioner and the police will never find out. In *An Eye For A Tooth* (1943) Mansel is particularly high-handed about taking on the job of the Austrian police without even asking. He comes across a body in the road, and immediately develops an elaborate plan to lure the killers into a position where he can persecute them with false telegrams, steal their passports and papers, and engage in armed conflict as well as outright murder. His motivation is simple: '"the law would have done no good, so we've taken it into our hands"'.[29] At the end of the novel, this extraordinary freedom of action is explained by Mansel as part of his role as a kind of extra-legal British law enforcer. When he meets his contact in Scotland Yard, he can't take Chandos with him to brief the police on their actions. '"He is within the law, and I am without the law; he is the right hand and I, sometimes, am the left: and the right hand must never know what the left hand does."'[30] This regularisation of Mansel's habit of involving himself in the political and criminal worlds of other countries simply allows him to continue carrying out executions at will.

At the beginning of *She Fell Among Thieves* (1935) Mansel justifies Yates's increasing habit of allowing his thriller heroes to act outside the law rather than helping the police: '"It must be obvious to you that, because of his birth and education, the range of the ordinary detective is strictly limited"'.[31] Mansel means that the police detective is lower class, thus never able to detect crime as conducted by the upper classes, and for this special men are needed whose activities the police will ignore, but will coming running to support as soon as the malefactor is found. Detective novelists had reinforced this attitude by making the police detective a man of the upper classes (Ngaio Marsh), or by giving the upper-class amateur detective the full confidence of the police by his very brilliance (Dorothy L Sayers). Leslie Charteris allowed The Saint to join the police in *She Was A Lady* in 1930, but Yates retained his modus operandi of the 1920s, while suggesting that Mansel's private projects to restore justice were a privilege for the upper classes, bestowed on them by a grateful nation.

In *Adèle & Co* (1931) the Pleydells are robbed of valuable jewellery, and they set out to find it themselves without the help of the French police. This comedy is also a thriller because it shares the thrillers' sense of personal injury and the personal meting out of justice. In these Yates creates an enclosed Arcadian setting for the crime and punishment which his particular social codes will sanction without disbelief from the reader. To maintain the necessary sense of the enclosed world of personal justice, Yates establishes that the Pleydells had been staked out for years as a target, and that the crime has been structured so carefully that the French police would be no help in solving it. Where the protagonists of other novelists would tease or mock the police in their plots, or admire and follow them, Yates's characters can simply ignore them. '"The police'll go their own way: if we like to go ours, there's no reason why we should collide."'[32] This personalisation of the crime has the advantage of quietly establishing how very important the Pleydells are, and their possessions, in the Yates world. Heightening the stakes also heightens the audacity of the crime, and the brilliance with which it is avenged by the gentleman investigators (sentimental disproportion again).

The crime is here sexualised: the narrative voice rages at how the jewel thief had 'insulted and robbed' the Pleydell women, while 'the five grown men who should have been their protectors had been of no more use than a pack of drunken servants that prefer their own amusement to the common duty they owe'.[33] Notice here the sense of class-based entitlement with which Yates imbues his narrative voice, intended to heighten the reader's sense of outrage at the crime.

Yates's protagonists resorted to legal arguments automatically. To support this, he developed a sweeping technique of reassurance that induces the reader to assume that the laws of England and Wales will hold sway in Carinthia, Austria and Riechtenburg. Legal advice like this seems unlikely to function outside Yates's customised version of central Europe.

> We could not help feeling that documents written in English would, as the saying goes, cut but little ice with a faithful Austrian staff [...] When we saw the lawyer, however, upon the following day, he laughed our suggestions to scorn, declaring that changes like this were taking place every day and that orders in English would run in any country where people could read and write.[34]

Yates's approach to legality in his novels is important because in the 1930s he reused the *Blind Corner* plot, in which the protagonists can claim a treasure that is about to be taken from them, and immediately make the law work for them to retain their rights. Their outrage is based on English legal reasoning, but mostly relies on the elevated tone and archaic vocabulary, and partly on a strong sense of entitlement, to convince. 'Dead Nicolas Ferrers had been most grossly betrayed and we, his heirs, had been deliberately spoiled. This by a man to whom we had always been civil, in whom our great-uncle reposed an absolute trust.'[35]

The sense of British political superiority that we saw in Buchan's *Castle Gay* and *The House of the Four Winds* is also present in Yates's novels when there is interaction with the natives. The Carinthians and Riechtenburgers need the help of the British to achieve the throne for the Prince, and the Duchess's escape, in *Blood Royal* and *Fire Below*. In the later *Safe Custody* (1932), the assumed British superiority of the heroes suffers a reversal and is deflated by the even greater superiority of the British villains, who leave the heroes without car, maps, letters of introduction or passports in a country where they don't even speak the language. (They do have money: Hubert carries a belt containing fifty gold sovereigns next to his skin, so we have to assume that English gold will also work in darkest Austria.) In this novel Yates felt assured enough to trick the reader by relying on the expectations of his style, making *Safe Custody* one of his strongest thrillers, with much to say about the legal maxim that possession is nine-tenths of the law. Strangely, the reader does not wonder whose law: it is enough that Yates has said so.

This selective application of English law mutates to an extraordinary attitude of almost colonial appropriation in the post-war novels. In *Cost Price* the fabulous jewels of the Castle of Hohenems, in Austria, are removed by Mansel and Chandos, with their owner's permission, and then offered to England for the national collection.[36] Justification for the complete ignoring of international law is that their owner, John Ferrers, is an Englishman. (He refuses a peerage for this gift.) The German interest in gaining possession of the jewels, before the Anschluss, is used as justification for an elaborate plot to smuggle the jewels through Austria to the Italian port of Trieste, and thence to the open sea. The much more important fact that Ferrers is only the owner of the jewels by his marriage to the Austrian noblewoman who owns the castle, is also ignored. Yates's tunnel vision concerning the paramount rights of Englishmen, and his abolition of married women's property rights, control this narrative point.

As we have already seen in the 1920s, Yates used extreme violence in his novels (and also in real life, when he had apparently attacked a 'Frenchman on the steps of the English Club [in Pau], thrashed him with a crop and broken his arm').[37] In *Storm Music* (1934) John kills the chief villain (who has demanded that Countess Helena strip to show him the tattoo under her left breast) by breaking his wrist and then breaking his back across a table.[38] In *She Painted Her Face* (1937) Exon kills the chauffeur by strangling him in mid-air, and also strangles Percy Virgil in the well. There are no qualms about murdering Percy, a future in-law, because Yates makes sure this death happens in a battle for survival. In *Gale Warning* (1939) Bagot kills Barrabas by cracking his skull with a paperweight, because the villain has just put his hand inside Lady Audrey's shirt. These highly dramatic killings are iterations of the Ruritanian requirement of the duel to conclude the plot,[39] and are carefully planned with due notice of who was the aggressor, whether due notice was given, and whether a lady was at risk of harm or threat, which is usually the deciding factor. A threat or an insult to women is usually the trigger for these outbreaks of murderous violence: Yates heroes do not indulge in casual torture or thoughtless death-dealing. In contrast, Buchan thrillers rarely contain a death, and his heroes almost never kill. The narrative focus on slow and decisive killing in Yates's thrillers is closely connected to his increasing use of sexual titillation, an acknowledgement that his brand could offer more physicality, unlike the highly moral and innocently clean adventures by Buchan. In this, Yates was keeping up with the times.

The attention Yates paid to due legal process, even when it was mostly his own invention, shows how his plots functioned as restorers of order and justice in a disturbingly out of order world. Even when his gentlemen heroes did not obey the law, a higher law based on class or imperatives of honour was invoked to give justification for their actions. The importance of following a code was essential for Yates's protagonists, and so policing these codes, and punishing their transgression, was their *raison d'être*.

In keeping with the new grittier reality in the thriller, in Yates's 1930s novels we can observe dramatic financial imperatives in the motivations of Yates's new, younger heroes. *She Painted Her Face* (1937) begins '"I became a beggar when I was twenty-two"'.[40] Yates invokes sentimental disproportion so his readers will feel sympathy for the gentleman who has had his rights withheld. This is the introduction to an almost Dickensian episode of saintly self-denial and the revelation of a secret from which the plot of the novel will spring. Once the hero has been established as a true and honest man, devoted in the service of his friend, he inherits an unexpected fortune from a conveniently dead uncle in Australia, so that his chivalric quest to set right an injustice can be funded lavishly, as befits his class. In *Gale Warning* (1939) John Bagot loses his father and his job on page one, is given an ideal job three lines later, loses it two pages later after he has spent the last of his capital on a training course, and then, on the fifth page, inherits £12,000. In *Shoal Water* (1940) Jeremy works like a slave for two years after failing to get his degree, but is then given three months' leave plus six hundred pounds by his benign uncles, his employers. The rapid reversals of fortune are so exaggerated in these opening pages of these novels that they seem almost routine, an expected route of suffering that gentlemen must follow to prove their worth.

Extending this argument to link to the didactic function of Yates's plots, the reader is expected to judge characters by their obedience to orders, and learn how servants, and those who give service, should obey the laws of Yates's coded society.

Service and class

In *She Painted Her Face* (1937) the devoted manservant Winter is the first servant in Yates's novels whose opinion matters. He is given a personality, and a back story, lives with a sister's family, and makes choices about his own career. Before this, Yates routinely wrote servants (excluding those in *Anthony Lyveden*) as automatons. In *Fire Below* (1930), Bell prefers to sleep in the Rolls rather than trust it to a strange garage abroad. In *An Eye For A Tooth*, written thirteen years later, he is 'a splendid servant. Whenever I wanted something he always seemed to be there'.[41] Barley in *Storm Music* (1934) is devoted and untiring: 'he did much more than his duty and used his brain'.[42] The servants in the Berry stories are extensions of the operations of the house, and those in the Ruritanian castles are characterless feudal serfs in livery. Where peasants can be chastised, this is done as a duty. In *Storm Music*, Countess Helena Yorick orders a man to be flogged because he has mistreated a horse, but speaks kindly to him every time she meets him afterwards, '"lest he should think that his offence is not purged and forgotten and that he has a mark forever against his name"'.[43]

These iterations of the duties of service and the correct way to give service can also be seen in the conduct of the protagonist who serves. For this, the history of Ruritania is responsible, since Yates is following a clear tradition, first set down by the novelist George Meredith in 1870–71, in *The Adventures of Harry Richmond*, and made famous by Hope's *The Prisoner of Zenda*, in which the English commoner hero may not marry the Crown Princess, despite having saved her and her tiny invented principality.[44] Meredith establishes the gulf that class and rank create between the lovers, and then allows the hero to leap the gulf by bravery and selfless deeds of honour in her service. Anthony Hope and Elinor Glyn were two important Edwardian British authors to have reused Meredith's Victorian trope in their own highly romantic novels. The twist that Yates creates is that the foreign princess, countess or duchess keeps her titles and lands if she stays in her own territory, but if she marries the Englishman and moves to England, she abandons her noble style. As such, the characters are able to conform both to the conventions of cardboard grandiosity and to modern English self-effacement. The reverse of this exchange is that if the English hero stays in the foreign land to marry the duchess, countess or princess, he will automatically assume her rank, by right if not by title. The local servants treat any such Englishman as a milord or boyar, and, in *Safe Custody*, they kiss his hand on his marriage.

Yates makes it clear that class barriers transcend poverty and the circumstances of earning a living. In *She Painted Her Face* the hero, Richard Exon, spends much time agonising over his hopeless love for the Lady Elizabeth Virgil, because he is a commoner, and is banned from marrying her. But a way round his unfortunate lack of noble rank is produced by the discovery that he once had owned a family estate. English gentility, plus adoption by the aged Countess of Whelp, is enough to make him eligible to marry Lady Elizabeth, Countess of Brief. This sudden rise in rank firms up the Ruritanian convention that allows him to take noble rank, but adoption confirms his ascension into Carinthian nobility. The castle's servants, of course, have long assumed his natural right to command.

Mansel's talent for finding the perfect inn with slavish servants is displayed in *She Fell Among Thieves* (1935).

> Mansel had a flair for good lodging. Except in the bigger cities he seldom, if ever, would stay at a well-known hotel, but would find some simple house whose clients were very few: his manner was so attractive and his address was so fine that the host would spare no effort to do what he pleased, and before the first day was out, Mansel and all who were with him, were lords of all they surveyed.[45]

This perfectionism seems to have been a new enthusiasm for Yates in the mid-1930s, as the same happens to the Pleydells (Mansel was with them) in *And Berry Came Too*, one year later. 'The garden was put at our disposal, a coach-house at that of the Rolls, and, before we had time to ask, our amiable host had proposed that our lunch should be served on the lawn in the shade of an oak.'[46] Yates clearly gloried in the idea of commanding service to exacting standards without question and with total discretion. Such a hotel is an extension of the perfect country house where the servants exist only to serve, without any failings. When the service fails – for example, the breakdown of the ice-machine in *And Berry Came Too* (1936) – the house is of course no longer habitable. When an inn-keeper fails to maintain the standards required, the party decamp. Service for Yates characters must be total and perfect. In *She Painted Her Face* (1937) the heroes visit 18 inns and reject them all because they are not perfect.[47] In *Safe Custody* (1932), when John and cousin Hubert decide to leave the Austrian inn where they have been staying for a few days,

> the hostess burst into tears such as we could not dry, while the host made up such a bill as we were ashamed to pay [...] nothing remained to be done but partake of the lavish refreshment which our friends had prepared in the place of a stirrup-cup. Upon this we wasted ten minutes, because we had hurt them enough [...] the woman weeping with her apron over her head, and the man with his arm around her, trying to lend her a comfort he did not know.[48]

This scene of exaggerated standards of hospitality, in which a host is offended if the guest does not eat and drink everything available, is more risible than impressive, since there is no logical reason in the plot for such extraordinary devotion to English travellers. The exaggeration in expectations of service is connected to how women should behave, since sex roles were deeply implicated in characters who served and were served.

Women's behaviour

In the 1930s Yates continued to be prescriptive about women's behaviour. The sequel to *Blood Royal, Fire Below* (1930), reveals the implications for a woman faced with marriage to a villain who is infinitely below her in morals and character as well as rank. Marya, a young widowed countess who has fallen in love with George Hanbury, is blackmailed into a marriage with the villain, Greig. She is willingly obedient to her new husband's requests simply because she has married him, not because she has any feelings for him.

> "You're going back?" I said.
>
> Marya nodded. "That's right. I must, of course. I've married the man. Unless and until he gives me cause to leave him –".[49]

Her behaviour is presented as aristocratic high-mindedness, utterly correct for a married woman, even if desperately inconvenient for her friends whom Greig is hunting, and tragic for her love story with

Hanbury. As mentioned earlier, Chandos needs to kill Greig singlehand-edly, because 'George, of course, could do nothing. For if he was to play the hangman, he could hardly expect to marry the widow he had made. Any woman must have recoiled from so grisly a bed'.[50]

The obstacle of sexual contamination is also about transferred guilt by subsequent congress, but is a tortuous definition of loyalty even for Chandos, who eventually rejects Marya's position:

"Can't you see that, just because he is my husband, he simply must not die at the hand of one of my friends?"

"No, I'm damned if I can. [...] the business smacks of the Stone Age."[51]

The contortions of plot that Marya's decision produces are brought to a climax by her suggestion of sexual self-sacrifice. 'Marya averted her eyes. "If I – I kept him at home tonight ...".'[52] And that, naturally, sends Chandos vaulting over the half-door, hunting for Greig so he can kill him before Marya has to sleep with the swine. Yates's focus on the sexual rights of the husband in this episode is more than obsessive, it is fetishistic, making the bond of marriage a many-layered metaphor as well as an axiom of faith.

A variation on this theme occurs in *She Painted Her Face* (1937) when Lady Elizabeth urges Exon not to let it be known that he has killed her cousin, because '"*It simply must not be known that the man whom I am to marry put Percy Virgil to death*"' (emphasis in the original).[53] It is not explained why her cousin's killer may not be her husband, and there is no obvious reason in the novel, apart from a potential murder charge. But Yates whips up the tension to gain a plot twist and to avoid having to explain its logic. In *Fire Below* Chandos has an extended flirtation with Lelia, a peasant girl (who later dies). This is unexpected since Chandos has previously not had eyes for anyone except his wife Leonie, but it is possible that Yates felt the need for a little Boy-like flirtation in this novel. Lelia is clearly the illegitimate daughter of a gentleman ('her face was fine and gentle and her figure was slight, and both argued some sire that had never set hand to a plough').[54] Upon this very dubi-ous foundation Chandos builds a fantasy that she is actually a proxy for his wife, and so it is perfectly fine to dally with her, even if he struggles briefly with marital guilt. Leonie, the Grand Duchess of Riechtenburg, does not react emotionally when he admits his behaviour, but she does remark that he has given the girl something that was not his to give. '"You drew a cheque upon my personal account. Do you think that I question your signature? Do you think that I would not honour it blindly, as you would mine?"'[55] This complex attitude towards honourable flirtations and marital continence has echoes in Yates's own life. His biographer spends some time discussing Yates's paranoia at this time, over imagined attentions to Bettine, his refusal to let her leave the car to talk to her friends, and the horse-whipping episode in Pau.[56]

As a more positive lesson, Yates offers models of ideal behaviour in the Berry stories. In *Adèle & Co* (1931), the three women – Boy's sister Daphne (Mrs Pleydell), his wife Adèle (also Mrs Pleydell), and cousin Jill (the Duchess of Padua) – are perfect in every way, each demonstrating different feminine qualities. Daphne as the eldest is the hostess, the lady of their joint house, and the one who shows most sense of responsibility. She is the usual liaison with the outside world. None of the ladies share the extravagant or rampaging characteristics expressed in Berry's intemperate discourse, and Daphne is the Pleydell woman least likely to do anything ridiculous or silly. She is also not given any sexuality or sexualised description. Adèle, as the narrator's wife, is the most evidently desirable, as we have seen in *Perishable Goods*. Jill, their young cousin, is described throughout Yates's oeuvre with a troubling lack of realism concerning her age and appearance – 'Though she was now a mother, she looked like a child of fourteen'[57] – but she and Adèle are the sexual focus of this novel.

Berry is incandescent with suppressed sexual jealousy when he thinks through what must have happened when the jewels were removed from their unconscious bodies. Naturally, the reader is invited to share these tantalising images. "'And when I think that that filthy slab of offal [...] not only drugged you but touched your lively beauty while you were asleep ... lifted those hands to strip them ... raised your heads to unfasten –".[58] Later, when Boy accuses the chief villain, he extends the metaphor: "'While they slept, you stripped them of all they had"'.[59] The sexual innuendo is quite apparent, as is the sense of ownership and the right of protection held by the male characters. The women characters make no comment on this outburst by Berry: they are quiescent and voiceless on the subject of their apparent violation by proxy. Yates's insistence on conflating a non-violent removal of jewels into a physical violation by its correlation with the violation of the rules of hospitality, is alarming and typical.

In high contrast, in the same novel Yates dresses up three of his male protagonists in drag, as a carnivalesque disguise to get them past the eyes of villains. The ease with which the men wear their dresses and the unembarrassed delight with which their wives assist with the costumes and make-up reflect well on the sexual and gender confidence that Yates gave these characters. None of the men show the slightest reluctance to drag up or play the fool. They are simultaneously described as grotesque and charming, a subversive dyad of repulsion and attraction. Berry, as Hortense, is loud, lurid and vulgar, which is a visual extension of his personality when roused. The youngest man involved, Piers, Duke of Padua, is initially teased for being likely to be 'a wonderful girl', and certainly comes up to expectations.

> He made a peach of a girl. His smart little dress of black silk, with cuffs and long, low collar of rose georgette, his broad-brimmed black-and-white hat and his rhinestone brooch served to set off his delicate boyish face, while his obvious shyness and the way in which he cast down his eyes bespoke to the life the blushing *ingénue*.[60]

What I find interesting about this riotously described episode, which is one of the funniest in this very funny novel, is the evident enjoyment Yates conveys in writing these men passing as women while flouting codes of social behaviour. They dress as women asking for donations to send children on seaside holidays, thus enacting the respectable request for alms for the poor. Berry comports himself outrageously in public, shrieking from the open car as Boy (also in drag) drives it (badly) past charabancs and carts, deliberately attracting attention as ridiculous novelties on the road. Yet their familiar exhibitionism reassures all who see them, including the villains. The only man to see them close up assumes that they are making a cinema film. Thus gaudy, vulgar women asking for money in the street are also good-hearted ladies respectably asking for alms for the poor; the ridiculous and the sublime. The attraction of the episode lies in its gusto and energy, but it carries an unexpected subtext that women who behave vulgarly like clowns in public are not a great surprise.

Safe Custody (1932) expresses some complex rules of behaviour for the heroine of the novel that reinforce the strictures of the plot. The Countess Olivia joins the protagonists in the empty castle to help find the treasure that two enemy parties are trying to steal. She has very strong views about how she may behave.

> "I can hardly believe that England's as lax as that. But you know Austria. I broke a good many rules when I shared your inn: but at least I hid my name, and it was a public hotel. But to stay with you here in this castle, for, possibly, two or three months ... You must be mad. [...] if I did this, no peasant in all Carinthia would take off his

hat as I passed. Instead, they'd spit on the ground. If I went to a farm and asked for cup of water, the farmer would try and kiss me, and if his wife was there, she'd order me off the place."[61]

This insistence on the fragility of a gentlewoman's reputation is a common pattern in Yates's thrillers, in which women are potential and violable hostages whom the heroes must invest considerable time and effort in guarding. In *Safe Custody*, this risk is taken a further, ludicrous degree when John Ferrars persuades Olivia that the only way she can participate in the enterprise as the only lady present (her maid, it seems, does not count as a chaperone) and not lose her reputation among the peasantry and servants, is to marry him (whom she has only known for a few days). And she agrees. Naturally they are already secretly in love with each other, so the marriage will end well, after inevitable misunderstandings and passages of pride. Their situation has a very high titillation quotient, and the extremely high guard on a lady's honour accentuates the privilege of John's eventual access to her body.

Nothing seems to have changed in *Storm Music* (1934), a novel almost identical in plot to its predecessor *Safe Custody* (the hero's name is still, confusingly, John).[62] The Countess Helena's noble birth also makes her reputation more than usually fragile. To protect her name while they are in hiding, John Spencer pretends that he is her brother. This tissue-thin fantasy goes awry when Yates tries to have his cake of titillation and eat it. John and Helena stay in a woodcutter's cottage, looking after the baby while the wife rushes off on an errand. Since the wife knows who Helena is, it seems that the need for Helena's reputation to be protected has been forgotten in Yates's determination to indulge in an Arcadian idyll, during which John and Helena share the cottage and baby and play house for several days and, most crucially, nights.[63] Not even the lax English would consider a baby a suitable chaperone, but when the question arises after the first night, Helena seems much more relaxed about her name than she had been 24 hours earlier. The games Yates makes them play are strangely divorced from the stringent comportment rules that he invokes at the same time. '"I mustn't be stained, my darling – I don't want your wife to be stained with a blemish that won't come off."'[64] Describing a woman's public reputation in such terms seems unnecessarily vindictive. It also suggests a particular interest in judging the degree of spotting or staining on a woman's reputation. Since this novel was written in the year of his divorce, reputation was on Yates's mind.

The mid-1930s shows Yates slackening his standards. *Storm Music* contains the episode of the leopard tattooed under Helena's left breast.[65]

Further titillation derived from the body of a naked woman occurs twice in *She Fell Among Thieves* (1935), when a dead housemaid is found naked on the courtyard stones, and when Jenny, the heroine, is first spotted through binoculars, bathing naked in a forest pool. '"I'd like to have a look at that girl. Not a peasant, you say. Well bred." [...] I think she wore next to nothing beneath her white linen dress.'[66] The episode of the naked forest girl takes a disturbing twist when it becomes obvious that though physically adult, she has the understanding of a child. This artificial retardation of her emotional development has been done to her for nefarious reasons, and she regains her adulthood quite quickly and easily when placed in the charge of a gentlewoman, but the result is still uneasy. Chandos, Mansel and the reader can freely ogle, or 'worship', as Yates might prefer to style their gaze, the beautiful body of an infantilised woman without her being aware of their scrutiny. When this novel was serialised in *Woman's Journal* from December 1934 to April 1935, the illustrations of Jenny were highly sexualised, something that the novel merely suggests.[67]

Further titillation is presented, and then incorporated into the plot, in *She Painted Her Face* (1937). After escaping from attempted murder in a well, Exon is sitting on the edge of Lady Elizabeth's bed wearing only his trousers at three in the morning, drinking whisky, while she is brushing her hair in front of the mirror in her underwear. The apparently pre- or post-coital tableau is compounded by Exon accidentally leaving his shirt on her floor, later discovered by her treacherous maid, and by Elizabeth's rapturous, breathy speech proclaiming Exon as her bridegroom. In *Gale Warning* (1939) John Bagot has to pretend to be in love with Lady Audrey Nuneham, and as part of the cover story he has to help her do up her dress before they go out dancing for the evening. Their intimacy is not dwelt on, but their whispered conversation at night in his hotel bedroom after a quarrel conveys it well enough to the reader. By page 103 Audrey admits that she has now lost her reputation, but this English gentlewoman is of stronger stuff than the nervous Austrian noblewomen, and disregards this rite of passage. By the end of the novel she has shared several erotic encounters with John, including being rubbed down naked after prolonged immersion in a river.

For Yates's heroes, sexualised encounters outside the upper classes were simply unseemly, and even a joke. In *Storm Music*, the Count of Yorick drinks himself senseless, thus allowing the village girl he had imported for the night to try on his sister's dresses. Naturally, she is too well-built to fit into the noblewoman's slender garments.

As we stood there, unseen and unheard, she proceeded to take it off, thrusting it up to her shoulders and over her head. The dress, too slight for her inches, clung to her breadth, and for thirty seconds or more a writhing, searing sack of crimson and gold was surmounting a thickset body and clumsy legs. The scene was too coarse to be comic.[68]

This grotesque image, invoking the obscene in its subversion of the refined behaviour of the protagonists, reflects on the count's taste in women as well as on the essential physical difference between the classes. It simply wasn't possible for a woman in a Yates novel to be slenderly beautiful and not be upper class. And without slenderness there could be no beauty, and a woman without beauty was not worth speaking of.

Echoes of Yates's unnerving stance that the ownership of women was their 'protection' appear in stories where an innocent and often penniless beautiful ingénue is threatened with forced marriage to a vile *parti*, but is abducted for her own protection by Yates's hero, a much better sort of man. This was not a new trope in Yates, but in the 1940s he was more explicit about the sale of women to repellent men. Because the heroine acquiesces, the abduction produces double standards in how women should regard their choices being made for them by men. If these are made by the right sort of man, then all is properly romantic. In 'My Lady's Chamber' Stephanie is being pandered by her guardian, to be sold off to 'a notorious evil-liver who had great possessions, had promised her "guardian" fifteen thousand pounds on the day he married the "child"'.[69] But Stephanie is rescued from harassment by him and other potential buyers by her new friend Patrick, who installs her in his own apartment. She thinks she has inherited this property in an unexpected bequest, and is looked after by his own servants (who are in the secret). She falls in love with Pat, who is waiting anxiously for her realisation that he is the man she loves before he moves back in. Georgette Heyer wrote similar best-selling plots with great gusto, set in the mid-eighteenth century and during the Regency, but there is something unpleasant, too close to a woman being bought and sold, in Yates's iteration of the trope of the modern-day King Cophetua. Pat's lawyer refers explicitly to Stephanie as a commodity – '"both of us know that Miss Beauclerk's body can command a very high price"'[70] – but the phraseology, while seeking to attract admiration for its straight-talking assessment of the facts, in fact has the opposite effect of reinforcing the similarities between a forced sale against her will, and a surreptitious purchase of her affections by the offer of security and comfort.

The same can happen to daughters as well as wives: in 'Way of Escape' (1943) the 17-year-old is cared for by her guardian on her father's apparent death, but when the father emerges unexpectedly as a drunkard whose behaviour is now 'impossible', the only way to save the daughter's reputation ('"she'd be *déclassée* before she'd made her *début*"')[71] is for her to marry her guardian.

Despite all these prescriptive and restrictive measures for the safety of women in Yates's fiction, the war made him give them at least one freedom of action. In 'Period Stuff', Lady Ursula Beechwood is able to use her gun, a present from her soldier brother, to shoot dead a German airman who had strafed her home and killed her dog. Such agency for a woman is dramatic in the story for its effective demonstration of how Yates (and presumably his readers) would have felt all enemy forces ought to be treated. It is also a quietly telling loosening of the restrictions on Yates women: they were finally allowed to defend themselves, and to do it successfully and without fuss. Infuriatingly, this did not seem to change Yates's attitude in subsequent fiction, since he only permitted this agency in wartime. In the year following this story's publication, *An Eye For A Tooth* (1943) was set in the late 1920s, in which the heroine is helplessly unable to do anything to defy her brutal and arrogant German husband because he is her husband. She has to be knocked out and taken by Mansel's Rolls Royce to a nursing home for her own protection, since she is incapable of doing anything herself.

The crisis in Yates's personal life that brought him to divorce his wife in 1933 marks a greater ferocity in his policing of the behaviour of women in his fiction after this date. Punishment and justice, and the control of inferiors, became stronger concerns in how Yates told his stories, and the attentiveness his characters have for the detail of the pursuit and execution of this justice. He and his fiction also moved away from England. In the 1930s and 1940s European settings became the testing ground for his characters, denoting the role of his works as escapist nostalgia in difficult political times. He ignored authoritarian politics in Europe until after war had broken out, and instead focused a very obvious need to restore justice on the corrupt lords of Carinthian and Austrian castles. This was an escape from the world in time as well as place, since his plots were archaic to the point of fable, and the characters were related as closely as they are in the traditional tale. The attention paid to the heroes' poverty, to their faithful servants, and to the prize of a princess-substitute, reinforces this reading.

7
Thirkell in Wartime, 1940–45

Thirkell's first wartime novel, *Cheerfulness Breaks In*, was published in December 1940, and had sold over 10,000 copies up to February 1941 in its US edition alone.[1] When thinking of a title for *Marling Hall* two years later (which Thirkell suggested needed something that would say 'people-living-in-the-country-under-war-conditions-and-carrying-on-through-difficulties-with-cheerfulness-breaking-in'), she considered 'that the title is not very important by now'.[2] The establishment of her brand and the frequency of her wartime reprints is quite remarkable considering that the supply of books grew progressively more limited as war went on. When Christina Foyle asked for *Growing Up* as a Book Edition in 1945, Thirkell's publisher James Hamilton was glad to have the increased print run using Foyle's paper allocation.[3]

Thirkell wrote novels about home front life during wartime, rather than war novels. This distinction, shared by many other writers in this period, was made by Elizabeth Bowen discussing her own writing during the Second World War, and is useful for reminding us that Thirkell's novels were about the times, not primarily about the war.[4] In wartime, Thirkell was writing about communities, rather than the families which had dominated her pre-war novels, and was considering how war was affecting towns and villages rather than the people of the great houses. *Cheerfulness Breaks In* (1940), *Northbridge Rectory* (1941) and *Marling Hall* (1942) illustrate the initial impact of war and increasing disruption to country society. *Growing Up* (1943) deepens the Barsetshire wartime saga by weaving together threads of stories set up in earlier novels and developing new areas of county life. *The Headmistress* (1944) and *Miss Bunting* (1945) are concerned with the wartime education of the young and the ignorant. All the novels deal with the effects of social and cultural invasion, by evacuee children, by refugees from within and outside Barsetshire, and from abroad.

Refugees and evacuees

Her wartime novels reflect the enforced cultural assimilation that the war brought to British society, and are associated with a new acidity in Thirkell's writing, at the expense of her humour. This was noticed by many reviewers, who found the change understandable, but regrettable.[5] The resentment of local change that Thirkell's characters express is a metonymic response to restrictions and alterations to a settled way of life. There was also a secondary fear of the unknown, which included the invasion forces of refugees, evacuees and soldiers in search of billets. In expressing this fear she was writing a new kind of novel that Yates could not. Buchan had died in early 1940, and Yates wrote little during or set in the war, being a refugee from France himself, in the Iberian peninsula and then Rhodesia until the end of the war. Thirkell, like many women writers, pioneered the Home Front novel, by using the setting of the small town and village to describe the impact of refugees and evacuation, written as contemporary accounts.

Only the soldiers are welcome in Barsetshire, because evacuee children are uniformly loathsome and sticky, and refugee women are overdressed and insolent. Panikos Panayi describes refugee demographics:

> During World War Two, two main groups of refugees entered Britain. The first, of 100,000, included Norwegians, Danes, Dutch, Belgians and French, who had made their way to the country following the fall of their countries to Hitler in the spring of 1940, and approximately 25,000 Austrian and German Jews who had fled these states previously.[6]

Interestingly, no refugees of these nationalities seem to enter Barsetshire. Thirkell had invented a mid-European Ruritanian origin for her Mixo-Lydian refugees in *Before Lunch*,[7] and they appear again in Barsetshire in *Cheerfulness Breaks In*, representing the refugees from Fascism who had been entering Britain since the middle of the 1930s. Since the Mixo-Lydians 'show a degree of determined ingratitude and unpleasantness',[8] Thirkell is clearly not interested in inducing sympathy for their homeless condition. Instead she uses them as a way of complaining about the rights and privileges refugees get that native Britons do not. They have an inexplicable ease in getting hold of other refugees as servants.[9] Their income and reserves are also suspect: Mr Pattern the lettings agent 'had let the upper part of the house at an excessive rent to various mid-European refugees who mysteriously always had plenty of money and got very good jobs, replacing local men and women who had been called up'.[10] The obvious tone of resentment here from Thirkell may be excused by its expression at the end of the war, but she is also outraged that refugees are not grateful enough for their safety. Polish and Czecho-Slovakian refugees are sniped at for being tedious servants because they keep talking about their own countries and how much better they are than Britain.[11] The angry Mixo-Lydian refugee Madame Brownscu is contemptuous of Barsetshire concerns, compared to her devastated homeland and the never-ending war between Slavo-Lydians and Mixo-Lydians. Her angry stories in bad French repay translation because they are outrageous faux-Slavic pastiches of revenge and persecution that Thirkell embroiders with malicious gusto.[12] Mme Brownscu becomes a farcical figure, but she cannot be ignored because she represents the nameless horrors of war taking place abroad.

Children from the London slums and their feckless parents were regarded by Thirkell as an invading, devouring army. Her reaction in the fiction appears to be an accurate reflection of what many people experienced. Ruth Adam observes that rural hosts who received urban refugees were appalled at their habits and condition: 'The disgust when the guests did arrive filled the correspondence columns for several days'.[13] Thirkell only mentioned the smell and the body vermin in her novels, but there was worse for real-life country hosts of city slum evacuees to endure, in hygiene or lack of. Thirkell pays no attention to the evacuees' own feelings or the psychological terrors of children accustomed to living in a crowded room, now expected to sleep alone and be grateful for it. She takes satisfaction in creating order among the fictional evacuees, and solves the country hosts' problem of having to cook for the refugee children by inventing the Northbridge Communal Kitchen.[14] Obedience and efficient management are her solutions to a problem to which she could not see an end. When 'the tide of evacu-ees surged back to London, with the exception of a certain number of the younger children whose parents were not disposed to tempt a Providence which had made it unnecessary for them to take any fur-ther financial or moral responsibility for their offspring',[15] Thirkell was outraged at the imposition on the country hosts, but not at the chil-dren's abandonment.[16] The lack of control over refugee children also annoyed her. In a private letter, she wrote that her friends 'the Barkers are having HELL with a dozen evacuees and 2 quite incompetent mas-ters who won't help at all'.[17] Useless and aggressive teachers crop up in several novels, and the wrong sort of teachers who cannot control children, and treat their billet as a hotel rather than a borrowed space, are ferociously attacked. Mr Keith 'had said he would rather have a hundred of the Barsetshire Light Infantry camping in the grounds, with the run of the squash court, tennis court and billiard room, than one child or one teacher'.[18] The British Army are also an invading force, but their organisation fits into Barsetshire country feudalism, something that the refugees are unable to understand. When Lydia Keith, burdened with luggage, is not able to find a seat in a railway carriage full of refugees and aliens, she stands in the corridor with soldiers and feels more comfortable there.[19]

New ways of behaving

Lydia's reluctance to sit next to the alien population of strangers is part of the wider sense that wartime Barsetshire is being invaded by many different groups. These included people who had not been seen in Barsetshire before, because Thirkell had not written before about the industrial classes. She also showed how daily lives were being altered by an invasion of new occupations.

In *The Headmistress* and *Miss Bunting* the gentry are at first amused at the blundering invasion of Mr Adams, with his money and influence and unexpected common sense. He is Thirkell's most important new character, since he represents an irresistible social mobility and incursion that Barsetshire needs and resents. He will be discussed in greater detail below, but for now it is enough to note that on his first appearance he is practically bestial, depicted in terms of vast size, hairy gloves and luridly unsuitable clothes. His arrival signals Thirkell's recognition that the war was prising open encrusted social practices to admit new blood, alarming new ideas and unwelcome possibilities. During the war, Lord Pomfret, in *Cheerfulness Breaks In*, and Miss Bunting, in *Miss Bunting*, die and are mourned. As if to replace their Victorian rectitude and rigid standards, the modernising and businesslike Mr Adams emerges energetically from the industrial town of Hogglestock, and does not go back.

Thirkell's novels are part of what Laura Hapke calls a 'Stiff-Upper-Lip school of war fiction', in that they show historically recognisable events in church, at dinners, in working parties and committee meetings.[20] They reflect the fact that 'by the early 1940s, one-third of all British women were in war work of one kind or another, from working in factories to caring for refugees and evacuees'.[21] A common war-related occupation is the sewing party making clothes for evacuees and refugees, for a selected group of upper- and middle-class ladies by invitation only.

In *Cheerfulness Breaks In* Mrs Keith's sewing party is a well-meaning but inefficient social circle, since it does not use a sewing machine. In *The Headmistress*, Harefield's sewing party functions as a social filter for new lady incomers. By the end of the war in *Miss Bunting*, Hallbury's camouflage netting work unit, also staffed by volunteer ladies, is impressively efficient, and productive. These contributions of increasing value, unanticipated by Thirkell but included by her over time as unconnected reflections of wartime life, function as reportage. Thirkell's wartime fiction would thus appeal as a record as well as an escape.

Yet it was a partial record. She restricted her wartime narratives to the home or village settings, and did not take the reader into the factories or hospitals, even though a few characters did have salaried war work outside the home. Ruth Adam's scrutiny of women's lives in the twentieth century allows us to assess how Thirkell used contemporary wartime details in her novels. We know that 'women registered with their age-groups at regular intervals, until by October 1942 all those from 45 downwards had registered'.[22] In *The Headmistress* Mrs Hoare does part-time work in a factory, but Lydia's year in the North, working on the land and in a factory, is only mentioned in hindsight. Laura Hapke observes that 'by 1941 all single women over 20 were required to register at government employment agencies as "mobile" labour for war factories': this is the background for Lady Fielding's fears about Anne's calling-up papers in *Miss Bunting*. Women were in 'Government departments or work[ed] in technical positions in the WRENS [*sic*], the WAAF, ATS and the Land Army'.[23] The Land Army in Barsetshire is a background rather than a foreground setting, with more women being involved in unspecified welfare work, probably under the aegis of the Women's Voluntary Service (WVS), because, in general, middle-class Barsetshire ladies do not do unskilled war work. Ruth Adam notes that 'by the middle of 1943, among women between 18 and 40 years old, 9 in 10 single women and 4 in 5 married ones were either in the services or in industry'.[24] But in *Miss Bunting* (1945) Jane Gresham, Mrs Merivale, Mrs Watson, Miss Holly and possibly Lady Fielding are all between 18 and 40 and none are 'in the services or in industry', only in part-time voluntary service at most (Miss Holly is a hired governess for the summer). The small town rather than urban nature of this small community might account for these women being unconnected with war work when they should have been fully occupied, but there is still a sense that Thirkell is reflecting only selective contemporary conditions that suited her plots.

We hear nothing of the Battle of Britain, the Blitz, or D-Day. Thirkell's only sustained integration of war events into her plots is in *Cheerfulness*

Breaks In (1940), which culminates with the news of the evacuation of the British Army from the French port of Dunkirk (27 May – 4 June 1940). Philip Winter returns from Dunkirk safely, but the novel ends as Lydia is about to open a telegram which will tell her if her fiancé Noel Merton is safe or not. Thirkell discussed the wisdom of using the real-life event in the novel with her publisher. 'The mention of Dunkirk does not seem objectionable. If we are all dead it won't matter. If we aren't, Dunkirk will not be forgotten and there are still (alas) people hoping that they will get news of those who didn't get back to England, and so it is not quite out of date.' She supplied an alternative ending for the novel, to avoid mentioning contemporary events, but made it a bitter-sweet declaration of love between Noel and Lydia, who cannot get married since there is no time. 'I couldn't feel a funny scene at the end. Noel and Lydia have to hold the stage.' In the event, Hamish Hamilton kept her 'Dunkirk' ending, which has more power for its truthful realism.[25] This reinforces Pryce-Jones's comment that Thirkell was writing fiction-alised journalism, since her account in this novel reflects A J P Taylor's later assessment that 'Dunkirk was a great deliverance and a great dis-aster', which is too often forgotten today in favour of sentimentalising the 'Little Ships'.[26]

No Barsetshire family loses a son or a husband in the war, though the Beedles wait patiently in *Growing Up* for their son to return from his prisoner of war camp, and Commander Gresham's 'missing' status comes to represent personal grief to his wife Jane.

> The longer Francis Gresham was missing the less she minded. It was not that she didn't love him, or that the dull ache at her heart, the dreary waking from dream to real life every morning grew any less; but the whole thing seemed so infinitely far away, and the longer he was absent the more difficult it would be, she feared, to begin their life again – if ever he came back. Sometimes she almost prayed to hear that he was dead. Then she blamed herself bitterly and knew that she would die of joy if the door suddenly opened and he were there. But of course none of these things happened, and she sank into an almost painless monotony of life and always thanked charm-ingly the people who asked if there was any news of her husband.[27]

This is an outstanding evocation of the feelings and social tensions felt by a service wife who does not know if her husband is dead or alive. Thirkell does not succumb to the clichéd ending of allowing the miss-ing husband to appear suddenly, but relies on the grinding slowness of realism, in the form of patient enquiries and the slowness of army communication with prisoner of war camps, to evoke the misery of no information. Her open discussion of Jane's need for closure, even widowhood, also rejects the romantic solution, and remains true to realistic feelings. Wartime conditions were altering how Thirkell wrote romance, in that she found herself able to transcend the formulaic marriage plot to write about a woman's feelings of arrested loss and longing that are constantly interrupted by the minutiae of caring for her son and dealing with the daily social round. Jane Gresham is a fine portrait of endurance, representing Thirkell's strongest wartime writing, not the least because her upper-class and naval codes of conduct are interestingly challenged by a fleeting consideration of an affair with Mr Adams. This is no more than the faintest of hints, and the service wife in Jane quashes her impulse, aided by Mr Adams's own good sense, but the episode is a deeply interesting exploration of cross-class romance that never was, representing the chaotic effect of war on the civilian's sense of social right and wrong.

When Pearl Harbour is mentioned, in passing, in *Marling Hall* (1942), the reference feels abrupt, a violent act intruding from reality. Emotion is thrust away with a wry rhyme about the Japanese. The defeats of British allied nations are given pathos and bathos by rapid name changes for Miss Hampton's dog, supporting the gallantry of the Ethiopians (Selassie), the Austrian struggle against the Anschluss (Schuschnigg), the Albanians (Zog), the Czechs (Benes), the Poles (Smigly-Rydz), and the Finns (Mannerheim) all through 1939.[28] We read about the trials of petrol and food rationing, of forgetting to carry a gas mask, of Air Raid Precaution wardens and the blackout regulations in *Cheerfulness Breaks In*; and Red Cross practices, siren and shelters, rumours of Fifth Columnists and enemy parachutists in *Northbridge Rectory*. We read almost nothing about the Home Guard, or about real bomb damage, only its rumour. We don't hear anything about road direction signs being removed, although in *Growing Up* the telephone exchange can get sticky about putting callers through to the hush-hush army unit, and the stationmaster calls out the names of blacked-out railway stations to passengers on stopping trains. There are no prisoners of war working on the land (although these are mentioned in *Private Enterprise*, in 1947, when Thirkell began retrofitting wartime Barsetshire). The requisitioning of large houses by London institutions, schools, the army and large companies is fully part of Thirkell's plots. But the astounding care and expense used by the army, and (borrowing from Dickens) the Ministry of Red Tape and Sealing Wax, to remodel Barsetshire mansions for institutional requirements is not part of history at all, in which 'very few of the temporary tenants showed any respect for their surroundings'. David Cannadine's account of the wreckage left by the army in requisitioned stately homes includes phrases like 'ploughed up', 'fabric decayed', 'broke the windows', 'forced the doors', 'cut to pieces' and 'knocked off by the soldiers'.[29] Mr Birkett's successful prevention of Nissen huts being built in the grounds of Southbridge School,[30] and the generous and respectful treatment of Beliers Priory, and, as we read after the war, of Gatherum Castle, are ahistorical. Likewise, Sir Harry's expectation that they will be able to get the Vicarage redecorated easily, in *Growing Up*, seems improbable given the very strict Ministry of Works regulations.[31] (Again, after the war, in *Private Enterprise*, Thirkell is much more accurate about the restrictive and ubiquitous need for permits, than when she was writing in wartime.) There is no mention (in the wartime novels) of Ruth Adam's point of 'the curious feature of illegitimate war babies [...] born to older mothers: almost twice the average to spinsters between 30 and 35'.[32] Most astonishing of all, where are the Americans? Hundreds of thousands of US troops were based in Britain from 1942 onwards, and are an essential part of British wartime history, but they only enter Barsetshire's war history as a brief, post-war, addition. Although she wrote about the effects of war on the individual as reportage, Thirkell departed radically from any sense of a historical record for her fiction when she needed to ameliorate reality and inject some reassurance into her plots.

During wartime Thirkell's depiction of Barsetshire is still based on her pre-war conception: an agricultural county of villages and small towns with a scattering of large estates. Thirkell followed Jane Austen, as noted by Raymond Williams, by focusing on land as 'an index of revenue and position – its visible order and control are a valued product, while the process of working it is hardly seen at all'.[33] (Again, after the war, she altered her attitude, and spent much time writing about farming worries.) Barsetshire's one industrial centre, Hogglestock, becomes important off-stage during the war, but only receives proper attention in 1949. Actual farming in Barsetshire during the war is largely the breeding of bulls and pigs. Owning the land, and viewing it with pride, is the most we see of farming as an activity. The ordering and control of land are more important for Thirkell than working the soil, and the eating of its products is emphasised whereas their growth and production are not.

Before and during the war, as in Trollope, Thirkell's fictional society is arranged around 'schemes of inheritance, with the interaction of classes and interests' that produces what Raymond Williams calls 'a social structure with pastoral trimmings', and 'no moral problem of any consequence'.[34] The towns and villages were drawn with texture and concern, since these were the social battlegrounds that she spent the war years illustrating. Williams observes that in wartime writing, there was

> a very different undercurrent: socially very similar to some elements of the reception of evacuated children from the bombed cities of the Second World War. Townspeople are seen [...] as louts and brats: not only in the obvious forms of litter and damage and noise, but also in deeper social forms of a hatred of the mob, of the unions, of the subverters of 'Old England' [...] rural life [had] that conscious reaction which was either a militant resident Toryism or, in one or two significant cases, an approach to and association with fascism.[35]

Wartime Barsetshire had stoutly upheld resentment for Communism, and sought to diminish its status. Former supporters of Communism discuss their ideology's failure as an adolescent aberration (Philip Winter in *Cheerfulness Breaks In*), or, against the background of the Nazi-Soviet pact of 23 August 1939, that it has let down the National Union of Teachers.[36] More generally, the wartime novels show that Communists cause all manner of ills, and are associated with shirking,[37] parsimony and class hatred,[38] and, of course, being a Fifth Columnist.[39] Mrs Keith's heart attack is caused by the billeted teachers being rude and pro-Communist in her drawing-room.[40] From *Marling Hall* onwards there is an increasingly uncritical adoration of Winston Churchill, as prime minister of a nation at war. Miss Bunting says sternly, "'If Mr Churchill wishes us to have Double Summer Time, He knows best'".[41]

This did not go unnoticed by the Left. Philip Toynbee regarded Thirkell's writing as 'the unscrupulous exploitation of contemporary [Left-wing] weakness. Perhaps the next epoch will call for factory epics and Stakhanovite heroines. Then we shall witness an *auto da fé* [...] and the tweeded dummies of this pygmy Barsetshire will be the first to burn'.[42] Other critics also objected to her astonishing class virulence in *Cheerfulness Breaks In*, especially her assertion that city-based teachers would not have encountered a dinner jacket or sherry before.[43] Enjoying a good dinner or a really beautiful drawing-room was a sign of class affinity. Hapke's discussion of wartime fiction by other women writers of the period reveals how limited Thirkell's subjects were.[44] She did not deal with rape, shell-shock, divorce, infidelity, suicide, treachery, spying, domestic bullying or desertion (except among the working classes). Thirkell's presentation of a threatened middle-class way of life was very digestible, to reassure and not alarm, while delivering self-assured warnings about the disruption of such niceness. She made her fictional world into a saga of conservative family values as a symbol of enduring strengths, rather than expose the weaknesses created by war.

Patricia Craig and Mary Cadogan consider that in the wartime best-seller, logic is substituted for 'a facile endorsement of social conventions – and the reader is led to believe that the popular sentiment is really, ultimately, the most sensible'.[45] Thirkell's wartime fiction, which consists largely of conversations and commentary from characters who all agree with each other, was designed to illustrate the conventions that she endorsed. It is very rare for Thirkell characters to have a sustained debate with opposing points of view being examined or even aired adequately: her characters are either Conservative or cranks, and if the cranks want to be accepted or get on, they have to become Conservative. Thus popular sentiment is agreed with by default as a patriotic gesture. After surveying hundreds of 'War Books' for Cyril Connolly's literary magazine *Horizon*, Tom Harrisson observed that 'in wartime it is socially difficult to criticize; easy to be uninformed and uniformed'. Thirkell's *Cheerfulness Breaks In* is one of the first on his list of books read and regretted, which is unfortunate since his final assessment of his reading is that it is a 'chaotic effluvia' and a 'cataract of tripe'.[46]

Phyllis Lassner's suggestion that 'British women writers interpret their World War II experiences in ways that unsettle our conceptions of political differences, social change and gender' is a useful way to consider Thirkell. She was entrenched in the 'regeneration of domestic ideology' that Lassner notes was a social marker of post-First World War fiction by the English middle classes.[47] Valerie Holman's interpretation of the popularity of conservative writers at a time when social change was expected is that during the war, 'good young writers were unavailable and had been replaced by ultra-conservatives whose minds were long ago made up and set against the modern world'.[48] Yet what Thirkell produced, as we have seen, was enthusiastically devoured by readers, who must have represented all political colours. In a Mass Observation survey of July 1942, 'Books and the Public', *Northbridge Rectory* was listed as the fifteenth most borrowed book, testament to Thirkell's great popularity with readers.[49]

As noted above, as well as showing a tendency to waspishness in her wartime writing, Thirkell also paid more attention to the comic mode. Occasionally this has been misread. Hermione Lee, for instance, cites the dreadful Mrs Spender of *Northbridge Rectory* as an example of 'the British myth of stoic domestic resilience against German aggression',[50] whereas this character is also the Unexpected Overnight Guest From Hell and a monstrous exaggeration of domestic tedium. Similarly, Thirkell's characters' rants were often simply hyperbolic fury used as a joke. She routinely mocked relentlessly cheerful characters, her narrative voice finding them as unbearable as did her heroes and heroines. She would mimic conversational speech patterns, especially for the comic night-mares like Mrs Spender and her banal monologues of self-important smugness. The purpose of such unbearable characters is to evoke the tedium of those amongst whom we live but must endure, whom the war has brought into a regrettable closer proximity. Elsewhere Thirkell would run on sub-clauses and tangential thoughts beyond their natural length to create comic surprise.

> It was a mysterious property of Harefield, as indeed it is of most vil-lages, that it was practically impossible to go off straight from one point to another because life, as Mrs Updike had said when a lorry carrying the trunks of several enormous trees came round a corner too sharply and crashed with its near front wheel into the wall of the alms-house while the tree trunks caught the laundry van full in the bonnet, was always going on to such an extent.[51]

Here, the truly eventful and image-packed words form the sub-clause of the main sentence, producing bathos (the extraordinary events take the subordinate position in the sentence). Thirkell follows Mark Twain's dictum that one of the tenets of successful comic writing is the slurring of the point of the joke, ensuring that it is half-hidden, as if the nar-rative voice does not realise its importance in the story.[52] The quoted passage is merely a commentary on the narrative, doing its work as comic background without developing its elements any further. Yet, at later moments in the novel, a lorry transports soldiers going on and off leave, Mr Belton is anxious about the tree-felling he has to arrange, and the unpredictability of the laundry van is a familiar worry for all Barsetshire housewives. These are fully integrated features of the story's setting, used initially in the construction of a richly detailed passage that quietly effaces itself while the real narrative carries on.

Other Twainian rules for comic writing that Thirkell followed include the dropping of the studied remark apparently without knowing it (for a good example of this, see the concluding remark by her narrative voice after Captain Hooper's failure in etiquette, p. 176 below), and stringing incongruities together in a wandering and sometimes pur-poseless way, apparently unaware that they are absurdities. Her ideas and examples remain well attached to their originating thought, and she never loses sight of her point, or her allusions, often returning to them with redoubled force.

This anecdote about the lightly disguised Ramblers' Association is a good example of well-planned discursiveness told with gleeful righteousness. Here the comic purpose has been subsumed in political and class loyalty, but the effect is still that of a thundering juggernaut of voice without apparent pauses for breath, ending with a highly subjective critical image.

> But no-one was more annoyed than the secretary of the local branch of the Hikers' Rights Preservation Society. This gentleman, who was a small chemist and a keen opposer of what he called feudal arrogance, spent most of his time walking over the field paths of the district [...] hoping to find evidence of arrogance in blocked, overgrown, or ploughed-up paths. But much to his fury the landlords, large and small, appeared to be as interested in the paths as he was, and Roddy Wicklow, the Pomfret estate agent, back on leave with a wound in his leg, meeting him one day near Six Covers Corner, had taken a malicious pleasure in forcing the champion of the people's rights to walk through three-quarters of a mile of a small sunk lane deeply embedded in thorn trees and brambles with a stream running down the middle of it, which lane had fallen into disuse simply because the public, and hikers in particular, were too lazy to use it, preferring to tread down Lord Pomfret's corn on one side, or frighten his gravid Alderney cows on the other. Each successive autumn since Mr Belton ploughed the park had this elderly Gracchus watched the ploughing with an auspicious (as hoping to get Mr Belton into trouble by its means) and a drooping (as one mourning the final extinction of Magna Carta) eye. And each successive autumn had he experienced the mortification of seeing the path neatly rolled out and Mr Belton taking a ceremonial walk across it, which did not prevent his doing a great deal of boasting at the H.R.P.S. yearly meeting.[53]

The classical reference embedded in the penultimate sentence, and the quotation borrowed from *Hamlet*, reinforce the political point Thirkell wished to make, that landowners do take care of the public rights of way, and that the rabidly left-wing protesters represented by the Hikers' Rights are hypocritical and malicious. Roddy Wicklow's wound reflects the trope familiar from Buchan and Yates that any man with a war wound has automatic moral authority. The damage caused to crops and stock is another assertion of the rights of the farmer's livelihood over the rights of the walker. This typically hyperbolic passage occurs in a novel in which the great family of the district (the Beltons) have had to rent out their home to an evacuated girls' school and live in a house in the village. Naturally they resent their displacement, but are resigned to waiting until better times return. So the theme of the (temporary) reorganisation of tenancy and land ownership (notice the reference to the Gracchi, who advocated reform of land ownership in favour of the people) is combined with the landowner's assiduous maintenance of rights of way, to produce a flourishing and very Conservative statement of How Things Should Be, by now a familiar refrain in Thirkell's Barsetshire. The Hikers' Rights Preservation Society was for her a manifestation of what Evelyn Waugh was to call, in *Brideshead Revisited* (1945), the Age of Hooper.[54]

Bernard Bergonzi remarked of 1930s writers that

> the prevalence of aristocratic nostalgia and images of indulgence [in their works] points to a different facet of wartime consciousness from the egalitarianism of 'thoughtful corporals', looking for a social democratic future and wider opportunity: the state of mind that Waugh, in a vein of ridiculous snobbery in *Brideshead*, exemplified in an odious young officer, Hooper.[55]

In a review of the 2008 film of Waugh's *Brideshead Revisited* Christopher Hitchens notes that 'one of Waugh's best minor figures is anything but aristocratic: the hapless clerk Hooper could have been invented by Charles Dickens or Arnold Bennett'.[56] It is far more likely that Hooper was invented by Waugh after reading Thirkell's character Captain Hooper, of *Northbridge Rectory* and *Growing Up*. He and Waugh's odious man are the new career soldiers, and are socially impossible. Thirkell's Hooper was presumptious and a bore, without the inculcated values or cultural references that had hitherto been default characteristics of the gentleman turned soldier. He is a sneering parody of the non-gentleman.

> Captain Hooper shook hands with Sir Harry, evidently thinking but poorly of him for not being someone else. One must not, he said, let etiquette go by the board even in these times of change, and he must introduce Lady Waring to Major Merton. Everyone behaved extremely well.[57]

Hooper's faux pas are to patronise older people (the Warings), in their own house (he assumes that his army rank gives him superiority over their position as local hosts doing him a favour), and to introduce an older and titled woman, in her own home, to a younger and untitled man, when it should be the other way round on all four counts. Hooper is an uncultured incomer who knows nothing, and places value on doctrines learned in books, not from experience. Noel Merton tries to remember that 'Captain Hooper was a conscientious soldier who had got promotion by hard work', but he has to be told this by Hooper himself, which rather spoils the effect.[58]

Regrouping values

Elizabeth Bowen's observation that 'durability was to be the theme of her war-time novels'[59] relates to the strongest aspect of Thirkell's wartime writing – her sense that life had changed very fast and abruptly, leaving a high tide of stranded social usages behind it. The characters endure, but they adapt, and they incorporate new blood to make them stronger. In her review of *Miss Bunting* Isabelle Mallet identifies exactly what has changed, and what Barsetshire has surrendered.

It is not Mr Adams' successful gate-crashing which unnerves us so much here as the fact that his progress is noticed at all. Gone is the old, tactless, kindly, absent-minded method of making Mr Adams feel ill at ease. Nicely brought up persons permit themselves to consider ways and means of dealing with him. Extreme 'insiders' and exceptionally old families discuss OUT LOUD for the first time in 600 years the whys and wherefores of Mr Adams' being.[60]

Mr Adams first appears as an easy butt of class-based criticisms, but develops over time into a well-integrated member of the social group who first looked at him askance. After the war he marries into the county, shows an innate appreciation of architecture (always important for Thirkell) and knows how to deal with people. His politics begin openly Socialist and end silently Conservative. Such a transformation was very unlikely to have been planned from his first appearance, but emerges over time as Thirkell identifies his place in her Conservative society. His alterations in each novel after his first appearance in *The Headmistress* reflect the increased flexibility of British society during the war. Mr Adams added variety to a socially limited set of characters, and incorporated other alterations in British society, an acknowledgement of changing social conditions between classes, and unprecedented social mixing caused by evacuation to Barsetshire from London.

Apart from *Cheerfulness Breaks In*, which is a continuation of *Summer Half* and begins with Rose Birkett's wedding, the wartime novels all begin with an elegy to beautiful domestic architecture, and describe how it has managed to survive to the present straitened times. *Northbridge Rectory* (1941) begins with a description of architectural perfection but we also see the Victorian rectitude that 'kept the railway at an extremely inconvenient distance from the town': this must be preserved, along with the High Street's perfect design.[61] *Marling Hall* (1942) begins with phrases such as 'in more golden days', 'owing to death duties and other ameliorative influences', and 'for want of woodmen'.[62] *Growing Up* (1943) begins with a paean to lost trains and railway services, which is also a lament for the loss of proper travelling privileges for the upper classes. *The Headmistress* opens with a description of a perfect village, the Great House and its family, followed by a lament for the family's financial decline. Thirkell works hard to win the reader's sympathy for the sad strictures that make it necessary for the Beltons to let Harefield Park for a very good sum, and to move to one of their other properties in Harefield itself. 'For five generations the Beltons had sat in their Palladian mansion looking over their own parkland. Now the sixth Belton since the nabob was sitting in a drawing-room, a parlour, in a house in the village street.'[63] *Miss Bunting* (1945) begins with a brief mention of the great Dukes of Omnium (borrowed from Trollope) and their resistance to railways, and the town of Hallbury. 'Until the coming of the railway it had remained almost untouched by progress', and 'it was the rising land that saved it from the degrading suburbs that so often accompany the march of progress'.[64] The emphasis on architectural value judgements in all her novels indicates, as Penelope Fritzer notes, 'a nice dichotomy between the upper-class taste for the late eighteenth- and early nineteenth-century beauty of such houses as the Old Bank House and [...] the mid- and late-nineteenth-century ugliness of houses such as Beliers Priory, Gatherum Castle and Pomfret Towers'.[65]

In *Marling Hall*, the community and family are led by Mrs Marling, rather than her husband the squire. 'If it were not for his wife he would have lost heart altogether by now.' But the qualities that make Amabel Marling so suitable for her role are not all beneficent. 'She had the tradition of service, the energy, capacity for taking pains and, let us frankly say, the splendid insensitiveness and the self-confidence that make the aristocracy of the county what it is.'[66] This toughness extends to the tone of *Marling Hall* itself, an astringent novel that has fewer jokes, and more distasteful encounters by invading non-gentry, than we are used to in Thirkell. The theme of the novel is the rescue of the elder Marling daughter Lettice from being crushed by her own family. This Darwinian process is observed by the elderly Miss Bunting, governess to the aristocracy, who upholds her values in the face of all change. She looks grimly at the new standards of behaviour indulged in by her favourite former charge David Leslie, last seen in *Wild Strawberries* (1934). In that novel David was a 1930s playboy; in this novel he is getting thinner on top, and is rejected by Lettice for his unreliability and self-centredness. These are not the values that will get the war won, or restore England to its proper condition. *Marling Hall* indicates a new anger in Thirkell's writing, that expresses resentment as well as sturdy resistance to change. There are very few wholly pleasant people in *Marling Hall*, as if Thirkell was simply too angry, some years into the war, to be loving or amusing without cynicism or bitterness. David Leslie is more selfish and manipulative than we have seen him before; the Harveys are a thoroughly unpleasant couple; and Mrs Smith the pilfering landlady is a nightmarish grotesque. These are people who have been brought together forcibly, and do not understand each other. By throwing these symbols of dissonance together, Thirkell shows us a society under stress.

Different worlds and social codes

In *Cheerfulness Breaks In*, the Hosiers' Boys Foundation School is to be evacuated from London to Southbridge School, causing a juddering shock of social values in collision. The sudden and unwanted close proximity of two teaching communities with such different backgrounds is mutually unwelcome. Thirkell was using cultural collision to express the fear of the unknown felt by the evacuees and their hosts, but her exploration of the certainties they cling to only extols the superiority of Southbridge, since they seem to learn nothing from the Hosiers' teachers. The Hosiers' teachers, in contrast, learn valuable lessons about how to be a gentleman and how to behave in polite (i.e. upper-class) society. But this is only true in the masculine sphere. When Mrs Birkett and Mrs Morland (representing Southbridge) pay a formal call on Mrs Bissell, wife of the headmaster of the Hosiers' Boys, they are discomfited and awed by their exposure to the cultural norms of a class they have never encountered before, and they come away feeling thoroughly ashamed of themselves for their preconceptions. Mrs Bissell, the remarkable former state school teacher, reminds these anxious gentry ladies of essential human values, and her quality is confirmed by her instant acceptance by her new neighbours.

However, the Southbridge social network is largely made up of local teachers and eccentrics, and they do not often appear at occasions where 'the county' gather. So the assimilation of the Bissells into Barsetshire is only partial. Mr Bissell is desperate to make a space for his own cultural norm of auto-didactic political debate. 'If they were to keep their balance in this new and peculiar world where no one knew what dialectic meant, they must somehow be alone in their spare time.'[67] To the reader's relief, the Bissells flourish in the halfway territory of Wiple Terrace, a No-Man's Land of social, and sexual, experimentation (see 'Camp' below).

Only the foolish, like Mary Leslie, think that children of different classes should be allowed to socialise together while 'they were too young to know the difference',[68] but she is rebuked by David Leslie who insists on the need to keep the different classes apart. Oliver Marling marvels at the gulf between the excellence of his office workers and their lack of interest in anything that he and his friends would want to talk about.[69] In *Northbridge Rectory* Mrs Villars the vicar's wife, 'who had realized long ago that one of her war duties would be to make friends with many people whom at other times she would have been able without discourtesy to avoid except as acquaintances, said she would love to come'.[70] She is a particularly revealing focaliser for Thirkell's monologue on the subject of class and social codes, since she is often being deferred to for her opinion. She finds her pastoral role difficult, and dreads the prospect of making contact with aggressive and rude evacuees in the village shops, since her accent and attitude classify her immediately as 'stuck-up'. 'Always, to be perfectly frank with herself, she would fear and shrink from contact with them. They didn't want to learn her language; she couldn't learn theirs.'[71]

Women are also judged by the narrative voice, from their class-defined dress sense. Miss Hampton, the dapper and gentlemanly lesbian in a tweed coat and skirt, rejects utterly the abomination of women in trousers,[72] yet another well thought-of character, Mrs Phelps the practical Admiral's wife, has never been out of trousers since the war began.[73] Lucy Marling the squire's daughter with a passion for outdoor work may look a sight in old and shapeless clothes, but when a stranger observes 'her well-groomed hair and her well-made, well-cleaned shoes and her well-fitting stockings' she is recognised for what she is: a lady.[74]

Thirkell instructed her readers how to judge other people's flouting of the social codes, using a caricature family called Warbury who flagrantly ignore all regulations possible, in *Cheerfulness Breaks In*. The Warburys, originally called Warburg, caused Thirkell's American publisher some concern. He wrote to her in September 1940 to ask her to reconsider their anti-Semitic depiction, and to change their surname to avoid offend-ing the prominent American Warburg family. Thirkell's irritated reply to Jamie Hamilton seems to miss the point, by saying that her original depiction of these three obnoxious characters was an accurate descrip-tion of people whom she had observed, and that they were 'no more representative of Jews than say Fagin is'.[75] She changed the name but the offensiveness of their description remains, and is still anti-Semitic by their association with the film industry, and their ostentatious dress and car. Their objectionable behaviour in a wartime setting of rationing and lighting restrictions was intended to show what the British were enduring, and how well they behaved, in contrast with these outsiders' wanton disregard for law and good taste. There was no need in plot terms to make the characters Jewish. Thirkell acts as a social barometer of her times by assuming that since she saw nothing wrong or repellent in this, neither would her readers.

Respecting the law is used again as an indicator of character, exem-plified by Frances Harvey admitting that she uses the black market to buy gin,[76] compared to Lord Stoke's strict adherence to petrol rationing regulations.[77] The visiting Mrs Hunter is silently rejected from future invitations to Mrs Perry's working party for failing to bring her own milk and sugar ration.[78] The laws of the community must be policed as strictly as the laws of the country. Laws of taste are similarly policed. When the Harveys and David Leslie inspect Mrs Smith's house they discuss its lower middle-class décor in sneering terms that are designed to signal their superior taste, and instruct the reader how to feel about certain items on the inventory. Mrs Smith's dialogue is itself a caricature of risible lower-class vocabulary that anticipates Nancy Mitford's 'U and Non-U' essay of 1956. Frances Harvey enjoys laughing with David Leslie at the very concept of guest towels, a class code revisited later in *Miss Bunting* when Heather Adams despairingly realises that 'proper people' don't use guest towels at all. '"Mrs Belton didn't. Lady Fielding doesn't. It's like fussing about doylies and things. Proper people just don't.'"[79] The correctness of vocabulary extends beyond conversational use to how one should think.

Lettice has to remind Geoffrey Harvey of this, when he goes too far in discussing his translation of medieval French poetry that includes the words 'breast' and 'wide-wombèd whore'. '"I simply cannot bear," said Lettice firmly, passing over this embarrassing sample, "poetry that has the word 'breast' in it. I don't know why. Modern poetry at least."'[80] We have already judged Frances Harvey for her perceptible cooling towards Oliver Marling when she realises that he will not inherit his father's estate.

Thirkell shows how unacceptable the Harveys' social codes are for Barsetshire when they quarrel in front of their guest. Their codes are simply inappropriate for the sphere in which they hope to move.

Class and snobbery

When her younger son Lance was finishing university in 1941, Thirkell mentioned in a letter Lance's plans to go into the Officer Training Corps and thence to service in the army reserve. 'He has been very lucky to get 2 years. Thank God the sons of gentlemen still have a little preferential treatment at the Universities.'[81] Thirkell was very preoccupied with the schooling of the sons of gentlemen, and her novels frequently judge one person to be acceptable or unacceptable because of where he came from, or to whom she was related. By exploring in such detail the nuances of the strangers in the camp – in *Cheerfulness Breaks In* these are the Hosiers' Boys, but there are invading strangers in every wartime novel – Thirkell's novels offer a remarkable record of how she expected people to judge each other, and how snobbery was a conservative force.

> "The Hosiers Boys, sir. But aren't those the chaps who had a week's camp down by the river the summer I left school. I mean they were very decent chaps –." There was a silence, so charged with agreement that Philip almost expected an immediate vengeance for snobbish feelings to fall on them all three.[82]

Nothing more need be said by the schoolmasters of Southbridge School, since it is obvious that 'very decent chaps' are not the same as 'chaps like us'. The same anxiety about judging others instinctively afflicts the women.

> "But Amy, though it seems snobbish to say so, perhaps Mrs Bissell doesn't have cards." Mrs Birkett thought this quite probable, which led to a discussion as to whether people who didn't have cards would think it an offensive act of Capittleism if people who had cards left them on them. As their premises were based on entire ignorance the argument was very inconclusive.[83]

Mrs Morland's anxious remarks reveal a colossal gap in her knowledge, on a comically redundant level of life (in)experience.

Class certainties are reinforced in *The Headmistress*, when Elsa and Charles are ferried home to Harefield village on a motorbike by an obliging Other Rank called Copper. Mrs Belton realises immediately that, helpful and generous though he has been, Copper cannot be asked to supper.[84] Her refusal to break class boundaries and offer hospitality that she would automatically have expected to give another young man of a higher social class is simply how Mrs Belton's class and generation are. 'All this mixing might be a good thing, but she felt too old for it and frankly hated it.'[85] Her younger and less reflective children have similarly fixed views, but without their mother's diffidence. Elsa Belton expresses herself stridently about her expectations of a lady's behaviour and choice of future husband, which is her right in a private family gathering,[86] but Charles shames his entire family in public. He is anxious about the Hosiers' Girls playing billiards on his former home's billiard tables.

> "Miss Sparling," said Charles, with the desperation of one who has been waiting to ask an indiscreet question for some time and can contain himself no longer, "when you said your girls played billiards at home, I thought the Hosiers' Girls School was a kind of secondary school. I don't mean rudely, but I saw some of the Hosiers' boys when they were at Southbridge School and they weren't quite what you would call a public school, I mean they did awfully well in exams, but they weren't – oh, well, you know what I mean, only it's so awfully difficult to say what one means, only they didn't seem as if they'd have billiard tables at home if it isn't rude to say so." By this time Charles' family would have been quite glad if he had been back in his billet in Shrimpington-on-Sea, and indeed Charles himself, hearing his own voice faltering in an embarrassed vacuum, wouldn't have been sorry if he could have been miraculously transported elsewhere.[87]

That Thirkell could joyfully expose a snobbish comment like this, which is so obviously anxious not to be rude, shows what an astute commentator she was on the delicate subject of class indicators. Charles' intention is to say that he didn't want the baize-covered billiard tables played on by schoolgirls who didn't know how to treat them, but as he could only judge the Hosiers' Girls by their cognates, the Hosiers' Boys, he did not expect them to know how the cloth ought to be treated. However, his error in assuming that both schools catered for children of the same (lower) class is interestingly wrong. As Miss Sparling explains to the Beltons,

> "[The Hosiers' Girls] are mostly the same as I am, only they have wealthy families and not so many books. In London my girls came

from good lower middle-class families, quite a lot of them well-off in a quiet way. When we were evacuated down here and became a boarding school, the people who had got rich quickly in war business began to send their girls to us."[88]

A page later, Miss Sparling's own background is established, very positively, as having good breeding, which is what really matters for Thirkell. The curious point for modern readers is that Thirkell rarely explains why breeding, class, rank, and so on, should matter so much. If she had, she would also be admitting that her readers were not like her, and represented the uneducated moderns she deplored. Statements like this – 'It may be snobbishness to think the better of a person because your Vicar has known her grandfather who was a Canon; but it lies deep at the roots of social life, and there is a good reason for it'[89] – are authoritative, but uninformative. When Thirkell has an example to work on, she is more forthcoming:

> [T]he status of [Hallbury New Town's] citizens was almost indefinable, but may be expressed in the words of Engineer-Admiral Palliser at Hallbury House who, inarticulately conscious of a house at least five hundred years old in parts, held by his family since the Commodore Palliser who did so well in the matter of prize-money under Lord Howe, remarked that these houses on the railway line were always changing hands, and so dismissed the whole affair.[90]

Thirkell is clear that age, continuity and inherited local status confer a high status, and that this applies to the peasantry as well: her county families are proud of their connection with the Margetts, Polletts, Bunces and so on, because those peasant-class families are as old as their own, if not older.

More definitively, the Hosiers' Boys headmaster Mr Bissell considers himself to be of a higher class than the unspeakable Mr Hopkins, also a Hosiers' Boys teacher. As we have already observed the essential decency and bravery of Mr Bissell, and have been shown and told nothing good about Mr Hopkins, we can draw the lesson that the more admirable the person is, the higher up the class scale they must be. (There are almost no unpleasant upper-class characters in Thirkell, except the Dreadful Dowager.) There are also degrees of behaviour. Mr Belton privately thinks Mr Adams 'a rank outsider and unmitigated vulgarian', but he does not say this to strangers and acquaintances, for such behaviour would not befit his class code of good manners.[91] Mr Adams's rise in these novels and the nuances of his increasing acceptance teach us how class works and how one may be accepted into a new social group with strict laws and invisible expectations.

Miss Bunting contains the most important lessons, since this novel is concerned with the education of Anne Fielding and her parents' social anxiety about her friends. Her governess, Miss Bunting, monitors Anne's relationships with the world to an extent that seems dictatorial today. Anne's friendship with Mr Adams's daughter Heather tests her budding social senses which struggle to work with two sets of social codes. The episodes of the embarrassingly ostentatious birthday presents, Miss Bunting's decisive ending of Anne's impromptu breakfast birthday party with the lower orders, Jane and Miss Holly realising that they have snobbishly misjudged Mrs Merivale on finding she can cap a quote from *Alice in Wonderland*, Jane's increasing attraction to Mr Adams despite (or because of?) his complete social impossibility, Miss Bunting's remarks about Barchester High School for Girls being '"all very well for the daughters of Barchester tradesmen, but most unsuitable for Anne"'[92] – these are lessons for the reader to absorb and learn from.

It is clear that Mr Adams will rise socially because his natural good sense and honesty is making him useful for the gentlemen that he deals with. '"We have elected him to the Barchester County Club, you know. A lot of members didn't want him, but he is extremely useful on committees."'[93] Expediency, and male business relationships, allow his foot to remain in the door, as does his own self-belief: Jane Gresham is stunned to find that Mr Adams thinks the very respectable Mrs Merivale a not quite good enough landlady for his gauche daughter. There is also the question of Mr Adams's political leverage. He employs a great many voters in Hogglestock, and thus could be a genuinely useful man to have in the upper layers of county leadership, all class questions aside. Lord Pomfret 'said seriously that what really mattered was how the fellow was going to vote. If he was the right sort they could do with a man like him on the County Council; someone who understood the growing class of industrial workers in and around Barchester, as well as old fogies like himself and Pridham, who thought more of the agricultural interest'.[94] When Jane admires Mr Adams as being the kind of person who gets things done, her father retorts, bristling, that that was what gave Hitler power.[95] How should we regard this discreet alignment of Adams and Hitler as anything but the threat of those who make a violent change to an old system?

It is clear that Heather Adams will never be a lady. Interestingly, neither Mr Adams nor Heather appear to want this, since she simply wants to go to Cambridge to study mathematics and then join her father in the Works. Thirkell is already lining up a husband for her, the son of a beer magnate who has done well in the war (the conservative marker of good character). But even though she and Anne have very little in common, they still like each other, and are both living in Hallbury for the summer. Why should they not be friends?

> Sir Robert Fielding recognised Mr Adams from their business meetings and hoped he would not have to introduce him to his wife. Not that he was more of a snob than most of us are, but he foresaw possible social complications for his extremely busy wife which were, to his mind, quite unnecessary. And they had heard enough from their daughter Anne about Adams's girl, for whom she seemed deplorably to have taken a liking to.[96]

There is a paradox here, for the anxieties expressed by both the Fielding parents are indicative of their less than secure social identity. Miss Bunting knows that the Fieldings, 'kind, delightful and intelligent people though they were, [they] could not be called county: not possibly'.[97] The clue may be that Lady Fielding is worried by the Adamses' existence, a sign of not-quite county-ness, since a truly aristocratic lady would not let anything bother her, but would take people as she found them, and remain secure in her own position.

Camp

In a very unexpected contrast, Thirkell's great lesbian creations of Miss Hampton and Miss Bent, who first appeared in Barsetshire in *Cheerfulness Breaks In*, are utterly secure in their position. They are two marvellous hard-drinking eccentrics in Southbridge unconnected with the aristocracy or the gentry. Their lesbianism is celebrated briskly with sly innuendo, and Miss Hampton is one of Thirkell's strongest authoritative figures. Their appearance reminds the reader that Thirkell had introduced homosexual characters in earlier novels, but with less affection or admiration.

The difference in her treatment is clearly gendered. In earlier novels Thirkell's male homosexuals were defined by their petty malignancy and coded dressing. In *Wild Strawberries* (1934) Lionel Harvest of the BBC wears his Fair Isle sweater tucked inside his trousers, and his friend Mr Potter has hair that 'waved quite naturally'.[98] Mr Harvest's aunt, Lady Dorothy Bingham, brays: 'I'd let my girls go out with him, but

I don't know that I'd let my boys'.[99] But when he inherits four thousand a year, this persuades Joan Stevenson to accept his proposal of a companionate marriage. Money will thus overcome effeminacy, and give a girl independence. Lionel continues to be associated with malice and petulance, in *Marling Hall* (1942), where he has written a book about the BBC after inheriting his fortune (so he no longer needs his job), but his scathing exposé hardly sells at all. The horrible Fritz Warbury does embroidery, which establishes him as being either a foreigner or camp, since no British male character since E F Benson's Georgie Pillson has embroidered in public. Thirkell's appreciation for the performance of male camp behaviour can be seen in an unpublished letter of 1945, in which she describes, maliciously, meeting Ivor Novello. 'Mr Novello is of course PERFECT – "The sincerity of his falseness, and the falseness of his sincerity" (as Denis said of J. M. B.) – the lingering handshake – DIVINE.' Her letter continues with 'It's a shocking display of conceit and pretension', which seems to refer to Mr Novello again.[100] Her resentful portraits of male homosexuals seem mean-spirited when contrasted with her wholly affectionate portraits of Miss Hampton and Miss Bent.

Miss Hampton's obvious homosexuality accentuates her social authority and the awed respect she receives for her capacity for strong drink. She is a noted author, and first appears in *Cheerfulness Breaks In* as 'a rather handsome woman with short, neatly-curled grey hair, not young, in an extremely well-cut black coat and skirt, a gentlemanly white silk shirt with collar and tie, and neat legs in silk stockings and brogues, holding a cigarette in a very long black holder'.[101] Her first words are 'Come in and have a drink', and she and her companion Miss Bent drink prodigiously with no obvious effects. She is also a direct challenge to mealy-mouthed attitudes to sex and sexuality. '"So you keep a boys' school; and in London; interesting; much vice? [...] We're all men here and I'm doing a novel about a boy's school, so I might as well know something about it. I'm thinking of calling it 'Temptation at St Anthony's'."'[102] British obscenity laws were stringent between the wars, making an amusing joke of Miss Hampton's award of the Banned Book of the Month.[103] Thirkell makes a number of stealth jokes about sexuality, like Lady Dorothy's joke about Lionel Harvest, that have a camp insouciance that is in strong contrast to her otherwise default tone of extreme social conservatism. Miss Bent mentions Rory Freemantle in passing, and the narrative voice adds a reference later to Aurora Freemantle, but only those who had read Compton Mackenzie's *roman-à-clef Extraordinary Women* (1928) would have known that she was a lesbian character.[104] Miss Hampton's louche though faithful lesbian lifestyle must have been eye-opening for conservative readers. '"Hampton does plunge so in bed when she is Writing."'[105]

The managing woman

Miss Hampton's sphere is writing, and Miss Bent organises their lives. Yet they are almost unique among Barsetshire women in not participating, at first, in the ordering and planning of local and small-scale service and activities. This range and number of these war-related activities on the Barsetshire home front is a further accurate reflection of the importance of British women's voluntary work in regional, but not national, organisation. They were a socially disruptive force. In Daphne du Maurier's play *The Years Between* (1944) a British airman returning home after a long absence during which his family had feared he was dead, calls his now-busy wartime volunteer wife '"one of those managing, restless women, always writing letters, going to meetings, arguing about ridiculous questions, having interminable conversations on the telephone"'.[106] This describes the wartime committee woman and the character of the patriotic and unpaid volunteer organiser, drawn largely from the middle classes. Northbridge is where Thirkell first lets loose the energies of a new population of Barsetshire housewives and county ladies, into a maelstrom of voluntary and social activity.

> In every war, however unpleasant, there are a certain number of people who with a shriek of joy take possession of a world made for them. Mrs Villars [...] suddenly found herself, rather to her relief, quite o'ercrowed by a number of women who had during what is mistakenly called The Last War driven ambulances, run canteens, been heads of offices, of teams of land girls, of munition welfare, and had been pining in retirement on small incomes ever since.[107]

Thirkell does not so much praise this army of underused women, as explore the personalities who relish performing voluntary tasks for no monetary gain, gaining as a by-product the invaluable reward of class approval. Before the war her socially privileged interfering woman was epitomised by the indulged and beloved Lady Emily Leslie in *Wild Strawberries*. Lower down the class scale the compulsive reorganiser Mrs Tebben clashes mightily with the haughtily theatrical Mrs Palmer in *August Folly*. We don't hear very much about these women during wartime, which is an odd omission. Instead, Thirkell focuses on women within communities.

In *Northbridge Rectory* Mrs Turner rises from the ranks by her diligent work running the Northbridge Communal Kitchen, and Mrs Paxon has more voluntary service uniforms than any other woman. According to James Hinton, it was unlikely that increased government funding for women's services at the beginning of the war 'opened up the privilege of wearing a WVS uniform to significant numbers of working-class women'.[108] This reinforces the reader's impression that these stalwart volunteers and community organisers are lower middle-class rather than working-class. They are used by Thirkell as didactic examples of how women may now work their way up the class hierarchies in a village through good community service, long since the province of the gentry and middle classes.[109] The unpaid organisational work of the county classes is held as the standard to which other women ought to aspire.[110]

Thirkell approves of women working very hard in the service of others, holding large responsibilities and fulfilling their class roles, for no pay (for example, Lady Pomfret, Mrs Marling and Lucy Marling). If the posts are part of their wifely or feudal/class duties, they receive praise. Women working in paid jobs are, however, inherently bad (Frances Harvey), or overwork themselves (Leslie Waring), or cannot make a family (Lydia Merton), or allow authoritative efficiency to overwhelm marriageable femininity (Elsa Belton). The steady, hearty teacher Miss Holly notes that '"Miss Belton has any amount of brains. Any amount. Too many perhaps. When we've got too many, we don't marry"'.[111] Teaching is exempt, of course, and Miss Sparling and Miss Holly (and even Miss Pettinger, long after the war is over) are praised for their exemplary good influence. Paid war service is acceptable, but it is much better from Thirkell's perspective for women to marry and *then* work for no pay.

Instructional texts

Thirkell's messages about how women should behave in their new social roles are conveyed through the changes in young women's characters on meeting young men they would like to marry, since marriage, or suitability for it, is the defining difference between a hoyden, a minx and a potential wife and mother. The resplendently awful Rose Birkett is a model of how not to behave, since she only learns partial self-control and good conduct many years into her marriage. She can also be seen as the modern 1940s girl in revolt against the rules of good behaviour, with which her husband sides as a representative of hierarchical and patriarchal society. Sometimes it is hard for the modern reader to sympathise with the strictures of the narrative voice, since Thirkell's determinedly old-fashioned views sit at odds with what we would consider now quite normal behaviour.

Another very important character in the wartime novels is Lydia Keith, since she transforms during the war from the hoyden of *Summer Half* to a serious and reliable officer's wife and lady of the manor in *Growing Up*. She avoids becoming a tyrant through the trials of wartime, developing the right way into the perfect kind of managing woman, and a good wife. Her depiction is almost an experiment on the effects of the war on a dominant personality. She no longer behaves like a trying and noisy schoolgirl, and her appearance is transformed; 'the well-groomed hair, the well-cut tweeds, the well-made shoes, even the well-kept hands'.[112] Her manners too have improved immeasurably. Lady Waring approves of Lydia's 'slight air of deference': 'it might come from the heart, it might be only an outward form; but it helped to keep civilisation going'.[113] Keeping civilisation going was, in the end, Thirkell's main concern in her wartime novels, and her hope was that it would remain thoroughly conservative.

It will be seen that this discussion has largely been about women. Thirkell did have a great many male characters in her wartime fiction, but since her focus was the changes that war was forcing on domestic life and community living, of which women were the first defenders, men were simply less affected by change. Most army-age men were away from home. The men who remained – the various vicars and retired gentlemen, Mr Downing the medieval scholar – were observers on the scene, hustled about by the women, or were absent in their offices and works. They return to fuller participation after the war, while the women were expected to sink back gratefully into inactivity.

8
Rewriting History: Yates and Thirkell, 1945–60

On writing fiction and history

Yates's new beginning for the Pleydells, in *The House that Berry Built* (1945), draws on his own experiences in leaving Britain in the 1920s and building his own house in south-west France, with a perfunctory detective mystery to unravel between construction *longueurs*. *The Berry Scene* (1947) delivers new 'Berry & Co' short stories set in different periods of their heyday, and his fictionalised memoirs *As Berry and I Were Saying* (1952) and *B-Berry and I Look Back* (1958) are denunciations of the changing times. Alternating with these are two thrillers, set before the war. *Red in the Morning* (1946) is Yates writing on top form, but *Cost Price* (1949) feels effortful, and the characters are tired. '"Tell me, William, why did we take this on?" "God knows," said I. "I've been asking myself for days."'[1] His historical novel *Lower Than Vermin* (1950) was a rewriting of the past for conservatives who feel hard-done-by, and was followed by a slight detective novel, *Ne'er-Do-Well* (1954). However, Yates's last novel and penultimate work, *Wife Apparent* (1956), was a triumphant return to his playful and witty style of the 1920s, an emotionally taut comedy of recovery from wartime brain damage, set in an English Arcadia.

In Yates's two volumes of fictionalised memoirs Berry Pleydell voices loathing, while Boy Pleydell and Yates himself, in a smooth demonstration of modernist metatextuality, are voices of moral smugness. The women are merely auditors, for whom Yates recalls episodes from the real-life past with a commentary that vilifies some historical characters (Oscar Wilde, Christabel Pankhurst) and praises others (judges from Yates's legal career). Despite Yates's prefatory Note – 'Perhaps I may be forgiven for repeating that the memories themselves are strictly true and that I have exaggerated nothing'[2] – the episodes read as highly subjective opinions on the past. The episodes that valorise the past at the expense of the post-war present are strangely unhistorical, and contain loathing for Germans in hindsight, during and after the First World War, in a way that he did not write at the time. He is obsessed with German spies in Britain,[3] and demonises German soldiers and civilians,[4] yet he never mentions the Nazis, and only cites Hitler twice in these catalogues of bitterness.[5] Yates's response to the Second World War is the misapplied bombast of a non-participant who does not understand its reality.

Yates made a point of proclaiming his veracity, in his works and in Notes or Prefaces, when his quasi-memoirs mixed history with invented stories. The obvious political messages in his later works are supported by 'truths' that his fictional characters relate, and that the narrative voice asserts as historical fact. Thus he obscures his fictions with selective history, by which he claims respectability for the whole of his work, while demanding the reader's trust as a celebrated author of invention. In *Lower Than Vermin* (1950) Yates's present-day interjections add an extra level of commentary to the story, in which the narrative voice makes its own observations. This technique, much like the metatextuality mentioned above, produces tensions between the understanding of history, and the boundaries between fiction and non-fiction.

This technique is used in *As Berry and I Were Saying* (1952), a series of conversations between William Mercer writing as Yates the author, who is also writing as his character Boy Pleydell, plus Berry, Daphne and Jill. The fictional characters congratulate Mercer the author in his alter ego persona of Boy Pleydell the character, for the success and accuracy of his earlier works, telling him which stories they liked best.[6] The fictional stories that Boy, Berry and Yates tell to the other characters are bracketed with writing tips by Mercer/Yates/Boy, by discussions of how Yates's real-life works were written, serialised and received by the public; and by name-dropping of Mercer's associations with famous people. The memories of Mercer the lawyer become the reminiscences of Yates the author voiced by Boy Pleydell, when 'he' recalls and admires the well-known author 'Saki' without mentioning that 'Saki' was Mercer's real-life cousin.[7] These complications of ego and authorial identity are enriched by obvious exaggerations, discussion of invented fictional characters who have appeared in earlier works, and selective recall of historical events.[8]

His practice of blending historical fact with the lives of fictional characters is disconcerting, as it presents them as part of real life, with real feelings and experience. An example from the novel *Lower Than Vermin* (1950) demonstrates this effect:

> Divorce has become so common that it bears no longer the stigma that it once did: but in 1908 to have figured in the Divorce Court meant, not, perhaps, social extinction, but a definite degradation – a stern reduction in rank. A great many doors were closed, as a matter of course. What was almost worse, there were flung open other doors, through which the de Guesclins would sooner have died than pass. Vivien was so much beloved that, she could, I firmly believe, have weathered the storm. But nothing on earth would ever have induced her to try. She would never have accepted the loyalty she could have had. And everyone knew as much, because they knew her.[9]

Notice how the narrative moves from historical fact (divorce becoming more common), to opinion ('definite degradation'), to the actions of the novel's characters (the de Guesclins), into a faux biography of the lead female protagonist ('Vivien was so much beloved'), described as fact ('I firmly believe'), and then character analysis as if of a real person ('she would never have accepted'). This is a complex progression of perspectives that affects the verisimilitude of the narration, and how the reader receives its implicit messages. Yates makes it impossible for the reader to trust the author, making the narrative voice alarmingly unreliable, yet in the later commentaries on *Lower Than Vermin* Mercer/ Boy insist that everything in the novel is true.

Yates's use of the conventions of historical fiction is suspect because they do not derive from, in the words of Georg Lukács, 'the individuality of characters from the historical peculiarity of their age'.[10] Yates describes a situation set in the past to describe it as moral degradation, a stance with which he would like his readers to agree, and then shows his characters as being too superior in morals or taste to participate in that degradation, unlike their fictional peers. Such characters are what Lukács calls 'eccentric figures, figures who fall psychologically outside the atmosphere of an age'.[11] Yates twists the rules of historical representation to emphasise his own authority,[12] and thus, following the reading of Jerome de Groot, 'provokes a certain anxiety and disquiet' in the reader.[13] Such a misrepresentation of history, or characters represented in a historical situation, is serious, as the novelist Sarah Waters has noted,[14] since Yates wants the reader to be reassured that the Yates narrative voice is still the voice of authority, no matter what fictional lies it may be telling.

Our task here is to scrutinise Yates, and Thirkell, as authors, to discern why they rewrote history as they did, and pressed their selective accounts on the reader as the whole truth. A brief comparison with the satirist Marghanita Laski contrasts with Thirkell's conservative nostalgia, which used the realistic narrative mode as well as utopian fantasy. Laski's novels *Love on the Supertax* (1944) and *Tory Heaven* (1948) are examples of the trend for Conservative apologia (in her case, anti-Conservative) in fiction that became a vogue in the later 1940s. Both these novels show the flaws in a Conservative utopia and ridicule politicised social codes, by separating the actions of the novels from the reader's own experience through the motif of a dream (as in *Tory Heaven*), or in a dystopic Tory nightmare (*Love on the Supertax*). Thirkell had constructed Barsetshire as the Conservative ideal for living: she did not need to create antithetical satire to produce humour. Thirkell's Tory Barsetshire was close enough to reality to be read both as affectionately ironical nostalgia, and also as a vision of the way things ought to be. Once the war had ended and the Conservatives had lost power, she rewrote Barsetshire's back history to better suit the way things ought to be, in a Brave New World of which she utterly disapproved.

David Pryce-Jones observed that for Thirkell, 'the war seemed a watershed: civilization and all things nice on the far side, and anarchy, snails and puppydog tails on this side'.[15] Just as Yates enlarged the White Ladies estate in retrospect, in Thirkell's post-war novels she systematically enhanced Barsetshire after the fact, by retrofitting its institutions and practices throughout the late 1940s and 1950s to account for things that she had not mentioned in the 1930s and during the war. This extended the Barsetshire experience, adding texture and detail to her characters' lives. As an example, the Barchester Women's County Club is first heard of in *Private Enterprise* (1947), but Thirkell describes it there as a long-established institution. It appears in this novel to stress the stringencies of post-war daily life for county women as a contrast to the comforts they had enjoyed in the past. It is a space for women to make arrangements in and to meet for lunch. It did not exist in *Before Lunch* (1939), say, or *Summer Half* (1937), because in the 1930s Thirkell expected women to make their social and county arrangements at home. After the war, in which her women characters had attained professional status and were given large public responsibilities, they needed a more professional meeting-place. A club gave them almost male status. This was hardly the 'anarchy' that Pryce-Jones invokes, yet it is clear that Thirkell regards the professionalisation of ladies as a poor substitute for pre-war gracious living.

Older lives and anger

In the 1950s Thirkell paid less attention to her junior romantic leads, and developed a new interest in writing the lives of the middle-aged and elderly. In *Jutland Cottage* (1953) Admiral Phelps's meagre service pension performs the function of the Wicked Stepmother, reducing middle-aged Margot Phelps to undeserved penury as Cinderella. The collapse of Miss Pemberton in *What Did It Mean?* (1954) is echoed by the decline of Admiral Phelps across several novels. The tone of *Never Too Late* has gravity deriving from Mr Halliday's decline into senility, and the slow-developing drama in George's anxieties over the estate that his father has forgotten to make over to him. Angus Wilson noted in 1951 that

> the great key theme of English fiction since the War has been nostal-
> gia. [...] It is, nevertheless, a school of death, nostalgic, wistful, even
> at its most loving expressing the kind of courage with which the
> aristocrats faced the inevitable guillotine. It has a lighter, gayer sister
> school, that of Nancy Mitford and Angela Thirkell, who attempt to
> reconstruct the same scene with some of the childhood laughter that
> rang through the nursery in the old Hall in those far-off days, but
> even this laughter comes to us a little hysterically though tears.[16]

Thirkell's 'tears' over the post-war condition are induced through an angry nostalgia. Elizabeth Bowen saw this clearly. 'Alas, after the 1945 Labour landslide, cantankerousness was to infect her work and begin to chill her admirers – they so wished she wouldn't ...!'[17] Thirkell's writing, still obstreperous into the 1950s, made her readers indignant at the plight of her characters. D J Taylor, after bitterly criticising her fiction, was able to scale back his feelings to admit that she had a point. 'The degree of genuine provocation – the note of class hatred in some of Bevan's speeches of the period – alarmed many a less excitable onlooker.'[18] The Labour Minister for Health Aneurin Bevan alarmed Yates as well: his title *Lower Than Vermin* was taken from one of Bevan's speeches describing the terrible conditions the Conservative government had inflicted on his family and community.[19] The continuing strong sales of the Conservative nostalgia offered by Yates and Thirkell indicates that their anger was shared.

By the end of the 1950s, Thirkell's grip on her characters and their families, marriages and births was failing, and her later novels contained genealogical and continuity errors.[20] Newcomers to Thirkell beginning with *Enter Sir Robert* (1955) or *Never Too Late* (1956) might have baulked at the excessive reintroductions to characters. This can be read as anxiety that her sprawling network of families would simply not be understood by new or lost readers. However, she maintained her standards in some areas. Her running jokes are still very good: Mrs Updike's serial domestic accidents, and the anecdotes about Glamora Tudor's films (see 'Sophistication' below) still comment wittily on current society. In *Close Quarters* the episode of the statues in the Harefield attics and the beautiful craftsmanship of its original seventeenth-century plans are persuasive, elegant and elegiac.[21] But these are highlights in novels that are increasingly old conversations we have heard before. To gain a better sense of how Thirkell's work responded to the changing times, we need to go back to the end of the war.

The effects of war

When the war ends, 'the hideous suspicion of peace bursting upon a war-wracked world' is either fine irony or comic displacement.[22] Thirkell continues the joke with: 'On the following Tuesday a day of national rejoicing burst by very slow degrees and barely recognised as such upon an exhausted, cross and uninterested world'.[23] Her treatment makes the point that disruption to beer and bread deliveries is more important to local life than world affairs. Barsetshire barely notices what others have had to suffer. After the atom bombs had been dropped on 6 and 9 August 1945, VJ-Day was reported in *Peace Breaks Out* in an extended rant in a housewife's voice, bitterly condemning the disruption to domestic routines.[24] The war that had ended was now a benign memory of community cooperation, and the acceleration of unwanted social change for the gentry classes. War bereavements are only mentioned in later novels, when new characters arrive to be healed by marriage.[25]

The most striking effect of the ending of war on Thirkell's characters is that the managing women of the war years are now exhausted. Barsetshire may not have suffered bombing or bereavement, but Thirkell's patient accounting of the debilitating details of life in wartime shows how war wore the civilian down. Lady Fielding, hitherto indefatigable, is 'thankful to have tea in peace. In more normal times she would have taken a committee and a dinner party in her stride, but after the strain of a long war and the almost greater strain of the recent peace, with all the upheavals and irritations and angers it had brought in its train, she felt her age'.[26] The strain of coping with emotional stresses as well as social and physical trials has its effect on the body as well as the mind. 'One is too bony, one's skin is coarsened, one's hands are not fit to show, one's neck and shoulders are better covered than uncovered; the very dresses look strange and out of place in the Foul New World.'[27] Thirkell's focus on how women of her own age have suffered from the war is extended to all women, and then to the state of the nation. We can see that her bitterness is aimed at those who have forced change on British society, not on the wartime enemy. 'All over England women of all ages, battered for six years by foreign enemies and increasing discomfort, far worse battered for the last year by discomfort and tyranny beyond what they had yet felt, mostly inflicted upon them by their own countrymen.'[28]

Thirkell pays particular attention to the unnecessary new Welfare State that Bevan had set up. Characters who notice it behave in two ways: either obstinately refusing to engage with it (Dr Ford refuses to have a panel; Mr Marling insists on paying his own way as he always has done; Margot Phelps pays for her father's care because she is 'certainly not' on the Health),[29] or proving what a waste it is (the young and healthy Edna and Doris get new false teeth just because they can; Jessie only wears her new teeth on Sundays because they are so uncomfortable).[30] Thirkell ignores the vastly improved daily medical and clinical care that her readers were enjoying.

Food, and rationing, were dominant topics of conversation.[31] Resentment at the continuation of rationing while exports were increasing to pay the war debt[32] was assuaged, partially, by some devious bypassing of permits for repair and decorating work and in farming.[33] American food parcels were gratefully praised in almost every post-war novel.[34] Thirkell's sense that the commercial structure of the nation was changing in line with social evolution was expressed in the rise of big business. 'To hear of yet another private enterprise being sucked into the insatiable and unfeeling maw of a big company made the tea-party quiet and sad.'[35] She describes the industrial town of Hogglestock for the first time, as its workers and needs become part of Barsetshire's civic and agricultural planning.[36] The post-war alterations that would reverberate all through Thirkell's novels derived from class, and how the class system was altering before her eyes. 'There is no book of etiquette, so far as we know, that deals with the difficulties when different social circles meet.'[37]

Class

Penelope Fritzer notes that, post-war, previously despised characters in Thirkell receive approval once they adopt the habits and tastes of the upper classes, specifically Mr Adams and the Parkinsons.[38] All three are incomers, and adapt themselves to county society. Mr Adams is toned-down and spruced up under Mrs Belton's guidance, and eventually marries into the county, making a home for Lucy Marling, who is otherwise a social liability. Thus he marries up, but proves himself worthy of it first. The Parkinsons are slightly different, in that he is an uneducated Church of England curate but deserves the respect due to his cloth. Their essential goodness, and lack of pride or presumption, also bring them respect. The county realises that although they are not of the right sort for former standards of social acceptance, they are absolutely the right sort for the village and the church. Mr Parkinson shows the right spirit by improving his English from Fowler's *Modern English Usage*, and reads the 'proper' *Pilgrim's Progress*.[39] They move to Greshambury New Town and suburbia, also becoming openly Conservative, as highly plausible indicators of British social evolution.

Things did not seem so hopeful elsewhere in Barsetshire for social mixing after the war. Class barriers were 'thin or cracking',[40] from the bottom up. Thirkell makes a point of writing bad behaviour from the lower classes in upper-class territory. 'Being a half-holiday it was on the cards that a boatload of the conceited, half-educated oafs and louts from Barchester might pass and help themselves to portable property.'[41] This reflects what Raymond Williams had noted as a post-war problem (also discussed in Chapter 7), that 'townspeople are seen [...] as louts and brats: not only in the obvious forms of litter and damage and noise'.[42] Notice that Thirkell implies pride and ignorance as a natural accompaniment to the presumptions of theft and bad character of lower-class urban youth. There are accusations of criminality deriving from post-war shock; rubbish and damage in Edgewood Church; criminal damage in the Pomfret Towers chapel, and at the Rising Castle protected ruins; and day trippers leave their rubbish behind.[43] Bad behaviour is associated with greater access for the lower classes to previously private estates.[44]

Thirkell insisted on proper demarcations between the classes, and worked hard at defining the mysterious quality of being 'county', analogous to her inarticulately expressed lessons about class in wartime. The wealthy and very pleasant Dean family had first appeared in *August Folly*, but were incomers with 'a kind of squatter's right' like the Perrys of Harefield,[45] and played very little part in the affairs of the upper classes or at parish level. After the war, they come to prominence as the importance of the landed classes decreases, yet the Deans rarely contribute to county causes, thus failing the 'service' requirement of the true upper classes. Susan Dean realises that her secretary, Eleanor Grantly, is much more county than she ever will be, because Eleanor knows all the Barsetshire family connections and is connected herself. The Deans are not connected, another failing in the county qualifications.[46]

All characters struggle to fit Mr Adams into their world-view because he cannot be ignored. Thirkell knew when she could not resist the social change that he represented, and used him to show how she wanted his rise in class to end: from impossible Socialist parvenu to decently useful and Conservative. Characters have difficulties in introducing Mr Adams to their friends; Lady Norton refuses to know him because he is rich and new; the Marlings think of him as an outsider even though he is to marry Lucy; and Mrs Marling recognises her own snobbishness about the suitability of Mr Adams's friends to be his best man.[47] In *Enter Sir Robert* (1955), Mrs Halliday and George encounter another, potential, Adams figure, but realise that Mr Cross(e) the bank manager (Thirkell changed the spelling of his name after his first appearance), and their tenant, is actually of their own class. He is the son of Lord Cross(e), he and George fought in the same area of France in the war, and he is 'seriously interested in finance, heir to a considerable amount of money'.[48] His wealthy sister Mrs Carter quietly takes over from Lady Graham as the lady of the Big House,[49] which indicates that Thirkell wanted class infiltrators to be the right kind of people.

Dornford Yates's novels offer an alternative view of how the conservative reader was expected to react to the changing times, using his postwar 'Berry' fiction to show how things ought to be done. Jill, erstwhile Duchess of Padua, is kind to a local Frenchwoman and her babies, which is received gratefully as a feudal condescension.[50] The Pleydells show their awareness of *noblesse oblige* in their new home in France, by opening the gardens and grounds to the public.[51] In an episode set earlier in their career they perform feudal service on behalf of their villagers by interceding over the closure of a right of way with the second Lord Withyham, whose overweening arrogance needs taking down a peg, as does his ignorance in trying to trample on the rights of the villagers who have lived there for 150 years.[52] The Pleydells are determined to protect their own people from the outside world's influence. '"Class hatred's a dreadful thing. It's been deliberately fostered for some years now – by certain politicians, to gain their ends. But it's never touched our parish – we've always been happy here."'[53] (Notice that 'we' means the landowners, not the peasants.) Yates associates class hatred with political opposition that will '"infect with the poison of envy the very tenants and servants he treats so well"'.[54] In the very defensiveness in Yates's stories we can sense an awareness of the world that is not present in Thirkell's writing. She wrote within her own protected world, albeit crossly, while Yates's voice feels more desperate, more exposed to post-war change.

Slipping standards

Thirkell filled her post-war novels with evidence of slipping social standards in the form of instruction. From the mid-1950s they taught the correct use of titles; how not to leave one's guests; whom it was possible to telephone to invite to dinner if one doesn't know them; and how to get out of a car in a skirt.[55] 'Hullo' and 'pardon' are criticised for not being correct; as are 'couch' for 'sofa' and 'lounge' for 'drawing-room'. Guest towels are still anathema.[56] As Yates did in his earlier 1940s novels (see Chapter 6), Thirkell shows how characters used first names to illustrate the social puzzle that existed across the post-war classes. Mrs Marling thinks it undignified to begin a new acquaintance by a telephone call, so she writes and posts a note instead.[57] Lady Cora and Sir Cecil are considered brave to use each other's first names early in their relationship.[58] Yet in *Jutland Cottage*, ten years later, Canon Fewling notices that in Wiple Terrace Christian names were used less than they had been during the war. Margot is confused by Wicks using her name for the first time; and doesn't know Mr Macfadyen's name until after they are engaged.[59] John-Arthur Cross(e) asks Edith to use his name, and she teases him when he forgets to use hers.[60] These anxieties about names usually occur when the characters are in interesting emotional situations, and act as metaphors for societal nervousness about intimacy as well as familiarity, reflecting changes in social usage.

In Chapter 7 I noted that Frances Harvey buying gin through the black market was an indication of her flawed character, compared to Lord Stoke's upright adherence to the law.[61] Yet, after the war, the upright characters Colin Keith and Lady Cora Palliser use petrol illegally, which was considered a normal use of privileged access.[62] This clearly breaks rules that earlier, wartime, characters had been assiduous in upholding, and suggests that Thirkell was reflecting a more relaxed attitude to obeying the regulations. There is also a political dimension: in wartime, disobeying the rules would have been defying Churchill's good guidance for winning the war, whereas ignoring rationing regulations after the war was only cocking a snoot at the new Labour government.

A more obvious example of slipping social standards, openness about illegitimacy, appears to have been a retrofitted detail that carries on into the peace.[63] There is a marked use of jokes between men about the chance of having an illegitimate child, and by the late 1950s even well-born county girls are joking about this themselves.[64] There is a veiled reference to contraception for vicars.[65] The much earlier hint in *The Brandons* (1939) about the Arbuthnot illegitimacy saga is recalled in full in *Private Enterprise* (1947), when Thirkell felt able to write openly about the adultery of a Victorian Indian officer's wife, and to develop a line of illegitimate Brandon descent.[66] There is no open adultery in Barsetshire itself, but Noel Merton strays in mind towards Peggy Arbuthnot, and is told off for this by Jessica Dean, since he is making Lydia unhappy.[67] Mrs Morland's views about divorce – '"I might *talk* about divorce in a dashing way in private, but it would never do for my books at all. The people who read them wouldn't like it"'[68] – are refuted in Thirkell's two successive novels, in which guests chat about divorce after dinner.[69]

In general, from the mid-1950s Thirkell is more relaxed about mentioning the unmentionable. She reveals that Lydia had had a miscarriage during the war, whereas in *Growing Up* (1943) Lydia was only described as having been ill.[70] She produces some more explicit doggerel verse about sex; invents a character in a play called Mrs O'Gonnoreagh, the name itself also mocking an Irish stereotype; and writes a scene suitable for a bedroom farce in which strapping young George Halliday emerges from his bathroom wearing only a towel and encounters the young lady guest.[71] She spends time making clear that the part of the mistress played by Jessica in *Two-Step for Three* was changed to be a wife; and George Halliday (again) calls keeping pornographic drawings under the bed 'dull'.[72] These moments of interest in the sex life of Barsetshire are startling in their sedate context. Taken together, they show an acculturation to modern openness about the body that Thirkell enjoyed exploring for comic effect.

Immediately after the war, Thirkell allows Barsetshire characters to be nastier about other people. Southbridge School rejects, with satisfaction, the applications for boys who had been sent to America for the war, punishing their families for their lack of patriotism, and for their choice of inadequate American education.[73] Young Lady Norton becomes the new haughty *grande dame* of the county, since Eleanor Grantly resigns rather than work with her, and she is catty about Lady Pomfret.[74] Francis Brandon is transformed into a bullying domestic tyrant, a dramatisation of what could happen when a son brings his bride to his mother's home instead of buying his own. This is a discreet but pointed commentary on domestic selfishness as well as on the national housing shortage.[75]

Dornford Yates did not allow any of his central characters to be self-ish. They had exquisitely good manners designed to show how perfect they were as individuals, and as representatives of their types. Berry introduces Jonah to Mr Hoby of the fairground (rather than the other way round, otherwise due to Jonah's class status) because Mr Hoby is a visitor, and a respected man, despite his class, profession, accent and way of life.[76] The stand-offs between the Pleydells and their antagonists are a joy to read because of Yates's genius in writing invective that played on class codes, showing how to be abusive while still demonstrating perfect manners. But Yates was not able to control critics of his style or subjects, outside his fantasy fan club in the memoirs. By rejecting his stories for their class attitudes, his critics rejected all that Yates had based his career upon, and so he took their criticism very personally.[77] He is superior about readers who correct his facts and his grammar.[78] Bad reviews were beginning to rankle.

> "Some – I repeat some – of those who review books today have neither the standing nor the background of the reviewers of other days. Such people allow their feelings to over-ride their duty, which is to review upon its merits every book that comes into their hands."[79]

This is a circular argument: 'I was not criticised by reviewers before the war: post-war reviewers who criticised my books after the war are not as good as pre-war reviewers'. It also betrays a skewed understanding of how reviewers operated and were paid in the 1940s and 1950s.

In strong contrast to his rigid rejection of modernity, Yates enjoys the relaxation of modern post-war mores enough to write sexuality more explicitly into his fiction. In a Victorian hunting scene in *Lower Than Vermin*, Lady Vivien, Yates's teenage heroine, is 'blooded' against her will (and against custom), by having her face wiped with the bloody end of the fox's brush.[80] This is a simulated rape, since the perpetrator is soon arrested for the rape and murder of a village girl. Lady Vivien's cousin agrees to marry a hunting boor, who systematically rapes her in marriage until she elopes with the right man. The young women characters in *Lower Than Vermin* are anachronistically willing to discuss sexual jealousy and marital rape in private, breaking, again, the conventions of historical unity.[81] These altering standards in his writing suggest his awareness of what was selling in modern thriller fiction, and how social mores were altering. Though this extra explicitness is largely restricted to one historical novel, it is still instruction for his modern readers.

Party politics

The dramatic general election of 1945 which brought a landslide Labour victory allowed Thirkell to patronise Richard Tebben's Communism as something that he will grow out of.[82] Frances Harvey is a Socialist (enough said) and by admitting that Geoffrey Harvey changed from Liberal to Labour because he saw more of a future in it, the Harveys are condemned for inconstancy, for being self-serving, and for their poor judgement in not supporting the Conservatives.[83]

The Liberals come in for sustained vitriol in Barsetshire. A well-loathèd character, Mrs Rivers, is a Liberal, and Sir Ogilvy Hibberd becomes a perpetual Liberal sacrifice. John Atkins notes of political fiction that 'the denial of claims of deference to the parvenu, for instance, because he is too new, or too crude, or too rich, or too contaminated with foreign connections, is a fertile source of alienation in society'.[84] Hibberd is a frequent butt of Conservative sneers, and personifies the kind of person Barsetshire does not want.[85] During the war he 'had come out at no personal inconvenience at all to tell the troops that the Italians were simple children who had been misled by their leaders and that practically all Germans were really domestic peace-loving Christians'.[86] On Hibberd receiving a peerage, his butler apparently has to teach him how to act like a gentleman. John Cross(e) is rude about him almost in his hearing at the White Hart, supported by the fawning head waiter. His modern mansion is insulted; the Mertons won't have him in their house; Lord Pomfret and the Duke of Towers hope he will lose money on the Stock Exchange. He invites himself to the Harcourt wedding but is rejected.[87] Decades of sneers about this unseen character make a strange running joke that loses its original political point, and leaves a nasty impression of pointless ritual scapegoating.

In contrast, there is only one political party of standing in Barsetshire. 'There was no need for [Anne] to add that her father was standing as a Conservative, for that was the only thing the people one knew did stand for.'[88] When Churchill resigned on 23 May 1945, 'millions of people felt a sudden sense of desolation, of being children deserted in a dark lonely wood; much as they had felt it in that black winter when their ruler deserted them. Other millions saw the dawn of an even Braver and Newer World, as if the present brave new one were not unpleasant enough'.[89] Thirkell embeds the election preparations into her fiction as she had done with the war: characters are involved, the election results are reflected in the events in *Peace Breaks Out*, and the new Rushwater bull calf is named after Churchill.[90]

The Barchester seat has two main candidates: Sir Robert Fielding is to stand for the Conservatives, and Mr Adams will stand for Labour.[91] Outside Barchester, other important characters naturally take the Conservative side. Sylvia Halliday canvasses unstoppably for the Conservatives among her obediently feudal voters in Hatch End.[92] Thirkell sticks grimly to the sad result in her novels, since her purpose is still to show how Britain is suffering. Mr Adams wins Barchester – a metaphor for his eventual conquering of the county – and Thirkell revenges herself on non-Conservative candidates by ensuring that the 'National Independent Crank candidate' loses his deposit.[93] Adams's progression from independent-minded Labour MP to a Conservative in all but name is a corollary to his passage across the class divide. '"Adams is a rum bird," said Sir Robert to his wife. "I wouldn't be in the least surprised if he turned up on the Opposition Benches one day. There's nothing so conservative as a good Labour man."'[94] He is a thorn in the side of his own party, and eventually well respected in the county.[95] Thirkell uses his actions to criticise the Labour party. 'If Mr Adams at some future time decides that his political views have changed, it will not be because he sees a reward: office, a title, a salary.'[96]

The Labour government stepped down on 5 October 1951, and the general election took place 20 days later. Noel Merton stands for the London constituency of Morristown, Mr Gresham is hoping for East Barsetshire and Lord Silverbridge has been nursing Barchester for years. All three are Conservative candidates, and Francis Brandon is on the Conservative Committee, which explains the triumphant result.[97] The incoming Carters subscribe to the Conservative Association with a 'gratifyingly large subscription', showing their commitment to the county. George Halliday's commitment to Conservative values, and his hard work as a farmer and landowner, brings him the invitation to stand for West Barsetshire County Council from Sir Edmund Pridham himself, a rite of passage for the Conservative gentleman, and acknowledgement that local political involvement and responsibility is the way to rebuild the county.[98]

Dornford Yates equates political education for the lower classes in his novels with left-wing agitation: the peasants would be better off not knowing anything.[99] In *The Berry Scene*, set in the 1920s, the Pleydells visit the Lyvedens, who have paternalistic plans to modify the model village on their land to such an extent that the villagers will all leave, leaving the houses free, in a new, workhouse-like form, for (undeniably deserving) disabled ex-soldiers.[100] Yates assumes that ex-soldiers will not be Leftist agitators, and that soldiers with impairments will be deserving and grateful for the feudal plan. A Communist agitator arrives, with a ridiculous name – Doogle – to educate the villagers to stand up for their rights as tenants, and is set up by Berry and Lyveden, who want him out of the way. Doogle is beaten up, ostensibly for his role in blackmailing the dead wife of the blacksmith (a convenient calumny from his past). The local power of the upper classes wins, and the gentlemen don't need to soil their hands with *canaille*, using the willing blacksmith to do their heavy work for them. These are positively eighteenth-century assumptions of the landowners' right to decree punishment, showing how out of touch Yates was with post-war politics, living as he was in self-imposed exile. There is no sense that his fiction related any more to the then present-day, or that he was aware of post-war living conditions.

Sophistication and the lady

Yates's early 1920s fiction, especially the stories of the Pleydells partying, was deliciously sophisticated. Yet he lost this knack as he and his characters grew older, so that portentiousness, rather than wit, became his dominant tone, and his interest in sexual morals became didactic. Thirkell was able to retain her mastery of sophisticated frivolity because she never stopped being amusing. The instructional function of her novels also enabled her to write about truly sophisticated characters with confidence, 'often by means of positioning the reader as much more knowing than the innocent protagonist [that] while dramatizing that protagonist's education, also present lessons in manners and models of successful and unsuccessful social behaviour'.[101] Faye Hammill goes on to suggest that 'novels and plays tend to understand sophistication primarily in relation to morality and values'.[102] Thirkell and Yates should be read as socio-political novelists who instruct as well as critique their own society's morals and values. Their characters carry this instruction through their actions – the Duchesse's sexual behaviour, below, shows that sophisticated behaviour was immoral[103] – and the narrative voices reinforce the instruction with remarks addressed to the reader directly. It is no coincidence that the nostalgic longing for the past from both authors was focused on the eighteenth and nineteenth centuries, since they were creating what Hammill calls literary 'nostalgia for the lost social structures of aristocracy and leisure [...] the 1950s and 1960s were nostalgic for both the "peak" of aristocratic culture in the eighteenth and nineteenth centuries and for its last days in the interwar years'.[104]

In *Private Enterprise* (1947), Barsetshire's actress makes her first adult appearance. Jessica Dean, still in her teens, is glamorous and entertaining, witty, and very wise. She enacts the part of the stage celebrity with her theatre partner Aubrey and her old acquaintance Peggy Arbuthnot: 'embraces were exchanged, affectionate and ritualistic, full of dears and darlings, signifying nothing'. She encourages sophisticated nonsense chatter at dinner parties, and she is the perfect mentor for women in need of a transformation.[105] Where did she come from, in Thirkell's pantheon of characters? Nothing like her has been seen since Rose Bingham in *Wild Strawberries* (1934). Phoebe Rivers of *Pomfret Towers* (1938) shares her glossy hardness and sophistication, but Jessica Dean is like a moving image compared to Phoebe's static attitudes. In 1945 (see Chapter 7) Thirkell had met Ivor Novello, and was responding rapturously if cattily to theatre life, so it is likely that Jessica Dean emerged from these encounters. She is the county's theatrical coach, and gives confidence and poise to the young (Lord Mellings) and inexperienced (Lucy Marling). Thirkell links her to the now famous musical composer Denis Stonor of *Before Lunch* (1939), who with Aubrey Clover and Jessica make a highly plausible theatrical trio for Barsetshire to enjoy. Yet they are outsiders still, since they live in London, and Barsetshire people who enjoy London's sophisticated nightclub lifestyle – Colin and Eleanor Keith, Oliver Marling, the Omniums and Hartletops – somehow lose social credit in Barsetshire.[106] Interestingly, Thirkell is less standoffish about London in her later novels, because Lord Lufton is allowed to become a friend of Princess Margaret, and Lord Mellings is always running up and down from town, but these two young noblemen are fulfilling their national aristocratic roles, and do not betray Barsetshire so much as add its lustre to London.[107]

The passion for performance in Barsetshire uses sophistication to impress the public. Peggy Arbuthnot and Francis Brandon tango, under Jessica's instruction, for the Barchester Amateur Dramatic at the Red Cross Cabaret; and the amateur but brilliant musical talents of the Omniums are to raise funds for the Conservatives.[108] But pleasing the public, and maintaining true Barsetshire values, keeps sophistication (tango-dancing) in its place. 'Lady Cora, as we know, had no particular voice, but she could please an audience and sang with no kind of self-consciousness' simple wartime songs.[109]

The most commonly perceived example of sophistication in Barsetshire never actually appears. Glamora Tudor's films are the epitome of working-class sophistication in 12 wartime and post-war Thirkell novels.[110] She is a role model for the ignorant village girl, and her many leading men have ridiculous names – Hash Gobbett is a particularly good one – showing Thirkell's appreciation of their relative unimportance compared to the cinematic siren.[111] There is still contempt in Thirkell's tone when describing the cinema and those who go there in her novels, yet she was sufficiently in tune with modern cinema culture for her characters to cite films in their conversation, showing that 'the presence of the modern' of the cinema was all-pervasive in the 1940s and 1950s in this supposedly retired and rural county.[112] *Young Woodley* (1930), *Pinocchio* (1940), *A Matter of Life and Death* (1946), *The Third Man* (1949) and *The Titfield Thunderbolt* (1953) are seen or discussed by the characters.[113] Mrs Carter uses the powerful effect of cinema sophistication to train a rather slow parlour maid, by taking her to a Scarlet Pimpernel type film 'where everyone said Sir and Madam [...] we've had nothing but Sirs and Madams ever since'.[114]

The effect of cinema stars and magazines set standards for women's appearance, and this too is offered in the novels as instruction. Face packs and cosmetics for older women are mentioned for the first time in *Love Among the Ruins* (1948). Lady Cora instructs Marigold the gormless maid with a Veronica Lake fixation on how to use make-up properly; Rose Fairweather, the epitome of insouciant public behaviour in matters of cosmetic mysteries, gives Edith Graham her first make-up lesson; and still makes up her face in public in the late 1950s. At the age of, presumably, 37, Thirkell wants us to feel that Rose really ought to do better.[115] She represents sophistication for the other classes, not for ladies. But a clear signal of her effortless leadership in femininity is that she, Jessica Dean and Peggy Brandon are the first women in post-war Barsetshire to wear a New Look dress.[116]

The New Look was a radical change in women's couture, presented most famously by Christian Dior in Paris in his first collection on 12 February 1947. It was a shocking and hugely popular new fashion for women, because it was so different from the post-war 'atmosphere of dismal poverty for all'.[117] Most women in Britain – when not in uniform – were wearing old and heavily-mended pre-war clothes, or dresses bought on coupons because there wasn't anything else. The status of clothes rationing as a contribution to the war effort made wearing Austerity, or old and mended clothes, a patriotic statement.

Only the rich and professionally fashionable could wear the New Look at first. Thirkell insisted that it was hopeless for the older woman to even try it, and that it wouldn't last, yet the perpetually impressive Miss Hampton wears a tailored suit with a 'slight but dashing' hint of New Look.[118] What went on underneath the New Look was crucial. The symbolic importance of ladies' underwear is central to the plots in *County Chronicle* (1950), and *Jutland Cottage* (1953), and deserves a detailed examination, since it has much to say about how Thirkell depicted women who needed help to become marriageable.

Lucy Marling is a hearty land girl, immature and ill-dressed. At 30 she is long past the age when she should be married with social responsibilities, but portrayed as emotionally around the age of 13, she has not yet crossed the threshold into womanhood. After her engagement she goes to stay with the very pregnant Jessica in London where she can get clothes for her married life. The crucial factor in this outfitting orgy is Lucy getting a 'good belt'. She has a good haircut too, and a facial, and a new wardrobe, but the 'belt' is the foundation of all this work.[119] This elastic corset, to step into and roll up or down, reaches from the tops of the thighs to below the bust and brassière, and holds the flesh around the bottom and abdomen firmly in place. Lucy owns one of these belts already, but since they can't be worn comfortably with breeches, she probably didn't bother much of the time.

Getting a good, or new, belt was a way of cramming Lucy not only into the conventional shape for a woman, but also of cramming her into the shape required by her class, and her married status. A feminist perspective would call the belt a tool of repression, but it is also a tool of support and morale: sexual confidence is also important. The instruction for Lucy and Thirkell's readers is explicit on the care of belts: '*roll* it off very carefully, not *pull* it, and remember to wear it alternately with her other belt'.[120] The results are apparent from the hearty Emmy's reaction to the sight of Lucy on her wedding day – 'a mixture of fear, scorn, and unwilling admiration'.[121]

Foundation garments are very important for Margot Phelps in *Jutland Cottage* (1953). She is a 'large spinster daughter of uncertain age', and 'would have been good-looking if she had ever taken the faintest trouble about her looks'. She stuffs her hands in her jacket pockets,[122] which is fatal for the silhouette, and her usual outfit is 'trousers and [a] shabby sports coat'. Her 'shabby and not very clean tweeds' are worn with 'cotton stockings of the type that does not have a back seam and falls into crumples over the instep'. She 'could see that Lady Cora's tweeds were quite different from her own and, quite without envy, wished that hers weren't quite so thick and shapeless'.[123]

However, the high state of polish on her shoes is a classic mark of the lady in fiction of the period: well-cared-for shoes make the difference (we have already seen this with Lucy in the war). In these clothes, 'during the war, Miss Phelps had tramped and bicycled and dealt with hens, ducks, pigs, goats and other recalcitrant animals [... They] were still in use and could never look like anything but what they were'.[124]

Margot is a Cinderella in all material aspects, but cannot do anything in a feminine way. She is only 40, but her 'life of a ceaseless round of toil, combined with her total lack of interest in herself, made her look more like a hearty fifty'. At least she has very good legs.[125]

Margot's transformation comes about because her family's friends realise that her hardworking existence offers no chance of a future, career or husband. Lady Cora sees straight to the heart of the problem by remarking to Rose Fairweather that they must 'talk to Margot about the importance of a good foundation belt'.[126] Rose buys Margot the new belt and a brassière, and a golden brown twinset to go with Lady Cora's gift of tweed that will be made up into a new suit. Margot wears the twinset to meet Canon Fewling at the County Club for lunch, and is emboldened to ask for a large whisky. Before she knows it Lady Pomfret has asked her to join a committee. She is taken to visit the Dowager Lady Lufton, who approves of her good character and pleasant looks, and asks Margot to join another committee. When this Cinderella comes home, and has to hide the new clothes from her father for fear of being made to take them back,

> 'Miss Phelps stood for a moment on the doorstep, feeling that her golden crown, her sparkling dress and her glass slipper were vanishing. Then she remembered that she was wearing the belt, the brassière and the twin set which were certainly as good as one glass slipper – and there was still the suit to come.'[127]

With the right clothes Margot has no trouble crossing the femininity threshold. By the end of this novel her book about keeping goats finds a publisher, and she receives three proposals of marriage. She accepts the man who had not objected to her wearing trousers. Five years later, Margot wears designer dresses from Florence that even Rose Fairweather envies.[128] Her apotheosis is a warm fulfilment of Thirkell's wishes in how she wanted the modern woman of the 1950s to behave, even if she was, by this time, filtering her expectations of good behaviour for the young through the sensibilities of a 60-year-old.

Women in the post-war world

Although most of Thirkell's post-war women characters are expected to marry, a surprising proportion are employed, after which they will, however, have to leave their jobs. Evelyn Kerslake and Janine Liladhar explain that in the 1950s 'firstly, there was the hire ban which prohibited the appointment of married women. Secondly, there was the retain ban which prevented the employment of existing women workers after marriage. Finally, there was the promotion ban which disallowed the promotion of married women workers to more senior posts, although still allowing them to remain in their existing jobs'.[129] Yet these rules only applied to the professional and educated classes: in Barsetshire, married and single women of the lower classes are expected to be available for domestic work, and Thirkell is firm about married women using their servants properly. The experiences of Lydia in *Private Enterprise* and Peggy in *Happy Returns* show that mothers with nannies should not spend time with the children when the master of the house has to be looked after.[130]

Jennifer Poulos Nesbitt notes that in her pre-war fiction Thirkell 'generally punishes women who work or pursue a university education',[131] but, post-war, university women are accepted as a fact of life. They also all – Joan Stevenson, Betty Dean, Clarissa Graham, Heather Adams – marry. The war had radically changed Thirkell's depiction of women in her novels, and women working for salaries have positive roles in most of her post-war novels. The marital home is still important as their ultimate destiny, but their freedom to prove their competence and intelligence in paid work is also a right that Thirkell defends implicitly.

Thirkell preferred her younger ladies to work in libraries. Susan Dean is an intimidatingly efficient Red Cross library official, as are Eleanor Grantly, Isabel Dale, Young Lady Norton, Miss Updike, Grace Grantly and Justinia Lufton.[132] Librarianship had been a well-known profession for single women in Britain since the late 1880s.[133] None of the women librarians in post-war Barsetshire work for more than a few years, and all display anxiety when they do not receive a marriage proposal, as do their well-wishers. 'Both ladies agreed it was high time Susan got married or she would settle down into one of the well-bred spinsters that inform the English countryside, and become a little more authoritative and efficient with each passing year.'[134] This reinforces the undesirability of the authoritative and efficient single woman.

Thirkell placed these women in these posts to show the blindness of men in love when thinking about their young women, since they cannot recognise or value their admirable skills outside the home. Colin Keith thinks only of Susan as someone who will help him in his work, whereas she is clearly far more efficient and important than he is. Oliver is horrified at the cost of the typing that Isabel has been doing for him for free, since now he will not be able to afford her.[135] Thirkell shows male embarrassment at the disconnect between the visible activity of these women, compared to the ideal of the leisured married lady at home. Eleanor rides the whirlwind and directs the storm in her office, to the discomfiture of her demobbed and unemployed brother Tom. His feelings of self-absorbed uselessness contrast bitterly with Eleanor's professional competence, since she will inevitably marry and become someone else's dependent, while he still needs to find both his vocation and the job with which to support a wife.[136]

Lady Lufton is a contrast in this group of women of organisation and public responsibility. She is a delightful yet ineffectual widow, but a fearsomely authoritative chairman of Women's Institute meetings and of committees. Mrs Villars has the same characteristic: blandly pleasant in private, but a formidable case study for Thirkell's instructions on how to chair a committee, as is Lydia's control of over-talkative nurses with her Committee Voice. Thirkell's description of the rush of women flinging themselves into community good works again at the beginning of the Cold War was partly a joke, but recognised that after their wartime responsibilities had ceased, these women were desperate for work to do.[137] The county lady volunteers in particular are singled out to demonstrate what Thirkell called 'a true aristocracy not only of blood but of the tradition of service'.[138] Their private diffidence showed that ladies knew that in the home their role was not the professional organiser, but the invisibly efficient manager. All these depictions show a surprisingly forward-thinking attitude from Thirkell, in embracing new expectations for women's lives.

However, as noted above, Thirkell was finding young women heroines more difficult to write in the 1950s, since she was in her sixties. In *Happy Return* (1952) she writes feelingly about the difficulty of managing teenage girls of good family, since they do not have the same restrictions that older women endured.[139] The younger women in Barsetshire also seem aimless and unwanted. Clarissa Graham, after defying the expectations for her class and sex to go to university to read engineering, decides that she does not want to work in Mr Adams's works after all, but to be married. Thirkell's uncertainty about this character suggests fluidity in 1950s expectations for young women. Jane Crawley refuses to take the school leaving certificate exam, since she is destined to be a gentleman farmer's wife and doesn't need Barchester High School's approval. Lydia worries that her daughter Lavinia won't marry and will thus be a bore.[140] With this reaffirmation of marriage came more openness in the novels about pregnancy, motherhood and nursing, and the events around childbirth.[141] Edith Graham spends almost three novels drifting around to no purpose, and is married off in what seems like half a page at the end of *A Double Affair* (1957). She next appears without personality or volition, about to give birth, in *Love At All Ages* (1959).

The 1950s pregnancies of Lady Cora, Mrs Parkinson and Octavia Needham, and their accouchements, become dramatic material in the novels. Thirkell's reduction of the roles for women to pre- and post-marriage situations is quite different to her descriptions of women's lives in the 1930s, as was her sustained interest in writing about the practicalities of marital life, rather than stopping, as she had done throughout the 1930s, at the moment of betrothal. This may be connected to the narrowing of her horizons.[142] Only a year or two earlier her novels had involved multiple settings, characters and conversations that tackled publishing, politics, class, the needs of the elderly, the rise of the bureaucrat and the struggles of the farmer. Her last three novels consist of conversations about things that had been recalled many times before at indistinguishable meals. The drop in quality and interest was due to Thirkell's age and illnesses.

In contrast, Dornford Yates experienced greater vitality during the 1950s, rather than an obvious decline (though we should recall that from 1950 to 1960 he published only five books, while Thirkell had published ten and was working on her eleventh when she died in 1960). *Lower Than Vermin* (1950) revises the historical experience of women of the upper classes. They still require mastering in Yates's innuendo-laden vocabulary of horsemanship, but there is a more knowing and ahistorical eroticism in how he uses the imagery. '"I'd never marry a man who'd let me have the reins [...] I almost expected him to run a hand down my legs."'[143] Yates is disturbingly interested in punishing women's sexual misbehaviour with suffering in this novel, and in policing upper-class society's sexual behaviour, in hindsight, apparently as an instructive lesson to modern readers. His talent for melodramatic plots and dramatic entanglements indicates the influence of the Victorian three-decker novel even in the 1950s. The rules of society in this novel are as rigid as Yates can make them, and the reader is expected to accept these as moral lessons for present-day conduct as well as warnings from a more censorious past.

A classic Yates episode in *Lower Than Vermin* uses exaggerated social mores to cause emotional outrage. In the *fin de siècle* the Duchesse de Sevignac is a serial adulteress, a frequenter of a club in Paris where 'people let themselves go but knew how to behave. Propriety was mocked, but not outraged. Abandon sat at the board, but she ate delicately. Every being there was in full evening dress, and every single woman was tightly masked'.[144] The Duchesse asks Philip where her lover Hubert is, since she wants him to father her next child. Philip lies that Hubert has been posted to Egypt, because Hubert is Philip's brother-in-law. In due course the Duchesse gives birth to her husband's son, who is 'born with a twisted leg', and is banished from Paris by her husband. The Duchesse wreaks vengeance for her rustication on Philip by secretly telling her infatuated suitor Andrew Ross, whose sister Ildico wants to marry Philip, that Philip is the father of her 'sick' child. Only Ildico's dogged refusal to believe the lie that Philip's line produces inbred characteristics enables her father and Philip's supporters to find out the truth from Andrew, after which he emigrates to Canada.[145] The heightened emotional tension in this extended episode derives wholly from Yates's views about how women should behave. The metaphor of the child's impairment for the mother's adulterous intentions is a particularly unfeeling aspect of Yates's storytelling, matched by the chilly eighteenth-century exchanges between Ildico and her father, Andrew and his accusers, and between the Duc and the Duchesse. In terms of style Yates makes a strong return in this novel to the classically formal conversation that characterises his most elegant fictional confrontations. In terms of society's rules for women and their lives, he presents rules closely associated with the woman's body, clearly intended for titillation as well as restriction.

Six years later Yates produced his last novel proper, *Wife Apparent*, with a very light touch. There are two surprising acknowledgements of modern mores in Yates's depiction of this contemporary marriage. Major Gore wants Niobe to keep working on her illustrations once they are married: '"Her stuff's never been on the market. When we are married, she'll give her talent rein"'.[146] They share a workroom, Niobe travels to London to sell her work through her agent, she is a professional artist and a married woman. This has a slight parallel in Thirkell, in Mrs Barton the acclaimed historical novelist in *Pomfret Towers* (1938), but none of Thirkell's young women are allowed to continue working after marriage. More interesting in terms of social advances, and much more typical of Yates's interests, is that Niobe agrees to live with Major Gore before their marriage. Although it is agreed by their friends and family that this is a radical step and a sacrifice, and that her reputation mustn't suffer, all agree that it is the right thing to do, due to the very complicated plot.[147] Preserving Niobe's reputation with the neighbours (the middle and upper classes), and their standing in the village (with the tradesmen and servant classes with whom Niobe must deal), becomes the *raison d'être* of the novel. Yates's purpose is clear: women must obey social rules, even to deceiving society in the most drastic of cases, as this one is, because the consequences of women breaking these rules are unimaginably terrible. Women are the mainstay of the home and their husbands' reputations, so nothing must conflict with this.

The long-lasting house

Thirkell's post-war novels usually began with the description of a home. In *Peace Breaks Out*, the opening passage describes the timeless topography of the Hallidays' Hatch House, and ends with a note of ownership opposing progress and access.

> The road is probably as old as history, always well out of reach of the higher floods, and follows the contours of the hilly land in a series of ups and downs, so that no motor bus can use it. This is a source of quite unreasonable pleasure and pride to its owners.[148]

The passage continues seamlessly into a grumble about the motor engine, although the train is admitted to be useful: a purposely Victorian perspective to establish that post-war Barsetshire has survived mechanical progress. Underlining the Hallidays' position in determinedly preferring the past to the present, the young Hallidays are described as having formed their impression of 'England's Lost Civilisation' from the family's bound volumes of *Punch*.[149] All this reinforces a familiar conservative landscape.

Yates began his first post-war novel, *The House that Berry Built* (1945), with a rather pompous scene describing the handing over of the Pleydell family mansion, White Ladies, to the nation, in 1937.[150] This positioning continues the aggrandisement of these characters and their importance in Yates's recreated version of Britain, since they do not sell their home: a gentleman does not sell his heritage.[151] The remainder of the novel concerns the planning and building of a new house for the Pleydell cousins on a hillside in the foothills of the Pyrenees, near Pau, where Yates himself had built his own mansion several years before. '"To build a house just now would do us a lot of good. It's a primitive instinct, of course: but it's none the worse for that."'[152] In contrast, in *Lower Than Vermin* (1950) the culminating blow to the staggering fortunes of the Earl of Ringwood is the takeover of some of his estate land for housing developments by the local council. He and his sister are distraught but stoic. It is unlikely that such a land takeover was legal at the time Yates was writing, which suggests, again, historical accuracy was jettisoned by Yates in pursuit of his political point.

Yates's choice of 'the nation' as the new owners of White Ladies, rather than the National Trust, reflects the Trust's relative newness in 1945. David Cannadine records that after the war 'many families considered giving their homes to the National Trust [...] There can be absolutely no doubt of the eagerness with which owners of once great houses sought to divest themselves of what had been the impossible responsibility of maintenance'.[153] In Thirkell's *Miss Bunting* (1945) giving land to the Trust is what landowners do to preserve it from developers. 'George said that the National Trust would jump at Bolder's Knob and that bit of Gundric's Fossway.'[154] The Trust's growing power in Barsetshire is evident, as is that of other new architectural guardians. In parallel, the Historic Buildings Council (the precursor to English Heritage) has taken over Rising Castle which has been Scheduled as a National Monument and can be visited, and the Society for the Protection of Ancient Buildings is disguised as the Society for the Prevention of Cruelty to Ancient Buildings.[155] The Georgian Group and the National Trust have a say in road widening in Barchester; and the Trust owns most of Greshambury, including Greshambury House.[156] The increasing strength of the power of civic interest was overcoming the wishes of the landed families, and it is indicative that Thirkell's tone is resigned rather than angry. The movement of ownership from the individual to the institution was not enough to get angry about.

The logical next step in transferring ownership to the Trust was opening up the house to earn its keep. David Cannadine notes that 'even in the inter-war years, there had never been anything quite like this. Occasional visitors might be tolerated out of a sense of noblesse oblige. But the idea of "refloating one's fortunes on a flood of half crowns, motor-coach parties and set teas" was something altogether different. [...] Between 1950 and 1965 six hundred houses were opened' to the public'.[157] Thirkell treats this with equanimity. She wrote uncertainty into her last novels about whether the Pomfret estates would be inheritable by the time Lord Mellings became 21.[158] The big houses of Barsetshire are gradually taken over by public bodies. Harefield House is leased to the Priory School; and Harcourt Towers is thought of for the County Asylum, but is taken over by the consortium led by Mr Adams and Mr Pilward for 'a kind of country club'. The Duke of Towers enjoys himself taking visitors round his home, incognito, and relishes the tips.[159] Pomfret Towers is similarly rescued, with Adams and Pilward renting its buildings and land for their new agricultural conglomerate offices and a golf course, and the Barchester Hunt renting the stabling.[160] These were miraculous solutions for Thirkell's preferred classes.

For those who had to move out of the great houses to more afford-able accommodation, Thirkell was sympathetic. 'For people who have lived in spacious houses – they need not necessarily be palaces or castles – they can never be really happy in a cosy little villa.'[161] But the 1950s had housing problems: there is nothing vacant in Northbridge due to evacuees and relocated government offices, nor in Pomfret Madrigal. There is a house free in Wiple Terrace in Southbridge for Peggy and Effie Arbuthnot, because they do their own cooking. When the Priory School moves to Harefield House, the young schoolmasters Swan and Charles each have a rare chance at married accommodation.[162] The housing demands of the gentry classes are different from those of the other classes, for whom the small flats made out of big houses and middling sized ones will be quite good enough.[163] Mr Mould's foreman describes a nice new house in Framley that Thirkell makes sound perfectly hor-rible. She feels similarly about the Greshambury houses in bright col-ours, 'with small poky rooms and cubic or spiral furniture'.[164] Despite examples of good modern house-building in Greshambury New Town, Thirkell dwells on the destruction or degradation of historic buildings. 'It is sad to see in many small country towns or large villages, how the more handsome of the houses are having to beg their bread as it were; to accept as lodgers people they would never have tolerated as owners.'[165]

This sense of a lost architecturally-based system of living, swamped by the modernity of the 1950s, is the rather sad ending to this examination of what these novels have to tell us. We have reached their last books. Yates died in 1960, and Thirkell died in 1961. The meaning of conserva-tism would change in the next few decades, and the cultural references of these writers would disappear from common knowledge, and become recondite, and desperately old-fashioned. Their novels were probably already old-fashioned in the 1930s, but by the 1980s and beyond they were almost beyond cultural notice, except for the readers who would not abandon the stories and the writers they loved so much.

9
Conclusion

Forty years from when we began, we have reached the end of the writing lives of Buchan, Yates and Thirkell. As I described in the Introduction, Buchan's literary reputation flourished after his death, and has achieved a critical renaissance since the early 2000s. Yates and Thirkell have not been so fortunate. Their publishers have kept some of their works in print, and Thirkell has had a very recent resurgence of popularity by the coming back into fashion of nostalgic writing by women, but Yates is still largely ignored except by readers who love his works. The insistent presence in the reading population of those who enjoy these authors, and hunt for second-hand editions to give to others and to replenish their own collection, is a significant indicator of reading pleasure, and is valuable for the study of readership and reception, also experiencing a critical renaissance. By focusing on how these authors gave pleasure in their writing, this book shows how reading the literary signs of their discourse can help us understand the messages their original readers read so avidly. Simon Eliot reminds us that the power of literature is predicated on its power over the reader: 'to surprise with joy, shock with facts or reason, or force us to see things from a disturbingly different point of view'.[1] Reading against the grain produces this reaction, and therein lies one of the importances of reading the authors who are unfashionable, disregarded or actively objected to. There are passionate emotions in these novels, and even more passionate emotions expressed by those who reject them.

As I said in Chapter 1, the consumer of fiction is as important as its author, because the reader continues the process begun by the author, in agreeing or disagreeing with the points of view in the fiction for sale. While I make the point in several ways that these authors should be studied because of their neglect by the academy, there are strong positive reasons for investigating their art and their impact. As writers they function as strong counter-balancing voices in the total picture of British literary production, which should be heard for its representation of the 'normate' reader, the default man and woman in the street against whose taste, politics, cultural tolerance and aesthetic preferences modernist and radical literature was cultivated and evolved. These three novelists venerated the continuity of tradition, and the importance of showing its value in a rapidly modernising society. Yates made social and cultural nostalgia a political position, and used his verbal invention to affirm his conservative view of post-war society, in which everything has changed for the worse. He incorporated elaborate decoration in his sentences, invoking a foundation of cultural power to resist change and uphold conservative values. Buchan's flexibility with language fleshes out the social hierarchies in his fiction and their willingness to accept new blood, as long as these conform to the values of the dominant group who already hold power. Thirkell demanded high standards of literary knowledge from her readers, and reinforced her views on social usage with high expectations of her readers. Reading fiction so saturated with these views introduces the reader to an encoded culture with specific expectations.

In Chapter 2, I established that the 1920s saw vigorous political churning in Britain, reflected by similarly vigorous activity in political activism and the loosening of social rules. Buchan's political training enabled him to create a detailed and highly plausible alternative political background for his characters, in which milieu he could experiment by engaging with specific social changes. His fiction delivered a means of escape, by offering individual characters a way out of economic and social ills, and reassuring readers that the traditional social systems of feudal relationships would support the war-impaired needy and destitute. The new enemy was unseen and everywhere, an Everyvillain to blame and be defeated by the forces of tradition. Women desiring new freedoms were similarly to be suppressed by the forces of patriarchy because there was a higher cause to serve than mere economic independence: the nation itself needed nurturing, and women and men must work together in traditional ways to restore Britain's stability. Buchan's attitude to intellectual challenge was much the same as it was to political or cultural avant-gardism: despite being a highly intelligent man himself, and an admirer of great thinkers and leaders of thought, Buchan did not revere those whose great thoughts wished to overturn social or political systems.

In Chapter 3 Yates is shown to be reactionary rather than stoutly resistant, as Buchan was. Yates invented idealised characters for a perfect world, and displayed a vehement antagonism against any influence or force that might threaten their continued existence. He began from the position of desiring a return to sanity in a mad world, offering a vision of traditional conservative standards and expectations as reasonable alternatives to his readers' reality. He spoke directly to his readers' experiences, as when he deplored a shortage of homes for his heroes, or the distressing independence of married women. He offered escape, through Gothic drama and fantasy Ruritanias, and through fantasies of wish fulfilment in everyday life for the upper classes.

Chapter 4 shows that Buchan was rethinking his 1920s vision of optimism as to how much the traditional social structures could support those in want: *A Prince of the Captivity* is overtly nihilistic in this respect. He acknowledges that modern times need modern heroes by developing his working-class heroes from *Huntingtower* into middle-class representatives of the press and academia, to join the new meritocratic politicians of the 1930s. Buchan was looking at national and European unrest and political instability in the 1930s, rather than at conditions on the streets, narrating from the ruling perspective: by 1935 he had become a baron. He died in 1940.

Chapter 5 introduces Thirkell's contribution to the range of conservative responses. Her particular gift, compared to Buchan and Yates, was for writing in the woman's voice, and locating the domestic setting as the centre of civilisation. She mediated social reportage through traditional marriage plot novels that served a double purpose: by reiterating the importance of and need for continuity in class and gender roles as a way to encourage stability in uncertain times, Thirkell also valorised the strength and solidity of these conservative traditional values. Indeed, Thirkell's focus on the woman's life and expectations introduce a very necessary grounding for the range of conservative visions that the novels in this book represent. She locates her ideological struggle in the living-rooms and on the streets, between parents and children and in the modern tendencies encroaching on a resistant society. Yet her interest in maintaining social control also introduces space for dissent, and the possibility of escape: to London, where those who are not quite Barsetshire must live and work, and to university, where only the very boring intelligent women end up.

In Chapter 6 we see the beginning of a rewriting of the past from Yates, after his traumatic divorce and a subsequent re-imagining of his salad days. His need to revise indicates a dependency on his created worlds that delivered an emotional validation as well as a living. Yates's recycling of his fantasies into fiction also released stronger sources of aggression in his vocabulary and plots: this reached new extremes in the 1930s and 1940s, reflecting the extremity of his own situation, an exile from Home, and a refugee from his home in France. He took refuge by enhancing the richness and complexity in his language and plots, but the sometimes disturbing results indicate that he was narrowing his range for an increasingly specialised readership. Policing women's behaviour, and the protection of class boundaries, remained his preferred subjects.

Chapter 7 describes Thirkell's apotheosis in terms of literary endeavour: her six novels of the Second World War are a major contribution to the literature of the Home Front. Her role as a social recorder is valuable and inspiring in her representation of civilian lives and wartime endurance under petty tyrannies. Her treatment of refugees and evacuees is important social evidence. Her representation of comedy and pathos from the new sources of class-collision adds to the detail of how British society was altering under the stresses of war. Before Waugh, Thirkell created the conservative response to the unstoppable destruction of pre-war society, recording and reworking her material to describe and comment on a revolution by rapid social engineering.

Chapter 8 explores how Yates continued to remake his past and redefine his present through his lens of encrusted conservative values. Thirkell also revises her past, but she merely added things that she had forgotten in the onrush of wartime changes, rather than rewrite history. The post-war novels of these ageing writers show considerable stresses, and produce unexpected flourishes. Yates's penultimate book is suffused with youth and gentleness, unlike his creaking and fictionalised memoirs. Thirkell found a new seam of rich writing in her angry rejection of the Labour government of the later 1940s. Her writing was re-energised by her resistance to the new order, and the attention she paid to getting her vast company of eligible county girls married off developed her ingenuity in extending Barsetshire's own mythology, remaking Trollope for her own purposes. She wrote about the old and the lives of those who could not marry. While Yates's characters told each other anecdotes and grumbled about how little the past was revered, Thirkell dealt energetically with the present. This difference between them is discernible throughout their careers, and also relevant to how we might think about them as influences.

I'd like to return to some questions I presented at the beginning of this book: how can we understand the work of Buchan, Thirkell and Yates as conservative novelists, and what assumptions can we make about how their readers absorbed their messages through their literary skill?

By studying this fiction as a longitudinal response to social and political change we can see that the politicised messages encoded in them could be received, from reader to reader, from extreme to perfectly sound. This suggests how political messages affect taste when reading for pleasure. Pierre Bourdieu's visual representation of the cultural field in late nineteenth-century French literature shows how we can consider how political and economic criteria affect the reader's positioning of literary works in relation to each other.[2] I also draw on Franco Moretti's use of mapping in fiction to explore how reading taste functions, because maps work 'as analytical tools: that dissect the text in an unusual way, bringing to light relations that would otherwise remain hidden'.[3] While Bourdieu worked with subgenres and readers, Moretti's work made maps from individual novels, but this approach can be extended to map the effect of novels as cultural agents. By 'placing a literary phenomenon in its specific space – mapping it – [...] one looks at the map, and thinks'.[4] Let us think about politics in the specific space of fiction.

The novelists this book discusses believed that their conservative ideologies could rebalance a society in flux, and would combat external threats, and so they wrote these messages into their fiction for their readers to learn from, and agree with. The adaptations in their instructional messages over time show that their rhetoric interacted with social change, and with society, to create a literary history of conservatism that was flexible rather than rigidly dogmatic. This is in concert with Moretti's thinking, which is that 'the only real issue of literary history [is] society, rhetoric, and their interaction'.[5]

The size of these authors' markets suggests that confirmation and reassurance were the predominant reasons for buying these books, since readers buying for pleasure – novels by Buchan, Yates and Thirkell were written primarily to give enjoyment – will rarely buy to experiment with something new. The novels would have reinforced what the readers already thought or felt, rather than changing their minds. Compounding the attraction of sharing the authors' opinions, these novels were good art. They fulfil David Smith's critique of socialist literature that I quoted in Chapter 1: 'to what extent is this book conveying its author's own conviction, and to what extent is it a satisfactory work of art?'[6] The conviction in these novels rests in how their high aesthetic values were sustained, and the emotionally satisfying writing that is stylistically innovative, delivering novelty with quality. The novels require to be taken seriously, since the authors take their readers seriously by offering a world-view that is coherent and sincere, and internally consistent. Even if the genre attraction of reading thrilling adventure, witty comedy or restrained English romance was the primary reason for choosing these novels, the conservative ideology was strong in how those stories were told, and in the values those stories advocated. There is no escaping conservatism when reading Yates or Thirkell.

Are there degrees in the conservative response to social change? Buchan is less forceful in his fiction, in many ways, than Yates and Thirkell, yet he was the professional Conservative, elected to represent constituents by promoting Conservative thought. These authors inhabit different positions on a continuum of engagement and pronouncement, on which the actions of one Member of Parliament speak in different ways than the words in the novels that reached millions of readers. In Chapter 1 I suggested the idea of a continuum as a tool for visualising relative positions of literary taste.[7] The relationships between the points produce value judgements, for instance of 'modernist' being 'better', or 'middlebrow' being 'easy', but it is the perspective that forms the judgement that is important. The reader applies their own preferences to a text or author, to form a judgement on it from their taste, and thus a relationship between preferences can be discerned. I argued that middlebrow, highbrow and lowbrow texts could be considered as points along a line, thus showing the importance of their relationships to each other in one dimension. For conservative popular fiction, we can extend the idea to incorporate cluster analysis when working with two axes rather than one.

Figure 9.1 shows a graph bordered by a horizontal axis of conservatism and a vertical axis of pleasure in reading, which represents a map of my own reading tastes, as an example. Yates sits in the centre to the far right, being, for my taste, middling popular and very conservative. Buchan sits further left but much further up, because I enjoy reading Buchan more than I enjoy reading Yates, and find him less stridently Conservative. Thirkell is further to the right than Buchan, but I enjoy reading her as much as I do him. Fitting other conservative authors in around these initial points indicates how, for instance, my taste assigns places to Evelyn Waugh, Georgette Heyer, Sax Rohmer and 'Sapper'. I instinctively compare Rohmer's fiction to that of Buchan, and to that of Waugh and Heyer, and I estimate the political distances between them and how much I enjoy reading them, in relative terms. To extend the ideological range, I also plot points in relation to the conservative authors plotted already, for Dorothy L Sayers, Rose Macaulay, Sylvia Townsend Warner, George Orwell, E M Forster and Ian Fleming, all of whom I enjoy, and whose work has a discernible political dimension. Figure 9.1 thus shows that my political range is bounded by Orwell and Yates: I am unlikely to enjoy reading fiction that extends further to the

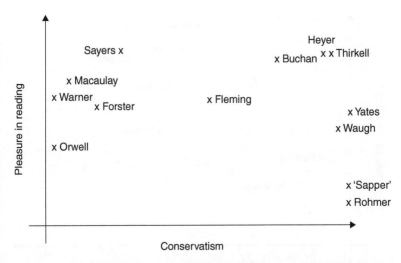

Figure 9.1 Graph indicating relative positions of authors, measured by the reader's reading pleasure against the conservatism of the author, for Reader 1 (KM)

Left or Right, respectively, than these authors. This suggests that fiction read for pleasure has a political dimension, and that the political elements function as a natural circumscriber of taste.

One reader's 'nice book' is another reader's 'cataract of tripe'.[8] A second reader's selection of authors might place Yates more in the centre of the conservative axis, and would not include Orwell or any other author from the Left, because, as we see in Figure 9.2, Reader 2 might consider Yates's political messages to be quite reasonable and middle-ground, and Orwell simply unreadable Marxist raving. Thus the taste of Reader 2 might frame a different selection of authors (I do not care for Dennis Wheatley or Anthony Powell), and probably also place them in different positions than mine. Reader 2 might think that Rohmer and Yates were central rather than extreme Right, and would not include Sayers, now off the map with Orwell, because of her feminist views. By relating politics to reading pleasure we exclude authors with political positions that are too far away from what our taste establishes as 'centre'.

A publisher might say that this is of course obvious: it is rare to find a Sylvia Townsend Warner enthusiast who also adores 'Sapper'. Yet the obvious has not been explained to show the hidden relationships. Relational mapping and simple cluster analysis offers a theoretical and evidential framework to separate out the clusters of loci denoting the combination of pleasure in reading (a middlebrow indicator)

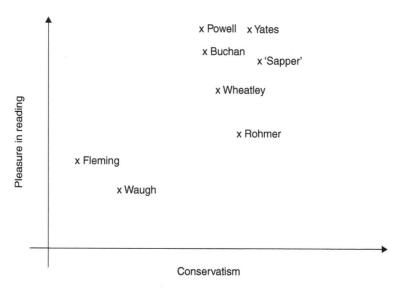

Figure 9.2   Graph indicating relative positions of authors, measured by the reader's reading pleasure against the conservatism of the author, for Reader 2 (anon.)

and political tolerance. Variation within the clusters becomes clearer when resolution is added to the scale. In Figures 9.1 and 9.2 there is an implicit ordinal scale to indicate degrees of political colouring between authors, but no exact measurements can be made. One can appreciate and understand any colour of political perspective in fiction, as an intellectual engagement, but this is not necessarily enjoyment, a reading choice made for pleasure, entertainment, amusement, excitement or escape. The study of popular fiction of any ideology should begin with the reader's affinity with the work, and its role in giving reading pleasure.

While this book has focused on three authors sharing one political affiliation, that fact that they operated successfully and for many decades while producing fiction sold in multiple genres indicates that genre alone is not a political indicator. Neither is a position on the 'brow' continuum: the most challenging and esoteric of the works of Wyndham Lewis or Ezra Pound was as fervently right-wing as anything Yates wrote at his least restrained. My purpose in writing this book is to open up ways for considering fiction read for enjoyment as a project of political avowal and persuasion. It may not necessarily be read by all its readers in its primary, politicised iteration, but critiques fiction as the reader's choice, rather than only the author's cultural production.

Appendix: The Fiction of John Buchan, Dornford Yates and Angela Thirkell

John Buchan

date of *The Dancing Floor* is 1926, not 1927
Only Buchan's fiction is listed here: volumes of short stories carry an asterisk *.
The variant American titles are in parentheses.

Sir Quixote of the Moors 1895
John Burnet of Barns 1898
*Grey Weather** 1899
A Lost Lady of Old Years 1899
The Half-Hearted 1900
The Mountain [unfinished chapters] 1901
*The Watcher by the Threshold** 1902
A Lodge in the Wilderness 1906
Prester John (*The Great Diamond Pipe*) 1910
*The Moon Endureth** 1912
Salute to Adventurers 1915
The Thirty-Nine Steps 1915
The Power-House 1916
Greenmantle 1916
Mr Standfast 1919
*The Path of the King** 1921
Huntingtower 1922
Midwinter 1923
The Three Hostages 1924
John Macnab 1925
The Dancing Floor 1926
Witch Wood 1927
*The Runagates Club** 1928
The Courts of the Morning 1929
Castle Gay 1930
The Blanket of the Dark 1931
The Gap in the Curtain 1932
The Magic Walking Stick 1933
A Prince of the Captivity 1933
The Free Fishers 1934
The House of the Four Winds 1935
The Island of Sheep (*The Man from the Norlands*) 1936
Sick Heart River (*Mountain Meadow*) 1941
The Long Traverse (*Lake of Gold*) 1941

Dornford Yates

As with the Buchan list, I have listed here only his books, not the separate publication of his short stories. Nearly all Yates's short stories were collected and published in book form after their magazine appearance, and these volumes carry an asterisk *. Titles in parentheses are the variant American titles.

*The Brother of Daphne** 1914
Eastward Ho! 1919 [a play written with Oscar Asche]
*The Courts of Idleness** 1920
*Berry & Co** 1920
Anthony Lyveden 1921
Jonah & Co 1922
Valerie French 1923
*And Five Were Foolish** 1924
*As Other Men Are** 1925
The Stolen March 1926
Blind Corner 1927
Perishable Goods 1928
*Maiden Stakes** 1928
Blood Royal 1929
Summer Fruit 1929 [a US omnibus edition of *Anthony Lyveden* and *Valerie French*]
Fire Below (Royal Command) 1930
Adèle & Co, 1931
Safe Custody 1932
Storm Music 1934
She Fell Among Thieves 1935
*And Berry Came Too** 1936
She Painted Her Face 1937
This Publican (The Devil in Satin) 1938
Gale Warning 1939
Shoal Water 1940
*Period Stuff** 1942
An Eye For a Tooth 1943
The House that Berry Built 1945
Red in the Morning (Were Death Denied) 1946
*The Berry Scene** 1947
Cost Price (The Laughing Bacchante) 1949
Lower than Vermin 1950
As Berry and I Were Saying 1952
Ne'er Do Well 1954
Wife Apparent 1956
B-Berry and I Look Back 1958

Angela Thirkell

The Barsetshire novels carry an asterisk *.

Three Houses 1931
Ankle Deep 1933

High Rising* 1933
Wild Strawberries* 1934
Trooper to the Southern Cross 1934
Demon in the House* 1934
O, These Men, These Men! 1935
The Grateful Sparrow 1935
The Fortunes of Harriet 1936
August Folly* 1936
Coronation Summer 1937
Summer Half* 1937
Pomfret Towers* 1938
The Brandons* 1939
Before Lunch* 1939
Cheerfulness Breaks In* 1940
Northbridge Rectory* 1941
Marling Hall* 1942
Growing Up* 1943
The Headmistress* 1944
Miss Bunting* 1945
Peace Breaks Out* 1946
Private Enterprise* 1947
Love Among the Ruins* 1948
The Old Bank House* 1949
County Chronicle* 1950
The Duke's Daughter* 1951
Happy Return* 1952
Jutland Cottage* 1953
What Did It Mean?* 1954
Enter Sir Robert* 1955
Never Too Late* 1956
A Double Affair* 1957
Close Quarters* 1958
Love At All Ages* 1959
Three Score and Ten* 1961

Notes

1 Introduction: Politics and Pleasure in Language

1. Virginia Woolf, 'Why Art To-Day Follows Politics' (1936), in Stuart N Clarke (ed.) *The Essays of Virginia Woolf, vol. VI, 1933–1941, and Additional Essays 1906–1924* (London: The Hogarth Press, 2011), 75–9, 75.
2. Woolf 1936, 76.
3. J B Morton wrote 'The Queen of Minikoi' in *Parody Party* (1936), as a pastiche of the Hannay adventure style. He also incorporated a pastiche of Dornford Yates's characters and style in *Pyrenean* (1938).
4. Letter from Angela Thirkell to P P Howe, 6 March 1942, Hamish Hamilton archive, Bristol University Library Special Collections (used by kind permission of the Estate of Angela Thirkell).
5. William Plomer, 'Fiction: *A Prince of the Captivity*', *The Spectator*, 151 (21 July 1933), 94.
6. *The Bookman*, LXXXVI: 513 (June 1934), back cover.
7. Raymond Williams, *The Country and the City* (Oxford: Oxford University Press, 1973), 12.
8. Alison Light, *Forever England: Femininity, Literature and Conservatism between the Wars* (London: Routledge, 1991), 18.
9. William Vivian Butler, *The Durable Desperadoes: A Critical Study of some Enduring Heroes* (London: Macmillan, 1973), 17.
10. Kate Macdonald, 'Writing *The War*: John Buchan's lost journalism of the First World War', *The Times Literary Supplement*, 10 August 2007, 14–15.
11. Kate Macdonald, *John Buchan: A Companion to the Mystery Fiction* (Jefferson: McFarland, 2009).
12. A J Smithers, unpublished postscript to his biography of Yates (private collection).
13. Butler 1973, 21.
14. Colin McInnes changed his surname's spelling to 'MacInnes' when he began his own career as a novelist.
15. Jill N Levin, *The 'Land of Lost Content': Sex, Art and Class in the Novels of Angela Thirkell, 1933–1960*, MA thesis, Washington University, St Louis, 1986, 11–12. The Leavis quote is from *Fiction and the Reading Public* (London: Chatto & Windus, 1932), 47.
16. Margot Strickland, *Angela Thirkell: Portrait of a Lady Novelist* (London: Gerald Duckworth & Co., 1977), 142, 150.
17. Hermione Lee, 'Good show', *The New Yorker*, 7 October 1997, 90–5, 90.
18. In this she was not alone. Tom Harrisson had noted the growing right-wing attitudes 'which he saw gathering "strength"' (Harrisson 1941, 419–20).
19. Diana Trilling, *Reviewing the Forties* (New York: Harcourt Brace Jovanovitch, 1978), 12.
20. Light 1991, 2.

21. Thomas J Roberts, *An Aesthetics of Junk Fiction* (Athens, GA: University of Georgia Press, 1990), 11, 15.
22. David Smith, *Socialist Propaganda in the Twentieth-Century British Novel* (London: Macmillan, 1978), 2.
23. Hans Jauss, *Toward an Aesthetic of Reception* (Minneapolis: University of Minnesota Press, 1982), 15.
24. John Carey, *The Intellectuals and the Masses: Pride and Prejudice among the Literary Intelligentsia, 1880–1939* (London: Faber & Faber, 1992), 6.
25. George Watson, *Politics and Literature in Modern Britain* (London: Macmillan, 1977), 84.
26. Light 1991, x.
27. Terence Rodgers, 'The Right Book Club: Text wars, modernity and cultural politics in the 1930s', *Literature and History*, 12:2 (2003), 1–15, 2.
28. Watson 1977, 87–8.
29. Watson 1977, 89.
30. Rodgers 2003, 1.
31. Rodgers 2003, 2.
32. Rodgers 2003, 2.
33. Rodgers 2003, 6.
34. Another competing book club set up in this period was the National Book Association (also established in 1937), but this 'was a propaganda mouthpiece for Chamberlain's National Government, and financed by Conservative Party Central Office'. Rodgers 2003, 7.
35. A J Smithers, *Dornford Yates: A Biography* (London: Hodder & Stoughton, 1982), 96.
36. Smith 1978, 2.
37. Mary Grover, *The Ordeal of Warwick Deeping: Middlebrow Authorship and Cultural Embarrassment* (Madison, NJ: Farleigh Dickinson University Press, 2009), 27.
38. Light 1991, 14.
39. Watson 1997, 90–1.
40. Janet Montefiore, *Men and Women Writers of the 1930s: The Dangerous Flood of History* (London: Routledge, 1996), 22–3, 47.
41. Rosa Maria Bracco, *Merchants of Hope: British Middlebrow Writers and the First World War, 1919–1939* (London: Berg, 1993), 69.
42. Light 1991, xii.
43. Nicola Humble, *The Feminine Middlebrow Novel 1920s to 1950s: Class, Domesticity and Bohemianism* (Oxford: Oxford University Press, 2001), 11.
44. Mary Grover's 2009 study of Warwick Deeping is an important, recent, exception.
45. Anon., 'Come in! and let's talk about Middlebrows', *London Opinion*, 16 August 1930, 136.
46. Kate Macdonald, 'Introduction: Identifying the Middlebrow, the Masculine and Mr Miniver', in Kate Macdonald (ed.) *The Masculine Middlebrow, 1880–1950: What Mr Miniver Read* (Basingstoke: Palgrave Macmillan, 2011), 1–23, 11.
47. Richard Usborne, *Clubland Heroes* (1953) (London: Hutchinson, 1983), 3.
48. Ann Rea, 'The collaborator, the tyrant and the resistance: *The Lion, The Witch and The Wardrobe* and middlebrow England in the Second World War', in

Kate Macdonald (ed.) *The Masculine Middlebrow, 1880–1950: What Mr Miniver Read* (Basingstoke: Palgrave Macmillan, 2011), 177–96, 190.

49. Williams 1973, 20.
50. Williams 1973, 21–2.
51. Dornford Yates, 'How Will Noggin was fooled, and Berry rode forth against his will' (1919), in *Berry & Co* (London: Ward, Lock & Co, 1920), 9–33, 31–2.
52. Smithers 1982, 19–23.
53. Paul Fussell, *The Great War and Modern Memory* (1975) (Oxford: Oxford University Press, 2000), 21.
54. Ted Bogacz, '"A tyranny of words": Language, poetry and antimodernism in England in the First World War', *The Journal of Modern History*, 58:3 (1986), 643–68, 645.
55. I am grateful to George Simmers for this suggestion.
56. Smithers 1982, 79.
57. Yates often took the opportunity, for later editions of his novels, to alter or replace the dedications. This one clearly dates from shortly before or after the Second World War.
58. Smithers 1982, 164.
59. Dornford Yates, *Berry & Co* (London: Ward, Lock & Co, 1920), 118–19.
60. George Simmers, pers. comm., 2009.
61. Dornford Yates, *Anthony Lyveden* (London: Ward, Lock & Co, 1921), 46–7.
62. Dornford Yates, *The Stolen March* (London: Ward, Lock & Co, 1930), 29.
63. Dornford Yates, *Blood Royal* (1929) (London: Hodder & Stoughton, 1941), 79.
64. Dornford Yates, *Storm Music* (London: Ward, Lock & Co, 1934), 96; *Gale Warning* (London: Ward, Lock & Co, 1939), 35, 149.
65. Robert Scholes, *Paradoxy of Modernism* (New Haven: Yale University Press, 2006), 171.
66. Scholes 2006, 173.
67. John Buchan, *Huntingtower* (1922) (Oxford: Oxford University Press, 1996), 107.
68. Buchan *Huntingtower*, 102.
69. Buchan *Huntingtower*, 149.
70. John Buchan, *John Macnab* (1925) (Oxford: Oxford University Press, 1994), 209–10.
71. Angela Thirkell, *Love Among the Ruins* (London: Hamish Hamilton, 1948), 363.
72. Angela Thirkell, *Marling Hall* (London: Hamish Hamilton, 1942), 151–2.
73. Thirkell *Marling Hall*, 152–3.
74. See Macdonald 2009, 11–14, and the bibliography, for an extensive discussion of critical writing on Buchan; also Kate Macdonald (ed.) *Reassessing John Buchan: Beyond The Thirty-Nine Steps* (London: Pickering & Chatto, 2009); Nathan Waddell, *Modern John Buchan: A Critical Introduction* (Cambridge: Cambridge Scholars Press, 2009); Kate Macdonald, 'The diversification of Thomas Nelson: John Buchan and the Nelson archive, 1909–1911', *Publishing History*, 65 (2009), 71–96; Kate Macdonald, 'John Buchan's breakthrough: The conjunction of experience, markets and forms that made *The Thirty-Nine Steps*', *Publishing History*, 68 (2010), 25–106; Kate Macdonald, 'Thomas Nelson & Sons and John Buchan: Mutual marketing in the publisher's series', in John Spiers (ed.) *The Culture of the Publisher's Series, vol. 1,*

Authors, Publishers, and the Shaping of Taste (London: Palgrave Macmillan, 2011), 156–70; Kate Macdonald and Nathan Waddell (eds) *John Buchan and the Idea of Modernity* (London: Pickering & Chatto, 2013).

75. Arthur C Turner, *John Buchan: A Biography* (Toronto: Macmillan, 1949); Janet Adam Smith, *John Buchan* (Oxford: Oxford University Press, 1965); Martin Green, *A Biography of John Buchan and his Sister Anna: The Personal Background of their Literary Work* (Lampeter: Edwin Mellen Press, 1990); Andrew Lownie, *The Presbyterian Cavalier: John Buchan* (London: Constable & Co, 1995); David Daniell, *The Interpreter's House* (Edinburgh: Thomas Nelson, 1975).
76. Archibald Hanna, *John Buchan 1875–1940: A Bibliography* (Hamden: Shoestring Press, 1953); Robert Blanchard, *The First Editions of John Buchan: A Collector's Bibliography* (Hamden: Archon, 1981); Kenneth Hillier (ed.) *The First Editions of John Buchan: An Illustrated Collector's Bibliography* (Clapton-in-Gordano: Avonworld, 2009). See also Macdonald 2010, 25–106, for the new amalgamated bibliography of Buchan's writing 1894–1915. A recent PhD thesis by Roger Clarke (University of the West of England, 2015) offers a bibliography of Buchan's journalism.
77. See Macdonald 2009, 13–14.
78. Usborne 1983, 1–2.
79. Yates himself objected to Usborne linking his writing to Buchan's novels, pointing out that his style was closer to that of Anthony Hope. Dornford Yates, *B-Berry and I Look Back* (London: Ward Lock, 1958), 147–8.
80. Usborne 1983, 1.
81. A survey I conducted on women readers of Buchan concluded that they were in a distinct minority, but that most had discovered Buchan's fiction while at school or from their parents: Kate Macdonald, 'Women readers of John Buchan', *The John Buchan Journal*, 23 (2000), 24–31.
82. The first to appear was the fourth Hannay adventure, *The Three Hostages* (1923). In 1956 eight further titles were published: *Greenmantle* (1916, the second Hannay novel); *Huntingtower* (1922, the first of the Dickson McCunn trilogy); *The House of the Four Winds* (1935, the last Dickson McCunn novel); *The Island of Sheep* (1936, the last Hannay novel); *Mr Standfast* (1919, the third Hannay novel); *The Thirty-Nine Steps* (1915, the first Hannay novel); *John Macnab* (1924, a Leithen novel); and *Castle Gay* (1930, the second McCunn novel). Two further Buchan titles, both historical novels from the 1930s, were reprinted in 1961 and 1963. See also Bill Schwartz on Buchan's republication by Penguin, in 'The romance of the veld', in Andrew Bosco and Alex May (eds) *The Round Table: The Empire/Commonwealth and British Foreign Policy* (London: Lothian Foundation Press, 1997), 65–125.
83. Usborne 1983, 98.
84. Usborne 1983, 6.
85. In the case of Hannay, his background became a retrospective acquisition as Buchan added to his background once he had become a success.
86. Clive Bloom, *Cult Fiction: Popular Reading and Pulp Theory* (London: Macmillan, 1996), 178.
87. Light 1991, 214.
88. David Pryce-Jones, 'Towards the Cocktail Party', in Michael Sissons and Philip French (eds) *Age of Austerity 1945–1951: The Conservatism of Post-War Writing* (London: Hodder & Stoughton, 1963), 215–39; D J Taylor, *After the*

War: The Novel and English Society since 1945 (London: Chatto & Windus, 1993), 11–13; Jenny Hartley, *Millions Like Us: British Women's Fiction of the Second World War* (London: Virago, 1997), 36, 75.

89. Laura Roberts Collins, *English Country Life in the Barsetshire Novels of Angela Thirkell* (Westport, CT: Greenwood Press, 1994).
90. Rachel Mather, *The Heirs of Jane Austen: Twentieth-Century Writers of the Comedy of Manners* (New York: Peter Lang, 1996), 67–95.
91. Penelope Fritzer, *Ethnicity and Gender in the Barsetshire Novels of Angela Thirkell* (Westport, CT: Greenwood Press), 1999; Penelope Fritzer, *Aesthetics and Nostalgia in the Barsetshire Novels of Angela Thirkell* (Angela Thirkell Society of North America, 2009).
92. Jennifer Poulos Nesbitt, *Narrative Settlements: Geographies of British Women's Fiction Between the Wars* (Toronto: University of Toronto Press, 2005).

2 From Communism to the Wall Street Crash: Buchan in the 1920s

1. See Smith 1978, 39; and Andrew Thorpe, *The Longman Companion to Britain in the Era of the Two World Wars 1914–1945* (London: Longman, 1994), 3–9, for useful background and chronologies of this period.
2. David Cannadine, *The Decline and Fall of the British Aristocracy* (1990) (London: Macmillan, 1996), 190.
3. Cannadine 1990, 196.
4. Adrian Gregory, *The Last Great War: British Society and the First World War* (Cambridge: Cambridge University Press, 2008), 1, 288.
5. Thorpe 1994, 29.
6. Thorpe 1994, 24, 31.
7. Smith 1978, 40.
8. Thorpe 1994, 32.
9. Thorpe 1994, 16–17.
10. Joe Hicks and Grahame Allen, *A Century of Change: Trends in UK Statistics since 1900*, House of Commons Library Research Paper 99/111, 21 December 1999, 20.
11. Gregory 2008, 270.
12. Hicks and Allen 1999, 7.
13. Hicks and Allen 1999, 7.
14. Lifebuoy Soap advert, *The Daily Graphic*, 22 July 1924, 4.
15. Daily Express, *These Tremendous Years, 1919–1939* (London: Daily Express Publications, 1939), 4.
16. Daily Express 1939, 3.
17. Daily Express 1939, 137. This would be equivalent to £766,574,200 in 2014.
18. Malcolm Baines, 'An outsider's view of early twentieth-century Liberals: Liberalism and Liberal politicians in John Buchan's life and fiction', *Journal of Liberal History*, 82 (Spring 2014), 6–15, 7.
19. Daily Express 1939, 112; Lownie 1995, 207–8.
20. Thanks to Michael Redley for clarification on these points.
21. Buchan *John Macnab*, 28.
22. Watson 1977, 90.

23. Watson 1977, 94.
24. Fowler 1991, 31.
25. Gregory 2008, 253.
26. John Buchan, *The Courts of the Morning* (1929) (Edinburgh: B&W Publishing, 1993), 9–10.
27. John Buchan, 'Conservatism and progress', *The Spectator*, 143 (23 November 1929), 754–5.
28. Buchan *Huntingtower*, 145.
29. John Buchan, 'A new defence of poetry', *The Spectator*, 129 (8 July 1922), 47–8, 47.
30. Buchan *Huntingtower*, 17.
31. It is interesting that Buchan chose not to allow the Die-Hards to follow the lead of the native Glaswegian Boys' Brigade (founded 1883), from which Baden-Powell developed the Scouting ethos. The BB was a strongly Christian movement, and it may be that the Die-Hards, as Buchan envisaged them, would not have tolerated the BB's focus on Sunday School, whereas their high level of post-war military efficiency aligned them more naturally with the Scouts.
32. Buchan *Huntingtower*, 132.
33. Buchan *Huntingtower*, 195.
34. Buchan *Huntingtower*, 159.
35. Buchan *Huntingtower*, 143.
36. John Buchan, *The Dancing Floor* (1927) (Oxford: Oxford University Press, 1997), 39.
37. Buchan *The Dancing Floor*, 47.
38. Buchan *Huntingtower*, 143.
39. Buchan *John Macnab*, 215–16.
40. Stephen M Cullen, '"The land of my dreams": The gendered utopian dreams and disenchantment of British literary ex-combatants of the Great War', *Cultural and Social History*, 8:2 (2011), 195–212, 205–6.
41. Buchan *John Macnab*, 104.
42. Gregory 2008, 267.
43. Thorpe 1994, 65.
44. Quoted in Michael Diamond, *Lesser Breeds: Racial Attitudes in Popular British Culture, 1890–1940* (London: Anthem Press, 2006), 73.
45. Susan Kingsley Kent, *Aftershocks: Politics and Trauma in Britain, 1918–1931* (Basingstoke: Palgrave Macmillan, 2009), 9.
46. John Buchan, *The Three Hostages* (1924) (Oxford: Oxford University Press, 1995), 149.
47. Buchan *The Three Hostages*, 123.
48. Kent 2009, 39.
49. Buchan *The Three Hostages*, 101.
50. Buchan *The Dancing Floor*, 48.
51. Buchan *The Dancing Floor*, 49, 52.
52. Kate Macdonald, 'Aphrodite rejected: Archetypal female characters in Buchan's fiction', in Kate Macdonald (ed.) *Reassessing John Buchan: Beyond The Thirty-Nine Steps* (London: Pickering & Chatto, 2009), 153–69.
53. Macdonald 2009, 169.
54. Buchan *John Macnab*, 156.

55. Cannadine 1990, 111.
56. Charles F G Masterman, *England after War: A Study* (London: Hodder & Stoughton, 1922), 40.
57. See Stephen Donovan, 'A very modern experiment: John Buchan and Rhodesia', in Kate Macdonald and Nathan Waddell (eds) *John Buchan and the Idea of Modernity* (London: Pickering & Chatto, 2013), 49–62.
58. Cullen 2011, 199.
59. Williams 1973, 115.
60. Buchan *The Three Hostages*, 7–8.
61. Thanks to Eileen Marsh for this opinion.
62. Terry Gifford, 'Ownership and access in the work of John Muir, John Buchan and Andrew Greig', *Green Letters: Studies in Ecocriticism*, 17:2 (2013), 165–74, 166.
63. Buchan *John Macnab*, 126.
64. Buchan *John Macnab*, 128.
65. Buchan *John Macnab*, 145.
66. Buchan *John Macnab*, 156.
67. Buchan *John Macnab*, 229.
68. Buchan *John Macnab*, 232.
69. John Atkins, *Six Novelists look at Society* (London: John Calder, 1977), 17.
70. Watson 1977, 11.
71. Cannadine 1990, 12–13.
72. Humble 2001, 13.
73. Vaninskaya 2011, 170.
74. Grover 2009, 26.
75. Buchan, *Huntingtower*, 206.
76. Buchan *The Three Hostages*, 20.
77. Buchan *The Three Hostages*, 159.
78. Buchan *The Three Hostages*, 161.
79. Buchan *The Three Hostages*, 197–8.
80. Buchan *The Three Hostages*, 268.
81. Buchan *The Three Hostages*, 270.
82. Buchan *John Macnab*, 16–17.
83. Buchan *John Macnab*, 34.
84. Buchan *John Macnab*, 118.
85. Buchan *John Macnab*, 82.
86. Buchan *John Macnab*, 64, 100.
87. Buchan *John Macnab*, 105.

3 Ex-Officers and Gentlemen: Yates in the 1920s

1. Gregory 2008, 270.
2. Laura Beers and Geraint Thomas, 'Introduction', in *Brave New World: Imperial and Democratic Nation-Building in Britain between the Wars* (London: Institute of Historical Research, 2011), 1–38, 2.
3. Butler 1973, 65.
4. Jill Greenfield, Sean O'Connell and Chris Reid, 'Gender, consumer culture, and the middle-class male, 1918–39', in Alan Kidd and David Nicholls (eds) *Gender, Civic Culture and Consumerism: Middle-Class Identity in Britain, 1800–1940* (Manchester: Manchester University Press, 1999), 183–97, 184.

5. Len Platt, 'Aristocratic comedy and intellectual satire', in Patrick Parrinder and Andrzej Gasiorek (eds) *The Reinvention of the British and Irish Novel 1880–1940* (Oxford: Oxford University Press, 2011), 433–47.
6. Winifred Holtby, *Letters to a Friend* (1937) (Adelaide: Michael Walmer, 2014), 110.
7. Ross McKibbin, *Classes and Cultures England 1918–1951* (Oxford: Oxford University Press, 1998), 479.
8. P N Furbank, 'The twentieth-century best-seller', in Boris Ford (ed.) *The Modern Age* (London: Penguin, 1961), 429–41, 435.
9. Furbank 434, 435–6.
10. Dornford Yates, 'Spring' (1923), in *And Five Were Foolish* (London: Ward, Lock & Co, 1924), 99–126, 100.
11. Cannadine 1990, 98.
12. Dornford Yates, 'Oliver' (1924), in *As Other Men Are* (London: Ward, Lock & Co, 1925), 105–29, 119, 121.
13. Dornford Yates, 'What's in a Name', in *The Courts of Idleness* (London: Ward, Lock & Co, 1920), 9–29, 10.
14. Yates *Anthony Lyveden*, 146.
15. Betty D Vernon, *Ellen Wilkinson* (London: Croom Helm, 1982), 4.
16. Cited in Smith 1978, 44.
17. Dornford Yates, 'Ann', in *And Five Were Foolish* (London: Ward, Lock & Co, 1924), 211–50, 211–12.
18. Yates 'Ann', 216.
19. S P B Mais, 'Books and their writers', *The Daily Graphic*, 5 September 1924, 13.
20. 'Saki', 'Tobermory' (1911), in *The Complete Stories of Saki* (Ware: Wordsworth Edition, 1993), 79–84.
21. Dornford Yates, *Blind Corner* (1927) (London: Ward, Lock & Co, 1957), 25–6.
22. Yates *Blood Royal*, 66, 76.
23. Yates *Blood Royal*, 78.
24. Yates *Blind Corner*, 9.
25. Smithers 27.
26. Hicks and Allen 1999, 11–13.
27. John Stevenson and Chris Cook, *Britain in the Depression: Society and Politics 1929–39* (2nd edn, 1994, Longman), 29.
28. See K Macdonald, 'The use of London lodgings in middlebrow fiction, 1900–1930s', *Literary London*, 9:1 (2011), http://www.literarylondon.org/london-journal/macdonald.html for more information on the nuances of housing choices in the immediate post-war period.
29. Dornford Yates, 'How Adèle Feste arrived, and Mr Dunkelsbaum supped with the Devil' (1920), in *Berry & Co* (London: Ward, Lock & Co, 1921), 219–49, 245.
30. Yates 'Spring', 124.
31. Smithers 1982, 145, 153–4, 157.
32. Dornford Yates, 'Susan' (1924), in *And Five Were Foolish* (London: Ward, Lock & Co, 1924), 281–311, 298.
33. John Buchan, *Mr Standfast* (1919) (Oxford: Oxford University Press, 1993), 216.
34. Jane Marcus, 'Corpus/Corps/Corpse: Writing the body in/at war', in Helen Margaret Cooper, Adrienne Munich and Susan Merrill Squier (eds) *Arms and the Woman: War, Gender, and Literary Representation* (Raleigh: University of North Carolina Press, 1989), 124–67.

35. Cannadine 1990, 84.
36. Dornford Yates, 'Jeremy', in *As Other Men Are* (London: Ward, Lock & Co, 1924), 11–39, 20–1.
37. Dornford Yates, 'Peregrine', in *As Other Men Are* (London: Ward, Lock & Co, 1924), 261–84, 265.
38. Dornford Yates, 'Sarah' (1922), in *And Five Were Foolish* (London: Ward, Lock & Co, 1924), 11–38, 20.
39. Dornford Yates, 'Force Majeure', in *Maiden Stakes* (London: Ward, Lock & Co, 1928), 131–60, 145.
40. Dornford Yates, *Perishable Goods* (1928) (London: Ward, Lock & Co, 1957), 19.
41. Yates *Blood Royal*, 157.
42. Yates *Blood Royal*, 158.
43. Macdonald 'Aphrodite', 153–69.
44. Dornford Yates, 'St Jeames' (1927), in *Maiden Stakes* (London: Ward, Lock & Co, 1928), 41–71, 57.
45. Yates 'Force Majeure', 132.
46. Yates *Perishable Goods*, 107.
47. Yates *Perishable Goods*, 114.
48. Dornford Yates, 'For Better or for Worse' (1919), in *The Courts of Idleness* (London: Ward, Lock & Co, 1920), 88–108.
49. Raymond P Wallace, 'Cardboard kingdoms', in *San José Studies*, 13:2 (1987), 23–34.

4 Political Uncertainty: Buchan in the 1930s

1. Richard Carr, *Veteran MPs and Conservative Politics in the Aftermath of the Great War* (Farnham: Ashgate, 2013), 50.
2. Taylor 559.
3. See Smith 1978, 39, and Thorpe 1994, 3–9, for useful background information and chronologies for this period.
4. Smith 1965; Lownie 1995; J William Galbraith, *John Buchan: Model Governor-General* (Toronto: Dundurn, 2013).
5. Galbraith 2013, 97.
6. Kate Macdonald, 'Witchcraft and non-conformity in Sylvia Townsend Warner's *Lolly Willowes* (1926) and John Buchan's *Witch Wood* (1927)', *Journal of the Fantastic in the Arts*, 23:2 (2012), 215–38.
7. Thorpe 1994, 16–17.
8. Thorpe 1994, 31.
9. John M Harrison, *The Reactionaries* (London: Gollancz, 1966), 34.
10. Thorpe 1994, 29–30, 32, 35.
11. John Buchan, 'After ten years of peace', *Daily Mirror*, 10 November 1928, 11.
12. Holtby 1937, 392.
13. These dates were handwritten at the front of his manuscript of the novel (National Library of Scotland Acc. 7214 Mf.MSS.325).
14. Hicks and Allen 1999, 15.
15. Hicks and Allen 1999, 14.
16. Andrew Martin Mitchell, *Fascism in East Anglia: The British Union of Fascists in Norfolk, Suffolk and Essex, 1933–40*, DPhil thesis, University of Sheffield, 1999, 49–83.

17. Thorpe 1994, 65–6.
18. Stevenson and Cook 1994, 12.
19. Hicks and Allen 1999, 21.
20. Hicks and Allen 1999, 26.
21. Stevenson and Cook 1994, 9.
22. Hicks and Allen 1999, 24.
23. Atkins 1977, 12.
24. Stevenson and Cook 1994, 5.
25. Stevenson and Cook 1994, 11.
26. Stevenson and Cook 1994, 12.
27. George Orwell, 'Inside the Whale' (1940), in *Selected Essays* (London: Penguin, 1957), 9–50, 41.
28. Orwell 1940, 30.
29. Andy Croft, *Red Letter Days: British Fiction in the 1930s* (London: Lawrence & Wishart, 1990), 24.
30. Croft 25.
31. Croft 185.
32. Croft 216. Published in 1926, its review in *The Spectator* notes: 'The Blue Shirts who play a part in an English revolution about ten or twelve years hence are a mixture of the O.M.S. and the Fascisti. The story is full of the same sort of adventures as those with which the reader is familiar in crook stories, the villains in this case being the revolutionaries. Ingenious, exciting, and we hope improbable' (*The Spectator*, 4 June 1926, 26). The OMS were the government-sponsored and non-political Organisation for the Maintenance of Supplies, set up in anticipation of civic disruption during the General Strike. Their popular and reactionary origins are strikingly similar to those of the BUF. See Anne Perkins, *A Very British Strike 3 May–12 May 1926* (London: Macmillan, 2006).
33. Peter Galway, cited in Croft 187.
34. John Buchan, *Castle Gay* (1930) (Kelly Bray: House of Stratus, 2001), 222.
35. Buchan *Castle Gay*, 197.
36. Buchan *Castle Gay*, 180.
37. *King Lear*, V.3.270–1.
38. Buchan *Castle Gay*, 180.
39. Buchan *Castle Gay*, 26.
40. Buchan *Castle Gay*, 86.
41. Buchan *Castle Gay*, 65.
42. Buchan *Castle Gay*, 271.
43. Buchan *Castle Gay*, 80.
44. Buchan *Castle Gay*, 2.
45. Simon Glassock, 'Buchan, sport and masculinity', in Kate Macdonald (ed.) *Reassessing John Buchan: Beyond The Thirty-Nine Steps* (London: Pickering & Chatto, 2009), 41–51, 47.
46. Buchan *Castle Gay*, 11.
47. Buchan *Castle Gay*, 181.
48. Buchan *Castle Gay*, 81.
49. John Buchan, *The Gap in the Curtain* (1932) (London: Thomas Nelson & Son, 1935), 132.
50. Buchan *Gap*, 27.

51. Buchan *Gap*, 133.
52. Buchan *Gap*, 153–4.
53. Cannadine 1990, 243.
54. Buchan *Gap*, 190.
55. Buchan *Gap*, 193.
56. Buchan *Gap*, 171.
57. Buchan *Gap*, 194.
58. Buchan *Gap*, 205.
59. Buchan *Gap*, 209.
60. Buchan *Gap*, 198.
61. Buchan *Gap*, 198.
62. Buchan *Gap*, 195–6.
63. Buchan *Gap*, 23.
64. Janet Adam Smith, 'Obituary: Alice Fairfax-Lucy', *The Independent*, 23 December 1993.
65. Lownie 1995, 175.
66. John Buchan, *A Prince of the Captivity* (1933) (Edinburgh: B&W Publishing, 1996), 188.
67. Buchan *Prince*, 100.
68. Buchan *Prince*, 101.
69. Buchan *Prince*, 116.
70. Cannadine 568–9.
71. Buchan *Prince*, 111.
72. Buchan *Prince*, 162.
73. Buchan *Prince*, 117.
74. Buchan *Prince*, 134.
75. Buchan *Prince*, 108.
76. Buchan *Prince*, 113.
77. Buchan *Prince*, 121–2.
78. Buchan *Prince*, 122.
79. Buchan *Prince*, 124.
80. Buchan *Prince*, 167.
81. Richard Kelly, *House of Commons Background Paper: Women Members of Parliament*, SN/PC/6652 (London: HM Government, July 2013).
82. Buchan *Prince*, 202.
83. Buchan *Prince*, 200.
84. Buchan *Prince*, 199.
85. Buchan *Prince*, 202.
86. Buchan *Prince*, 165.
87. Buchan *Prince*, 165.
88. Buchan *Prince*, 170.
89. Buchan *House*, 58.
90. John Buchan, *The House of the Four Winds* (1935) (London: Hodder & Stoughton, 1937), 176, 153.
91. On page 50 Jaikie is instructed to give the Juventus salute, but this is a raised left hand, not an outstretched right arm.
92. Buchan *House*, 317.
93. Buchan *House*, 38.
94. Buchan *House*, 231.

95. Buchan *House*, 150.
96. Buchan *House*, 103–4.
97. Buchan *House*, 103.
98. Cicely Hamilton, *Modern England, As Seen by an Englishwoman* (J M Dent, 1938), 72.
99. Buchan *House*, 113.

5 Novels of Instruction: Thirkell in the 1930s

1. Levin 1986, vii.
2. Pryce-Jones 1963, 215–39, 222.
3. Angela Thirkell, *Never Too Late* (1956) (London: Moyer Bell, 2000), 155.
4. Levin 1986, 66.
5. Light 1991, 214.
6. Heather Ingman, *Women's Fiction Between the Wars: Mothers, Daughters, and Writing* (Edinburgh: Edinburgh University Press, 1998), 2.
7. Nicola Beauman, *A Very Great Profession: The Woman's Novel 1914–39* (London: Virago, 1983), 196; Nicola Humble, 'The feminine middlebrow novel', in Maroula Joannou (ed.) *The History of British Women's Writing, 1920–1945* (London: Palgrave Macmillan, 2013), 97–111, 109.
8. Levin 1986, 107.
9. Levin 1986, 109–10.
10. Montefiore 1996, 22.
11. Lee 1997, 90.
12. Trilling 1978, 12.
13. Humble 2013, 105.
14. Light 1991, 210.
15. Humble 2013, 108.
16. Light 1991, 212.
17. Levin 1986, 87.
18. Lee 1997, 91.
19. Cannadine 1990, 578.
20. Cited in Lee 1997, 94.
21. Angela Thirkell, *Three Houses* (1931) (London: Allison & Busby, 2012), 98–9, 13, 41–2.
22. Strickland 1977, 73.
23. Elizabeth Bowen, 'Introduction', in *An Angela Thirkell Omnibus* (London: Hamish Hamilton, 1966), vii–ix, vii.
24. Strickland 1977, 69–70.
25. Strickland 1977, 38.
26. Strickland 1977, 90–1.
27. Strickland 1977, 94.
28. Her father J W Mackail was a distinguished classicist, the Oxford Professor of Poetry (1902–06) and President of the British Academy (1932–36).
29. Strickland 1977, 106.
30. Strickland 1977, 116.
31. Angela Thirkell, *The Brandons* (1939) (London: The Hogarth Press, 1988), 171.
32. Ruth Adam, *A Woman's Place, 1910–1975* (1975) (London: Persephone Books, 2000), 180.

33. Light 1991, 212.
34. Angela Thirkell, *Before Lunch* (1939) (Harmondsworth: Penguin, 1951), 10.
35. Angela Thirkell, *Pomfret Towers* (1938) (London: Virago Press, 2013), 27.
36. Thirkell *Before Lunch*, 63.
37. Angela Thirkell, *Summer Half* (1937) (London: The Hogarth Press, 1988), 140.
38. Thirkell *Summer Half*, 122.
39. Thirkell *Summer Half*, 121.
40. Thirkell *Summer Half*, 108–9.
41. Thirkell *Summer Half*, 161.
42. Angela Thirkell, *O, These Men, These Men!* (1935) (London: Moyer Bell, 1996), 30.
43. Thirkell *O, These Men*, 34.
44. Thirkell *O, These Men*, 48.
45. Thirkell *O, These Men*, 39.
46. Angela Thirkell, *Wild Strawberries* (1934), in *An Angela Thirkell Omnibus* (London: Hamish Hamilton, 1966), 319–467, 338.
47. Thirkell *The Brandons*, 70, 76.
48. Letter from Angela Thirkell to Jamie Hamilton, 1 June 1939, Hamish Hamilton archive, Bristol University Library Special Collections (used by kind permission of the Estate of Angela Thirkell).
49. E M Forster, *Howards End* (1910) (London: Penguin Books, 1989), 93.
50. Williams 1973, 22.
51. Williams 1973, 253.
52. Alex Potts, '"Constable Country" between the wars', in Raphael Samuel (ed.) *Patriotism: The Making and Unmaking of British National Identity, vol. 3, National Fictions* (London: Routledge, Kegan Paul, 1989), 160–86, 160.
53. Ian Baucom, *Out of Place: Englishness, Empire and the Locations of Identity* (London: Yale University Press, 1999), 35.
54. John J Su, 'Refiguring national character: The remains of the British estate novel', *Modern Fiction Studies*, 48:3 (2002), 552–80, 555.
55. Su 2002, 555.
56. Su 2002, 557.
57. Thirkell *Wild Strawberries*, 342.
58. Thirkell *Wild Strawberries*, 347.
59. Thirkell *Before Lunch*, 265.
60. Thirkell *Pomfret Towers*, 1.
61. Thirkell *Before Lunch*, 75.
62. Humble 2013, 104.
63. Alan Kidd and David Nicholls, 'Introduction: History, culture and the middle classes', in Alan Kidd and David Nicholls (eds) *Gender, Civic Culture and Consumerism: Middle-Class Identity in Britain, 1800–1940* (Manchester: Manchester University Press, 1999), 1–11, 1.
64. Len Platt, *Aristocracies of Fiction: The Idea of Aristocracy in Late-Nineteenth-Century and Early-Twentieth-Century Literary Culture* (Westport, CT: Greenwood Press, 2001), xv.
65. Platt 2001, xv.
66. Humble 2013, 104.
67. Thirkell *Summer Half*, 199–200.
68. Thirkell *Summer Half*, 196.

69. Thirkell *The Brandons*, 175.
70. Thirkell *Before Lunch*, 15.
71. Thirkell *Before Lunch*, 140.
72. Thirkell *Wild Strawberries*, 348.
73. Thirkell *Before Lunch*, 63, 104.
74. Hazel Bell, 'A tale told by an index: Collating the writings of Angela Thirkell', *Angela Thirkell Society North American Branch Conference Papers* (Hatfield: Angela Thirkell Society North American Branch, 1998), 1–8, 1.
75. Mather 1996, 95.
76. Angela Thirkell, *High Rising* (1933), in *An Angela Thirkell Omnibus* (London: Hamish Hamilton, 1966), 163–315, 204, 205, 252, 274.
77. Angela Thirkell, *August Folly* (London: Hamish Hamilton, 1936), 47.
78. Thirkell *Summer Half*, 51.
79. Thirkell *Before Lunch*, 206–7.
80. William Deecke, 'Angela Thirkell's crime novelists', *Angela Thirkell Society North American Branch Conference Papers* (Hatfield: Angela Thirkell Society North American Branch, 1998), 15–16.
81. The pseudonym of Mary-Ann Dolling, née Sanders, Lady O'Malley, 1889–1974.
82. Thirkell *Pomfret Towers*, 59, 62, 68–9, 117, 119–20, 176, 227–8.
83. Thirkell *Before Lunch*, 46. There is also an affectionate parody of the genre in *Northbridge Rectory* (London: Hamish Hamilton, 1941), 304–6.
84. Mary Grover, 'Thirkell, Angela 1890–1961', in Virginia Blain, Patricia Clements and Isobel Grundy (eds) *The Feminist Companion to Literature in English* (London: B T Batsford, 1990), 248–50, 249.
85. Thirkell *Summer Half*, 197; *Pomfret Towers*, 87.
86. Thirkell, *Pomfret Towers*, 68, 95, 224–6, 248–50.
87. Christopher Hilliard, *To Exercise Our Talents: The Democratisation of Writing in Britain* (London: Yale University Press, 2006), 72, 74.
88. Angela Thirkell, 'Henry Kingsley', *Nineteenth-Century Fiction*, 5:3 (December 1950), 175–87.
89. Thirkell *Wild Strawberries*, 371.
90. Thirkell *Wild Strawberries*, 376.
91. Thirkell *Summer Half*, 221.
92. Light 1991, 215.
93. Macdonald *Companion* 2009, 142, 100, 171–8. He also wrote the script for the pioneering documentary naval film *The Battle of Coromandel and the Falklands* (1927), re-released by the British Film Institute in 2014.
94. Thirkell *O, These Men*, 77, 93.
95. Thirkell *O, These Men*, 129.
96. Thirkell *The Brandons*, 57.
97. Thirkell *Before Lunch*, 117.
98. Thirkell *High Rising*, 184.
99. Thirkell *High Rising*, 174.
100. Thirkell *High Rising*, 173.
101. Humble 2001, 39.
102. Thirkell *Summer Half*, 54.

6 Aggressive Reactions: Yates in the 1930s and 1940s

1. Smithers 1982, 130, 145, 157–64.
2. Smithers 1982, 179.
3. Quoted in Tom Sharpe, 'Alias Dornford Yates', *The Times Saturday Review*, 17 July 1976.
4. Smithers 1982, 223. While researching his biography of Yates, Smithers found evidence that Richard Mercer was homosexual, and he discussed this in a letter to a Mercer family friend, Hilary Eccles-Williams, some seven years later: 'I am told by those in a position to be certain that [Richard] became addicted to what is politely called unnatural vice and for that reason was turned out of Rhodesia'. 'In [his 1982 biography of Yates] I had to be careful what I said.' Note by A J Smithers, 31 August 1979; letter from A J Smithers to Hilary Eccles-Williams, 16 September 1986 (private collection).
5. The dedications of *Berry & Co* (1920), *Jonah & Co* (1922), *Valerie French* (1923), *And Five Were Foolish* (1924), *Blood Royal* (1929), and *Fire Below* (1930) were all originally to Bettine, but were altered after 1933 to remove her.
6. Dornford Yates, *Lower Than Vermin* (London: Ward, Lock & Co, 1950), 214.
7. Butler 1973, 22.
8. Usborne 1982, 43.
9. David Salter, pers. comm., 28 May 2014.
10. Dornford Yates, *Fire Below* (London: Hodder & Stoughton, 1930), 28.
11. Dornford Yates, 'Period Stuff', in *Period Stuff* (London: Ward, Lock & Co, 1942), 297–319, 317.
12. Dornford Yates, 'Preface', *Period Stuff* (London: Ward, Lock & Co, 1942), 8.
13. Dornford Yates, 'And Adela, Too' (1941), in *Period Stuff* (London: Ward, Lock & Co, 1942), 197–218, 202.
14. In *The Courts of Idleness* (1920) there are further consanguineous relationships. There is some debate in Yates circles over whether the Jonah of the Berry books is the same character as the Jonah in the thrillers.
15. Yates *Adèle*, 54.
16. Dornford Yates, *The House that Berry Built* (London: Ward, Lock & Co, 1945), 284. After Yates's second marriage in 1934, to Doreen Elizabeth Bowie, he always called her Jill, to which she willingly answered for the rest of his life.
17. Dornford Yates, *The Berry Scene* (London: Ward, Lock & Co, 1947), 48.
18. Wallace 1987, 29.
19. Dornford Yates, 'How Adèle broke her dream, and Vandy Pleydell took Exercise' (1920), in *Berry & Co* (London: Ward, Lock & Co, 1921), 250–80.
20. Smithers records in his biography of Yates that the magazine denied having serialised this novel. Graham Harrison showed me his copy of an undated letter from a reader, Leonie Walters, to Smithers, written after she had read the biography, in which she states that she recalled reading the serial in *Woman's Journal* under this alternative title. Richard Greenhough traced the relevant issues in the British Library, for which I owe them both thanks.
21. Dornford Yates, *This Publican* (London: Ward, Lock & Co, 1938), 166.
22. Yates *This Publican*, 204–13.
23. Luke 18.13–14.
24. Macdonald *Companion*, 40–4.

25. Dornford Yates, *And Berry Came Too* (1936) (London: Ward, Lock & Co, 1958), 53.
26. Butler 1973, 94.
27. Yates *Fire Below*, 145.
28. Yates *Fire Below*, 148.
29. Dornford Yates, *An Eye For A Tooth* (London: Ward, Lock & Co, 1943), 57.
30. Yates *Tooth*, 244.
31. Dornford Yates, *She Fell Among Thieves* (1935), 1.
32. Yates *Adèle*, 21.
33. Yates *Adèle*, 21.
34. Dornford Yates, *Safe Custody* (London: Ward, Lock & Co, 1932), 18.
35. Yates *Custody*, 15.
36. Dornford Yates, *Cost Price* (London: Ward, Lock & Co, 1948), 247.
37. Smithers 1982, 158.
38. Yates *Storm Music*, 283.
39. Wallace 1987, 29–30.
40. Dornford Yates, *She Painted Her Face* (1937) (London: Ward, Lock & Co, 1944), 9.
41. Yates *Tooth*, 42.
42. Yates *Storm Music*, 16.
43. Yates *Storm Music*, 86.
44. Wallace 1987, 23–34, 23.
45. Yates *Thieves*, 3.
46. Yates *Berry Came Too*, 45.
47. Yates *Face*, 31.
48. Yates *Safe Custody*, 171.
49. Yates *Fire Below*, 195.
50. Yates *Fire Below*, 141.
51. Yates *Fire Below*, 197.
52. Yates *Fire Below*, 199
53. Yates *Face*, 264.
54. Yates *Fire Below*, 166.
55. Yates *Fire Below*, 307.
56. Smithers 1982, 145, 157–8.
57. Yates *Adèle*, 10.
58. Yates *Adèle*, 148.
59. Yates *Adèle*, 246.
60. Yates *Adèle*, 234.
61. Yates *Safe Custody*, 162.
62. It is also possible that the distress of 1933, the year of the divorce, had made Yates struggle to produce a new plot, so he reused a proven winner for convenience.
63. Yates *Storm Music*, 127.
64. Yates *Storm Music*, 208.
65. Yates *Storm Music*, 266.
66. Yates *Thieves*, 62, 67.
67. My thanks to Richard Greenhough for this observation.
68. Yates *Storm Music*, 177–8.
69. Dornford Yates, 'My Lady's Chamber' (1927), in *Period Stuff* (London: Ward, Lock & Co, 1942), 11–38, 31.

70. Yates 'Chamber', 31.
71. Dornford Yates, 'Way of Escape', in *Period Stuff* (London: Ward, Lock & Co, 1942), 273–94, 285.

7   Thirkell in Wartime, 1940–45

1. Postcard from Angela Thirkell to P P Howe, 21 March 1941, Hamish Hamilton archive, Bristol University Library Special Collections (used by kind permission of the Estate of Angela Thirkell).
2. Letter from Angela Thirkell to P P Howe, 6 March 1942, Hamish Hamilton archive, Bristol University Library Special Collections (used by kind permission of the Estate of Angela Thirkell).
3. Letter from Angela Thirkell to James Hamilton, 23 April 1944, Hamish Hamilton archive, Bristol University Library Special Collections (used by kind permission of the Estate of Angela Thirkell).
4. Mary Cadogan and Patricia Craig, *Women and Children First: The Fiction of Two World Wars* (London: Victor Gollancz, 1978), 194.
5. R D Charques, 'Other new novels', *The Times Literary Supplement*, 2181 (20 November 1943), 564; 'War-time Barsetshire', *The Times Literary Supplement*, 2238 (23 December 1944), 617; Jan Stephens, 'A model Barset', *The Times Literary Supplement*, 2119 (12 September 1942), 449; Marjorie Hand, 'Novels of the week', *The Times Literary Supplement* 2066 (6 September 1941), 434; Lee 1997, 90, 93.
6. Panikos Panayi, 'Immigrants, refugees, the British state and public opinion during World War Two', in Pat Kirkham and David Thoms (eds) *War Culture: Social Change and Changing Experience in World War Two* (London: Lawrence & Wishart, 1995), 201–8, 203.
7. Thirkell *Before Lunch*, 204.
8. Angela Thirkell, *Cheerfulness Breaks In* (1940) (London: Hamish Hamilton, 1949), 139.
9. Thirkell *Cheerfulness*, 180.
10. Angela Thirkell, *Miss Bunting* (London: Hamish Hamilton, 1945), 10.
11. Thirkell *Cheerfulness*, 165.
12. Jan Gore and Hilary Temple, 'Cheerfulness Breaks In: Relusions', The Angela Thirkell Society. http://www.angelathirkellsociety.co.uk/storage/CHEERFULNESS%20%20BREAKS%20%20IN.pdf [accessed 16 July 2014].
13. Adam 1975, 195.
14. Thirkell *Cheerfulness*, 212–15, 282, 232–3, 246–7.
15. Angela Thirkell, *Growing Up* (1943) (London: The Book Club, 1945), 10.
16. Adam 1975, 225.
17. Letter from Angela Thirkell to James Hamilton, 13 September 1939, Hamish Hamilton archive, Bristol University Library Special Collections (used by kind permission of the Estate of Angela Thirkell).
18. Thirkell *Cheerfulness*, 118.
19. Thirkell *Growing Up*, 66.
20. Laura Hapke, 'An absence of soldiers: Wartime fiction by British women', in Paul Holsinger and Mary Anne Schofield (eds) *Visions of War: World War II in Popular Literature and Culture* (Bowling Green, OH: Bowling Green State University Popular Press, 1992), 160–9, 161.

21. Hapke 1992, 161.
22. Adam 1975, 205.
23. Hapke 1992, 161.
24. Adam 1975, 221.
25. Letter and MS of an alternative ending for *Cheerfulness Breaks In* from Angela Thirkell to P P Howe, 9 July 1940, Hamish Hamilton archive, Bristol University Library Special Collections (used by kind permission of the Estate of Angela Thirkell).
26. A J P Taylor, *English History 1914–1945* (1965) (Oxford: Oxford University Press, 1975).
27. Thirkell *Miss Bunting*, 7.
28. Thirkell *Cheerfulness*, 84.
29. Cannadine 1990, 628.
30. Angela Thirkell, *Peace Breaks Out* (London: Hamish Hamilton, 1946), 152.
31. Cannadine 1990, 629.
32. Adam 1975, 223.
33. Williams 1973, 115.
34. Williams 1973, 174, 175.
35. Williams 1973, 253.
36. Thirkell *Cheerfulness*, 156.
37. Angela Thirkell, *Marling Hall* (London: Hamish Hamilton, 1942), 23.
38. Thirkell *Cheerfulness*, 196, 198.
39. Thirkell *Cheerfulness*, 331.
40. Thirkell *Cheerfulness*, 118.
41. Thirkell *Marling Hall*, 79.
42. Toynbee 1942, 294.
43. Richard Charques, '*Cheerfulness Breaks In*', *The Times Literary Supplement*, 20 May 1940, 505.
44. Hapke 1992, 165.
45. Cadogan and Craig 1978, 100.
46. Tom Harrisson, 'War books', *Horizon*, December 1941, 416–43, 418, 436.
47. Phyllis Lassner, *British Women Writers of World War II: Battlegrounds of Their Own* (Basingstoke: Macmillan, 1998), 8, 12.
48. Valerie Holman, *Print for Victory: Book Publishing in England, 1939–1945* (London: British Library, 2008), 58.
49. Holman 2008, 53.
50. Lee 1997, 93.
51. Angela Thirkell, *The Headmistress* (London: Penguin Books, 1944), 55.
52. Mark Twain, 'How to tell a story' (1897), *How to Tell A Story and other Essays* (New York: Harper & Brothers, 1897). http://www.gutenberg.org/files/3250/3250-h/3250-h.htm [accessed 24 July 2014].
53. Thirkell *Headmistress*, 37.
54. Evelyn Waugh, *Brideshead Revisited* (1945) (London: Penguin Books, 1981), 395.
55. Bernard Bergonzi, *Wartime and Aftermath: English Literature and Its Background 1939–1960* (Oxford: Oxford University Press, 1993), 39.
56. Christopher Hitchens, 'It's all on account of the war', *The Guardian*, 27 September 2008. http://www.theguardian.com/books/2008/sep/27/evelyn-waugh.fiction [accessed 5 July 2014].
57. Thirkell *Growing Up*, 46.

58. Thirkell *Growing Up*, 51.
59. Bowen 1966, ix.
60. Isabelle Mallet, 'Miss Thirkell, and Barsetshire, face up to war', *New York Times Book Review*, 17 February 1946, 7.
61. Angela Thirkell, *Northbridge Rectory* (London: Hamish Hamilton, 1941), 10.
62. Thirkell *Marling Hall*, 5.
63. Thirkell *Headmistress*, 10.
64. Thirkell *Miss Bunting*, 5.
65. Fritzer 2009, 5.
66. Thirkell *Marling Hall*, 5.
67. Thirkell *Cheerfulness*, 77.
68. Thirkell *Marling Hall*, 37.
69. Thirkell *Marling Hall*, 144.
70. Thirkell *Northbridge*, 67–8.
71. Thirkell *Northbridge*, 133.
72. Thirkell *Cheerfulness*, 82, 192.
73. Thirkell *Cheerfulness*, 162.
74. Thirkell *Marling Hall*, 131.
75. Letter from Angela Thirkell to P P Howe, 14 September 1940, Hamish Hamilton archive, Bristol University Library Special Collections (used by kind permission of the Estate of Angela Thirkell).
76. Thirkell *Marling Hall*, 229.
77. Thirkell *Growing Up*, 107.
78. Thirkell *Headmistress*, 65.
79. Thirkell *Miss Bunting*, 145.
80. Thirkell *Marling Hall*, 122.
81. Letter from Angela Thirkell to James Hamilton, 12 June 1941, Hamish Hamilton archive, Bristol University Library Special Collections (used by kind permission of the Estate of Angela Thirkell).
82. Thirkell *Cheerfulness*, 26.
83. Thirkell *Cheerfulness* 150. Spelling as in the original.
84. Thirkell *Headmistress*, 28.
85. Thirkell *Headmistress*, 34.
86. Thirkell *Headmistress*, 34.
87. Thirkell *Headmistress*, 40.
88. Thirkell *Headmistress*, 47.
89. Thirkell *Headmistress*, 134.
90. Thirkell *Miss Bunting*, 6.
91. Thirkell *Headmistress*, 84.
92. Thirkell *Miss Bunting*, 50.
93. Thirkell *Headmistress*, 150.
94. Thirkell *Miss Bunting*, 178.
95. Thirkell *Miss Bunting*, 136.
96. Thirkell *Miss Bunting*, 133.
97. Thirkell *Miss Bunting*, 158.
98. Thirkell *Wild Strawberries*, 370.
99. Thirkell *Wild Strawberries*, 450.
100. Letter from Angela Thirkell to James Hamilton, 1 October 1945, Hamish Hamilton archive, Bristol University Library Special Collections (used by

kind permission of the Estate of Angela Thirkell). 'Denis' was Thirkell's younger brother, the novelist Denis Mackail, and 'J.M.B.' is the playwright and novelist J M Barrie, Thirkell's godfather, whose biography Mackail wrote. In 1949, the first performance of Novello's musical comedy *The King's Rhapsody* took place on 15 September. The book included a character called Madame Koska, as a deliberate compliment to the most famous character of Angela Thirkell's alter ego Mrs Morland (source: letter of 12 January 1950, AT to Roger Machell, Hamish Hamilton archive, Bristol University Library Special Collections (used by kind permission of the Estate of Angela Thirkell)), but the character is a courtier rather than a detective–dress designer. The mixed messages in this brief private report of the encounter are retransmitted to the world in *Love Among the Ruins* (1948), in which Thirkell describes the otherwise wise and delightful theatrical couple Jessica Dean and Aubrey Clover by 'the most sincere falsehood, the falsest sincerity in the world' (Thirkell *Ruins*, 344).

101. Thirkell *Cheerfulness*, 83.
102. Thirkell *Cheerfulness*, 84.
103. Hilliard 2006, 145.
104. Gore and Temple.
105. Angela Thirkell, *County Chronicle* (London: Hamish Hamilton, 1950), 141.
106. Ina Habermann, *Myth, Memory and the Middlebrow: Priestley, du Maurier and the Symbolic Form of Englishness* (London: Palgrave Macmillan, 2010), 197 (emphasis in the original).
107. Thirkell *Northbridge*, 11.
108. James Hinton, *Women, Social Leadership and the Second World War: Continuities of Class* (Oxford: Oxford University Press, 2002), 35.
109. Hinton 2002, 39.
110. Thirkell *Cheerfulness*, 130, 201, 214, 301; *Miss Bunting*, 60–1.
111. Thirkell *Headmistress*, 51.
112. Thirkell *Growing Up*, 53.
113. Thirkell *Growing Up*, 75.

8   Rewriting History: Yates and Thirkell, 1945–60

1. Yates *Cost Price*, 118.
2. Yates *B-Berry and I*, 9.
3. Yates *House*, 282; *Berry Scene*, 105, 111–12, 122.
4. Yates *Red*, 96; *Berry Scene*, 67–74, 109; *Cost Price*, 54, 79, 88, 94, 174, 193, 277; *Vermin*, 301.
5. Yates *As Berry*, 57.
6. Yates *As Berry*, 73–6, 182.
7. Yates *As Berry*, 128.
8. The exaggerations include the many reminiscences of German behaviour, e.g. *As Berry*, 58, 194–5, 198, 200 and the cabmen's beef as a symbol of the benevolence of Edward VII's reign in *Vermin*, 201; the invented characters that Yates, or Boy, expect the reader to accept as real include the lawyers Coles Willing (a fictional character in *Vermin* and a lawyer in real-life legal cases described by Boy/Yates in *As Berry*) and Forsyth (the 'house' solicitor

in many Yates stories and novels from the 1920s).The episodes of selective recall include the extended account of the suffragette trial in *As Berry*, 22–4.

9. Yates *Vermin*, 225.
10. Lukács 1962, 15.
11. Lukács 1962, 65.
12. Jerome de Groot notes how historical accuracy in the historical novel is an assertion of authority (de Groot 2010, 7).
13. De Groot 2010, 9.
14. Cited in de Groot 2010, 10.
15. Pryce-Jones 1963, 215–39, 219.
16. Angus Wilson, cited in McSweeney 1983, xi–xvi, xii.
17. Bowen 1966, ix.
18. Taylor 1993, 12–13.
19. The quotation from Aneurin Bevan's speech on 4 July 1948 to a Labour meeting at Manchester runs 'That is why no amount of cajolery [...] and no attempts at ethical or social seduction, can eradicate from my heart a deep burning hatred for the Tory Party that inflicted those bitter experiences on me. So far as I am concerned they are lower than vermin'. David Kynaston, *Austerity Britain, 1945–1951* (London: Bloomsbury, 2008), 284. Thanks to Richard Greenhough for this reference.
20. In *County Chronicle* (1950) Lady Cora meets Isabel Dale for the second time, but this is presented as the first (223). In *A Double Affair* (1957) Edith's best friend is apparently Jane the Archdeacon's grand-daughter (whom we have not yet met), but some pages later Jane doesn't know who Edith is (135).
21. Thirkell *Close*, 194–201.
22. Thirkell *Peace*, 115.
23. Thirkell *Peace*, 119.
24. Thirkell *Peace*, 256–7, 258–60.
25. Thirkell *Chronicle*, 50, 231, 311.
26. Thirkell *Peace*, 129.
27. Angela Thirkell, *Private Enterprise* (London: Hamish Hamilton, 1947), 33.
28. Thirkell *Private*, 88; and also in 132, 189, 206–7, 305, 322; *Ruins* 57, 133–4; Angela Thirkell, *The Old Bank House* (London: Hamish Hamilton, 1949), 9; *Chronicle*, 120.
29. Thirkell *House*, 135; *Chronicle*, 8; *Close*, 212.
30. Thirkell *House*, 138–9; *Close*, 214.
31. Thirkell *Peace*, 49; *Private*, 89, 188, 197, 247, 280, 291; *Northbridge Rectory*, 28, 126–9, 169, 212; *Marling Hall*, 108, 224–6; *Growing Up*, 136.
32. Thirkell *Private*, 51.
33. Thirkell *Private*, 108; *House*, 249, 392.
34. Thirkell *Private*, 206; *Ruins*, 120; *House*, 309; *Daughter*, 168; Angela Thirkell, *Happy Return* (London: Hamish Hamilton, 1952), 166; Angela Thirkell, *Jutland Cottage* (London: Hamish Hamilton, 1953), 149; *Enter*, 8; *All Ages*, 148.
35. Thirkell *Ruins*, 13, 354.
36. Thirkell *Ruins*, 347–51.
37. Thirkell *Close*, 40.
38. Fritzer 2009, 9.
39. Thirkell *Private*, 58; *Chronicle*, 204–6; *Happy*, 77–8.

40. Thirkell *Peace*, 85.
41. Thirkell *Private*, 26; and also *Close*, 111; *House*, 151.
42. Williams 1973, 253.
43. Thirkell *Daughter*, 15; *Enter*, 139; *Close*, 228; *Never*, 90; *Enter*, 137.
44. Thirkell *All Ages*, 45–6; *Ruins*, 277.
45. Thirkell *Ruins*, 51.
46. Thirkell *Ruins*, 70–2, 187, 320–2; *House*, 123–4.
47. Thirkell *Ruins*, 144–5; *House*, 126, 200; *Chronicle*, 63.
48. Thirkell *Enter*, 115.
49. Thirkell *Never*, 121.
50. Yates *House*, 212.
51. Yates *House*, 279.
52. Yates *Berry Scene*, 47–9.
53. Yates *Berry Scene*, 51.
54. Yates *Vermin*, 133.
55. Thirkell *What*, 24; *Enter*, 39, 109; *What*, 46, 92; *Enter*, 200; *Never*, 132; *All Ages*, 133, 308.
56. Thirkell *Private*, 370; *Ruins*, 135; *House*, 170; *What*, 100; Angela Thirkell, *A Double Affair* (London: Hamish Hamilton, 1957), 159, 290; *Close*, 84, 136, 218; *All Ages*, 74, 223, 252; *Close*, 25.
57. Thirkell *Chronicle*, 49.
58. Thirkell *Daughter*, 144.
59. Thirkell *Jutland*, 59, 155, 279.
60. Thirkell *Enter*, 153, 206.
61. Thirkell *Marling Hall*, 229.
62. Thirkell *House*, 100; *Chronicle*, 179.
63. Thirkell *Private*, 134; *Ruins*, 17, 44, 44; *House*, 8, 11, 85, 178, 275; *Close*, 13.
64. Thirkell *Jutland*, 41, 95; *What*, 31, 89, 126; *Enter*, 77, 120, 160, 210, 213, 260; *Never*, 16; *All Ages*, 55, 211.
65. Thirkell *Private*, 251.
66. Thirkell *Private*, 358–9.
67. Thirkell *Private*, 350.
68. Thirkell *Jutland*, 106.
69. Thirkell *What*, 107; *Enter*, 231.
70. Thirkell *What*, 25, 120.
71. Thirkell *What*, 73, 81, 209; *Enter*, 59, 75.
72. Thirkell *Enter*, 188; *What*, 310; *Enter*, 213; *Double*, 270.
73. Thirkell *Private*, 157, 241–2.
74. Thirkell *Private*, 162.
75. Thirkell *Chronicle*, 137; *Happy*, 46, 241, 248–9.
76. Yates *Berry Scene*, 58.
77. Yates *B-Berry*, 140, 151–2.
78. Yates *As Berry*, 107.
79. Yates *B-Berry*, 150–1.
80. Yates *Vermin*, 35.
81. Yates *Vermin*, 46, 93.
82. Thirkell *Ruins*, 86, 89.
83. Thirkell *Chronicle*, 291, 306.
84. Atkins 1977, 17.

85. Thirkell *Happy*, 70; *Peace*, 7.
86. Thirkell *Peace*, 90. For further instances see Thirkell *Ruins*, 180; *House*, 163; *Jutland*, 180.
87. Thirkell *Never*, 66; *Double*, 235; *All Ages*, 21, 68, 71, 236.
88. Thirkell *Peace*, 69.
89. Thirkell *Peace*, 127.
90. Thirkell *Peace*, 251.
91. Thirkell *Peace*, 150.
92. Thirkell *Peace*, 172–7.
93. Thirkell *Peace*, 253.
94. Thirkell *Peace*, 255.
95. Thirkell *Private*, 260; *Ruins*, 7; *All Ages*, 158.
96. Thirkell *House*, 228.
97. Thirkell *Happy*, 69, 83, 67, 76, 83–4.
98. Thirkell *Double*, 216; *Never*, 144.
99. Yates *House*, 187.
100. Yates *Berry Scene*, 141–3, 148–9.
101. Faye Hammill, *Sophistication: A Literary and Cultural History* (Liverpool: Liverpool University Press, 2010), 3.
102. Hammill 2010, 4.
103. Hammill 2010, 145.
104. Hammill 2010, 165.
105. Thirkell *Private*, 90, 94, 95, 209, 308.
106. Thirkell *House*, 161; *What*, 131; *House*, 333.
107. Thirkell *Daughter*, 83.
108. Thirkell *Private*, 317–18, 368; *Chronicle*, 239–40.
109. Thirkell *Chronicle*, 304.
110. Thirkell *Miss Bunting*, 207; *Ruins*, 63; *House*, 142, 279, 286; *Chronicle*, 121, 147, 240; *Happy*, 146, 171; *Jutland*, 17, 100; *What*, 26; *Enter*, 69; *Never*, 100, 268; *Double*, 82; *Close*, 6, 246; *All Ages*, 73, 240; *Three*, 80.
111. Thirkell *Ruins*, 30; *Peace*, 245; *Private*, 187; *Ruins*, 23.
112. Hammill 2010, 146.
113. Thirkell *Ruins*, 41; *Never*, 253; *Daughter*, 314, 356; *What*, 38.
114. Thirkell *Double*, 50.
115. Thirkell *Ruins*, 141; *Daughter*, 155; *Double*, 160; *Jutland*, 170, 217; *Double*, 94.
116. Thirkell *House*, 122, 217; *Chronicle*, 135, 239.
117. Adam 1975, 230.
118. Thirkell *House*, 48, 169, 179; *All Ages*, 218; *Chronicle*, 132.
119. Thirkell *Chronicle*, 61.
120. Thirkell *Chronicle*, 75, emphasis in the original.
121. Thirkell *Chronicle*, 76.
122. Thirkell *Jutland*, 47, 48.
123. Thirkell *Jutland*, 123, 71; information from Pamela Taylor of the Angela Thirkell Society; Thirkell *Jutland*, 73, 185, 187.
124. Thirkell *Jutland*, 77–8.
125. Thirkell *Jutland*, 69, 154, 188, 214.
126. Thirkell *Jutland*, 171.
127. Thirkell *Jutland*, 211–12.

128. Thirkell *Close*, 238.
129. Evelyn Kerslake and Janine Liladhar, 'Angry sentinels and businesslike women: Identity and marital status in 1950s English library career novels', *Library History*, 17 (July 2001), 83–90, 87.
130. Thirkell *Private*, 293, 295.
131. Nesbitt 2005, 80.
132. Thirkell *Private*, 150; *Chronicle*, 223; *Daughter*, 61; *Happy*, 35, 89; *Jutland*, 234.
133. Julia Taylor McCain, 'Women and libraries', in Alastair Black and Peter Hoare (eds) *The Cambridge History of Libraries in Britain and Ireland, vol. 3, 1850–2000* (Cambridge: Cambridge University Press, 2006), 543–7, 544–5.
134. Thirkell *Ruins*, 35.
135. Thirkell *Private*, 325; *Chronicle*, 292.
136. Thirkell *Private*, 165; *House*, 146.
137. Thirkell *Happy*, 127; *Jutland*, 224, 130; *What*, 64; *Never*, 199; *What*, 187.
138. Thirkell *What*, 32; *Close*, 7.
139. Thirkell *Happy*, 231.
140. Thirkell *Double*, 200; *All Ages*, 165.
141. Thirkell *Chronicle*, 31–2, 60, 117; *Happy*, 11, 14, 244, 256; *Jutland*, 141; *Enter*, 126, 134, 213, 249; *Never*, 187–8; *Double*, 106.
142. Strickland 1977, 171.
143. Yates *Vermin*, 92.
144. Yates *Vermin*, 140.
145. Yates *Vermin*, 161, 184–92.
146. Dornford Yates, *Wife Apparent* (London: Ward, Lock & Co, 1956), 146, 258.
147. Yates *Wife*, 222.
148. Thirkell *Peace*, 6–7.
149. Thirkell *Peace*, 15.
150. Yates *House*, 9–11.
151. Yates *House*, 151–2.
152. Yates *House*, 39.
153. Cannadine 1990, 632–3.
154. Thirkell *Peace*, 69.
155. Thirkell *Never*, 90; *Private*, 128.
156. Thirkell *Happy*, 314; *Jutland*, 19; *Double*, 148.
157. Cannadine 1990, 647.
158. Thirkell *Private*, 300.
159. Thirkell *Ruins*, 190; *Chronicle*, 217; *Daughter*, 328, 245; *What*, 194, 233; *All Ages*, 15; *Double*, 151.
160. Thirkell *All Ages*, 20, 21.
161. Thirkell *Happy*, 276.
162. Thirkell *Private*, 10, 42, 88, 44; *Happy*, 151.
163. Angela Thirkell, *Three Score and Ten* (London: Hamish Hamilton, 1961), 25.
164. Thirkell *House*, 56; *Jutland*, 21; *Close*, 8, 18.
165. Thirkell *Close*, 12; *Enter*, 84, 106.

9 Conclusion

1. Simon Eliot, 'Foreword', in Katie Halsey and W R Owens (eds) *The History of Reading, vol. 2, Evidence from the British Isles, c.1750–1950* (Basingstoke: Palgrave Macmillan, 2011), xiii–xv, xiv.
2. Pierre Bourdieu, *The Field of Cultural Production* (New York: Columbia University Press, 1994), 49.
3. Franco Moretti , *The Atlas of the European Novel 1800–1900* (London: Verso, 1998), 3.
4. Moretti 1998, 7.
5. Moretti 1998, 5.
6. Smith 1978, 2.
7. Macdonald 'Introduction' 2011, 11.
8. Harrisson 1941, 436.

Works Cited

Unpublished sources

John Buchan, manuscript of *A Prince of the Captivity*, National Library of Scotland Acc. 7214 Mf.MSS.325.

Roger Clarke, *Towards a Critical Edition of John Buchan's Uncollected Journalism*, PhD thesis, University of the West of England, 2015.

Wendy Gan, 'Comic crossings', at Crossing the Space Between, 16th annual conference of the Space Between: Literature and Culture, 1914–1945, Institute of English Studies, University of London, 17–19 July 2014.

Ashley Maher, 'Architectural inhospitality: Modernist architecture's disruption of social order in Evelyn Waugh's *Decline and Fall*', at Everydayness and the Event, 15th annual conference of the Modernist Studies Association, University of Sussex, Brighton, 29 August–1 September 2013.

Andrew Martin Mitchell, *Fascism in East Anglia: The British Union of Fascists in Norfolk, Suffolk and Essex, 1933–40*, DPhil thesis, University of Sheffield, 1999.

Note by A J Smithers, 31 August 1979 (private collection).

Letter from A J Smithers to Hilary Eccles-Williams, 16 September 1986 (private collection).

A J Smithers, unpublished postscript to his 1982 biography of Yates (private collection).

Letter from Angela Thirkell to James Hamilton, 1 June 1939, Hamish Hamilton archive, Bristol University Library Special Collections (used by kind permission of the Estate of Angela Thirkell).

Letter from Angela Thirkell to James Hamilton, 13 September 1939, Hamish Hamilton archive, Bristol University Library Special Collections (used by kind permission of the Estate of Angela Thirkell).

Letter and MS of an alternative ending for *Cheerfulness Breaks In* from Angela Thirkell to P P Howe, 9 July 1940, Hamish Hamilton archive, Bristol University Library Special Collections (used by kind permission of the Estate of Angela Thirkell).

Letter from Angela Thirkell to P P Howe, 14 September 1940, Hamish Hamilton archive, Bristol University Library Special Collections (used by kind permission of the Estate of Angela Thirkell).

Postcard from Angela Thirkell to P P Howe, 21 March 1941, Hamish Hamilton archive, Bristol University Library Special Collections (used by kind permission of the Estate of Angela Thirkell).

Letter from Angela Thirkell to James Hamilton, 12 June 1941, Hamish Hamilton archive, Bristol University Library Special Collections (used by kind permission of the Estate of Angela Thirkell).

Letter from Angela Thirkell to P P Howe, 6 March 1942, Hamish Hamilton archive, Bristol University Library Special Collections (used by kind permission of the Estate of Angela Thirkell).

Letter from Angela Thirkell to James Hamilton, 23 April 1944, Hamish Hamilton archive, Bristol University Library Special Collections (used by kind permission of the Estate of Angela Thirkell).

Letter from Angela Thirkell to James Hamilton, 1 October 1945, Hamish Hamilton archive, Bristol University Library Special Collections (used by kind permission of the Estate of Angela Thirkell).

Letter from Angela Thirkell to Roger Machell, 12 January 1950, Hamish Hamilton archive, Bristol University Library Special Collections) (used by kind permission of the Estate of Angela Thirkell).

Lance Thirkell, 'Assassination of an Authoress, or, How the Critics Took my Mother to the Laundry', paper given to The Sixty-Three Club, 11 December 1983, 4.

Published sources

Ruth Adam, *A Woman's Place, 1910–1975* (1975) (London: Persephone Books, 2000).

John Atkins, *Six Novelists look at Society* (London: John Calder, 1977).

Anon., 'Come in! and let's talk about Middlebrows', *London Opinion*, 16 August 1930, 136.

Malcolm Baines, 'An outsider's view of early twentieth-century Liberals: Liberalism and Liberal politicians in John Buchan's life and fiction', *Journal of Liberal History*, 82 (Spring 2014), 6–15.

Ian Baucom, *Out of Place: Englishness, Empire and the Locations of Identity* (London: Yale University Press, 1999).

Nicola Beauman, *A Very Great Profession: The Woman's Novel 1914–39* (London: Virago, 1983).

Laura Beers and Geraint Thomas, 'Introduction', in *Brave New World: Imperial and Democratic Nation-Building in Britain between the Wars* (London: Institute of Historical Research, 2011), 1–38.

Hazel Bell, 'A tale told by an index: Collating the writings of Angela Thirkell', *Angela Thirkell Society North American Branch Conference Papers* (Hatfield: Angela Thirkell Society North American Branch, 1998), 1–8.

Bernard Bergonzi, *Wartime and Aftermath: English Literature and Its Background 1939–1960* (Oxford: Oxford University Press, 1993).

Robert Blanchard, *The First Editions of John Buchan: A Collector's Bibliography* (Hamden: Archon, 1981).

Clive Bloom, *Cult Fiction: Popular Reading and Pulp Theory* (London: Macmillan, 1996).

Ted Bogacz, '"A tyranny of words": Language, poetry and antimodernism in England in the First World War', *The Journal of Modern History*, 58:3 (1986), 643–68.

The Bookman, LXXXVI: 513 (June 1934), back cover.

Pierre Bourdieu, *The Field of Cultural Production* (New York: Columbia University Press, 1994).

Elizabeth Bowen, 'Introduction', in *An Angela Thirkell Omnibus* (London: Hamish Hamilton, 1966), vii–ix.

Rosa Maria Bracco, *Merchants of Hope: British Middlebrow Writers and the First World War, 1919–1939* (Oxford: Berg, 1993).

John Buchan, *Mr Standfast* (1919) (Oxford: Oxford University Press, 1993).

John Buchan, *Huntingtower* (1922) (Oxford: Oxford University Press, 1996).

John Buchan, 'A new defence of poetry', *The Spectator*, 129 (8 July 1922), 47–8.

John Buchan, *The Three Hostages* (1924) (Oxford: Oxford University Press, 1995).

John Buchan, *John Macnab* (1925) (Oxford: Oxford University Press, 1994).

John Buchan, *The Dancing Floor* (1927) (Oxford: Oxford University Press, 1997).

John Buchan, 'After ten years of peace', *Daily Mirror* (10 November 1928), 11.

John Buchan, *The Courts of the Morning* (1929) (Edinburgh: B&W Publishing, 1993).

John Buchan, 'Conservatism and progress', *The Spectator*, 143 (23 November 1929), 754–5.

John Buchan, *Castle Gay* (1930) (Kelly Bray: House of Stratus, 2001).

John Buchan, *The Gap in the Curtain* (1932) (London: Thomas Nelson & Son, 1935).

John Buchan, *A Prince of the Captivity* (1933) (Edinburgh: B&W Publishing, 1996).

John Buchan, *The House of the Four Winds* (1935) (London: Hodder & Stoughton, 1937).

William Vivian Butler, *The Durable Desperadoes: A Critical Study of some Enduring Heroes* (London: Macmillan, 1973).

Mary Cadogan and Patricia Craig, *Women and Children First: The Fiction of Two World Wars* (London: Victor Gollancz, 1978).

David Cannadine, *The Decline and Fall of the British Aristocracy* (1990) (London: Macmillan, 1996).

John Carey, *The Intellectual and the Masses: Pride and Prejudice among the Literary Intelligentsia, 1880–1939* (London: Faber & Faber, 1992).

Richard Carr, *Veteran MPs and Conservative Politics in the Aftermath of the Great War* (Farnham: Ashgate, 2013).

Richard Charques, *'Cheerfulness Breaks In'*, *The Times Literary Supplement*, 20 May 1940, 505.

R D Charques, 'Other new novels', *The Times Literary Supplement*, 2181 (20 November 1943), 564.

R D Charques, 'War-time Barsetshire', *The Times Literary Supplement*, 2238 (23 December 1944), 617.

Laura Roberts Collins, *English Country Life in the Barsetshire Novels of Angela Thirkell* (Westport, CT: Greenwood Press, 1994).

Andy Croft, *Red Letter Days: British Fiction in the 1930s* (London: Lawrence & Wishart, 1990).

Stephen M Cullen, '"The land of my dreams": The gendered utopian dreams and disenchantment of British literary ex-combatants of the Great War', *Cultural and Social History*, 8:2 (2011), 195–212.

Daily Express, *These Tremendous Years, 1919–1939* (London: Daily Express Publications, 1939).

David Daniell, *The Interpreter's House* (Edinburgh: Thomas Nelson, 1975).

William Deecke, 'Angela Thirkell's crime novelists', *Angela Thirkell Society North American Branch Conference Papers* (Hatfield: Angela Thirkell Society North American Branch, 1998), 15–16.

Jerome de Groot, *The Historical Novel* (Abingdon: Taylor & Francis, 2010).

Michael Diamond, *Lesser Breeds: Racial Attitudes in Popular British Culture, 1890–1940* (London: Anthem Press, 2006).

Stephen Donovan, 'A very modern experiment: John Buchan and Rhodesia', in Kate Macdonald and Nathan Waddell (eds) *John Buchan and the Idea of Modernity* (London: Pickering & Chatto, 2013), 49–62.

Simon Eliot, 'Foreword', in Katie Halsey and W R Owens (eds) *The History of Reading, vol. 2, Evidence from the British Isles, c.1750–1950* (Basingstoke: Palgrave Macmillan, 2011), xiii–xv, xiv.

E M Forster, *Howards End* (1910) (London: Penguin Books, 1989).

Bridget Fowler, *The Alienated Reader: Women and Popular Romantic Literature in the Twentieth Century* (Harlow: Harvester Wheatsheaf, 1991).

Christina Foyle, 'The bookseller and the reading public', *Royal Society of Arts Journal*, 101:4908 (18 September 1953), 779–87.

Penelope Fritzer, *Ethnicity and Gender in the Barsetshire Novels of Angela Thirkell* (Westport, CT: Greenwood Press, 1999).

Penelope Fritzer, *Aesthetics and Nostalgia in the Barsetshire Novels of Angela Thirkell* (Angela Thirkell Society of North America, 2009).

P N Furbank, 'The twentieth-century best-seller', in Boris Ford (ed.) *The Modern Age* (London: Penguin, 1961), 429–41.

Paul Fussell, *The Great War and Modern Memory* (1975) (Oxford: Oxford University Press, 2000).

J William Galbraith, *John Buchan: Model Governor-General* (Toronto: Dundurn, 2013).

Terry Gifford, 'Ownership and access in the work of John Muir, John Buchan and Andrew Greig', *Green Letters: Studies in Ecocriticism*, 17:2 (2013), 165–74.

Simon Glassock, 'Buchan, sport and masculinity', in Kate Macdonald (ed.) *Reassessing John Buchan: Beyond The Thirty-Nine Steps* (London: Pickering & Chatto, 2009), 41–51.

Jan Gore and Hilary Temple, 'Cheerfulness Breaks In: Relusions', The Angela Thirkell Society. http://www.angelathirkellsociety.co.uk/storage/CHEERFULNESS%20%20BREAKS%20%20IN.pdf [accessed 16 July 2014].

Helen Gosse, 'Folly Field', *Fortnightly Review*, 138 (November 1933), 637–9.

Martin Green, *A Biography of John Buchan and his Sister Anna: The Personal Background of their Literary Work* (Lampeter: Edwin Mellen Press, 1990).

Jill Greenfield, Sean O'Connell and Chris Reid, 'Gender, consumer culture, and the middle-class male, 1918–39', in Alan Kidd and David Nicholls (eds) *Gender, Civic Culture and Consumerism: Middle-Class Identity in Britain, 1800–1940* (Manchester: Manchester University Press, 1999), 183–97.

Adrian Gregory, *The Last Great War: British Society and the First World War* (Cambridge: Cambridge University Press, 2008).

Mary Grover, 'Thirkell, Angela 1890–1961', in Virginia Blain, Patricia Clements and Isobel Grundy (eds) *The Feminist Companion to Literature in English* (London: B T Batsford, 1990), 248–50.

Mary Grover, *The Ordeal of Warwick Deeping: Middlebrow Authorship and Cultural Embarrassment* (Madison, NJ: Farleigh Dickinson University Press, 2009).

Ina Habermann, *Myth, Memory and the Middlebrow: Priestley, du Maurier and the Symbolic Form of Englishness* (London: Palgrave Macmillan, 2010).

Katie Halsey, '"Something light to take my mind off the war": Reading on the Home Front during the Second World War', in Katie Halsey and W R Owens (eds) *The History of Reading, vol. 2, Evidence from the British Isles, 1750–1950* (Basingstoke: Palgrave Macmillan, 2011), 84–100.

Cicely Hamilton, *Modern England, As Seen by an Englishwoman* (J M Dent, 1938).

Faye Hammill, *Sophistication: A Literary and Cultural History* (Liverpool: Liverpool University Press, 2010).

Marjorie Hand, 'Novels of the week', *The Times Literary Supplement*, 2066 (6 September 1941), 434.

Archibald Hanna, *John Buchan 1875–1940: A Bibliography* (Hamden: Shoestring Press, 1953).

Laura Hapke, 'An absence of soldiers: Wartime fiction by British women', in Paul Holsinger and Mary Anne Schofield (eds) *Visions of War: World War II in Popular Literature and Culture* (Bowling Green, OH: Bowling Green State University Popular Press, 1992), 160–9.

John M Harrison, *The Reactionaries* (London: Gollancz, 1966).

Tom Harrisson, 'War books', *Horizon*, December 1941, 416–43.

Jenny Hartley, *Millions Like Us: British Women's Fiction of the Second World War* (London: Virago, 1997).

Joe Hicks and Grahame Allen, *A Century of Change: Trends in UK Statistics since 1900*, House of Commons Library Research Paper 99/111, 21 December 1999.

Christopher Hilliard, *To Exercise Our Talents: The Democratisation of Writing in Britain* (London: Yale University Press, 2006).

Kenneth Hillier (ed.) *The First Editions of John Buchan: An Illustrated Collector's Bibliography* (Clapton-in-Gordano: Avonworld, 2009).

James Hinton, *Women, Social Leadership and the Second World War: Continuities of Class* (Oxford: Oxford University Press, 2002).

Christopher Hitchens, 'It's all on account of the war', *The Guardian*, 27 September 2008. http://www.theguardian.com/books/2008/sep/27/evelynwaugh.fiction [accessed 5 July 2014].

Valerie Holman, *Print for Victory: Book Publishing in England, 1939–1945* (London: British Library, 2008).

Winifred Holtby, *Letters to a Friend* (1937) (Adelaide: Michael Walmer, 2014).

Nicola Humble, *The Feminine Middlebrow Novel 1920s to 1950s: Class, Domesticity and Bohemianism* (Oxford: Oxford University Press, 2001).

Nicola Humble, 'The feminine middlebrow novel', in Maroula Joannou (ed.) *The History of British Women's Writing, 1920–1945* (London: Palgrave Macmillan, 2013), 97–111.

Heather Ingman, *Women's Fiction Between the Wars: Mothers, Daughters, and Writing* (Edinburgh: Edinburgh University Press, 1998).

Hans Jauss, *Toward an Aesthetic of Reception* (Minneapolis: University of Minnesota Press, 1982).

Richard Kelly, *House of Commons Background Paper: Women Members of Parliament*, SN/PC/6652 (London: HM Government, July 2013).

Susan Kingsley Kent, *Aftershocks: Politics and Trauma in Britain, 1918–1931* (Basingstoke: Palgrave Macmillan, 2009).

Evelyn Kerslake and Janine Liladhar, 'Angry sentinels and businesslike women: Identity and marital status in 1950s English library career novels', *Library History*, 17 (July 2001), 83–90.

Alan Kidd and David Nicholls, 'Introduction: History, culture and the middle classes', in Alan Kidd and David Nicholls (eds) *Gender, Civic Culture and Consumerism: Middle-Class Identity in Britain, 1800–1940* (Manchester: Manchester University Press, 1999), 1–11.

David Kynaston, *Austerity Britain, 1945–1951* (London: Bloomsbury, 2008).

Phyllis Lassner, *British Women Writers of World War II: Battlegrounds of Their Own* (Basingstoke: Macmillan, 1998).

Hermione Lee, 'Good show', *The New Yorker*, 7 October 1997, 90–5.

Jill N Levin, *The 'Land of Lost Content': Sex, Art and Class in the Novels of Angela Thirkell, 1933–1960*, MA thesis, Washington University, St Louis, 1986.

Jill N Levin, 'Lady novelists in Britain, 1920–1960', *The Journal of the Angela Thirkell Society*, 11 (1991), 24–6.

Jill N Levin, 'Inhibition, silence and speech in the novels of Angela Thirkell', *Angela Thirkell Society North American Branch Conference Papers* (Hatfield: Angela Thirkell Society North American Branch, 1998), 19–21.

Lifebuoy Soap advert, *The Daily Graphic*, 22 July 1924, 4.

Alison Light, *Forever England: Femininity, Literature and Conservatism between the Wars* (London: Routledge, 1991).

Edward Living, *Adventures in Publishing: The House of Ward Lock* (London: Ward, Lock & Co, 1954).

Andrew Lownie, *The Presbyterian Cavalier: John Buchan* (London: Constable & Co., 1995).

Georg Lukács, *The Historical Novel* (1962) (Harmondsworth: Penguin, 1969).

Kate Macdonald, 'Women readers of John Buchan', *The John Buchan Journal*, 23 (2000), 24–31.

Kate Macdonald, 'Writing *The War*: John Buchan's lost journalism of the First World War', *The Times Literary Supplement*, 10 August 2007, 14–15.

Kate Macdonald, *John Buchan: A Companion to the Mystery Fiction* (Jefferson: McFarland, 2009).

Kate Macdonald, 'The diversification of Thomas Nelson: John Buchan and the Nelson archive, 1909–1911', *Publishing History*, 65 (2009), 71–96.

Kate Macdonald (ed.) *Reassessing John Buchan: Beyond The Thirty-Nine Steps* (London: Pickering & Chatto, 2009).

Kate Macdonald, 'Aphrodite rejected: Archetypal female characters in Buchan's fiction', in Kate Macdonald (ed.) *Reassessing John Buchan: Beyond The Thirty-Nine Steps* (London: Pickering & Chatto, 2009), 153–69.

Kate Macdonald, 'John Buchan's breakthrough: The conjunction of experience, markets and forms that made *The Thirty-Nine Steps*', *Publishing History*, 68 (2010).

Kate Macdonald, 'The war-wounded and the congenitally impaired: Competing categories of disability in John Buchan's *Huntingtower* (1922)', *Journal of War and Culture Studies*, 4:1 (2011), 7–20.

Kate Macdonald, 'Thomas Nelson & Sons and John Buchan: Mutual marketing in the publisher's series', in John Spiers (ed.) *The Culture of the Publisher's Series, vol. 1, Authors, Publishers, and the Shaping of Taste* (London: Palgrave Macmillan, 2011), 156–70.

Kate Macdonald, 'Introduction: Identifying the Middlebrow, the Masculine and Mr Miniver', in Kate Macdonald (ed.) *The Masculine Middlebrow, 1880–1950: What Mr Miniver Read* (Basingstoke: Palgrave Macmillan, 2011), 1–23.

Kate Macdonald, 'The use of London lodgings in middlebrow fiction, 1900–1930s', *Literary London*, 9:1 (2011). http:// www.literarylondon.org/london-journal/macdonald.html [accessed April 2014].

Kate Macdonald, 'Witchcraft and non-conformity in Sylvia Townsend Warner's *Lolly Willowes* (1926) and John Buchan's *Witch Wood* (1927)', *Journal of the Fantastic in the Arts*, 23:2 (2012), 215–38.

Kate Macdonald and Nathan Waddell (eds) *John Buchan and the Idea of Modernity* (London: Pickering & Chatto, 2013).

S P B Mais, 'Books and their writers', *The Daily Graphic*, 5 September 1924, 13.

Isabelle Mallet, 'Miss Thirkell, and Barsetshire, face up to war', *New York Times Book Review*, 17 February 1946, 7.

Jane Marcus, 'Corpus/Corps/Corpse: Writing the body in/at war', in Helen Margaret Cooper, Adrienne Munich and Susan Merrill Squier (eds) *Arms and the Woman: War, Gender, and Literary Representation* (Raleigh: University of North Carolina Press, 1989), 124–67.

Charles F G Masterman, *England after War: A Study* (London: Hodder & Stoughton, 1922).

Rachel Mather, *The Heirs of Jane Austen: Twentieth-Century Writers of the Comedy of Manners* (New York: Peter Lang, 1996).

Julia Taylor McCain, 'Women and libraries', in Alastair Black and Peter Hoare (eds) *The Cambridge History of Libraries in Britain and Ireland, vol. 3, 1850–2000* (Cambridge: Cambridge University Press, 2006), 543–7.

Ross McKibbin, *Classes and Cultures England 1918–1951* (Oxford: Oxford University Press, 1998).

Kerry McSweeney, 'Editor's Introduction', in Kerry McSweeney (ed.) *Diversity and Depth in Fiction: Selected Critical Writings of Angus Wilson* (London: Secker & Warburg, 1983), xi–xvi.

Janet Montefiore, *Men and Women Writers of the 1930s: The Dangerous Flood of History* (London: Routledge, 1996).

Franco Moretti, *The Atlas of the European Novel 1800–1900* (London: Verso, 1998).

Jennifer Poulos Nesbitt, *Narrative Settlements: Geographies of British Women's Fiction Between the Wars* (Toronto: University of Toronto Press, 2005).

George Orwell, 'Inside the Whale' (1940), in *Selected Essays* (London: Penguin, 1957), 9–50.

Panikos Panayi, 'Immigrants, refugees, the British state and public opinion during World War Two', in Pat Kirkham and David Thoms (eds) *War Culture: Social Change and Changing Experience in World War Two* (London: Lawrence & Wishart, 1995), 201–8.

Anne Perkins, *A Very British Strike 3 May–12 May 1926* (London: Macmillan, 2006).

Len Platt, *Aristocracies of Fiction: The Idea of Aristocracy in Late-Nineteenth-Century and Early-Twentieth-Century Literary Culture* (Westport, CT: Greenwood Press, 2001).

Len Platt, 'Aristocratic comedy and intellectual satire', in Patrick Parrinder and Andrzej Gasiorek (eds) *The Reinvention of the British and Irish Novel 1880–1940* (Oxford: Oxford University Press, 2011), 433–47.

William Plomer, 'Fiction: *A Prince of the Captivity*', *The Spectator*, 151 (21 July 1933), 94.

Alex Potts, '"Constable Country" between the wars', in Raphael Samuel (ed.) *Patriotism: The Making and Unmaking of British National Identity, vol. 3, National Fictions* (London: Routledge, Kegan Paul, 1989), 160–86.

David Pryce-Jones, 'Towards the Cocktail Party', in Michael Sissons and Philip French (eds) *Age of Austerity 1945–1951: The Conservatism of Post-War Writing* (London: Hodder & Stoughton, 1963), 215–39.

Ann Rea, 'The collaborator, the tyrant and the resistance: *The Lion, The Witch and The Wardrobe* and middlebrow England in the Second World War', in Kate

Macdonald (ed.) *The Masculine Middlebrow, 1880–1950: What Mr Miniver Read* (Basingstoke: Palgrave Macmillan, 2011), 177–96.

Thomas J Roberts, *An Aesthetics of Junk Fiction* (Athens, GA: University of Georgia Press, 1990).

Terence Rodgers, 'The Right Book Club: Text wars, modernity and cultural politics in the 1930s', *Literature and History*, 12:2 (2003), 1–15.

Sonya Rose, *Which People's War? National Identity and Citizenship in Wartime Britain* (Oxford: Oxford University Press, 2003).

'Saki', 'Tobermory' (1911), in *The Complete Stories of Saki* (Ware: Wordsworth Edition, 1993), 79–84.

Robert Scholes, *Paradoxy of Modernism* (New Haven: Yale University Press, 2006).

Bill Schwartz, 'The romance of the veld', in Andrew Bosco and Alex May (eds) *The Round Table: The Empire/Commonwealth and British Foreign Policy* (London: Lothian Foundation Press, 1997), 65–125.

Tom Sharpe, 'Alias Dornford Yates', *The Times Saturday Review*, 17 July 1976.

Janet Adam Smith, *John Buchan* (Oxford: Oxford University Press, 1965).

Janet Adam Smith, 'Obituary: Alice Fairfax-Lucy', *The Independent*, 23 December 1993.

David Smith, *Socialist Propaganda in the Twentieth-Century British Novel* (London: Macmillan, 1978).

A J Smithers, *Dornford Yates: A Biography* (London: Hodder & Stoughton, 1982).

Jane Southron Spence, 'England in War', *New York Times Book Review*, 2 March 1941, VI, 7:1.

Jan Stephens, 'A model Barset', *The Times Literary Supplement*, 2119 (12 September 1942), 449.

John Stevenson and Chris Cook, *Britain in the Depression: Society and Politics 1929–39* (2nd edn, 1994, Longman).

Margot Strickland, *Angela Thirkell: Portrait of a Lady Novelist* (London: Gerald Duckworth & Co., 1977).

John J Su, 'Refiguring national character: The remains of the British estate novel', *Modern Fiction Studies*, 48:3 (2002), 552–80.

A J P Taylor, *English History 1914–1945* (1965) (Oxford: Oxford University Press, 1975).

D J Taylor, *After the War: The Novel and English Society since 1945* (London: Chatto & Windus, 1993).

Hilary Temple, 'Wild Strawberries: Relusions', The Angela Thirkell Society. http://www.angelathirkellsociety.co.uk/storage/Wild%20Strawberries.pdf [accessed 22 May 2014].

Angela Thirkell, *Three Houses* (1931) (London: Allison & Busby, 2012).

Angela Thirkell, *Ankle Deep* (1933), in *An Angela Thirkell Omnibus* (London: Hamish Hamilton, 1966), 3–159.

Angela Thirkell, *High Rising* (1933), in *An Angela Thirkell Omnibus* (London: Hamish Hamilton, 1966), 163–315.

Angela Thirkell, *Wild Strawberries* (1934), in *An Angela Thirkell Omnibus* (London: Hamish Hamilton, 1966), 319–467.

Angela Thirkell, *O, These Men, These Men!* (1935) (London: Moyer Bell, 1996).

Angela Thirkell, *August Folly* (London: Hamish Hamilton, 1936).

Angela Thirkell, *Summer Half* (1937) (London: The Hogarth Press, 1988).

Angela Thirkell, *Pomfret Towers* (1938) (London: Virago Press, 2013).

Angela Thirkell, *Before Lunch* (1939) (Harmondsworth: Penguin, 1951).

Angela Thirkell, *The Brandons* (1939) (London: The Hogarth Press, 1988).

Angela Thirkell, *Cheerfulness Breaks In* (1940) (London: Hamish Hamilton, 1949).

Angela Thirkell, *Northbridge Rectory* (London: Hamish Hamilton, 1941).

Angela Thirkell, *Marling Hall* (London: Hamish Hamilton, 1942).

Angela Thirkell, *Growing Up* (1943) (London: The Book Club, 1945).

Angela Thirkell, *The Headmistress* (London: Penguin Books, 1944).

Angela Thirkell, *Miss Bunting* (London: Hamish Hamilton, 1945).

Angela Thirkell, *Peace Breaks Out* (London: Hamish Hamilton, 1946).

Angela Thirkell, *Private Enterprise* (London: Hamish Hamilton, 1947).

Angela Thirkell, *Love Among the Ruins* (London: Hamish Hamilton, 1948).

Angela Thirkell, *The Old Bank House* (London: Hamish Hamilton, 1949).

Angela Thirkell, *County Chronicle* (London: Hamish Hamilton, 1950).

Angela Thirkell, 'Henry Kingsley', *Nineteenth-Century Fiction*, 5:3 (December 1950), 175–87.

Angela Thirkell, *The Duke's Daughter* (1951) (London: Moyer Bell, 1998).

Angela Thirkell, *Happy Return* (London: Hamish Hamilton, 1952).

Angela Thirkell, *Jutland Cottage* (London: Hamish Hamilton, 1953).

Angela Thirkell, *What Did It Mean?* (London: Hamish Hamilton, 1954).

Angela Thirkell, *Enter Sir Robert* (1955) (London: Moyer Bell, 2000).

Angela Thirkell, *Never Too Late* (1956) (London: Moyer Bell, 2000).

Angela Thirkell, *A Double Affair* (London: Hamish Hamilton, 1957).

Angela Thirkell, *Close Quarters* (London: Hamish Hamilton, 1958).

Angela Thirkell, *Love At All Ages* (London: Hamish Hamilton, 1959).

Angela Thirkell, *Three Score and Ten* (London: Hamish Hamilton, 1961).

Andrew Thorpe, *The Longman Companion to Britain in the Era of the Two World Wars 1914–1945* (London: Longman, 1994).

Philip Toynbee, 'New novels', *The New Statesman and Nation*, 31 October 1942, 292–4.

Diana Trilling, *Reviewing the Forties* (New York: Harcourt Brace Jovanovitch, 1978).

Arthur C Turner, *John Buchan: A Biography* (Toronto: Macmillan, 1949).

Mark Twain, 'How to tell a story' (1897), *How to Tell a Story and Other Essays* (New York: Harper & Brothers, 1897). http://www.gutenberg.org/files/3250/3250-h/3250-h.htm [accessed 24 July 2014].

Richard Usborne, *Clubland Heroes* (1953) (London: Hutchinson, 1983).

Anna Vaninskaya, 'The political middlebrow from Chesterton to Orwell', in Kate Macdonald (ed.) *The Masculine Middlebrow, 1880–1950: What Mr Miniver Read* (Basingstoke: Palgrave Macmillan, 2011), 162–76.

Betty D Vernon, *Ellen Wilkinson* (London: Croom Helm, 1982).

Nathan Waddell, *Modern John Buchan: A Critical Introduction* (Cambridge: Cambridge Scholars Press, 2009).

Raymond P Wallace, 'Cardboard kingdoms', in *San José Studies*, 13:2 (1987), 23–34.

George Watson, *Politics and Literature in Modern Britain* (London: Macmillan, 1977).

Evelyn Waugh, *Brideshead Revisited* (1945) (London: Penguin Books, 1981).

Raymond Williams, *The Country and the City* (Oxford: Oxford University Press, 1973).

Virginia Woolf, 'Why Art To-Day Follows Politics' (1936), in Stuart N Clarke (ed.) *The Essays of Virginia Woolf, vol. VI, 1933–1941, and Additional Essays 1906–1924* (London: The Hogarth Press, 2011).

Dornford Yates, 'For Better or for Worse' (1919), in *The Courts of Idleness* (London: Ward, Lock & Co, 1920), 88–108.

Dornford Yates, 'How Will Noggin was fooled, and Berry rode forth against his will' (1919), in *Berry & Co* (London: Ward, Lock & Co, 1920), 9–33.

Dornford Yates, 'How Adèle Feste arrived, and Mr Dunkelsbaum supped with the Devil' (1920), in *Berry & Co* (London: Ward, Lock & Co, 1921), 219–49.

Dornford Yates, 'How Adèle broke her dream, and Vandy Pleydell took Exercise' (1920), in *Berry & Co* (London: Ward, Lock & Co, 1921), 250–80.

Dornford Yates, 'What's in a Name', in *The Courts of Idleness* (London: Ward, Lock & Co, 1920), 9–29.

Dornford Yates, *Anthony Lyveden* (London: Ward, Lock & Co, 1921).

Dornford Yates, *Jonah & Co* (London: Ward, Lock & Co, 1922).

Dornford Yates, 'Sarah' (1922), in *And Five Were Foolish* (London: Ward, Lock & Co, 1924), 11–38.

Dornford Yates, 'Spring' (1923), in *And Five Were Foolish* (London: Ward, Lock & Co, 1924), 99–126.

Dornford Yates, 'Ann', in *And Five Were Foolish* (London: Ward, Lock & Co, 1924), 211–50.

Dornford Yates, 'Jeremy', in *As Other Men Are* (London: Ward, Lock & Co, 1924), 11–39.

Dornford Yates, 'Oliver' (1924), in *As Other Men Are* (London: Ward, Lock & Co, 1925), 105–29.

Dornford Yates, 'Peregrine', in *As Other Men Are* (London: Ward, Lock & Co, 1924), 261–84.

Dornford Yates 'Susan', in *And Five Were Foolish* (London: Ward, Lock & Co, 1924), 281–311.

Dornford Yates, *The Stolen March* (1926) (London: Ward Lock & Co, 1930).

Dornford Yates, *Blind Corner* (1927) (London: Ward, Lock & Co, 1957).

Dornford Yates, 'My Lady's Chamber' (1927), in *Period Stuff* (London: Ward, Lock & Co, 1942), 11–38.

Dornford Yates, 'St Jeames' (1927), in *Maiden Stakes* (London: Ward, Lock & Co, 1928), 41–71.

Dornford Yates, 'Force Majeure', in *Maiden Stakes* (London: Ward, Lock, & Co, 1928), 131–60.

Dornford Yates, *Perishable Goods* (1928) (London: Ward, Lock & Co, 1957).

Dornford Yates, *Blood Royal* (1929) (London: Hodder & Stoughton, 1941).

Dornford Yates, *Fire Below* (1930) (London: Ward, Lock & Co, 1931), 145.

Dornford Yates, *Adèle & Co* (London: Ward, Lock & Co, 1931).

Dornford Yates, *Safe Custody* (London: Ward, Lock & Co, 1932).

Dornford Yates, *Storm Music* (London: Ward, Lock & Co, 1934).

Dornford Yates, *She Fell Among Thieves* (1935) (London: J M Dent, 1985).

Dornford Yates, *And Berry Came Too* (1936) (London: Ward, Lock & Co, 1958).

Dornford Yates, *She Painted Her Face* (1937) (London: Ward, Lock & Co, 1944).

Dornford Yates, *This Publican* (London: Ward, Lock & Co, 1938).

Dornford Yates, *Gale Warning* (London: Ward, Lock & Co, 1939).

Dornford Yates, *Shoal Water* (1940) (London: Ward, Lock & Co, 1946).

Dornford Yates, 'And Adela, Too' (1941), in *Period Stuff* (London: Ward, Lock & Co, 1942), 197–218.

Dornford Yates, 'Preface', *Period Stuff* (London: Ward, Lock & Co, 1942), 8.

Dornford Yates, 'Period Stuff', in *Period Stuff* (London: Ward, Lock & Co, 1942), 297–319.
Dornford Yates, 'Way of Escape', in *Period Stuff* (London: Ward, Lock & Co, 1942), 273–94.
Dornford Yates, *An Eye For A Tooth* (London: Ward, Lock & Co, 1943).
Dornford Yates, *The House that Berry Built* (London: Ward, Lock & Co, 1945).
Dornford Yates, *The Berry Scene* (London: Ward, Lock & Co, 1947).
Dornford Yates, *Cost Price* (London: Ward, Lock & Co, 1949).
Dornford Yates, *Lower Than Vermin* (London: Ward, Lock & Co, 1950).
Dornford Yates, *As Berry and I Were Saying* (London: Ward, Lock & Co, 1952).
Dornford Yates, *Wife Apparent* (London: Ward, Lock & Co, 1956).
Dornford Yates, *B-Berry and I Look Back* (London: Ward Lock, 1958).

Index

Note: 'n' after a page reference denotes a note number on that page.

First World War
 returning soldiers, 41, 46, 48–9
 social changes, 36, 43, 52, 66
Fleming, Ian, 222
Forster, E M, 11, 222
 Howard's End, 123
Fowler, Bridget, 41, 46
Foyle, Christina, 13, 164
Fritzer, Penelope, 34, 178, 197
Furbank, P N, 70
Fussell, Paul, 19

Galbraith, J William, 90
gay and lesbian characters, 186,
 187, 88
gender, 24, 30, 34, 37, 64, 81, 83, 126,
 158, 173, 186, 219
General Strike (1926), 37, 39, 237n32
Gentleman Outlaw genre, 5
gentry, 39, 52, 196, 216
 in Buchan's work, 44, 56, 108, 110
 in Thirkell's work, 114, 115, 116,
 126–7, 137–8, 167, 179, 186, 189
 in Yates's work, 71, 73, 76
George VI, 90, 91
Germany, 38, 90
Gibbons, Stella, *Cold Comfort
 Farm*, 134
Gifford, Terry, 56
Glyn, Elinor, 154
Gollancz, Victor, 13
Grahame, Kenneth, *Wind in the
 Willows, The*, 87
Great Depression, 39
Greenfield, Jill, 66
Gregory, Adrian, 37, 41, 49, 64
Grosvenor, Susan, 4, 33
Grover, Mary, 13, 59, 131, 229n44

Haggard, H Rider, 19, 96
Hamilton, Cicely, 112
Hamilton, James, 118, 164, 180–1
Hamish Hamilton Ltd., 118
Hammill, Faye, 205
Hapke, Laura, 167, 168
Hardy, Thomas, 18
Harrisson, Tom, 173, 228n18
Hatry, Charles, 39
Henty, George Alfred, 19

Hewlett, Maurice, 19, 141
Heyer, Georgette, 12, 77, 222
Hibberd, Ogilvy, 125
Hilliard, Christopher, 132
Hinton, James, 189
historic preservation, 215
historical novels, 4, 19, 25, 91, 130,
 191, 202, 231n82, 238n12
Hitchcock, Alfred, *39 Steps, The*, 31
Hitchens, Christopher, 176
Hitler Youth, 111
Hitler, Adolph, 122, 165, 185, 192
Hodder & Stoughton, 2, 76, 131, 140
Holman, Valerie, 173
Holtby, Winifred, 67, 92
homosexuality, 143, 149, 180,
 186–8, 242n4
homosocial loyalty, 143
Hope, Anthony, 18, 154
 Prisoner of Zenda, The, 113, 141, 154
Horizon, 173
House of Lords, 36
Hudson, W H, 18
Hulme, T E, 11
Humble, Nicola, 15, 58, 114, 116,
 126, 127, 136
Hunt, Holman, 117
Huxley, Aldous, 15, 66

illegitimate children, 157, 171, 201
immigrants, 38
Imperial Fascist League (IFL), 37
imperialism, 3
Independent Labour Party, 37, 45, 92
Industrial Revolution, 19
influenza epidemic (1919), 38
Irish Republican Army (IRA), 93
Isherwood, Christopher, 11

John, Augustus, 13
Johnson, Samuel, 68

Kent, Susan Kingsley, 49, 50
Kerslake, Evelyn, 209
Kidd, Alan, 126
King, Mackenzie, 91
Kingsley, Henry, 30
 Ravenshoe, 132
Kipling, Josephine, 117

Printed and bound by CPI Group (UK) Ltd, Croydon, CR0 4YY